LIMITED EDITIC
EIGHT /75
MH Liardet

KILROY WAS THERE

A tale of amazing pranks, wizard prangs and wanton women, by the man behind the infamous WWII graffiti

From the memoirs of
Pilot Officer Kilroy, CdeG(F), DM(joint)

MIKE LIARDET

TO DAVE -
THERE'S A CHARACTER CALLED
DONTON IN THERE (BRIEFLY*) -
NOT YOU OF COURSE!

Mike

*P146

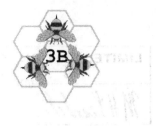

Published by 3B Publishing: ThreeBPub@Hotmail.Com.

ISBN 978-1540624024

Copyright © Mike Liardet 2016 MikeLiardet@Hotmail.Com.

The right of Mike Liardet to be identified as the author of this work has been asserted by him in accordance with the Copyright, Designs and Patents Act 1988.

All rights reserved. No part of this publication may be reproduced, stored in or introduced into a retrieval system, or transmitted, in any form, or by any means (electronic, mechanical, photocopying, recording or otherwise) without the prior written permission of the publisher. Any person who does any unauthorized act in relation to this publication may be liable to criminal prosecution and civil claims for damages.

3B Publishing has no responsibility for the information provided by any websites you obtain from this book. The inclusion of website addresses in this book does not constitute an endorsement by or association with us of such sites or the content, products, advertising or other materials presented on such sites.

This book is entirely a work of fiction. The names, characters and incidents portrayed in it are the work of the writer's imagination. Any resemblance to actual persons, living or dead, events or localities is entirely coincidental.

This book is sold subject to the condition that it shall not, by way of trade or otherwise, be lent, re-sold, hired out, or otherwise circulated without the publisher's prior consent in any form of binding or cover other than that in which it is published and without a similar condition including this condition being imposed on the subsequent purchaser.

Printed by CreateSpace {1.1}.

DEDICATION

To the 70,253 men and women of the Royal Air Force
who gave their lives in World War II

And to two who survived

CONTENTS

EDITOR'S NOTE

I imagine you don't want to linger here so I'll be brief. I'll have a story to tell later, on how I came by this memoir, but it contains spoilers so you should read it in its proper place.

The main text is Kilroy's but the footnotes, inserts and other extras are my doing. If you don't welcome this sort of distraction then don't read them! They are not essential reading but, for the keen researcher, there is some useful background material. After much agonising I decided on weblinks (and especially the Wikipedia) rather than academic style references, as being readily accessible to all – my apologies to the serious historian. To make life easier for readers of the paperback edition I have presented all these links as "tinyurls". Type the links as given into your web browser and Tinyurl automatically redirects you to the right place on the world wide web. For example http://tinyurl.com/Kilroy001 will take you to https://www.youtube. com/watch?v=c08wiEyVuak, where you will be treated to Fred Astaire and Ginger Rogers performing *Let's Face the Music and Dance* (turn up the volume!).

Finally be assured I've checked the history, pored over the account, checked Kilroy's writing and rechecked and rechecked. No matter how crazy it might read it's all true.

M.H.L. 2016

FOREWORD

"Kilroy Was Here". You must have seen that graffiti countless times. You know, the little man with his head poking over a wall. Mind you, it's nothing like as popular now as it was in the war. All over the place it was then. You would sit down in your Spitfire cockpit and there he would be, scratched in the paintwork of the instrument panel, or you would take your girlfriend to the Gaumont and find him nestling between you and her on the armrest. He really got around during the war he did, literally everywhere.

Picture this. The Potsdam Conference. 1945. There's Stalin, Churchill and President Truman, all grim and statesmanlike, carving up the world between them. Uncle Joe excuses himself. He's off to "drop a depth charge" as we used to say, and he's not heading off to use just any old latrine. He's going to a special executive outhouse, purpose built in finest marble, one despotic backside for the use of. And security is as tight as a nun's knickers. They would have had a minesweeper patrolling in there if they could have floated one in. No, not in the nun's knickers, I mean the latrine of course. So, a few minutes later Stalin comes back, scratching his moustache and looking worried. He turns to Churchill. "Oo iz diz Kil-rov?' he says.

I should point out that I wasn't even at the conference, not that one anyway, so it wasn't my doing. But that's to show just how popular I was then.

But I forgot to tell you. You see it was me who started it. I'm Kilroy. I mean *the* Kilroy. Not intentionally you understand, but it was my shenanigans early in the war that had a few people doing it locally and then one thing led to another and before you knew it the little Kilroy figure was everywhere.

Or so I thought... For years I'd enjoyed some small celebrity for starting this Kilroy business then one day a well-meaning acquaintance sent me an American press cutting, all yellowed and faded, about how some oaf with my name, but not related I can assure you, claimed back in the late forties that he had started the "Kilroy Was Here" graffiti. That was not a happy day to put it mildly, and I'd read the clipping and reread it several times and even when I'd reread it, with the aid of a large glass of malt, I still can't say I felt greatly cheered by it.

The next day I managed to track down the interloper, a Mr James Kilroy, residing somewhere in Massachusetts, and had a transatlantic call put through to him. I started by saying that I was happy for him to keep the wretched tram car he'd won – I'm not making this up, he was the proud recipient of a tram car seemingly – but said that I would like the credit for starting the whole business. He wasn't having any of it and he told me a tedious story about scratching his name in a ship's bilges or some such. 'That's why we call you Limeys,' he rounded things off, incorrectly as it happens, 'You always want to steal our limelight.'*

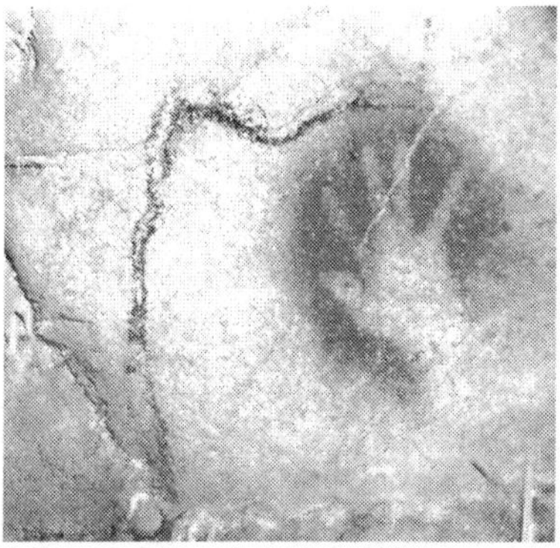

Drawn by Kilroy's ancestor 35,000 years ago.

Now don't get me wrong. I'm very fond of our cousins on the other side of the ocean. God knows, over the years I've fornicated with enough of their women and enjoyed aplenty their menfolk's friendly banter, not to say friendly fire. But if they have a fault, and some would say it's only a minor one, they do have a teensy weensy habit of taking credit where it's not theirs to take. You know the sort of thing I mean: Hollywood heroics in Burma when barely a GI ever set foot in the place,† and, oh I don't know – if you believe what a Septic Tank tells you it would seem they invented everything from the submarine to the rectal thermometer.‡

So this is why I have started this little memoir. A true tale of my service in the fight against Adolf Hitler. Set the record straight and all that. And there is much more to it than a bit of graffiti, although you will find out about that in due course. And I might add you will discover I had a lot more interesting places to put my moniker than a blinking ship's boiler.

---

* There are many claims to have originated the graffiti, but as "our" Kilroy's account predates them all by some margin, it seems likely that he was indeed the originator.

For more information, albeit from the US perspective, there is an extensive website on the graffiti at: http://tinyurl.com/Kilroy005. See also Wikipedia *Kilroy Was Here*: http://tinyurl.com/Kilroy006.

† Kilroy is probably referring to *Objective Burma!,* released in 1945, and which so offended the British that it was withheld from UK release for many years.

‡ Kilroy *doesn't* know in this instance. The first military submarine *was* invented by an American, David Bushnell, in 1775. The origins of rectal thermometry are evidently lost in the mists of time.

PART ONE: PEACE

1929-38

There may be trouble ahead
But while there's moonlight and music and love and romance
Let's face the music and dance

First performed by Fred Astaire (and Ginger Rogers) in
Follow the Fleet (1936)
Words and Music by Irving Berlin
Youtube: http://tinyurl.com/Kilroy001

CHAPTER 1

'Never wrestle with a chimney sweep,' my mother once said to me, which was an odd thing to tell an eight year old, especially as she ran off with one a month later. Pater wasn't much bothered. In New York City in those frantic last days of the twenties there was no time to be bothered about anything much. He arranged for someone else to sweep the chimney and promptly found solace in the ample form of Helga, my mother's maid.

I've always called him Pater and I carry his surname but he isn't, in fact, my father. My real father had had what you might call only a fleeting acquaintance with my mother and had fled the crime scene long before my first toot, breach first and expertly extracted (I'm told) by a Mr Mablet at Lord Reading's establishment in London.[*]

I remember little of the many countries and the several years before my first encounter with the man I now call Pater. It was in 1929 when we'd just come from Bremerhaven on the SS Bremen[†] and my dear Mutti, who you are no doubt suspecting of being a tad flighty, met him at some drunken reception at the Russian in New York, while I was lodged in our rooms at the Roosevelt, eating candy and playing Ludo with the bellhop. The next day she returned with the news that we had a new home. I think Mutti's eager new paramour barely noticed my arrival, hidden somewhere in the luggage train, and throughout their brief and passionate affaire he largely ignored me, barring the odd clip around the ear.

A few weeks later she was gone. It was only when he was chucking out the empty hatboxes into the yard that Pater discovered she had left behind more than just bills. 'Helga,' he cried. 'Helga, look what the hell we have here.'

---

[*]At the time of Kilroy's arrival (20th January 1921) Lord Reading was preparing to leave London to take up his appointment as Viceroy of India. The next day he announced in *The Times* his intention to let his Mayfair house. One of the agents was a Mr Mabbett (Kilroy mentions a "Mablet") so it is possible that Kilroy was brought into the world by an estate agent. Lord Reading: http://tinyurl.com/Kilroy007.

Lord Reading's house, Kilroy's birthplace, still stands at 32, Curzon Street in Mayfair in London. There is a commemorative blue plaque on the front elevation (surprisingly, with no mention of Kilroy). Google Maps Streetview: http://tinyurl.com/Kilroy008.

[†] This must have been the maiden voyage of the SS Bremen, leaving Bremerhaven on 16 July 1929. She arrived in New York four days, 17 hours, and 42 minutes later, capturing the prestigious (westbound) Blue Riband for Germany from the Mauretania, with an average speed of 27.83 knots (51.54 km/h). http://tinyurl.com/Kilroy009.

I thought he was going to throw me out there and then along with the other rubbish but Helga stayed his hand. 'The lieb-chen has nowhere to go,' she chided him in her soft German lilt, as I sucked my thumb and sunk my face into her bosom for good measure.

'One week,' he said, as he jerked his thumb at the door. 'One week.'

Three days later the Wall Street Crash turned all our lives upside down. Pater was trading in commodities, I found out later. He could have just lost a pile in the ordinary way that historic October day but he had to go one better. 'Gold,' he had said, 'that's where there's money to be made.' As the price of gold subsequently went through the roof while everything else fell off a cliff my life would have been so different had he actually gone out and bought gold, but what he had meant was he was going to make his fortune by doing the exact opposite, that is betting against it, or selling "short" as they say.

I well remember that day at the breakfast table as he sat with his head propped in his hands and the Wall Street Journal lying unopened before him. 'What's to do?' he kept asking, to no one in particular. As I said, he didn't just lose a pile, which might have entailed selling the yacht and the family estate in the Hamptons, a bit of a comedown surely but sustainable. What he had done was so much worse than that, that is he had bet and lost with money he didn't have. 'Maranzano's boys will be here this Friday and that's all I have to give them.' He waved at a battered carton of Rice Krispies, which was wedged between the milk and the toast.*

'What about the boy?' said Helga.

'Why in hell would they want him?' he spat out.

Of course he had misunderstood her. You see my mother may have been flighty but she was also a great granddaughter of Count Otto von Bismarck and seemingly there was a flotilla of von Bismarcks back in Germany – cousins, uncles and what-not, who were a little tired of my mother's wild ways. Helga, who had met a few of them in the course of her duties, thought they might, just might, be prevailed upon to fork out a little if a responsible American financier were to take Mutti's little blow-by under his wing and provide a stable home for him.

I was kept in the dark at the time but I've since found out that, over the next couple of days, telegrams bounced backwards and forwards across the Atlantic and the long and short of it was that in the time it takes a shipping clerk to fill an inkwell we, that is me, Helga and my new found guardian

* The 1929 Wall Street Crash took place over several days at the end of October that year and the market continued its slide in the following year. The worst days were Black Monday (28th October) and Black Tuesday (29th) when the market dropped 13% then 12%. The crash signalled the beginning of the ten-year Great Depression that affected all western industrialised countries. The Dow Jones did not recover to its 1929 peak until 1954. http://tinyurl.com/Kilroy014.

were standing on the second class promenade deck of the SS Albertic, watching the receding skyline of New York as we sailed for Liverpool and a new life.*

Pater looked at his watch and exhaled loudly. 'Made it,' he said, 'with 24 hours to spare.' It was Thursday.

White Star Line – SS Albertic.

* The SS Albertic sailed from New York just after the Wall Street crash, routing via Boston and docking at Liverpool's White Star Terminal on the morning of Monday 4th November 1929. http://tinyurl.com/Kilroy015.

CHAPTER 2

We didn't linger long in Liverpool. 'Penniless since the slave trade ended,' was Pater's parting shot as we boarded the train for London. There he set about the important business of re-establishing his fortune while I was sent off to get an education. There was a merry-go-round of Prep schools, each less eager to take me than the previous, before I finally landed a more permanent berth at the Herne Bay College for the offspring of the seriously deluded.

The years went by without further expulsion but with plenty of thrashings, icy showers and dismal food. My summer vacations were enlivened with visits to my mother's family in Germany, resulting in a solitary examination success (Modern Languages) and then it was May 1937. I had just turned 16, had grown into a man (almost) and had become what they called a senior boarder, one of a party of eight selected to shout, cheer and generally wave the school banner at the coronation of our new king, George VI.

We set off for London the day before. I didn't know it at the time but I was to be enmeshed in an adventure that would end with the sacking of a key government minister – a dismissal that is largely forgotten now but at the time was a matter of some moment on our troubled European stage. Mind you, my stepfather must take some of the blame for this too. Leastways it was Pater who, in a rare fit of generosity, had given me a grubby pound note for my birthday, with a sober instruction to spend it wisely. And then... well you will see presently what other part he had to play in it all.

The day started innocently enough, on a train chugging alongside the Thames estuary towards London. As the fields and villages slid past we lounged in our seats, puffed on cigarettes and chatted about the usual things older boys talk about – sport, girls and the school catering as I recall. Apart from Jennings I didn't know my companions so well. They were in the year above ours and were what we called "the anointed ones", bedecked with the braid and badges of the high table whereas Jennings and I, well, I did wonder why Old Man Blenkinsop – our headmaster – had allowed us to join the party in the first place. Perhaps he had hoped we'd be useful if things turned ugly or, more likely, he'd been told it was going to rain – and it did too.

Two of the others, Peters and Smythe, had been going on at some length about the bowling line-up of the New Zealand tourists* when Jennings, who had been yawning in the corner, asked if anyone would like to hear about his brother's recent encounter with *une horizontale*. I think all of us had heard as much as we needed on Curly Page's slow-medium pacers and whether or not they would get the better of Wally Hammond's cover drive so the consensus was that we would indeed like to hear about Jennings Senior's recent antics.

First Jennings had to explain what a horizontal lady was to Peters, mouth agape, then we settled down for the usual debauched tale that young men like to hear. It was all she-couldn't-sit-down-for-a-week-afterwards sort of stuff and mainly made up I'm sure, but Jennings insisted it was true. And, if any of us doubted it, we were free to try the establishment concerned, this very night if we liked, as it was in central London and very much open for business as usual.

That had me thinking. Jennings and I went back a way. We had been what you might call very roughly acquainted on occasions, and as he had always been a big lad for his age these encounters hadn't generally worked out to my advantage. Now, at the ripe old age of 16, I thought that open warfare was most probably behind us but I did wonder if I could trust anything he said. On the other hand I reckoned that this establishment, if it existed at all, would be a useful place to know about. I asked him for the address, pulled out my note book and jotted it down.

'Ooh,' said Jennings, as he elbowed Smythe and pointed at me. 'Do you fancy going then?'

'Well, I don't see why not,' I replied, trying to sound casual. I'd realised it was just a short walk from Pater and Helga's place.

'How much have you got?' he asked.

I started rummaging in my trouser pockets.

'No, not how much of *that*,' he said, quick as a flash, 'I meant how much *money* have you got?'

The others laughed and when I pulled out Pater's paltry offering, Jennings thought this was hilarious. 'A quid,' he said, 'a lousy pound won't even get you through the front door, matey. This place is in Shepherd Market, old boy, not Shepherds Bush.'

Peters, Smythe and the rest had a good chuckle at that. 'Okay,' I said, trying not to show my irritation, 'anyone else like to visit Fornicating Fifi's or whatever the damned place is called?'

Looking around the compartment I was treated to a series of nods, mutterings and 'ooh yesses' and so on. I suspected that not all of them

* The New Zealand cricket team had recently arrived in England and was playing warm-up games in London in the week of the coronation, at the Kennington Oval and at Lords.

would have the nerve to go if it came to it, but no one wanted to admit it there and then. One thing was certain: all of us, including Jennings, were short of the readies.

Jennings and Smythe exchanged a look. 'I know,' piped up Smythe, 'let's pool our money and draw for it. Aces high and the winner gets the night of his life, eh?' He looked around at each of us. 'And, he can report back to one and all later. What say?' he added, elbowing me none too gently in the ribs.

'Good idea.' Jennings jumped in a little too quickly I thought, and dumped the contents of his pocket on the table.

What the others didn't know and I did was that Jennings was a born persuader. I'd been taken in a few times in the past by his persuasive powers and reckoned that if it suited his purposes he could sell bubble bath to Hitler or nerve gas to Gandhi – both of which, by the way, he claimed to have done when I bumped into him after the war.

A few minutes later there was a pile of notes and coins on the table – about six or seven pounds I reckoned – and all eyes were on me. I stared at Jennings but his face was impassive. I felt sure he was up to something but couldn't think of a way out without losing face. I idly flicked through the pile, and found a shirt button lying at the bottom. 'Yours, I believe,' I muttered as I handed it to him. 'I suppose I'm in then,' I added with a sigh.

In the end we didn't draw cards to determine the winner because of course Jennings had had a better idea – a "totty tournament" as he called it, based on some game with matchsticks that he called Limbo. I'm not sure any of us wanted to play the silly game but, as I said, Jennings could be very persuasive.

Half an hour later and more by luck than any great skill, I found myself sitting across the table from Jennings for what he called 'the best of three grand final' – winner takes all. The others were crowded around us as the train rattled its way through the outer London suburbs. 'Your start,' said Jennings as I made little piles of the matches. He looked even larger than usual sitting just opposite me as he theatrically rolled his shoulders and flexed his muscles like a prize fighter.

I hadn't come across Limbo before but it is a simple enough game. You take it in turns to remove matches in line with some straightforward rules that I won't bore you with and the player who gets to remove the last match is the winner. It sounds easy enough but the strange thing is it is not at all obvious how to play it well. There is a point, around about halfway, when the outcome is certain and if you are in a bad position, no matter what you do, your opponent can easily keep you there – you are just bound to lose. Jennings, I noticed, had seemed pretty hopeless when we were messing around with trial games but had played with a calm assurance once the tournament proper had started. Sure enough, in our first game, I was quickly on a loser. 'Limbo, limbo,' he exclaimed each time he replied to my move, then 'Judgement Day, matey,' as he snatched up the winning match. 'One nil to me,' he cried, eying the pile of money.

I'm sure the next game would have gone the same way if we hadn't gone into a railway tunnel soon after it started. I'd noticed earlier that when Jennings was about to move he'd rest his forehead on his fist, as if concentrating intensely, but I could see his eyes were only half closed. Suddenly the outside went black as we entered the tunnel. It was Jennings move at the time and so he was "thinking" as usual, when I casually wiped the condensation from the window alongside us. In the reflection I just caught a glimpse of the inside of his wrist before he dropped his arm down on the table. There were several rows of numbers on it.

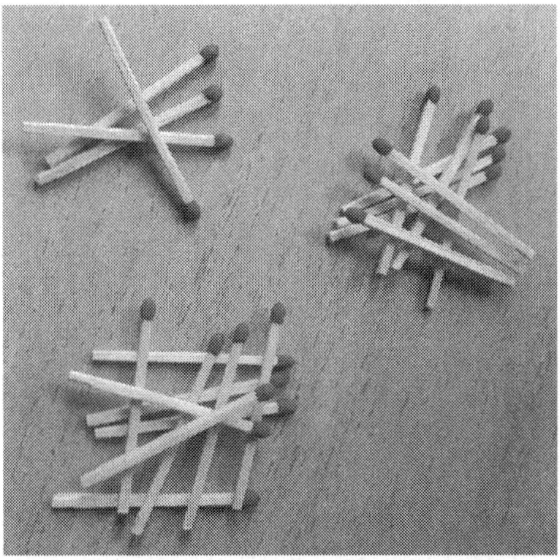

Nim, AKA "Limbo". Game in progress with piles of 4/9/10 matches. Remove one from the pile of four matches to win.

Jennings himself was a duffer at maths but I recalled his father was a mathematics professor, and putting two and two together, well, it didn't need his old man to tell me that it wasn't five. An immediate unmasking I ruled out. A few months earlier Pater had come home one night with a missing tooth and an angry bruise across the bridge of his nose. 'Nether thell a genthelman thee's a cad,' he had said as Helga patched him up, 'not when he's bigger than you, anyways.'

I started singing. 'One, two, three, four, five,' I trilled in wobbly tones, 'once I caught a fish alive.'

I could see Jennings frowning and his lips moving as he sat in his familiar thinking position. Some of the others were pretending to wince as they stuffed their fingers in their ears.

'Six, seven, three, nine, eight – then I went to fornicate.'

Feeble stuff I know but those who could bear to listen still had a chuckle at it. Jennings had been about to move but stopped with my improvised line, frowned and went back to his thinking pose.

'Five, four, seven, up your bum,' I went on but I needn't have bothered as I could see by Jennings' furious expression that he had well and truly lost the thread. He sighed, looked up and glared at me from across the table as he made his move quickly, grabbing a handful of matches and throwing them to one side.

Whatever move he should have made it was evidently the wrong one as I easily found a winning reply. 'Judgement day two,' I cried a few minutes later, as I snatched up the last match. Some of the lads patted me on the back as I set up for the next game, trying not to look too pleased with myself.

Victoria Station, London.

The train had slowed and, looking out the window, I could see the grimy outline of Victoria station in the middle distance. This meant we had only five minutes left to complete our "titanic struggle" as Smythe was calling it. 'No more bloody singing,' was all my opponent could say as I made my first move.

Once again a railway tunnel came to the rescue. That and a game of Happy Families I had once played with Helga when she taught me the "Tenkai" Palm. If you can palm Mrs Bung the Brewers Wife then you will have no trouble with a couple of matches. By the time we emerged into daylight all that Jennings could do was sit, open mouthed, and stare at a position that wasn't fully of his own making. 'Made another mistake, old boy?' I asked, all innocence.*

The train shuddered to a halt as I scooped up the last match and pocketed the cash. 'Must dash, chaps,' I shouted over my shoulder as I jumped down and ran off down the platform.

---

* There is no record of a game called Limbo in the 1930s, but most likely Kilroy and the others were playing "Nim". Nim is an ancient game, played by two players with piles of matches, pebbles or any convenient counters. To the uninitiated there is no obvious winning strategy but in fact one was discovered in 1901 and it is relatively easy to apply, at least for the mathematically astute. Since, by Kilroy's account, Jennings was not very mathematically able, it is likely that he had instead noted various key combinations on his arm – these too would have helped him to win.

See *End Note (1)* for more detail on the method and an account of the fascinating Nimatron machine, which was exhibited at New York's World Fair in 1939.

A few hours later I was walking the smart streets and lanes of Mayfair. This part of town was familiar territory to me of course so I soon found the house I wanted, only a few doors away from the site of my grand arrival at Reading's old place, and a short hop from Pater and Helga's too. This is London at its finest I thought. Fornication, finance and politics make natural bedfellows so it made sense that they would all be within easy reach of one another, and in one of London's finest quarters at that. I paused outside the door but then thought it wise to first cross to the other side of the road to verify the establishment's credentials so as to speak. Like most of the houses in that district it was an elegant Georgian property, and with its shining marble steps leading to an imposing front door it looked every inch the sober town house. But not so the comings and goings. In the short time I stood there, men of all shapes, sizes and religious persuasions made their discreet entry and exit and, more spectacularly, there was the arrival of a curvaceous young blonde, greeted as Hayley, who even found time to wink at me on her way in. So, I concluded, it was safe to assume Jennings had given me a genuine address, if nothing else, and now it was time to move on to phase two of Operation Bordello.

I confess that at that very moment I did start to wonder if this was really such a good idea. Still, I told myself, 'faint heart never won fair lady,' as Shakespeare would say.* I took a deep breath, buttoned my jacket, climbed the steps, and affecting a confidence I scarcely felt, smartly rapped the polished brass knocker. After a short delay, the door opened a crack. I could just make out a pair of eyes peering at me from the gloom within. 'Deliveries round the back,' came a voice, and the door started to close.

I stuck out my foot. 'No, I'm not here for that,' I declared.

The gap widened a touch and this time I could see the person I was addressing. It was a maid, smart and businesslike, with both arms wrapped around what looked like a weighty ledger. She stared back at me, her eyebrows raised, and said nothing.

'Well, I...' I started. 'I er..., I er...' and then I blurted out why I was there.

Her eyes widened and I began to wonder if Jennings had made up the whole story. It flashed through my mind that she might call the police and I was wondering about the consequences of that when, to my relief, she smiled. 'Lordy, lordy,' she said. 'Does your mother know you're out?' and I could hear her chuckling as the door clunked shut in my face.

I paused for a moment and briefly considered knocking again but somehow didn't have the heart for it. I turned around to head back home.

Salvation came as I reached the bottom of the steps in the form of a tall fair haired man, a few years older than me, dressed in a smart lounge suit.

* The origins of the saying are obscure but it did not originate with Shakespeare.

'Pardon me,' he said in a clipped German accent. 'Do you want to gain entry, so as to spik, at the house there?' He nodded at the front door.

There didn't seem much point in denying it.

He smiled back and gestured at a pub across the road.

Over a half of mild, Axel – for this was my companion's name – soon had my story. 'And so, you'd like the, er, services of, er, 'ayley?' He drained his glass and put it back on the table.

I nodded.

'Good choice, my friend, hif you don't mind my saying so?' He smiled and patted me on the back. 'How much money haf you?'

I had counted my winnings when I arrived back home. There was a fair amount of loose change and it had come to seven pounds six shillings and four pence. Alex's eyes widened as I dumped it, in its paper bag on the table in front of him.

He opened the bag and poked around inside with his finger. I could just see Pater's grubby note nestling in there amongst the mound of copper and silver. 'How old are you?' he asked.

'Eighteen,' I lied.

His hand reached out and roughly stroked my cheek. I jerked my head away but he just smiled and stood up. 'Right, young shafer. Trust me,' he said, as he picked up the bag and stuffed it in his pocket. 'Gif me two minutes.'

Half an hour later and I was thinking that I had seen the last of Axel and my money when he came breezing back into the bar, ordered himself a drink and sat back beside me.

'All tekken care of,' he whispered.

I looked questioningly.

'Go on. Go on.' He gave me a gentle shove. 'Just ask for 'ayley.'

'She is there then?'

'Oh yes, she's there and villing all right,' he spluttered into his beer.

A few minutes later I was standing outside Suite 11, as the maid had called it. I was wondering whether or not to knock, when the door swung open.

Her pale blue eyes flashed at me. 'Ah, it's you,' she smiled.

Close up I could see how young she was – perhaps only a couple of years older than me, and looking utterly arresting in a black silk evening gown. 'Er...'

'Come in, come in, my lovely. Don't just stand there like a commie at a coronation.' She crooked her finger.

I found myself wondering who exactly *was* in the Russian delegation. 'Er...'

'Crikey, big boy, you've not much to say for yourself.' She grabbed my tie and gently pulled me into the room.

I knew Stalin wasn't coming. Perhaps it was Molotov?* I heard the door click shut behind me. 'I...'

'Your brother told me what you liked.'

'Eh...?'

'Your brother, sweetie,' she said, as she stood on tip toe and put both her arms around my neck. I could smell her sweet perfume and feel her breasts pressing against my chest. I sensed her warm breath in my ear. 'Now give me a hand with this dress,' she whispered.

Five minutes later I was back in the pub.

'Well?' asked Axel.

I felt it might be appropriate to make some ribald comment. 'Er, I...' I replied then lost my thread and all that came out was a sigh.

Axel thought this was a huge joke, and slapped me on the back. 'Mission accomplished, little brother, eh?' he asked.

I weakly nodded and he chortled some more.

And there ends the happy tale of my first visit to a busy Mayfair knocking shop. You are probably wondering by now what this has to do with the downfall of a government minister and speculating about Russians caught out by hidden cameras or how I might have blundered into the Chancellor of the Exchequer in a room full of choir boys. Nothing of that nature happened but the seeds were now sown and they were about to be watered, in the form of a nasty surprise.

Somebody sat down at the table next to us and as I turned to see who it was I found myself face to face with Pater.

'What are you doing here?' we both asked simultaneously.

***

The unexpected encounter with Pater went rather well in the end. He looked like he didn't believe a word of my feeble excuse for being there but didn't seem in any hurry, I noticed, to explain *his* presence either. I half expected him to give me my marching orders for being out and about and underage but instead he seemed much distracted by Axel, and started bombarding him with questions.

Axel fielded them admirably. Yes, he was here for the coronation, from Berlin, and, no, Hitler wasn't coming and yes he was staying at the embassy and no he would not be in the Abbey as, ha-ha, he was way too junior for that honour.

I suppose my stepfather had guessed that Axel had a silver spoonful of blue blood somewhere, so he had to get him on file and this meant he had to know everything. Pater may not have been up to much with the technicalities of stock market trading but he made up for it by being the

* It was Litvinov and Tukhachevski who represented the Soviet Union at the coronation. Molotov succeeded Litvinov as Foreign Minister in 1939.

world's leading social climber. He was oft given to tapping his nose and telling anyone who'd listen, 'It's not what you know but who you know' – or insider dealing as we call it nowadays. Soon he had dragged the whole family history out of Axel – everything from his sister's forthcoming marriage through to what the cat liked for breakfast.

'Phew,' declared Axel after he left. 'Another drink?'

The rest of the evening was a blur. For our last drink I recall Axel proposed a toast. 'To my blood brother,' he said.

I asked him why he called me that.

'Because, little brother,' he said with a mischievous twinkle in his eye, 'we have supped at the same well.'

***

I didn't make the coronation the next day. I slept in.* The only excuse I can offer now is that I must have felt exhausted by my Herculean performance with Hayley the previous night. But then again, for all the impact world events had upon me in the months to come, I might as well have been asleep for the rest of the year. Chamberlain becomes Prime Minister? In the sixth form common room, basking in the glory of said Herculean labour. Northern Spain falls to the Falangists? Puzzling over the chemical properties of Sodium. Hitler maps out his plans for world conquest? My mother came to visit.

I can't be blamed for missing Hitler's plans. Everybody else did too. We now know that in the November of that year he sat down with his military leaders, von Neurath, von Blomberg and the others and told them that, yes *they* would be taking Austria and, yes, *they* would have to move on Czechoslovakia and Poland too and, by the way, he didn't want to hear any fuddy-duddy Prussian reservations about what weedy old Britain and France may or may not get up to in response.†

---

* The coronation ceremony, on 12th May 1937, was in Westminster Abbey, which was filled to capacity with dignitaries from all over the world. Outside, the streets along the procession route were packed, despite the poor weather. It was a busy time socially for everyone, with delegates attending functions and celebrations in London while the general populace held street parties and gatherings all over the country.

This was the first coronation to receive wide media coverage, on radio, television and newsreel. http://tinyurl.com/Kilroy016

† This meeting took place on November 5th 1937, and was summarised in a document which has come to be known as the Hossbach Memorandum. Along with Hitler, in attendance were: von Neurath, the Foreign Minister; von Blomberg, the War Minister; and von Fritsch, Raeder and Göring, the army, navy and air force commanders. Neurath, Blomberg and Fritsch were the conservatives, urging caution. Historians still argue over the importance of this meeting, with some saying it was just a run-of-the-mill discussion of economic matters while others claim it was the first airing of Hitler's plans for the European war. http://tinyurl.com/Kilroy017.

I'd seen precious little of dear Mutti since her sudden exit all those years back in New York. She'd been in Europe mostly and would occasionally turn up out of the blue, deliver a quick hug, shed a light tear and then be gone, with only a faint waft of Chanel to tell me she had been there at all. This visit was on a cold November day, with both of us standing shivering in the school driveway while her latest beau sat in a Bugatti just outside the gates – a pristine yellow type 57S I recall, engine rumbling all the while. She'd knitted me a cardigan. I think she really had too – this one had three arms and was four sizes too small. More importantly she brought something else, for my educational needs she said, an envelope she dropped into my hands as she left. I had it ripped open before she reached the car. Five pound notes were a lot, lot bigger in those days, reflecting the fact that they represented a week's wages for some. There were five of them.

George VI coronation procession. Admiralty Arch, London, 12th May 1937.

As soon as I was home for the Christmas break I wasted no time putting my educational windfall to good use at the horizontal palace. And while I was enjoying the delights of Hayley, the Nazis were, for once, also concerned with affairs of the heart. Field Marshal von Blomberg, a key participant at the November meeting, was to be wed, and on such a momentous occasion it could only be Hitler himself for best man and Göring, who wouldn't be left out, would have to make do as bridesmaid. The wedding date was set for early January, which would leave plenty of time for von Blomberg to have his honeymoon and be back in harness and poised to put the boot in on Austria in early spring, although we allies knew nothing of this at the time. He was one of the old school military who had tried to act as some sort of brake on the mad corporal's ambition and was therefore not always favoured, but at that moment he must have thought the world was at his feet – Minister of War with a society wedding and a new young bride at his side.

Twenty five pounds seemed like a small fortune at the time but Mayfair isn't exactly the cheapest part of London for nefarious activity and there was a very real danger the whore would be over by Christmas. Fortunately

Helga came good with a further Yuletide educational subsidy and Hayley herself, who seemed to have taken a liking to me, agreed to 'let me in for half price' as she put it. Thus I managed to keep up an appearance throughout the Christmas break and, in particular, was in attendance there one evening early in the new year.

I like to think that I had improved my delivery a little after my first visit. Practice makes perfect they say and there is nothing like having a master, or rather a mistress, to teach you. At any rate Hayley and I had just completed an energetic romp and I was picking up the chaise longue where it had tipped over and was generally straightening the furniture as I looked for my clothes. A pile of postcards had fallen on the floor and I gathered them up and started flicking through them. 'Oh I say,' I said, 'one of these chaps still has a sock on.'

'They're a sort of menu,' said Hayley, wobbling on one leg as she attempted to slide the other into a stocking.

'Really? So what's this dish?' I asked waving a card at her, 'Game bird stuffing?' I found another. 'Or this? Sausage surprise?'

Hayley frowned. I'd noticed she could be surprisingly prim when it suited her and this would seem to be one of those moments. 'Don't be vulgar,' she said as she strode over and wrenched them from my hand.

A couple of the cards fell out of the pile. I picked them up, glanced at one and then the other. They both featured the same woman, acrobatically receiving what I might call the full gamut of male attention. I gulped. 'Blimey,' I said, 'I know who she is.'

'Not likely,' said Hayley. She looked at her watch and then at the door. 'Look, can we discuss this next week?'

'No, really,' I continued, 'I have seen this woman before. I'm sure it's her. Either that or her twin sister. In fact her photo is lying on our mantelpiece this very Christmas.'

'Not, looking like that, I hope,' smirked Hayley, as she gave me a gentle shove through the doorway.

Later that night, after I returned home, I laid out Hayley's postcards, along with the photo from our mantelpiece, on my bed. The photo was innocent enough. It showed an elderly man with his arm around a young woman. There is an age beyond which it is not a great idea to wear lederhosen, I reflected, and he had certainly passed that by many years. His companion was, well, very young, very pretty and mercifully more conventionally attired, which is to say not looking like she had just dropped in from an Alpine picnic. But the more I looked at her picture alongside the two postcards the more I was convinced it was the same woman. The problem, as I saw it, was whether or not to tell Axel.

Over six months had passed since I'd met Axel, and I'd almost forgotten about him when he surprised me with a large Christmas hamper that arrived at the house. Nestling between the bottles of Hock, sausage and pies was a note attached to a photograph – *the* photograph that ended up on our mantelpiece of course. 'To my blood brother,' the note said and beneath, the one line: 'Es gibt kein größerer narr als ein alter wolf!' which means 'There is no greater fool than an old wolf!'

Along with the cat's dietary preferences, I recalled that Pater had uncovered that Axel's widowed father had an eye for young beauty, so it was obvious what this was about and that is why, when I saw Hayley's postcards, I was amused if not alarmed to discover what manner of "lady" his old man had taken up with. I am older and wiser now and of the view that a fruity young tart can make an excellent companion for a gentleman of some age and means but at the time and armed only with the misplaced indignation of a brothel creeping sixth former I felt I had to do something about it.

The next day, returning from the post box, I found Pater waiting for me in the hallway. 'Come to my study,' he said and I followed behind him, alarm bells ringing.

I stood awkwardly in front of the desk as Pater levered himself into his worn leather chair. There was a large blotter on the desk top, bearing the imprint of several years worth of correspondence. Lying on the blotter, face down, was a postcard.

'Where did you get this filth?' He turned it over.

I'd been careless. The previous night, after selecting the marginally less lurid postcard for my missive to Axel, I should have secreted its partner somewhere a little less obvious than beneath an old *Daily Telegraph*. I looked at the picture again, as Pater waited for my response. Previously, what with wondering about facial resemblances I hadn't given much thought to what was actually going on, or rather in, in the picture itself. Crikey, I thought, it was eye-wateringly explicit.

'Do you find this funny?'

'Why, no sir.' Pater had a quick temper and I could see him eying the cupboard alongside the fireplace – the home of Master Whippy. Master Whippy and I had not met up for quite a while. Now that I had grown bigger than Pater, I liked to think that he had been pensioned off, but would prefer not to put this theory too closely to the test. I muttered something about acquiring it from one of my schoolmates.

'Hmmm,' he said. 'Last I heard, these sort of pictures were doing the rounds of certain, er, joints in Soho.' He had both elbows planted on his desk and was turning the card over and over as he spoke.

'On the menu in Mayfair too, I shouldn't wonder,' I replied without thinking.

'Who told you that?' he replied and I could see his face colour, whether with anger or something else I couldn't be sure.

I could see I was getting on dangerous ground here but, as sometimes happens, you find inspiration in your darkest hour. 'Actually, sir, do you not recognise the young, er, lady in the picture?'

'You goddammed cheeky beggar.'

I realised immediately I hadn't introduced this new direction with much tact. He had risen from his chair. His face had taken a bright ruddy hue, redder than I'd seen for quite a while, and he was heading towards the cupboard. 'No sir, I didn't mean that,' I added hastily. 'What I meant was: do you not think she's a dead ringer for the woman here?'

I scrambled in my pockets, pulling out the photo from the mantelpiece. He looked doubtfully at me but at least he stopped and returned to his seat. I placed the photo on the desk, alongside the postcard.

'Oh ho,' he exclaimed as he examined them both. 'From that chap Axel?' He picked up a magnifying glass and I waited in silence while he gave them further scrutiny. 'Oh ho,' he repeated. He looked up and stared at me long and hard but I could see his mind was far away. His eyes looked like they were glazed over with dollar bills. At last he picked up the magnifying glass again. 'Very interesting, very interesting,' he said, as he continued his examination. I stood there in silence, until abruptly and without looking up, he waved at me to leave.

Later that day I heard Pater on the phone, to Teddy. Teddy, when he wasn't loafing around in the House of Lords, was useful to Pater for his contacts on the New York Stock Exchange. Phone calls to him always meant that Pater was up to something. To this day I can't say exactly what it was but on this occasion, at the heart of it, was the fact that he had found out that the US Motor industry, specifically General Motors and Ford, were selling armaments to the Nazis. They really were too – it all came out after the war.* So Pater had discovered this and, knowing how he liked to operate, I can be pretty sure he would have been looking for a lever on one of the top men in the affair, at the Nazi War Ministry, say. 'Give me the right lever and I can lift a goldmine,' Pater was fond of saying. I didn't know it at the time but I had just provided him with the lever he needed.

A couple of days later I caught Pater in the kitchen as he was making himself a pot of coffee. He took it through to his study and I heard him lift his phone and give the operator a telephone number, in Berlin.

---

* Both General Motors and Ford owned and controlled German subsidiaries at this time: Opel and Ford-Werke. Ford-Werke supplied the Wehrmacht – the German military – with heavy trucks and troop carriers while Opel manufactured a three ton truck, called "the Blitz" which was used in the Blitzkrieg invasion of Poland and throughout the war thereafter. Executives from both companies (Henry Ford himself and James D Mooney of GM) were honoured by the Nazis with the award of the Grand Cross of the German Eagle, the highest medal Germany could bestow on a foreigner. See *End Note (2)*.

The coffee must have been stone cold by the time operator came back to him. Pater could speak quite reasonable German and was given to shouting down the phone so I had no trouble hearing what took place. 'Von Fritsch,' he bellowed. There was a pause, then 'Never mind who I am. Put me through to the Generaloberst.' There was another pause then 'No, not his driver, I want the Generaloberst himself.' This time I could just make out a voice at the other end, explaining something at some length and I was wondering how much longer it would be before Pater's short fuse would blow. 'Look dummkopf. This is a matter of national security. Put me through, I say.'

Ford Werke army lorry.

By then Helga had joined me in the hallway to see what all the fuss was about. It was clear that Pater's charm offensive wasn't working too well as there was a considerable pause this time, while no doubt some lowly telephone operator explained that the general was on holiday/ indisposed/ asleep or whatever. I could imagine Pater's face getting all puffed up and turning the familiar beetroot red. Finally his patience snapped. 'Very well. Tell the general that Field Marshal von Blomberg has married a whore. Have you got that? Married a whore I say.' He slammed down the phone, strode out of his study past Helga and me and stomped up the hallway.

I realised I'd been a tad slow off the mark. Two things: I'd switched off after a while when Pater was busy grilling Axel on the eve of the coronation and missed the little nugget that his old man was the infamous von Blomberg; then, later in the year, I had not been keeping up to speed with Nazi matrimonial matters at all and thus had failed to notice that the Field Marshal was getting spliced. What with that and the pictures it all fell into place when I heard Pater's words.

It all fell into place for von Blomberg too. I hadn't thought about the ways of a police state earlier but it was inevitable that my well intentioned letter with card within was lying on Himmler's desk within a few days and never reached Axel. Pater's outburst on the phone was soon reverberating around the corridors of power as well. They never discovered who the caller was but that didn't stop him being widely quoted. Von Blomberg had lots of enemies, many more in Berlin than in Paris and London, and his job, as Minister of War, was coveted by Göring, Himmler, von Fritsch, not to mention Hitler himself. Within a few days he was out, in exile and in disgrace. He was offered the honourable option of divorcing his tainted bride and the even more honourable option of a revolver to the temple, but declined both, to live out the war quietly with his wife on the island of Capri. In the end I guess Pater and I did him a favour as his contemporaries all ended up committing suicide or being hanged at Nuremberg, but with all

Opel Blitz trucks in convoy during the Blitzkrieg, near Rouen, 1940.

the Nazi war crimes still in the future he was free of any blame for what they got up to after he left.

I would love to have had an ear to the wall when Göring broke the glad tidings to Herr H on the recent society match, although surely anywhere within half a mile would have been near enough. The bride and groom had been much fêted in the Nazi press and the wedding snaps showed their most honourable guests proudly standing in the wedding line-up on their special day. But this was a period when the Führer had an unerring ability to find the right line. So, instead of covering up this one real scandal like any normal politician would do, the Nazis boldly *invented* another, where von Fritsch, the head of the army, the one who had been out to lunch when Pater called, was accused of homosexuality with rent-boys. It all goes to show how important spelling is, as it was actually someone else, a von Frisch (without the "t" for "trousers"), who had been found in the bushes, but this was a detail they conveniently overlooked at the time. In the aftermath there was the inevitable restructuring of the High Command, and of course this meant that Hitler ended up with just the people at the top who would bend to his will, which is what he had wanted all along of course. It was a case of being careful what you wish for. Many, on both sides of the Channel, had hoped for someone stronger than von Blomberg, to rein in Hitler's ambition, but what Europe ended up with was Field Marshal Keitel who was all but invisible. So, there we were in January 1938 with Austria about to be toppled, and with only a 'Ja, mein Führer' to stand in Hitler's way. Now call this the musings and meanderings of an old man but I do wonder what might have happened if von B had still been there, which he would have been if I'd left those damned postcards alone, or maybe never met Axel, or just not visited the brothel in the first place. Fate they call it, I suppose.

***

There's a routine I've seen many women perform. In fact it's so common that I believe it's a behaviour pattern in-built from birth in the female half of the species. There are many ways to initiate it: try dismantling a carburettor on the dining room table, or bring back the wrong child after a trip to the park, or present your beloved with night attire which, inevitably, is too small, in the wrong colour and not exactly built for warmth and comfort. The lady in question will glance at her accomplice (if available), raise her eyes heavenward, exhale loudly and utter the one word: 'Men!' This is usually followed by a weary shake of the head.

Hayley's eyebrows shot up. She exhaled loudly and uttered the one word: 'Men!' with a weary shake of the head.

I was only 17 years old and this was my first ever experience of this phenomenon, but I had a ready riposte, the same one I've used ever since. Quick as a flash I replied, 'What!?'

'How could you?' she replied, still shaking her head.

It was Easter and the mansion of earthly delights was, of all things, having a year-end stock-taking. I'm sure the stocklist would have made for interesting reading but I never got to see it. All I know is that postcards were items very much to be accounted for, so I had been asked to return the ones I'd "borrowed". I found the one we still had, somewhere in Pater's files, and by dint of explanation for the missing one brought along the photo. It wasn't long before the whole story had tumbled out.

'So this von Blomberg fellow was disgraced for marrying a harlot?' Hayley asked.

I nodded.

'Let me see the pictures again.'

I handed them over and that's when Hayley said it. 'Men!' she said.

To play a full part in the routine it is necessary for the man concerned to have no idea what the woman is on about. This is usually easy enough in my case. 'I've no idea what you are on about,' I said.

'These two women are not the same person,' she said, stabbing at each in turn with her finger, and looking a little triumphantly in my direction.

'But...'

'Compare the mouths – one big and the other small.' She continued stabbing at each picture as she spoke. 'And you can just see the left earlobe in both. Completely diff... oh, look, wait here and I'll show you.'

She thrust the pictures back in my hand and bustled out of the door. A few minutes later she was back, with a companion. 'This is Marie,' she said as she ushered her into the room.

German Embassy, Carlton House Terrace, in the 1930s.

I nodded to the newcomer and realised with a jolt that she looked strangely familiar.

'Marie's the one who posed for those postcards.'*

* War Minister Werner von Blomberg, along with Admiral Otto Schultze, represented Germany at the coronation and von Blomberg brought his son and daughter, Axel and Dorothea, to London with him. They were not there in any official capacity but stayed with von Blomberg in the German Embassy, then in Carlton House Terrace in St James. This is only a short walk from Mayfair, where Kilroy was "visiting" on the day before the coronation.

Kilroy's story concurs with the well known account of what became known as the Blomberg-Fritsch affair, but he also sheds new light upon it. As Kilroy mentions, both parties were disgraced and Hitler used the opportunity to restructure the High Command, introducing people he could easily dominate. It has previously been thought that von Fritsch's homosexuality was fabricated but von Blomberg's bride, Erna Gruhn, really had been a prostitute. Kilroy offers the interesting possibility that Erna Gruhn, too, was misrepresented. Hitherto the identity of the belligerent caller to von Fritsch was unknown but he has at last been identified here, as Kilroy's stepfather. http://tinyurl.com/Kilroy018.

CHAPTER 3

I had only just returned to school after the Christmas break, all full of the joys of Hayley, when I went down with pneumonia. That saw me in the local hospital and thence to the school sick bay under the care of Mad Mungo's wife. Mad Mungo, or Mr Clarke I should say, was not that well known to us boys at this time as he had only recently been appointed, as head of Geography. This was a remarkable achievement for someone who could no more read a map than I could read Chinese and, moreover, who looked (and smelled) like Robinson Crusoe after a rough night out. More happily for the school his wife had turned out to be a game young stick, willing to muck in with any of the multitude of tasks that can crop up in any badly run educational establishment. By the time I had made it to the sick bay Mungo's trouble and strife had already had a turn as school cook, secretary and gardener. Now she was trying her hand as matron.

Fortunately Mrs C was a much better matron than she was a cook or I doubt I'd be here now to tell the tale. My pillows were plumped, temperature taken *and* charted regularly and once my appetite picked up she administered some wholesome broth (not of her devising obviously) which brought my strength flooding back.

To begin with I enjoyed all the attention and the luxury of lying in bed all day whilst my classmates sweated over the Tudors and trigonometry, but once my only co-resident was sent home, broken leg and all, I became bored. Two of my pals brought me some reading material. Bertie Cavaray came with a Raymond Chandler, bless him, while Nige Nicolson rather wickedly turned up with *The Twelve Caesars*, gleefully informing me that in my absence I'd missed all of them bar Tiberius and Caligula.

I'd already read the Chandler and so, after supper, I thought I might as well try wrestling with Caligula, which is not a good idea at the best of times. If you have never read *The Twelve Caesars* I can certainly recommend it as a racy read: politics well-laced with debauchery, greed and violent death – not much has changed in 2,000 years. Unless you like being tortured and/or bored witless don't even think about the schools edition, which is in Latin with all the juicy bits removed. This was of course what I was reduced to that evening.[*]

I like to think I have a gift for most languages but up until then, Latin wasn't one of them. After half an hour I was still on the first page,

[*] *The Twelve Caesars*, in full and in English, can be downloaded as an e-book (for free) from Gutenberg: http://tinyurl.com/Kilroy019.

mouthing the words and frowning as Matron walked in. 'What are you reading?' she asked brusquely.

I told her it was Suetonius at his best and she replied, 'I can see that, but what bit?'

I hesitated.

'C'mon. In your best Latin.' She smiled as she snapped her fingers.

'Qua-rum vir-tu-tum fruct-um...' I stumbled.

'Caligula?' she asked, and I nodded.

'Fourth paragraph?'

I nodded again.

'Quarum virtutum fructum...' she replied and then delivered the whole of it, word perfect, without drawing breath.

'Oh, I say,' I replied, wondering why old man Tank was still in a job when the school had talent such as this at close hand.

'I just *love* the Classics.' She looked dreamily out of the window as she plonked herself on my bed. 'Just imagine that we are seeing those words today, as fresh as they were when written nearly two thousand years ago.'

I nodded, although at the time I was wishing that someone had had the good sense to quietly lose them in the centuries between.

She turned to face me, staring intently. 'Now what do they mean?'

'I... er... I think...' I took a breath. 'Of which valour fructum most luxuriantly...'

'Good golly,' she winced. 'You're *murdering* him.' She plucked the book from my hand. 'Go straight to the verb. "Tulit". Means?'

'Er, I...'

'From fero. To bear. Third conjugation. Yes?'

She smiled as she waited for my reply. All I've said about her so far was that she was the matron and that she was married to the horror show that was Mad Mungo, but don't picture an old hatchet-face in a starchy uniform threatening unspeakable things with a thermometer. Actually she wasn't in uniform at all, just in the everyday dress of a teacher's wife, which was a rather pretty frock on this occasion. I guess she was a fair bit younger than Mad Mungo but hidden beneath all that facial hair (his, I mean) it was hard to be sure of this. Of course all the teachers and their wives seemed unspeakably old to us boys, but with her animated enthusiasm for her subject it suddenly struck me she was probably quite young – not a great deal older than Hayley I realised. There was a pause as we both stared at each other, and I don't know what came over me but I found myself reaching out and gently touching her breast.

'It's irregular,' she said.

I started at that and was about to remove my hand but she grabbed it and held it there, still staring intently at me. 'Oh, I see,' I said. 'You mean the verb. Irregular, eh? Ho ho. Tuli, tuilsti, tulit and all that?'

'Perfect,' she said and to this day I can't tell you if she was referring to a Latin tense or to what I was doing with my hand.

She let me hold it there for what seemed like an age and I noticed she was breathing a little heavily and there was a little colour to her cheeks. Come to that I was getting a little hot under the bedclothes myself.

'Abrogare tunicam meam,' she declared suddenly.

'Eh?'

'Christ, does that fool Tank teach you boys anything?' she exploded. 'I said "Undo my tunic."'

'But you are not wearing a tunic,' I said, rather forlornly.

Her eyebrows shot heavenward. 'Here, let me show you,' she replied and with one movement she was on top of me.

The next ten minutes were what I can only describe as frantic and confused. I remember her frock – there's no Latin word for "frock" seemingly – being peeled off and chucked on the floor, with the bedding, pillows and miscellaneous undergarments all rumpled and thrown around. Of course I was game for anything but it didn't help the smooth running of the show that she kept whispering instructions to me in Latin. 'Flora me voca' – 'you may call me Flora,' I interpreted okay but not 'Est nocendum pectus tuum cubito,' which means 'your elbow is digging into my breast.' Then there was 'Plaga mea cunnus,' which she hissed in my ear at one point.

'My cunning plague?' I asked, incredulously.

She growled what was needed, in English, or to be more precise in Anglo Saxon and I found it means something quite different.

A few minutes later, she was back to being Matron again. The frock was back on, her stockings retrieved from the fruit bowl and my bedding neatly rearranged. 'Healthy exercise seems to agree with you,' she exclaimed. 'I do declare you are looking much better today,' she added as she breezed out of the door, looking pretty pleased with herself.

The next day I was deemed fit to be back in class. I resisted the temptation to tell my classmates what had transpired and instead made some sort of attempt to focus on my schoolwork. This was difficult as my thoughts kept straying back to Mrs C, or rather Flora as I now thought of her, and then when I wasn't thinking about Flora there was Hayley too to divert me from the life-cycle of the earthworm. The difference between them I realised (and I refer to Flora and Hayley here, not the earthworm) was that whereas Hayley was snugly tucked up in some whorehouse 50 miles away, Flora was dangling before me, only just out of reach, across the quadrangle. And now I'd had a taste I simply had to get back to grips with her for some more. The question was how?

I saw my opportunity after church the next Sunday. Flora had fallen behind the other teachers as we were walking back to the school and I adjusted my pace to catch up with her. 'Perhaps we could go for a walk this afternoon?' I asked.

She smiled at me. 'In Latin.'

I was ready for this. 'Possumus hoc meridianus ambulant,' I trotted out confidently.

She came over all thoughtful as she caught my eye. I could see the tip of her tongue as she moistened her lips. 'Er, I think that would be unwise,' she finally blurted out.

'But surely...' I continued.

'I said "no,"' she hissed and I noticed she was gazing past me, over my shoulder.

Herne Bay College.

I was just about to remonstrate further when I realised somebody had come up behind me.

'Everything okay dear?' It was Mad Mungo of course.

And that would have been that but for the annual rugby tourney with our arch-rivals, Dover College. I wasn't exactly noted for my prowess on the playing fields, but we had several injuries at that time and so I was picked as full back for the third fifteen.

On the big day it turned out that our game was last to finish. I will spare you the intricacies of the scoring system for the Hannibal Cup but suffice to say that, with five minutes to go, if we could avoid conceding yet another "try" Herne Bay would win it. Then their "number eight" forward got the ball, just inside our half.

In the game of rugby the number eight position is usually filled by the biggest strongest brute in the team and I don't know where Dover College had found this specimen – London zoo springs to mind – but he was a dangerous piece of goods. I'd managed to keep well out of his way thus far in the game but this time he was heading straight for me, with a full head of steam, his massive chest out proud and elbows and knees flailing around like whirling jack-hammers.

I noticed that everyone else had contrived to do what I'd been doing all game when he had the ball, which was to be somewhere else on the field, so there was only me between him and glory. My first instinct was to busy myself with tying a bootlace and pretend I hadn't seen him but it was too late for that. So, as his pounding size 14s drew near, I clamped my mouth tightly closed, shut my eyes and hurled myself at his feet, hoping he would have the good sense to jump over me.

There was a sickening crunch, followed by a fierce blow to my chest that knocked the wind out of me and then a loud bang that left me seeing stars. That is all I remember. I suppose I must have been knocked out because the next thing I knew I was lying on a stretcher with what seemed like the whole school crowding around and congratulating me. 'Best take him to the sick bay,' I heard a master say.

And this was the pattern of my schooling over the next few months: three days in the sick bay with wasp stings after I'd hung a chamber pot at the top of the old oak in the quad; five days after nearly drowning while attempting to swim under Herne Bay pier, and then, best of all, a week following concussion in the cricket nets when I stopped a full blooded drive with my chin.

You are probably wondering how we managed things when there were other occupants in the sick bay but, as they say, true love finds its own path.* There was a locked medicine cabinet which, conveniently, was in Mr and Mrs C's apartment which, conveniently, was just along the corridor. Thus I became the "medicine monitor", a task that involved spending an inordinate amount of time with Mrs C in the flat, eventually returning, all flushed and cheerful, with a trayful of medical goodies for my fellow patients.

My Latin improved as well. Old man Tank could hardly believe it. 'Kilroy,' he'd say, turning to me, 'your conjugation is near perfect.'

It was a good year. My other studies picked up as well and my dalliances with Mrs C were certainly giving new meaning to the idea of extra-curricular activity. It was all rather splendid, but as the days went by and the medicine monitor sessions got longer we became careless.

There was a couch in the corner by the medicine cabinet, which is where we usually performed the carnal act, that is if we didn't get too carried away too quickly, in which case we might resort to the rug, table or, in fact, any other roughly horizontal surface that came to hand. This time, we had made it to the couch.

If I have a weakness, and some would say I have many, it is a tendency to nod off after such joyous occasions. Even as a young man I was susceptible and now I am of, er, middle years I'm even worse – and when I care to think about it, it has got me into trouble more times than, than, well, I care to think about. So there I was, dozing pleasantly, face down and stark naked, in the sure knowledge that Mad Mungo was far far away on a field trip when the front door banged, accompanied by a loud 'Hoolloo.'

* Kilroy has mangled Byron here. Byron's quote is 'Love will find a way through paths where wolves fear to prey.'

CHAPTER 4

So many famous people have been expelled from school that it hardly counts as a distinction these days. In the arts and literature the poet Shelley, Salvador Dali and Ian Fleming got their marching orders before matriculation. For the scientists it was Buckminster Fuller and Albert Einstein who were caught nuking the chemistry lab. Then there were Hearst and Bogart and... well I'd better stop there because the list is long, but I'll wager that few on that list were expelled, as I was, in the middle of the summer vacation. It takes some, well, not exactly skill but certainly timing to incur the wrath of the beak when you are not even at the scene of the crime.[*]

I well remember the day – in late August 1938, with my final year beckoning. I had recently returned from what turned out to be my last summer visit to my mother's Onkel Otto in Bremen and could sense trouble as soon as I walked through the door. The atmosphere was not generally that cosy when Pater was around and there he was, sitting at the fireside as usual, reading *The Times*. I could see the overfull glass of whisky by his side and old Krupp dozing at his feet. Everything *looked* normal, for sure, but there was definitely an atmosphere. Looking over Pater's shoulder I caught a glimpse of a headline. *Turning Point in Prague.* Funny how you hold onto these things, but I've always remembered it. I suppose it's because that day was a turning point in my life as well.[†]

As soon as he heard me my stepfather put down the paper and stood up. 'Come to the study.'

'Where's Helga?'

'Never mind about her. Follow me. Quickly now.'

This was a familiar routine for both of us, played out many times over the years, from the botched whisky-porridge experiment (aged nine) through to the Grand Postcard Inquisition earlier that year. Even had I

---

[*] There is however the case of a Jonathon Burrows, 11, who managed to be expelled from school before he had even had his first lesson. This was long after Kilroy wrote these words and it must be said that Burrows has not (yet) revolutionised physics, been influential to several generations of poets or become famous for devising a wartime graffiti, but it was certainly an impressive achievement. See *Daily Mail*: http://tinyurl.com/Kilroy020.

[†] *The Times* of 31st August 1938 carried an article under this heading. It was reporting on the escalating tension between the allies and Germany over what came to be called the Czechoslovakian crisis.

known then that it was to be the last time I was to tread that path (as indeed it was) I can't say I would have felt any easier as I followed him down the hallway.

And so I stood before his desk. As usual, it was clear except for the main exhibit. Where once had stood an 1882 vintage Glenfiddich with a strange gluey suspension within, and very much later a candid snap of my friend Axel's step-mama (supposedly), I could see a letter, lying in the middle of the blotter. I recognised the stationery and could feel my fists tense involuntarily as my stepfather picked it up and extracted a single page. 'It seems you have been expelled.'

'But, Pater, we are in the middle of the vac.'

'It says here something about, er,' he paused to find the right place, '"conduct unbecoming of an Hernebayvian." I think you had better explain yourself.'

I caught a whiff of the peaty tang of Laphroaig on his breath and could see him gazing idly at Master Whippy's home in the fireside cupboard. 'I don't know sir. I'd like to shed some light, but I've not even been anywhere near the school since the end of summer half.'

'And, so, Mr Ellery Queen, what does that tell you?'

I paused for thought. Usually it was a sign of good humour when Pater started jabbering on about his favourite detective but there were exceptions. 'Well, I...'

'It tells you, you young idiot,' he paused and started stabbing at the letter as he spoke, 'that it's something you did earlier and it's only come to light now. Right?'

It looked like today might be one of the exceptions. 'Well, yes, sir.'

He sighed and glanced again at the letter. 'Right. Good. So now I'd like to hear your side of it, in your very own words and maybe you can even manage the truth this time, before I phone Mr Blenkinsop.' He glanced at the telephone beside him. 'Okay?'

My first thought was that my dalliance with Matron had somehow caught up with me but I really didn't feel like raking over that with Pater. But then there was also another possibility and I didn't want to discuss that with him either. It would have to be one or the other though, I thought and the problem was, which to confess to, which of course required I work out which was the most likely of my crimes for which I was being hanged. I found myself standing on my toes to try to get a glimpse of the page he was reading but he spotted what I was up to, folded it and placed it on the desk.

'Come on laddie.' He looked at his watch. 'I've not got all day.'

'Pater, it's only a small thing, but I was sort of involved in a sort of club.'

The old boy has been in his grave for many a long year now so I suppose it is safe to tell all here. Some time before the Mungo-not-on-a-field-trip incident, the 'sort of club' started as I was taking out the medicine, following a matronly romp. Around that time Mad Mungo was marking the entries for the school's Wills-Burke Award. This had been set up by some Australian former pupil, Don Bradman's great uncle so the rumour went, and was named for two supposedly heroic early Australian explorers who starved to death on their quest, after shooting at the very aborigines who were trying to help them.* The idea was that the writer of the best travel essay each year at the school be rewarded with a week's outward bound course in the easter vac, located in some suitably damp corner of Wales. I hadn't entered but many of my classmates had and, apparently, they hadn't done too well. 'Not one of you made even 50 per cent,' Mrs C told me, rather gleefully I thought, as she held open the door for me.

A few days later I was back in class and in the break we were discussing the Award. Jennings and I had largely kept out of each other's way since the totty tourney the previous year, but he was one of the group talking about it and he seemed to think that he might be in the frame to win it. Others thought that *they* might have a chance so there was some lively discussion ongoing.

'50 per cent,' I said to Jennings.

'What?'

'I'd bet my shirt you don't even make 50 per cent,' I said. As you are probably surmising I was taking a leaf out of Pater's book. 'Knowledge is king,' he'd often say, when he really meant 'Money is king,' but that one way to make lots of it was to profit from others' ignorance.

Jennings looked flabbergasted. As I mentioned earlier, he was a dunderhead at maths and science but he certainly made up for it with his literary skills. By common consent he was the best essayist in our year. He turned to the others for support, who merely looked amused at me, and some with what I took to be pity. Eventually he just snorted and attempted to wave me away.

I was about to propose a straightforward wager, ten shillings or so but then, and I don't know how it came to me, I had an idea. 'If you make over 50, I'll give you sixpence for every percentage point you make over.'

He looked keen enough on that idea alright.

'But,' I said, as I counted on my fingers in front of him. 'But if you make under, you pay me sixpence a point for every point you fall short. Can't say fairer than that, eh?' I held out my hand.

---

* Burke and Wills, in 1860, led an expedition from Melbourne, in the south of Australia, attempting to forge an overland route to the Gulf of Carpentaria in the north. Only one man returned from the bungled quest, with both leaders and five other men losing their lives. Shortly before they died Burke shot at a group of friendly aborigines, causing them to flee. http://tinyurl.com/Kilroy021.

Nobody bet like that in those days and, of course, sums weren't Jennings' strongpoint so I had to run through my proposal again a couple of times. Once he had the hang of it the thought of easy money was too much for him and he held out his hand. 'You're on.'

There was an unexpected bonus when others wanted a share of the action. Of course I was always pleased to have one over Jennings but if I felt a pang of guilt for the rest of them it didn't last long. So, safe in the knowledge from the horse's mouth so as to speak, I was soon the holder of half a dozen or so of these novel wagers.

The results were pinned on the notice board the next day and Jennings was top, with a mark of 85 per cent I think it was. He couldn't wait to find me and I had to write him an I.O.U. on the spot, before trudging into town to empty my post office account. Several of the others had scored over 50 as well and I was only saved from an embarrassing bankruptcy by the Springer twins who both clocked well under 30.

It was some days before I managed to confront Mrs C. Eventually I came upon her coming out of the science block. We walked around the corner, out of view. 'I don't see what's the problem?' she muttered as she pushed her hair off her forehead, smiling all the while.

'You told me no one in my class scored over 50.' I was trying, not successfully, to avoid sounding petulant.

She reached out for my tie, wrapping it around her finger and pulling me towards her. 'You're looking very poorly,' she said, her lips pouting as she looked up at me. 'I think you need another spell in the sick bay. Yes?'

I caught a waft of her perfume and, what with those hazel brown eyes staring up at me I nearly made a grab for her there and then but common sense prevailed – just. I pulled myself away, unwinding my tie from her grasp as I did so. 'About that class score...'

'Oh that,' she said looking disappointed, 'that wasn't your lot, that was 4C I was talking about.' She frowned. 'Or was it 4B? Oh I don't know. Well, you didn't enter anyway, so what's it to you?'

Which all goes to show that if you have inside information then make damned sure it's reliable before you go jumping in at the deep end. And no, this is not one of Pater's old sayings, it's one of mine and from a lesson learned the hard way.

Oddly, that loss was the beginning of a very prosperous period for me. The turnaround came a few days later when we had a *Publice Vindicatum*, which offered the spectacle of our Head soundly thrashing some second year, young Bobby Simpson I think it was, in front of the entire assembled school. Second only to expulsion, these occasions were infrequent and so were much discussed beforehand. I think Simpson had been caught tippling his housemaster's sherry or something. Had he been caught with his trousers down with one of the older boys they would most probably have been given house points for initiative or, at worst, a mild ticking off. And if all that seems nuts nowadays, well, that's an English Public School education as was and the basis of Britannia ruling the waves. No one saw fit to argue with it at the time.

So, on P.V. minus one day, there was much speculation as to the extent of punishment. The common room was divided between those who thought three or four strokes for a first offence and those who reckoned on a round dozen because "demon drink" was involved. I thought this seemed like a good moment to reintroduce my novel betting scheme. Jennings and the others had done a good job with advance publicity, telling one and all how they had cleaned me out, so I had no shortage of takers. Everyone had different ideas about how much of a thrashing would be administered, so I held several different types of bet in the end, with the demon drink brigade mainly staking a shilling a stroke over the eight I think it was, while the first offence stalwarts lined up at sixpence for every whack under five.

This time around I had something better than Mrs C's woolly information to work with. In the days after the Wills-Burke fiasco, my social life had been necessarily curtailed, with a fair bit of time spent in the library. This is where I had stumbled upon a weighty work on the science of mathematical probability by a John Maynard Keynes, a name that meant nothing to me at the time, although he is very famous now.* I spent many an unhappy hour trying to make sense of it but it was worth it in the end, when I came to the conclusion that for whatever event we might look at, as long as I didn't bet myself and set the odds with due deference to the complexities of probability, I couldn't lose. I think Simpson copped a nine in the end, but what did I care? Some of my classmates I paid out and some paid me but it was all fair and above board and, whatever happened, I made a few bob. Even Simpson himself was happy – I think he took half a crown off me.

So one thing led to another over the following weeks and there was no shortage of opportunities for a little flutter: elapsed time in assembly before physics master Tat Gardiner picked his nose (32 seconds); how long before France changed premier (never long)† and, best of all, how long Austria would hold out to the Nazis (two days).‡

---

* The book to which Kilroy refers is most probably *A Treatise on Probability* by John Maynard Keynes, published by Macmillan in 1921. It can be downloaded as an eBook (for free) at Gutenberg: http://tinyurl.com/Kilroy022. Keynes is better known as a leading economist who argued against the "free market" and for state intervention to avoid the boom and bust economic cycle and high unemployment, which of course figured heavily in the western economies of the twenties and thirties. See *End Note (3)*.

† The Third French Republic had more than 20 changes of leader in the 1930s, from Théodore Steeg, the incumbent in 1930, through to WWI hero, Marshal Pétain, who was

It was all very pleasant and free and easy, until that day when I was dozing pleasantly, face down and stark naked, on the couch, in the sure knowledge that Mad Mungo was far far away on a field trip when, in fact, he wasn't. The first we knew that things had gone awry was the front door banging and the loud 'Hoolloo.' This was followed by the sound of the new arrival stomping up the hallway. The old boy didn't sound in good humour either, damning and blasting about some problem with 'the bloody trains.' Mrs C, I could see, was at least dressed and decent but the thought flashed through my mind that the sight of my backside, winking at him from within his wife's boudoir would hardly likely improve his mood. With only seconds before our door crashed open I reckoned I had only two options, both quite desperate – dive under the settee or out the window. Both manoeuvres have proved occasionally successful over the years but on this occasion I did neither.

Mrs C must have seen me braced for flight. She tapped me lightly on the shoulder. 'Hush. Stay where you are,' she whispered as she pushed my face back down into the seat. I didn't have time to argue and so I just lay there. The next 20 seconds were a master class in what people can get away with *in extremis*.

The door crashed open. Being facedown, with eyes clenched shut in any case, I could only hear the exchange.

'Oh, good evening, darling. You're back early.' This was Mrs C, sounding a bit preoccupied.

Then we had Mad Mungo's gruff bark, so near I reckoned he must have been standing over me. 'Oh, I see. Bit late for that, isn't it?'

'Some supper in the oven, darling. Be with you presently.'

And with that, I could hear him shuffling out of the room, quietly humming to himself.

I was on the point of turning over and congratulating Mrs C, on whatever devious ploy she had pulled over the old boy when I felt an agonising pain down below. Having enjoyed the full benefits of a public school education I can safely say it exceeded anything meted out by the most sadistic master or even prefect and can only describe it as feeling like somebody was attacking my backside with a blowtorch. With the shock as

---

saddled with the task of capitulating to Germany in June 1940. In Kilroy's Spring Term, 1938, Chautemps gave way to Blum on 13th March and, less than a month later, Blum gave way to Daladier, on 10th April.

‡ It was *less* than two days. The German Army crossed the Austrian border on the morning of 12th March 1938, to be met with cheers, Nazi flags and flowers. The *Anschluss* (German for "union" or "annexation") was ratified the following day. http://tinyurl.com/Kilroy023.

much as anything, I found myself crying out loud and lustily, in a voice that could probably be heard right across the school grounds.

The pain only lasted a second perhaps, no longer than it took me to turn over, tears springing from my eyes and see that Mrs C was, indeed, holding a lighted blowtorch. 'What the...?' I gasped.

Hitler accepts the ovation of the Reichstag after announcing the "peaceful" acquisition of Austria. Berlin, March 1938.

'Well, young man,' she exclaimed theatrically, 'no more problems with nasty old Mr Boil now, I think.' She lit a cigarette from the flame before extinguishing it.

'What the...?' I repeated.

'A new treatment,' she said, blowing a smoke ring in my direction. 'Quicker than a needle apparently. Read about it in *Woman's Own*.' She drew again on the cigarette. 'Or was it in *Tit-Bits*?' She pointed at her ample bosom with a suppressed giggle and winked at me.

'But, I don't have a...'

She clamped her hand over my mouth. 'He... doesn't... know... that,' she hissed, then added in a loud voice: 'Best get dressed young man and back to the sick bay.' She slapped a plaster on the affected area as she spoke.

There was nothing else for it but to gather my garments, taking care to dress extra carefully over my newly tenderised posterior. Once I had made myself decent I was aiming to creep down the hallway, hopefully without bumping into Mad Mungo, but of course that didn't happen.

'Kilroy, isn't it?' he asked sharply as I was only a yard or so from the front door.

'Yes sir.'

'Ah, got some homework for me I see?'

He had spotted an exercise book under my arm and before I could stop him he had plucked it from my grasp. I watched as he flicked it open.

I had recently been taking wagers on the number of acquittals at the "Trial of 21" in Moscow (none, although three escaped execution)* and there had been little interest. With still a few days to go before the verdicts were handed out I'd had hopes of interesting some of my fellow inmates in the sick bay.

'What is this?' Mungo was frowning as he turned the pages.

I'd used up about half the book by this stage, the accumulated jottings of several "events", all with wagers carefully recorded and signed for. I realised it would make no sense to anyone really and toyed with the idea of inventing some innocent explanation for Mungo, but all I could think about at that moment was that I had a throbbing backside. 'It's a sort of game, sir.'

Well, of course, Mungo wasn't to be deflected by that, so it wasn't long before he had dragged the whole story out of me. 'You had better come with me.'

I followed him back down the hall, taking the opportunity while his back was turned to frantically gesture at Mrs C to get me out of there.

He turned suddenly. 'What are you up to?'

'Er, nothing sir, just an itch.' I only just managed to avoid looking at Mrs C as I said it, wondering if beneath all that hair he really did have eyes in the back of his head.

We resumed our way to what turned out to be his study. 'Flora, make us a pot of tea, there's a love.'

Unseen by him, I noticed her eyebrows shoot heavenward, but she went off to the kitchen nonetheless.

'So, let's get this straight. You take bets, on, er, pretty well anything where you can count up an outcome?'

I nodded.

'The number of rainy days in April, or...' He glanced out the window. 'Or how long it takes old Baz Hope to mark out a rugby pitch?'

'Ha, ha, sir. Wait for ever for that I suppose, but yes, you could have a betting scheme even for that, sir.' I was thinking that the old boy might be as mad as a demented dervish but he seemed fairly quick on the uptake.

'So, tell me again about that young idiot, Simpson, and the *Publice Vindicatum*?'

---

* This was the last of the Moscow show trials, instigated by Stalin. It took place in March 1938 and the defendants included Bukharin, Rykov and Yagoda, all formerly leading Bolsheviks. There were no acquittals, although Rakovsky, one time ambassador to Britain, Pletnev and Bessonov escaped the death penalty. http://tinyurl.com/Kilroy024.

I started on the story of Keynes and his probabilities but he soon shushed me.

'Yes, yes, well you seem to know what you are on about.' He flicked through the book, squinting at the figures at the bottom of each page, where I had calculated my net winnings. 'I think we can overlook your little breach of school rules with this...' He tapped my exercise book. 'If...'

I said nothing although I had a feeling I knew where this might be leading. I had already decided I would agree to anything he came up with if only it would get me out of there.

'If...' He poured himself a tea and one for me as well I noticed. 'If, er, well, you know there are a few people in the staff room who like a bit of a flutter?'

I tried to look surprised as I nodded.

'And, tomorrow we have another P.V., don't we? I think we could have a little partnership here...'

'Oh, no sir, I couldn't do that. That wouldn't be right.'

His head swivelled around and he stared back at me in alarm.

'I mean, sir, if one of your people is giving out the thrashings the others are hardly going to place bets on the outcome.'

He hardly looked best pleased by this news and I was wondering where that was going to lead when I had a moment of inspiration. There was a copy of the *Daily Mirror* sitting on his desk and I snatched it up, turning to one of the inside pages. 'Look sir. Your colleagues aren't going to bet on schoolboy beatings, but what about sport? Football? Cricket and so on?'

I could see he was doubtful and, to be truthful, I was just making it up as I went along. I blundered on anyway. 'Preston North End versus Manchester City this Saturday?'* I stabbed at the fixture in the paper. 'How about the total number of goals scored? Or, er, the number of goals Preston North End score in April? The winning margin in the boat race? Or the number of fallers in the National?'

Nowadays I gather people will bet on the number of times a referee ties his bootlaces, but this sort of betting was unheard of then, so it took a while to work through what I had in mind. I tried some more examples.

'So we don't bet on who is going to win, but on other things like the number of teeth that that chap Schmeling will get knocked out?' he asked.†

---

* Manchester City entertained Preston North End on March 19th in a first division tie. The score was 1-2. This must have been a busy time for Kilroy's syndicate. The invasion of Austria, the show trial in Moscow and two changes of Premier in France all happened around then.

† German Max Schmeling was scheduled to fight Joe Louis for the Heavyweight Championship of the world in June 1938. He lost the fight but at least kept all his teeth. http://tinyurl.com/Kilroy025.

Eventually we carved out a deal, or to be more accurate he told me what the deal was. I would do all the work, work out the margins, keep the books and so on and in exchange he would turn a blind eye to my own modest financial shenanigans with the class. Oh yes, and he would pocket the proceeds from the staffroom.

And so the days passed. Bluebells blossomed, fledglings twittered in the trees and the path to the village turned from ice to mud to dust. We had the FA Cup Final and Benny Newbold's round dozen, Wimbledon fortnight and Simpson caught at the sherry again. I only remember one argument, over the number of times Czechoslovakia was mentioned in *The Times* in one day (26 I thought, others claimed 32*) but apart from that both classroom and staffroom seemed happy with our little extra-curricular activity. I'd splashed out on a rather natty HMV Medium Wave wireless and I noticed that Mungo had acquired a shiny red Raleigh bicycle, complete with the latest cable brakes *and* a Sturmey Archer three speed.

Then the summer vacation was upon us. I packed my trunk, had a final mad tumble with Mrs C, said my cheerios and set off for Bremen. A few weeks later I was back home and there I was standing before my step-father's desk.

As you have no doubt guessed I had decided it would be prudent to spare Pater the ins and outs of my little arrangement with Mrs C and just admit to the gambling syndicate. Money, odds, chance and all that chicanery were right into his top pocket, so it was with some relief I saw that the matter of my unscheduled exit from school was put to one side when I brought down my exercise book and he could question me on how I calculated the margins, collected the debts and paid out the winnings and so on.

He looked puzzled. 'So nobody's been cheated and everyone's happy?'

I nodded.

'Well, something's not right. Expulsion for a gentlemanly flutter seems a bit extreme. When I was in High School, we had a little Blackjack syndicate and nobody made a fuss as long as we did our homework on time.' He scratched his head and flicked through the last few pages. 'What's going on here?'

---

* The Czechoslovakian question – whether or not its largely German Sudetenland should join Austria in the Greater German Reich, as Hitler wanted – was a major news story for much of 1938. It is not clear which issue of *The Times* Kilroy is referring to, but to take one at random, Saturday 21st May carried no fewer than seven news stories concerning Czechoslovakia. The name also appears in the index and as an item under Stock Exchange Dealings, neither being directly concerned with the Sudetenland crisis, and this may possibly have been a source of argument.

I glanced at the page. 'R.A.F.'s recruitment drive,' I answered. 'Number of pilots, observers enlisted and so on. *The Times* has an update every Monday.'*

'But what about all these bets placed? You have not even been at the school?'

'No, but Mad, I mean, er, Mr Clark has been. No interest to us boys in the vac, ha ha, but some of the staff are still around and they seem to have been pretty keen on it, if all the betting slips he's sent me are anything to go by.'

That seemed to leave him content, that is until he turned to the last page. 'This isn't R.A.F. recruitment is it?' He thumped the page as he spoke and looked again. 'Jesus H. Christ. I know what this is.'

'What is it Pater?'

'Who's bet on this?' he barked.

'I don't know Pater. The slips only arrived this morning.'

'Go and get them. Be quick now.'

I ran upstairs, grabbed the envelope from my dressing table and ripped it open as I ran back down.

He grabbed them from me and before I could stop him had started filling in the names and amounts in the book. There were some very large sums there.

'What is it?' I asked again.

'Cricket. You Limeys and your game of cricket,' he said with a sigh, 'Baseball's a lot safer, I'm telling you.' He kept tutting as he continued writing. 'You were away for all the fuss last week, weren't you? Look it up in the paper.' He gestured at a pile of newspapers in the corner.

It didn't take me long to find what he was talking about. Just before the end of term Mad Mungo asked me to calculate the margins for England's last test match against the Australians. At the time England

* In June 1938 the Royal Air Force started a recruiting campaign with the aim of enlisting 31,000 pilots, observers, airmen and boys. By August, 600-700 a week were joining up, with progress duly reported each Monday in *The Times*.

were looking much the weaker side and I could see from Pater's work with the betting slips that most of the staff room had thought they would continue to fare badly in this last game. *The Times*, as ever, flagged the occasion with an understatement –"New Cricket Records" was the bland headline*.

I frantically scoured the article trying to pick out the essentials and there it was: England had scored a world record 903 runs and one of their players, Len Hutton had notched up 364 on his own account, which was more than the entire team had amassed in two attempts in the previous test.† So England had demolished the opposition and rewritten the record books while doing it. I looked at Pater's calculations. All well and good I thought, good for Mad Mungo and his staffroom takings and good for England's future prospects, but it shouldn't make much difference to me one way or the other. I was wrong on all points as it happened.‡

Scoreboard for England's historic innings at the Oval in 1938.

Looking at Pater's jottings I could see that most of the teachers had taken some sort of hit on the game but the biggest loser by far was our dear headmaster who stood to be down 350 pounds I think it was. I guessed that this would be not far short of his year's salary.

A few minutes later and Pater had been put through to the school. As usual for him it was a one-sided conversation although on this occasion he wasn't the one doing all the talking. I couldn't hear what the other party was saying but he certainly seemed very animated. All Pater could manage was

* This was reported on August 24th 1938.

† Not quite. England had lost the previous test match, in Leeds, in July. For their first innings of that test they scored only 242 runs and in their second they collapsed with a meagre 123 on the board, totalling 365 runs which is just one more than Hutton's tally in the final test.

‡ Kilroy was certainly wrong on England's future prospects. In the event they played little cricket after this, before the war intervened. There was a tour to South Africa in the winter and the West Indies visited the following summer, just before the outbreak of hostilities, but England's performance was mediocre in both series and there was no continuation of the devastating form they had found for that last test match at the Oval.

Thereafter test cricket and virtually all other international sport shut down for the duration. The next tests played by England were in 1946 by which time most of the old team had retired, although not Len Hutton, the scorer of the 364.

the odd 'Yes, but...' and 'You see, headmaster...' but this barely stemmed the torrent.

Eventually he just dropped the phone back on its cradle while the person I presumed was now my ex-headmaster was still in full flight. 'Asshole,' my stepfather said.

I started at that because Pater rarely swore.

'And your friend Mungo, I mean Mr Clark's, has been chopped as well,' he added with a sigh. 'And all because that godammed effing asshole can't be a man and just pay his godammed debts.'

I merely nodded. This didn't seem like the moment to remind Pater of his unscheduled exit ten years earlier from North America.

'Now what's to be done with you?' he asked.

Strange to relate, my stepfather's attitude to me seemed to have eased a little with this recent turn of events. It was hard to be sure, but I thought he seemed mildly pleased that I had shown some aptitude for the sort of business he liked best. The honeymoon wasn't to last of course but I'm running ahead of myself now. More immediately we had Helga to deal with.

Supermarine Spitfire K9795, the 9th production Mk I, with R.A.F. 19 Squadron in 1938.

A few minutes later and we were standing either side of her as she sat at the kitchen table with her head in her hands. 'But I wanted the boy to be a fock turd,' she said.

Pater and I exchanged looks. 'What was that, my dear?' he asked.

'A fock turd,' we heard between muffled sobs. 'I wanted him to be a Harley Street fock turd.'

Pater looked relieved. 'Oh, I see, a doc-tor, dearest. But there's going to be a war. Before the year's out if I'm not mistaken.' He gestured at me to put the kettle on. 'No time for studying medicine anyway. It will have to be the army for him.'

That was not the wisest thing to say to Helga at that moment or indeed at any time. She had lost four brothers on the Western Front in the previous show. Fighting for the other lot of course but dead and missed just the same.

Pater and I stood around awkwardly as we waited for the sniffling to subside. After a decent interval I poured the teas. You might notice that I hadn't had much to contribute thus far on the subject of my future. I decided to make my move. 'There's always the R.A.F.'

They both looked at me and said nothing. The papers had been full of stories of our new fighters, the Spitfire and the Hurricane, and I rather fancied myself, standing by the bar, an ATS girl on each arm whilst modestly refusing to talk about the number of Jerries bagged. What a fool I was. We all were. If I'd known what was in store I'd have begged to go back somewhere, anywhere that would have me, keep my head down and study my darnedest to be a fock turd.

English Electric Lightning.

Helga was the first to speak. She turned to Pater. 'Couldn't he start with you in the family business?'

Pater had just taken a sip of his tea and most of it landed back in the cup. 'Good God no. With his appetite for risk we'd have another Wall Street Crash in no time.'

If I had any thoughts about Pater's own performance in the last Wall Street Crash I kept them to myself, but I do recall protesting that thanks to my cunning calculations I had in fact made a small but steady income. Pater, though, was convinced it was beginner's luck and, in short, I'd just been 'goddamned lucky' as he put it. And of course he had to have the last word. 'Let the R.A.F. have him,' was his verdict. 'The City will be much safer for him being at Cranwell.'

And so it was to be, although as you will see shortly my induction into the R.A.F. was anything but smooth. At any rate, years later, with the war safely behind us all, I discovered Pater's instincts about me had been right. It was in the late fifties when I was in the States on a mission to sell the Lightning to the Yanks.* On a night off I had ended up in a poker school with some Mathematics professor, MacNeil was his name and while we were winding down after the game I got around to telling him about my schoolboy syndicate. I was surprised he was so interested but on his prompting I eventually managed to dredge up the ins and outs of my method. He was horrified. 'Jeez,' he said, 'You've just murdered Bayes Theorem.† You can't do that.' He then sketched out on the tablecloth where I'd gone wrong. Well, there you are. So it was beginners luck after all,

* The English Electric Lightning was in R.A.F. service from 1959 to 1988. With an astonishing Mach 2 performance and a 50,000 feet per minute rate of climb it would outperform most of today's fighters. The Americans never bought it. http://tinyurl.com/Kilroy026.

† Bayes Theorem is a mathematical result widely used in statistics and probability and so possibly applicable to gambling.

but I still took over a hundred bucks off MacNeil at the game. And the waitress made him fork out an extra five dollars too, it being a linen tablecloth.*

* The Mathematics professor Kilroy refers to could be Charles K. McNeil, from the University of Chicago. McNeil is credited with inventing spread betting in the 1940s and is also noted as a one-time tutor of John F Kennedy. Kilroy's betting methodology sounds remarkably similar to spread betting and so preceded McNeil by several years, even if his calculation of the odds was flawed. McNeil in http://tinyurl.com/Kilroy027.

CHAPTER 5

It was a Thursday, a few weeks later, and I was sitting behind two hundred throbbing horse power, the most powerful engine that Leyland produced. Position: Feltham. Destination: Heston Aerodrome in West London. Quite possibly you know that Leyland Motors never made aero engines so I might as well confess that I was not sitting at the controls of a powerful war-bird but was rather positioned on a bench seat just behind the driver on a grubby red liveried double-decker London bus – rumbling along the 152 route as I recall.

There were a dozen or so other passengers with me in the downstairs compartment, all yawning and stretching as we watched the sun rise over the factories and offices nearby and generally wishing we were still abed. At this time Heston Aerodrome was not used for military operations, training or otherwise, so you might now be wondering whether said hero's glittering aviation career had in fact not got off to the much anticipated glittering start. It hadn't.

Following my untimely exit from Herne Bay's House of Horrors, Pater had swung into action with, what seemed to me, alarming efficiency. He was on the phone first thing the next morning to a contact at the Aviation Ministry. Then it was a matter of only a couple of hours for the obliging desk pilot to amend some paperwork, tweak a paperclip, ping a couple of rubber bands and suddenly the Royal Air Force had a most promising recruit. The very next week I was dispatched, hair shaven to a bristle and clad in my newly acquired Saville Row suit, to the famous R.A.F. officer training college at Cranwell in Lincolnshire.

It did not take long to discover there was an impediment to my plan for becoming a famous fighter ace en route to an appointment as the youngest air marshal in history. As an essential part of my introduction to the College I was taken up on a series of "air experience" trips in a Tiger Moth, the little open seater bi-plane that was very popular with the R.A.F. in those days. This is where I found there was a disagreement between my visual perception of motion and my vestibular system's sense of movement. That is how the medical officer described it anyway. All I knew was that I had air sickness. We tried everything: dried olives, cracker biscuits, lemons, in short enough canapes and condiments for a Buckingham Palace garden party, but the end result was always the same. I was fine until we took off, but as soon as the wheels left the ground I'd feel the sweats and dizziness starting. I would grip the sides of the cockpit, trying to concentrate on what the instructor was telling me through the crude intercom, but then I would get a whiff of petrol and that would be it, usually straight back down my speaking tube.

After a miserable couple of weeks I was back home and once again sitting around the table with Pater and Helga. This time our conference was

Royal Air Force College, Cranwell.

in the kitchen – cook being off sick as I recall – so the three of us sat there gloomily munching on crusty sandwiches as my future was once again to be mapped out.

Helga was quick to point out that 'Nelson suffered seasickness all his life,' to which my stepfather grunted something about how Nelson, when he wasn't busy thrashing all those Frenchies single-handed, had the common sense to throw up over the side. I think I might have mentioned motor torpedo boats at this point but Pater was dead against any career on anything that moved he said and was speaking broadly in favour of sending me down a coal mine when Candice breezed in.

'What the lad needs,' she said, 'is continual exposure to the problem and then he'll get over it.' She filled a glass from the tap and, without waiting for a reply, breezed out leaving the tap running, with the rest of us staring after her.

I haven't mentioned Candice before, because until then, she had played little part in my life. She was Pater's daughter from some way back, before his fling with Mutter obviously and had spent most of her childhood with *her* mother, in the States. She had been over to visit a couple of times during the years and now she was with us for a few days, on her way to some hoity-toity educational establishment in Switzerland.

Candice's remark started a debate between Helga and Pater about the pros and cons of various motion sickness cures, argued with the stubbornness of two people who know nothing whatsoever about the subject. I was happy to let them get on with it. At any rate my recent shortcomings were temporarily forgotten, so I quietly got up from the table and walked through to the living room.

Candice was sitting sideways in an armchair, legs draped over one of the arms as she read a book, humming quietly to herself. We were about the same age and, as I said, we hadn't seen a great deal of each other but I can't say we'd got on when we did. I guessed that she found my forced polite English ways a little pansyish for her liking and although she was a pretty young thing, for my part I'd always found her as snooty as a room full of duchesses.

'Be a darling,' she drawled without looking up, 'and make me a caw-fee.'

I pointedly ignored her, picked up a newspaper and sat down opposite.

Pater and Helga were still squabbling in the kitchen. Then I heard Pater sigh. There was a final 'Oh, for God's sake woman,' followed by the sound of a chair scraping on the kitchen floor and then he was with us in the living room. 'Why don't you two do something useful?' he barked.

We eyed each other warily.

'Come on you two. Get to know each other, eh?' He clapped his hands. 'I know. Why don't you play that game we were playing last night – the one Candice brought over with her? With the houses and hotels?'

Candice raised her eyebrows at me but she got up nonetheless and fetched it from the shelf. Pater was talking about the Monopoly board game of course. It had been invented only a couple of years earlier in the States and, so Candice had told us, *everyone* was playing it over there. She unfolded the board on the coffee table and set up all the cards and pieces while I tried to look interested. The four of us had indeed played the game the night before and I had found it pretty tedious – four hours of shuffling my silly little Scottie dog token around the board with all of four and ninepence ha'penny* to spend, until at last I landed on two of Helga's hotels on successive moves and was wiped out. Pater had loved it. Well that was pretty inevitable really and of course he won easily.

This time around was more enjoyable. Without having to contend with Pater's bullish tactics and Helga's Machiavellian ways I found, unexpectedly, that I was doing quite well. Candice and I seemed to be getting on marginally better too. That is I ignored her attempts to cheat and she let pass my wisecracks about American footballers.

I guess a couple of hours must have passed as if in an instant, with Pater and Helga having slipped out almost unnoticed by us, when we had a break. Candice made the tea. It tasted like it had been brewed with Pater's socks but it represented some small improvement in North Atlantic relations I thought. I took a last sip from my cup, taking care not to grimace and threw the dice. It was a six and a one. I'll always remember it. A six and

* Four shillings and nine pence halfpenny in Sterling currency would, at the time, have been worth approximately one dollar, the smallest note used in the US Monopoly game.

a one. I moved my counter and it landed on a vacant red square. 'Yes!!' I cried. 'Kentucky Avenue. Another set!'

Candice pursed her lips and flicked through the property cards. She pulled out the one I needed and waved it in my direction. As I reached out she snatched it away.

I sighed. 'Come on Candice. Give me the card.'

I reached towards it again but she just repeated the manoeuvre.

'Please Candice,' I declared, 'Give me the card. Stop faffing around.'

I must confess that at that moment I had become so engrossed in the game that all I could think about was that with Kentucky Avenue in my portfolio, I could put some more hotels on the board and very likely win. At this stage we were sitting on the floor with the board on the coffee table between us so I crawled around to her side to claim the card. Still Candice was having none of it. But by then I had seen the funny side of it all and we were both giggling as we fought for the card. At one point I recall I grabbed both of her wrists but she managed to wriggle one hand free and, before I could stop her, she had slipped it down the front of her blouse.

'Jesus, Candice,' I exclaimed.

There are a lot more interesting things than Kentucky Avenue in a woman's blouse, as I was soon reminded. Candice didn't seem to mind as I pretended to make a hash of trying to find my treasure, as I called it. All the while she just lay quietly, on her back on the floor, with a sort of amused quizzical look on her face, her arms stretched above her head as if in surrender. 'Are you enjoying yourself in there?' she asked eventually.

'Just taking a Chance with the Community Chest m'dear, I said. I looked down and could see a tinge of colour to her face. 'And er... I was wondering where I might find Marven Gardens?'

Her eyes widened and I wondered what she was going to say but then her mouth crooked into a smile, her arm reached out behind my neck and she pulled me to her.

If you have never played the US version of Monopoly I can highly recommend it. Over the next few minutes I cruised slowly up Park Place, hung a right along Broadwalk, almost took a wrong turn up Baltic Avenue, before finally overcoming only token resistance in Wall Street. By then, the Pennsylvania Railroad had built up a full head of steam and so was in perfect time for its triumphant arrival at Grand Central Station.*

---

* At the time Kilroy was playing this game a British version of Monopoly was available, with its property locations named after well-known London districts, but it would seem the Kilroy family was unaware of it (Mayfair, where they lived, is the most expensive property in British Monopoly). The locations featured in the US version of Monopoly are in Atlantic City and not New York as is often supposed by non-Americans. Kilroy has recalled most of them correctly, but not Wall Street and Grand Central Station which are

Afterwards we just lay alongside each other, in silence. I don't know what Candice was thinking but my thoughts were along the lines of 'What the hell was I thinking of?' With the madness no longer upon me I realised with a jolt that we were, well, brother and sister, well, sort of. Fortunately, I reflected, she was only going to be around another couple of days and if we... And that was as far as I got with my plans because at that moment I heard the front door bang.

'The best laid schemes of mice and men gang aft agley.' Rabbie Burns wrote those words 200 years ago. And he knew a thing or two about women because, you might notice, he said nothing of *their* blinking schemes going *agley* or indeed going anywhere else.* You might recall that I'd already been treated to Mrs C's scheming in a tight corner and so, there I was again with only a desperate hope that Candice would deliver something equally enterprising.

Candice was indeed to be enterprising but not quite as I hoped. Picture the scene: Candice, hair unkempt, items of underwear strewn around the lounge, blouse undone and skirt hoisted to her armpits. Then there was me: well, even now, I still can't bear to think of the sight I presented – let's just say the Monopoly was in disarray. The door crashes open and, framed in the opening, Pater with Helga just behind him.

'What the...?' cried Pater.

I leapt to my feet, attempting to adjust my dress, as they say. Candice jumped up, pulling down her skirt. I was wondering what I might do, what she might do and then I saw her, without a moment's hesitation, run to her father. 'Daddy,' she cried.

'What the...?' Pater repeated.

Candice threw herself into his arms. I couldn't quite make out what she said next, her voice being directed into his shoulder. It might have been 'Thank God, you are here Daddy.' I do recall she raised a very convincing sob. Mind you I felt like sobbing myself right then.

'It's not what it seems, sir...' I started bravely. I was hopping on one foot while trying to put a sock on the other. I've no idea what I might have come up with had I been asked to explain myself further but there didn't seem much chance of that happening.

---

indeed in New York and play no part in the original US game. http://tinyurl.com/Kilroy028.

*The line is taken from the noted Robert Burns poem, 'To a mouse, on turning her up in her nest with the plough,' written in 1785. Burns had numerous relationships with women in his short life, most famously with Jean Armour, who bore him nine children. His complete works (including this poem) can be downloaded (for free) at Gutenberg: http://tinyurl.com/Kilroy029.

'You viper. You vile...' Fortunately he was lost for words at this point. 'Stay there,' he shouted. 'You stay right there.' He turned around and led Candice away.

Helga had been very quiet throughout. I'm not sure what she had made of it all. As I turned to look at her, her lips pursed and I thought she was going to say something but in the end she just shook her head and followed Candice and Pater upstairs.

With the room to myself, at least I had a chance to make things look decent. I smartened myself up, straightened my tie, found my other sock, picked up the Monopoly pieces and generally tried to make things look like, well, look like things hadn't happened. Candice's brassiere I found in the corner and for wont of somewhere to lose it I stuffed it in a flower pot. All the while, I heard shrieks and sobs from upstairs.

Twenty minutes later I was out in the street. It was almost a relief to be thrown out. Evidently the possibility of pressing criminal charges was still being considered but in the meantime, my stepfather said, I could just get out. I attempted to protest that I had no money and nowhere to go but he wasn't interested. In the end I thought it safest to leave before he stuck an axe in my head.

London is a great city but not much fun on a Saturday night for a young man with no money and only the clothes he stands up in. I remembered that my old sparring partner, Jennings, lived nearby. I went around to ring his doorbell but had forgotten it was term time and so he wasn't there. There was nothing for it but to spend the first night of my new life in the park – that's Hyde Park, which was only a short walk away. It was of course a disturbed and mainly sleepless night but I must have nodded off on a park bench at some stage because I recall being awoken with my face being licked. I opened my eyes to find that it was daylight and I was face to face with Rex, next door's dalmatian.

Normally I couldn't stand the beast but on this occasion the reminder of times past, my own lecherous folly and all that I'd lost almost brought tears to my eyes. I gently patted him, choosing to ignore his bad breath and in return he wagged his tail and slobbered over my shoes. There was a cry in the distance. Rex's ears pricked up and he turned and loped off towards a young woman pushing a pram. I knew her of course. It was Ida, next door's nanny, out bright and early with the young Master Snooty for his morning constitutional I guessed. I could see her look in my direction. She did a double take, hesitated for a few seconds then, to my relief, gave only a quick wave before she headed off.

Half an hour later Helga was with me. Not surprisingly she was in one of her no-nonsense moods. 'How could you?' she asked abruptly, as she sat down at the far end of the bench.

Fortunately the park was still largely deserted because conversation was necessarily a little loud. I stared into middle distance. 'Well I...' I began.

'You should be ashamed of yourself. With *Candice* of all people?' Helga wouldn't look at me I noticed. She sniffed as she rubbed at a handkerchief clasped in her hands.

'You see, er...' I began. Of course I couldn't think what to tell her, but fortunately Helga wasn't giving me much chance to say anything.

'She says you, er, well you...' Her voice trailed off. 'Well, Pater says hanging's too good for you and that bad blood will out. He won't have you back. It's impossible, you know?'

I nodded. I'd sort of guessed that. I was just wondering how to claim *some* mitigation in that Candice had been a little more willing than she now chose to admit, when Helga solved the problem for me.

'Oh, you fool. You absolute fool,' she pronounced. 'How could you be so stupid as to take up with that absolute *hussy*?' She spat out the word and banged the bench with her fist.

I tried to look surprised. It hadn't escaped my notice the previous evening that Candice had certainly made all the right moves during our little encounter, and with what seemed like well-practised ease, but I'd hardly felt I could say this.

'Why, your stepfather doesn't know the half of it, with all her wide eyed innocence and simpering.' Her face hardened. 'Anyway, I know the cut of her jib alright. And she's no better than, than... that Hayley woman.'

That set me back a bit. My ongoing arrangement with Hayley was supposed to be my little secret but then I should have known that Helga, with a nose for intelligence that would have put Mata Hari to shame, was more than capable of homing in on my supposedly innocent comings and goings just around the corner.

Helga rose and sat down again beside me. She took both my hands and looked me full in the face. I could see she had been crying. 'Now, what's to be done with you, you young rascal?'

I must have muttered something about joining the navy but she shushed me.

'No. I know a place you can stay.'

I looked hopeful, thinking that anywhere would be better than a park bench. She reached into her handbag, pulled out a business card and handed it to me. It read "Cecil McKenzie, Import and Export – no consignment too small, no finance too great". His address, I noticed, was somewhere out in the suburbs, in Surrey. 'That name sounds familiar?' I asked.

'Yes, Pater did some business with him once.'

And fell out, I remembered. He had been at the house only once, there had been what might be called a full and frank exchange of views and then he was gone, back out the front door not long after he had come in through it.

'And how do *you* know him?' I asked.

Helga coloured slightly. 'Never mind with your questions, young man. Go and see him. He's at home today and he's expecting you.'

'But...'

'Don't argue. Just go.' She reached into her bag again, pulled out a five pound note and handed it to me. 'You'd better have this. Now be gone with you before you get into any more trouble.'

CHAPTER 6

'What do you make of this?' he blurted out, glaring madly at me like a preacher who's overdone the communion wine.

I tried to figure out what he was holding but as he was jiggling it up and down so quickly I wasn't quite sure. 'It's er, er... It's a toothbrush!' He slowed a little and I could see that I was right.

'No, young man.' He pointed the object at me. 'This... this is the future,' and he slapped it down on the table between us.

I paused. Over the years I was to become used to conversation with him but this was my first day. As you've probably guessed the madman with the toothbrush was the, er, friend of Helga, that is Cecil McKenzie ('Call me Mac, young feller – everyone else does') and it was indeed he who was my new landlord.

I picked up the toothbrush, which looked like, well, a toothbrush.

'Ny-lon,' he pronounced.

I stared back.

'Invented by some boffin in the States. Soon they will be making *everything* with it. Rope, tents, ladies stockings, everything.'

'Won't they find them rather bristly?' I asked.

He ignored me. 'Look,' he snatched it back and pointed at the head. 'Soft, durable and hygienic, eh? Marvellous, what? Now stand back – watch this,' he started flexing the shaft, 'so wonderfully supp...' It snapped. He tossed the remains over his shoulder and continued, unfazed. 'The question is: would a young fellow like you happily fork out half a crown for one?'

I nodded my head doubtfully.

'Well I hope so. I've got 50 boxes of the little buggers piled up in the garage.'[*]

And that was Mac in a nutshell. Import and Export it said on his business card and the evidence of this was in the boxes, cartons and packing cases of all shapes, sizes and nationalities, piled all around us, along the hallway and in most of the rooms as far as I could tell.

[*] Nylon was first produced in 1935 at Dupont's research facility in Delaware in the US. Its initial commercial application was as the bristles in toothbrushes, but not the shaft, and this is possibly why the toothbrush in Kilroy's account snapped. Ladies stockings came later – in 1940, after it had been introduced as a fabric at the New York World's Fair in 1939. http://tinyurl.com/Kilroy030.

Later that evening, when clearing a place to sleep, I came across a consignment of Packard Lifetime-Lektro Ladies Shavers. I managed to blow up one of them before I had even shaved one leg. There was also a box containing some funny looking pens, called "Biros", fitted with a small ball bearing instead of a nib – ink indelible on both skin and bed linen I discovered[*] and, best of all, years later when I was clearing his loft, under a dusty pile of 1930s *Paris Match* magazines, a funny looking typewriter with wires and plugs hanging out the front, housed in a polished mahogany box with a brass nameplate embossed with the word "Enigma". In short, if something was novel, mad or daft enough Mac would buy it.[†] Those were his imports and I dread to think what he exported – Thames Valley mudpacks no doubt. He had his fair share of disasters one way and another but overall he did well enough to live in some comfort and not a little chaotic splendour in Waverley Towers (actually a bungalow) just outside London on the famous Claremont estate.[‡]

Claremont Estate, Esher, near London.

---

[*] Colonel Jacob Schick patented the "shaving machine" in 1930. By the late 1930s many US companies were selling electric shavers. http://tinyurl.com/Kilroy031.

László József Bíró invented the ballpoint pen and patented his design in 1938. Its development was interrupted by the war. http://tinyurl.com/Kilroy032.

[†] It would have been easy for someone like Cecil McKenzie to obtain an early Enigma coding machine before the war. In the 1920s, its inventor, Arthur Scherbius, produced a range of Enigmas for commercial use and some of them found their way to the UK. However, Kilroy's description points at the later military Enigma (which was an enhanced design and a lot more secure) and it seems extraordinary that McKenzie could have obtained one of them back in the 1930s. Certainly the code breakers at Bletchley Park would have loved to have had it but because their work was so secret he would have been unaware of this. It was nearly two years into the war before one was captured intact, from a sinking U-boat and it wasn't until 1974, with the publication of *The Ultra Secret* by F. W. Winterbotham, that the general public became aware of the Bletchley code-breakers and the enormous contribution they had made to the war effort. http://tinyurl.com/Kilroy033.

[‡] Claremont is just outside Esher, to the south west of London. It was once a royal estate and the home of George IV's daughter, Princess Charlotte, who would have reigned instead of Queen Victoria had she not died young. In the twentieth century Claremont House was taken over by a private school and its landscape gardens were acquired by the National Trust. The rest of the grounds were developed into an exclusive private estate with homes which proved to be very popular with the rich and famous. George Harrison, of the Beatles, lived at 16, Claremont Drive in the 1960s. Google Maps

Mac's web of contacts wasn't quite up to Pater's standards but did include someone called Harold Balfour – he's not widely remembered nowadays but was a man of some influence in his time. Evidently there had been a phone call just before my arrival and the result was that I had a job waiting for me at my new abode, in aviation of all things, as a "cabin boy" with British Airways.* As I was about to discover, air cabin boys were the dogsbodies of the industry, expected to load luggage, man the gang plank, soothe the passengers, get the pilot his favourite sandwiches or whatever. And, as you've no doubt guessed, the job necessarily entailed being aboard an aeroplane as it bounced around the sky.

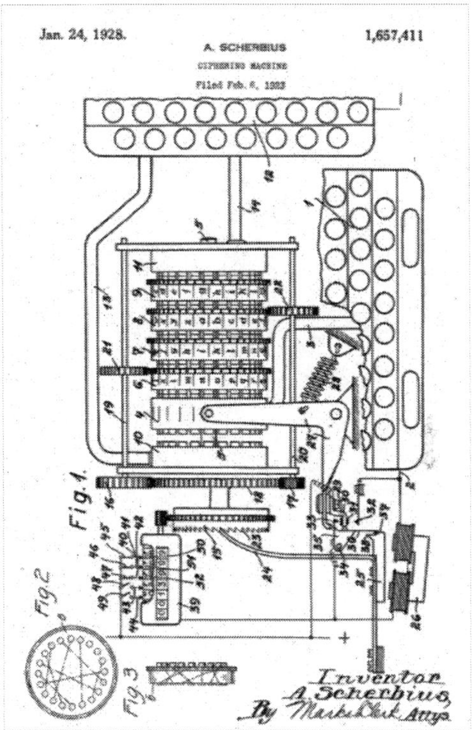

US Patent for "commercial" Enigma cyphering machine, number 1,657,411, granted in 1928.

'Yes,' said Mac as he gave me the glad tidings, he had thought about that. He'd heard about my little problem at Cranwell and did I know that with regular exposure it would soon go away? At the time I couldn't think where I had heard that before so I just gulped – not for the last time over the next couple of weeks – and merely nodded in reply.

Thereafter I was busy. Mac was busy. Claremont was busy. The whole country was busy. Never mind the little ins and outs of my life – the early bus to work each day and the ups and downs of the Paris mail run – but more importantly dear old Blighty was on the brink of war and we ordinary citizens had plenty to worry about, in the shape of the Luftwaffe.

Streetview: http://tinyurl.com/Kilroy034 Claremont School: http://tinyurl.com/-Kilroy035 National Trust: http://tinyurl.com/Kilroy036.

* The company has only a tenuous connection with the present day national carrier of the same name. Harold Balfour, WWI flying ace, politician, who subsequently became Lord Balfour, was influential in aviation in the 1930s and was at that time a director of British Airways Ltd. http://tinyurl.com/Kilroy212.

It was 1938 so you'll know we didn't go to war in the end, not that year anyway. How that came about and my part in it I will deal with presently, but for those few frantic weeks of autumn we all thought we *would* be at war and then, as our prime minister had kindly assured us, 'the bomber would always get through.'* So we'd lie awake at night, clutching our gas masks and wondering if we'd be alive come Christmas, but being British we'd say nothing about it by day and busy ourselves with "preparations". There were children to be evacuated, shelters to be built, monuments to be sandbagged, trenches to be dug and balloons to be flown. No loafing around listening to the wireless after a hard day's cabin-boying – I was out with a spade digging a trench across next door's lawn – he was furious when he returned – or helping Mac put up some daft construction called an "Anderson shelter" in his back garden.† The R.A.F. was on our doorstep as well, not with a squadron of Spitfires or anything useful like that, but *with* some ridiculous balloon and *without* anyone who knew how to fly it. We served them tea and biscuits while their lorries chewed up the golf course opposite.‡

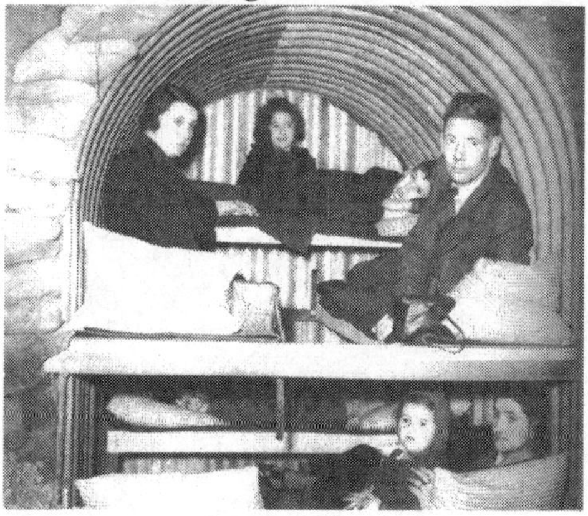

Anderson air-raid shelter.

Adolf Hitler was at the core of the problem of course. Having clobbered Austria while I was busy with Matron and the betting syndicate

* It was not Chamberlain but an earlier prime minister, Baldwin, who had said in 1932 that 'the bomber will always get through.' In the event he was overly pessimistic but it was widely believed in the late 1930s.

† The Anderson Shelter, named after Sir John Anderson, the man responsible for the country's air raid precautions at that time, was a cheap structure made primarily of galvanised corrugated steel panels, which could be assembled in any back garden and could then accommodate up to six people. The one Kilroy refers to here must have been a prototype as the Anderson was not generally available to the public until February the following year. http://tinyurl.com/Kilroy037.

‡ Barrage balloons were used throughout the war as a defence against low flying bombers, each with a tethering steel cable which was intended to bring down any aircraft that may strike it. Balloon defences were first organized by the R.A.F. into a Balloon "Group" in 1937, and later (in November 1938) a larger Balloon "Command". The Balloon Centre at Hook, in Surrey, was near Claremont and its balloons were deployed at various locations nearby. http://tinyurl.com/Kilroy038.

he had next set his sights on Czechoslovakia. The difficulty here was that we had a treaty with the Czechs and were obliged to defend them from their nasty neighbour.[*] So while I had been busy throwing up over my flying instructor, Prime Minister Neville Chamberlain invented shuttle-diplomacy, flying backwards and forwards to Germany in an attempt to soothe Herr H without losing too much face in the process.

We all thought he'd failed and were bracing ourselves for the inevitable when, with some desperate diplomacy, the prime minister secured a final meeting with Hitler, to be held in Munich. He was to fly out there early in the morning of the 29th September and, as he was being driven out of London in a motorcade, I was sitting yawning on a 152 bus. We were both heading for Heston Airport.[†]

---

[*] Not strictly true. The French had a treaty with Czechoslovakia and the UK had a treaty with the French.

[†] During the 1930s London had two airports. Croydon, to the south, was used by Imperial Airways to serve the Empire while Heston, to the west, was home to British Airways Ltd for the European routes. After the war Heston survived as a USAAF base for a short time but with Heathrow nearby and under rapid development it was soon side-lined. Today the airport is buried under a housing and industrial estate, with the M4 motorway cutting through it. http://tinyurl.com/Kilroy039.

CHAPTER 7

I knew he was coming. The whole country knew. And as I stepped off the bus that morning I could see that most of West London had descended on Heston for the occasion. I should have been in my finest British Airways uniform for the occasion but that was at the dry cleaners (again). Instead I was wearing my best Savile Row suit, figuring that as the newly recruited and randomly vomiting cabin boy, it would surely pass muster. I didn't expect to be much involved with anything important in any case.

There were people everywhere – young, old, men and women, short, fat and tall, all standing on tiptoe and spilling off the pavement to stare back up the road as I slowly threaded my way through them. Outside the terminal building I had to push hard to make any way at all. 'A bigger turnout than the Arsenal,' I heard a burly copper mutter as I squeezed past him. Near the main entrance I was surprised to find I recognised some of the faces: Sir John Simon, Walter Elliot, Hailsham and others. It seemed that, in a rare moment of solidarity, the cabinet had showed up to lend their support and, by the look of the jaundiced pasty faces and stifled yawns alongside them, I guessed there was a fair turnout from our national press too.

At that moment a procession of police cars, Humbers, Wolseleys and other vehicles drew up. Somewhere in the middle, coming to a halt precisely by the entrance was a Bentley. The crowd broke into applause, so I gathered the hero of the hour had arrived. I took the opportunity to push through the doors and, once inside, I decided to hang around awhile in the entrance hall. A few seconds later I heard a commotion, someone opened the doors and for the first time in my life I came face to face with a world statesman. There was a pause as he stopped, with the others holding back behind him while we eyed each other. With the silence that followed I started to feel embarrassed, wondering if I should bow. Then, I confess, I had a sudden ridiculous impulse to curtsey. I was saved when Old Man Balfour appeared. I'd earlier been told to make sure I jumped to it if he was around, but my idleness was the last thing on his mind at that moment. He came breezing out of his office, smiled warmly at one and all and gestured at the PM to come to the waiting room. The PM nodded at me and I exclaimed, 'Good luck, sir,' as he and the others swept by.

After he had passed I found myself wondering why I had bothered to smarten up for the occasion. Pater had had gardeners better dressed than our PM that day. At least he wasn't carrying his talisman umbrella* for this occasion, but I remember noticing that his hair was lank and greasy and thinking that his little winged collar didn't do much for him either – it was formal diplomatic dress in those days but at the time it just made him look like he was a relic from a bygone age. Over the years I've discovered that famous people always look different when you see them in the flesh for the first time but the main thing that struck me that morning was that he looked so worryingly frail. He was in his late sixties, which was not so old for a politician in those days, but as it turned out he had only two years left to live. Some say that he enjoyed excellent health up to the end but to me, on that morning at Heston, he looked like a doomed man. Which he was in so many ways, I suppose.

As the new boy I was only to be entrusted with loading the comestibles for the flight and that was it. I was rather hoping to loaf around in the terminal a while longer but Balfour soon had me directed out to the apron, where two gleaming silver aeroplanes stood side by side. The airline had just taken delivery of the latest in flight-line technology, in the shape of American Lockheed Super Electras. They may have been the pride of the fleet but aviation still had a way to go in the thirties. In short the new planes could carry only 12 passengers apiece and, with about 20 souls on this last desperate mission to Germany, we'd had to lay on another flight.

A Lockheed Super Electra over Manhattan in 1938, and piloted by Howard Hughes.

I strolled up to the aeroplanes but could see there was not a lot happening at this point. The sun had risen and was starting to bake the ground below. The pilots were strolling around their mounts, waggling the control surfaces on the wings, kicking the tyres and generally joshing each other about who would get there first. Parked nearby was an Austin van, with the word "Savoy" written on the side in bright gold lettering. It was my job to unload it, distributing its contents equally between the two galleys. I remember thinking that the world might be in crisis but, by crikey, our team of negotiators wasn't going to go hungry. There were little picnic hampers with neatly typed labels inscribed with "Grouse", "Caviar" and "Salmon", crates containing bottles of beer, claret and cider, best linen

* The PM was seen so often with his furled umbrella that he was nicknamed 'Umbrella Man' and often shown with it in cartoons. http://tinyurl.com/Kilroy040.

napkins, glasses, shiny white plates and gleaming cutlery. And that was only the starters. It was a struggle fitting it all in.

Only then did I remember that I had a camera with me, lodged in my jacket pocket. A typical camera in those days needed to be carried around on wheels (well, just about) so something that you could slip into your pocket was certainly remarkable. I pulled it out, took a couple of snaps of the planes and, in the absence of any more elite subject matter, attempted a close-up of a pigeon doing its business on the roof of the van. The camera was another of Mac's speciality imports, called a "Minox" and designed by some genius in Latvia, with all the necessary optics and whatever else crammed into a slim-line package not much bigger than a cigarette lighter. No doubt you know the sort of device I'm talking about – they've since turned up in plenty of post-war spy films, but back then nobody had seen anything like it. And, as you will see, it was to have an important part to play in the Munich mission, but not in the way you might expect.*

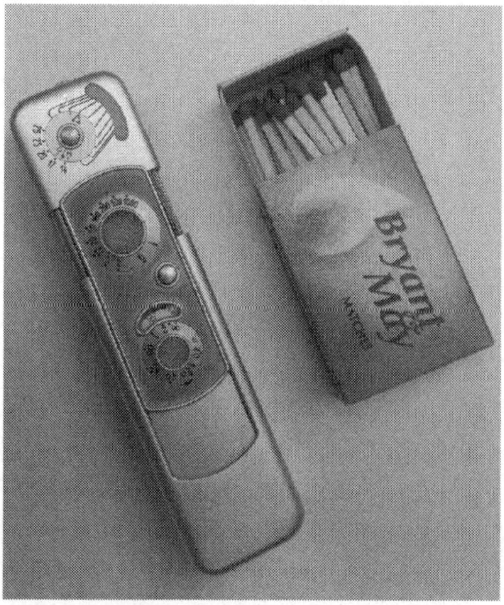

A post-war Minox camera, the design largely unchanged.

My photo session didn't last long. Old Man Balfour came out to chivvy things along, clutching his pocket watch and looking worried. By then I'd finished my chores and was on my own on the apron – the pilots had finally kicked enough out of their tyres and had moved up to their flight decks, where they were flicking switches, folding maps and consulting clipboards. They both gave Balfour a thumbs up and so he waved his hand, beckoning to the passenger terminal and people started to file out. I stood by the ladder of one of the planes, ready to render assistance if needed.

* The Minox 'subminiature' camera was invented in 1936 by a Baltic German, Walter Zapp and first produced in Latvia. It was a remarkable achievement for the time, measuring just 80 × 27 x 16 mms and weighing 130 gms – not much bigger than a cigarette lighter, as Kilroys says. It possessed all the functionality and quality optics of a much larger device. After the war, production resumed in Germany, and continued with essentially the same design into the 21st century when it was finally overtaken by digital technology. http://tinyurl.com/Kilroy041.

Chamberlain was not there at this point and so, apart from Wilson and Dunglass,* who I had seen pictured on previous diplomatic missions over the summer, I didn't recognise anybody. I could see the group divide into two parties as they approached and gathered that there was a planned demarcation as to who was to go on which plane. My plane was getting

some burly looking chaps in heavy macintoshes – security obviously, whilst the other was going to hold the Westminsterites. My charges formed an orderly queue as I pointed them up the ladder into the passenger compartment while, out of the corner of my eye, I could see our elected

* Sir Horace Wilson, the PM's most senior advisor and Lord Dunglass (later Prime Minister Sir Alec Douglas-Home) his parliamentary private secretary. http://tinyurl.com/Kilroy042 (Wilson); http://tinyurl.com/Kilroy043 (Dunglass).

representatives a few yards away on the apron, squabbling over who should board first and who should sit where.*

I ushered the last burly macintosh aboard knowing there were still some places left. Behind them was a small posse of even larger gentleman and I realised I had seen them earlier on the way into the terminal. Those ruddy unhealthy faces were quite unforgettable and I was sure I must have been right first time – the press corps, although I could not imagine how they had wangled their way on the trip.

The last one to board looked especially peaky, like he had lingered a little late with the Liebfraumilch. I was not that surprised when, as he was levering himself through the doorway, I noticed what I might delicately describe as a wind of change. Without thinking I called after him, 'Gut fahrt, mein herr,' which is German for 'Good journey, my man.' Now that may not be the funniest thing you ever heard but the remark certainly precipitated a very interesting 24 hours for yours truly.

Being busy helping the cops and loafers aboard I hadn't noticed that the PM had arrived on the apron and was waiting to board the other plane. When he heard me speak he looked over, turned and said something to the man standing alongside him. They both came over and stood before me.

'What did you just say?' asked the PM.

'Well sir, um, I said...' I didn't feel particularly anxious to repeat it right then.

'Was that German I heard you speak? Do you speak the language?'

'Jawohl, mein Führer.' I clicked my heels.

I could see his companion frowning at me. The PM peered curiously at me. There was a keen intelligence behind those tired glassy eyes. He turned to his companion. 'Syers, speak to the laddie.'

Syers straightened himself, coughed and started, 'I say, it's a bit windy for...'

'In German you idiot.' I gathered our first minister was not of the positive reinforcement school of management.

'Hallo, wie heissen Sie?' Syers asked and I told him my name.

We exchanged some further pleasantries, about the likely weather in Bavaria and so on. I could hear his German was workable but not fluent.

'Enough,' said our leader, interrupting our discussion on our preferred type of sausage. 'I think we should take him.'

Syers looked doubtful.

* Kilroy doesn't mention it but he would have been expected to check everybody's ticket. As with any ordinary commercial flight, each passenger had to have a ticket and, indeed, Prime Minister Chamberlain's original ticket has survived through the years and, most recently was auctioned in 2014 at Spinks in London, where it fetched £16,800. The original price of the return flight would have been around £20 per person.

'He could be useful,' he said, looking shrewd. 'While we exchange pleasantries with the Tepichfresser...' – that means 'carpet chewer' by the way – '...er, that is with Herr Hitler, our friend here, that is Mr, er, Kilroy can mix with the belowstairs brigade.'

He looked up at me and, as I couldn't think what else to do, I nodded.

'So, Mr Kilroy, you can mix with those young SS types, share a bierstein * or two and report back to me. Could be useful to know about the thinking down in the ranks. How eager *they* are to go jack-booting into central Europe, what?'

I have to say, I thought then and I still think now, that it was a positively daft idea but I wasn't going to gainsay him. I did have one bright idea of my own though. 'I haven't got any money with me sir.'

The PM looked puzzled.

'I'll need some dosh, I mean, Deutschmarks sir, for hospitality purposes. Help get the tongues wagging and all that?'

He sighed and looked heavenward. 'Syers, give him some money.'

Syers looked even less pleased and dug into his wallet, pulling out a few grubby notes.

'Climb aboard lad. There is plenty of room on the other plane,' the PM said.

There, as in so many ways, he was wrong and so Syers had to get the passenger list, which the PM carefully perused before deciding. 'This one isn't coming,' he said, stabbing at the page.

This one turned out to be the foreign correspondent from the *Daily Mirror*, I think it was. There was an awful kerfuffle when he was given the glad tidings. Eventually one of the burly macintoshes had to intervene. 'Take your hands off me,' I heard him protest. 'Don't you know who I am?' he cried as he was propelled down the aisle to ironic cheers from his colleagues. Some of them were calling out that he could get the train instead and how they would bring him back a Fraulein if he wanted. He glared at me as he passed and I slipped into his seat.

We were soon above the clouds and I sat there gazing at the bright blue world overhead, trying to take stock of the day so far. I'd had my first encounter with a prime minister and remember thinking what a mundane man he was. Of course I was a young man then and didn't know it all. I have met many top politicians and leaders since and not one of them was mundane. I have come to the conclusion that they are all, as a breed, either great actors or master criminals. The best of them, and I mean this in the political not the moral sense of the word, are both. Neville Chamberlain, I was presently to find out, was a great actor. One of the best.

* "Bierstein" is actually an anglicisation for a German stone beer mug. The Germans themselves use other words like "bierkrug"(beer mug). http://tinyurl.com/Kilroy215.

I took a look around at my fellow passengers and reflected that, inexperienced as I was as an aviator, I had flown more times in my short and un-illustrious career than most of them. I could see some concentrating furiously on the interior bulkhead and tightly gripping their armrests, while others were gazing a little too fixedly at the view below. Only one or two, the seasoned regulars I guessed, lazed back in their seats, chatting or reading a book or newspaper or whatever.

And this is how I first met Commander John McNulty. I could hardly fail to notice him, just across the aisle from me, with his eye-patch and bow tie and his highly polished brogues stuck out in the gangway. It was he who earlier had so expertly expelled my delegation predecessor and now he was in his element, that is he was in full flow, talking to the journo behind him on the history of flight and politics.

His broad Glasgow accent took some getting used to but, thoughtfully, he provided one and all with plenty of opportunities to do so. Apparently Chamberlain was *not* the first prime minister to fly. Rrrr-amsay Macdonald took to the air in 1929. And if you wanted to include non-British prime ministers? He looked questioningly at the journalist, who could only blink back at him with the glazed look of someone who wished he hadn't asked the question in the first place. For non-British prime ministers there was Joseph Lyons and... He was holding his index finger in his other hand and was clearly on the brink of providing a fistful of pioneering premier aeronauts when someone butted in with another question.

'Of course, it's safe, man,' he said. The finest avionics, dual control, and the seven hundred and sixty horse power radials, tested, tuned and fresh from Wright's state of the art facility in New Jersey.

I was beginning to wonder if he was a close relative of Wilbur and Orville themselves as he launched into a full itemisation of cylinders, gaskets and connecting rods. I asked a question of my own.

'The karzee, as you quaintly put it,' he said, glaring at me with his one good eye, 'is identical to the fac-ee-lities you will find in first class on the Pennsylvania Railroad.'

There is not really much you can say in response to that. I decided not to risk asking if he was the one aboard to look after it. 'Are you the spare pilot or something?'

'Good God laddie. No time for that. I'm in security for...' His voiced trailed off and he tapped his nose, looking through the porthole for the other plane.

'Are you telling me you're in,' I lowered my voice, 'espionage?'

He laughed. 'Ah, not afraid to ask the direct question. I can see the PM has not made such a bad choice of young recruit to sneak around the gutters and serving girls of Munich.'

In truth I had hardly had an exhaustive briefing from our lord and master so hadn't realised quite what my target area of investigation on this trip was to be. On reflection, I thought, the latter sounded quite promising but hopefully I'd avoid much of the former.

He stared at me long and hard and I could see he was thinking but couldn't guess his thoughts. After what felt like an hour he asked, 'Fly hauf?'

'Er, pardon?'

'Fly hauf, laddie. D'ye play at fly half?' He stubbed out his cigarette and caught me in his gaze again.

'Oh I see. Well, no, I'm more a full back type, actually.' And I wasn't going to tell him I'd only just made it into the third fifteen.

He leaned across and tweaked my bicep. It felt like I was being tested by a shark. 'A lean strapping lad like you should play further forward than that.'

Over the years I've learned to avoid people like him, avoid them at all costs. Not because he was a know-it-all bore, which he was, or because he was a Scotsman or wore an eye-patch or smoked a Gauloise through a silver cigarette holder, all of which are true, but because of something else. Partly it was his penetrating look. The steely gaze told me he had me figured out right away, that was for sure. Then there was his iron grip, which spelled iron control and... really, I can't explain it but in short, I have an instinct where people like him are concerned and the rule of thumb is steer clear as they will only lead you into trouble.

'I'll gi' you some advice, laddie.' He grabbed my arm for another bite. 'When you are in the field, go where they don't want you.' He had me fully in his gaze and his eye acquired a look of what I can only describe as missionary zeal. 'Go where they don't want you. And probe where they least expect it.'

'Well, er, thank you.' Escape seemed like an excellent idea, which is how it occurred to me that we might as well make use of the copious refreshments I had recently loaded. I made my excuses and took it upon myself to organise this. The plane seemed to be cruising along very evenly, with only the faintest hint of turbulence so I cautiously made my way back to the tiny galley, where I broke open the hampers.

I soon discovered that there were plenty of willing helpers to aid me with their consumption. Within a few minutes I had everyone happily munching on the smoked salmon and grouse or poking suspiciously at the little biscuits loaded with caviar.

Somebody asked about drink and so, naturally I had to dig out the beer and claret. I noticed that some of the press corps had come with their own supplies in any case. I caught sight of a bottle, wrapped in brown paper, being passed from one of them to the other. The nervous new flyers were looking a little less worried by this time and things were becoming more convivial. Police and press are natural bedfellows of course. A pack of cards appeared. Elsewhere the conversation turned to sport. Some were keen rugger fans – I think it was Harlequins that was mentioned – while others preferred to follow the noble game in the shape of Arsenal.

When you look back on these things you can't imagine how it came about but half an hour later we were all having a rollicking good time and in summary I can say that anyone aboard with any aviation nerves, including my good self, had forgotten all about them.

Unfortunately it was at this point that two of the journalists had a disagreement about, of all things, a game called British Bulldog. I won't even attempt to describe it. Just imagine a pub brawl, only rougher, but being British, of course it had to have rules. There lay the dispute. One said a reciprocating headlock was legal at any time while the other said it was only permitted to disengage a testicle twist. Foolishly I tried to intervene and found myself immediately caught in the role of demonstration dummy. Others tried to intervene on my behalf and, inevitably, one thing led to another. Thankfully, when it got to the point where there were several large struggling bodies on top of me, I could just make out the muffled, pleading voice of our co-pilot.

'Gentlemen, gentlemen, please desist.'

He had to repeat this several times to make himself heard over the wild cries of 'Ouch', 'Take that you bastard' and so forth. One by one people peeled away until from somewhere at the bottom of the pile I at last managed to stagger to my feet.

We were causing too much "in-cabin turbulence" we were informed, which was knocking "George" – that's the term for the automatic pilot – out of kilter. We all tried to look knowledgeable and suitably concerned at this announcement but I suspect most of us just felt plain sheepish. I know I did and I tried not to catch his eye as he stood there, glaring at me like a school prefect, while I dusted myself down and hobbled back to my seat.

Once he felt he'd safely restored good order our trusty aviator returned to the flight deck, banging the door shut behind him. I was concerned that this little incident might reappear as another black mark on my record. In my short tenure as cabin boy I had already picked up one blot in the ledger when I'd fallen asleep in the baggage hold at Schipol so by my reckoning it wasn't looking like a great first week for British Airways' latest recruit. It wouldn't hurt to make amends, I thought, in the shape of some light sustenance for the flight crew.

I made my way back to the galley to find that much of the food had gone, or been sat on, spat out or generally trodden underfoot by twelve good men and true. Eventually I managed to piece together some pâté on biscuits, which looked quite presentable on the elegant china Savoy plates. Balancing them carefully in one hand I took them forward.

Compared to Cranwell's queasy Tiger Moth, with little more than a compass and broken air speed indicator to distract me, the flight deck of the world's latest and fastest airliner was a blaze of dials, gauges, levers and switches.* I could make little sense of it all at the time, but pilot training is a wonderful thing and, courtesy of HMG and its extreme anxieties over the situation in Europe, I was about to be inducted (again) into the mysteries myself. Within a couple of years I would be flying a Hudson, that is the military version of this very aeroplane, with the wonderful Valla aboard and into occupied France. Of course all that, and especially the lovely Valla, was still ahead of me. All I could do that morning was to marvel at the nonchalance of the flight crew as I stood behind them clutching my two plates of biscuits.

Victor Flowerday, Chamberlain's Munich pilot, promotes Services Shockproof watches.

Through the windscreen I could see snow-capped peaks far below. We seemed to be just floating over them. The co-pilot was humming quietly to himself, buried in the day's copy of *The Times*. There was a summit conference going on in Munich, it said on the front page, rather predictably.† Our captain was sipping from the dregs of a cup of tea, with his Thermos parked on the dash board in front of him, partially obscuring

---

* The Lockheed Model 14 Super Electra *was* quite possibly the fastest airliner in the world at that time – just – although all-out speed wasn't the only consideration for the airlines. Its competitors, the Douglas DC-2 and DC-3 (the Dakota – which was to become the celebrated WWII transport aeroplane), were not quite as fast but were more efficient, and ultimately outsold the Lockheed by a considerable margin. But the Electra certainly must have seemed very futuristic at the time, an all-metal monoplane, which could carry up to 14 passengers, cruise at 215 mph at 25,000 feet with a range of 850 miles. At Munich it had not been long in service, having first been operated by Northwest Airlines, in the US, in October 1937. A few months before the conference, a Super Electra, piloted by Howard Hughes, had flown around the world in just four days, at an average speed of 206.1 mph.http://tinyurl.com/Kilroy193 (Super Electra). http://tinyurl.com/Kilroy192 (Hudson – the military version)

† *The Times* on 29th September 1938 had the bizarre headline *'Herr Hitler Holds His Hand'*, which certainly scores high on alliteration but very low on clarity.

the wonderful view. I couldn't help noticing a large stain on his shirtsleeve and a small puddle by his feet on the cabin floor.

The engines were thrumming reliably, with a gentle slow oscillation in pitch. All the gauges were rock steady. George was doing his stuff obviously. I coughed loudly and they both turned around and eagerly took the plates when I offered them. The pilot could see I was studying the instrument panel with some interest and took it upon himself to explain what some of the gauges were for.

For the second time that day I was treated to a pep-talk about how trusty and reliable these aeroplanes were. 'They are the best money can buy.' He stroked the dashboard lovingly and pointed through the windscreen to the other aeroplane, some distance in front of us, before rattling off a load of figures about altitudes, air speeds and so on. 'It's the modern way,' he continued. 'Herr Hitler has been flying all over Germany for years now and it doesn't seem to have done him much harm, does it?'

I did wonder if some might wish aviation was a mite more hazardous in that case but kept that thought to myself. Instead I ventured, 'So, it's really as safe as houses then?'

He yawned. 'Safer.'

Well, it's a funny thing, but I have an instinct where plane crashes are concerned. Yes, I've been in quite a few over the years (mainly of my own doing too) but I often have a strange feeling of foreboding, a sort of shiver down my spine, when I feel one may be imminent. And, for the first time, I experienced that feeling that brilliant sunny morning, high over the Alps, just as the pilot was reassuring me of the opposite. Of course, as the whole world knows, our PM and delegation all arrived back from Munich unscathed (if not unhumiliated) but... oh it's another story, but I've often wondered if there was anything I could have done or said that morning that, a few weeks later, just might have saved the plane and the brave pilot I was talking to.*

There was a certain amount of mess strewn around the cabin, following our impromptu set-to earlier and lying near my seat, between a squashed sandwich and an apple core I spotted some pages that had fallen out of somebody's travel reading. I picked them up and was surprised to find that I was holding a fragment of *Mein Kampf.* I'd never read it of course. I had heard that it was the most awful drivel but started idly flicking through it.

* Aviation was hazardous in those days as illustrated by the remarkable number of crashes worldwide during the Super Electra's service career. For example: at the time Kilroy flew to Munich, British Airways Ltd operated a fleet of four and not one of these planes made it to honourable retirement. In particular the two aeroplanes on the Munich mission were both lost shortly after they returned, with one of the crashes killing Eric Robinson, one of the Munich pilots. See *End Note (4)*.

Jock McKnow-All spotted what I was doing. 'Should be compulsory reading for anyone locked in negotiations with Herr Hitler,' he ventured.

I looked questioningly at him and he took the pages from my hands.

'See here,' he said, 'Mr Hitler, whatever you think of him, makes no bones about what he wants.' He frowned, looked down the page and read, 'The plough shall be the sword and the tears of war shall water the bread of future generations.' He looked up. 'Cheerful stuff, eh?'

Konzentrationslager (KZ) Dachau.

I didn't answer.

'Or what about this?' He'd found a new page. 'When we speak of new territory in Europe today we must principally think of Russia and its border states.' He tossed the pages back on the floor. 'You don't need to read it from start to finish, although I have of course. Just choose a page at random and you'll see what his game is.'

I picked up a couple of the loose pages and of course he was right. War, invade, conquer, Germany, power, land. Over and over again, and that was only the non-racist stuff. I remember thinking that it was the rantings of a madman maybe, but a chillingly consistent rant that was for sure. I asked McNulty what he thought would happen with the talks today.

'My, you're a one for the questions aren't you?' he replied. 'Let's just say Chamberlain hasn't read this tedious work but Churchill has. I'll not go any further than that but I'll tell you what I think will happen eventually anyway.' He paused to consider what to say. 'Win or lose around today's top table, Hitler won't stop until he is either dead or has what he wants in there.' He pointed at the papers lying on the floor.

He looked out the port-hole. 'We're nearly there.'

The engines were still in the cruise and I could detect no change in course so I asked how he knew. He beckoned me over and pointed downwards at what I took to be an enormous chicken farm.

'Dachau,' he said. 'Ten thousand offenders of the Third Reich. Commies, Jews and Catholics mainly.'* He sighed. 'It's only a few miles outside the city but you won't find *that* in any of the guide books.'

* At the time Kilroy flew over it, Dachau was mainly filled with German political prisoners, including many Catholic priests. Most of the remainder were Jews. http://tinyurl.com/Kilroy044.

CHAPTER 8

We queued in the aisle in the airplane and slowly made our way through the doorway and down the waiting steps, blinking and stretching as we took in our new surroundings. It was a fresh sunny day, with a light breeze ruffling my hair and, in the distance, as I had expected, the backdrop of the Alps prodding upwards from the horizon. More immediately, we had the massed ranks of Hitler's finest arrayed before us, all rigidly to attention with flags waving in the breeze. The French and Italians were also invited to the party so their tricolours were in evidence alongside our flag and the Nazi emblem of course.

Most airfields in those days were pretty much just that, boggy fields with a few hangars and rough buildings at the edge, but this one had a sparkling new passenger building and, a big novelty, a hard concrete runway.[*] There were a hotch-potch of aeroplanes standing nearby and, discreetly parked alongside one of the hangars, a half dozen of what I guessed must be the new German fighter, the famous Messerschmitt 109, presumably just back from its recent triumphs in Spain.[†]

I recognized Ribbentrop at the head of the party to greet us at the airport. He was the German Foreign Minister, known to all sides as Brickendrop, which tells you all you need to know about his skills in the art of diplomacy. He swooped upon the PM and ushered him into a waiting limousine, having delegated an enormous Aryan to keep an eye on the rest of us.[‡] There was an SS guard of honour with a military band, all looking immaculate in their black uniforms, with fixtures and fittings gleaming in the midday sun. It took me a while to work out what the band was playing.

---

[*] The Munich mission landed at Oberwiesenfeld airport, outside Munich. Shortly afterwards all Munich civil operations were transferred to the newer and larger Flughaven München-Riem so it seems likely the airport where Kilroy landed was not as fresh and modern as he describes. Today, Oberwiesenfeld lies under the Olympic Park, built for the 1972 Summer Olympics. http://tinyurl.com/Kilroy045

[†] The Messerschmitt Bf 109, arguably the most successful fighter of WWII, first saw action in Germany's Condor Legion, fighting for the Nationalists in the Spanish Civil War. In Spain, the Germans had over two years in which to perfect the design of their fighter (and other combat planes) and to refine aerial combat tactics under field conditions. http://tinyurl.com/Kilroy046 (109) and http://tinyurl.com/Kilroy047 (Condor)

[‡] This was most probably Alexander von Freiherr Dörnberg, a commander in the SS and the 'Chef de Protocol' who was present at most of the Hitler-Chamberlain conferences. He was reputedly two metres tall. http://tinyurl.com/Kilroy048

Eventually I decided it must be the Marseillaise, but with a possible Wagnerian improvisation, and felt a little heartened by the thought that the famed German organisation and efficiency could sometimes be wanting.

Someone had thoughtfully laid out rope barriers to mark our way to the cars but I had fallen a little behind the others and jumped over one of them to take a shortcut across the grass. I instantly regretted doing it as it was muddy of course. I'm sure our Aryan giant would have liked to whisk me off to Dachau for getting out of line but, apart from a long glare, he did nothing.

A fleet of cars awaited us, open-topped, polished to perfection and the best that Herren Mercedes and Benz had to offer. We were shown to our vehicle and, once we were all loaded, the procession took off, rumbling along at a leisurely pace.

It was only a short drive through the streets of Munich but all along the route the pavements were crammed with men, women and children, shouting, cheering and waving flags. I spotted one small family group, conducted by *Vater* I guessed and making a pretty good job of "Rule Britannia". Further on I was surprised to see a troop of Boy Scouts, and clearly British too, from their cries of 'Good show, sir', 'Wizard try' and so on.* Equally memorable was a gang of elderly men in felt hats and leather shorts, all raising their near empty biersteins to us as we swept by. Herr und Frau München were out in force to greet us that day. You would have thought we had just successfully concluded a war, rather than being on the brink of starting another one.

As we neared our destination the streets became narrower and the buildings seemed to tower over us. There was bunting hanging overhead, stretching from window to window and the cheers and shouts from the crowd seemed even louder in the confined space. I had half expected to see the famed Nazi architecture everywhere but looking up all I could see was a traditional Bavarian cityscape – colourful buildings with high sloping roofs intermixed with some dull purposeful municipal stuff. I found out later that Hitler had had plans to demolish much of the area we drove through and rebuild it in his own image. In the end he had half his wish, courtesy of the allied air forces, but back in 1938 it was all untouched and very pleasantly Bavarian.

Königsplatz, or Kings Square, was another matter. I had seen it a few times in newsreels and knew what to expect, but was still greatly taken in by

---

* The Scout movement was banned in Germany at this time, with boys expected to join the Hitler Youth and girls the BDM – the Bund Deutscher Mädel or League of German Girls. However overseas Scouts *were* tolerated and so it is entirely plausible that there were British scouts in Munich when Kilroy visited. The Alps are nearby and it is a popular area for hiking and climbing.

the scale and grandeur of the place. Hitler had bulldozed the old gardens in the middle and laid polished granite instead, making a huge expanse which was just perfect for massed jackbooting, and for bonfires too – it was where the burning of the books took place.*

Jock McK-A had to tell me that it was only thirty seven point two five per cent of the size of Nuremberg, but to compensate it did contain the holy of holies: the Ehrentempel or Temples of Honour. These were two neoclassical open air structures, impressive but not huge as they stood like sentinels, side by side in the middle of one of the long sides of the square. Within them lay the remains of 16 brownshirt thugs or, if you prefer, martyrs, of the failed Nazi putsch in the twenties. Every year on the anniversary of their death there was an immense quasi-religious ceremony held in the square to commemorate their demise. Fortunately we would not be there for it.

Just alongside one of the temples was our destination – the Führerbau, the Nazi headquarters. It had been completed only a few weeks before our arrival and was a spectacular example of the new National Socialist architecture, not original at all but still magnificent, borrowing heavily from ancient Rome. The building was of some extent, finished in gleaming cream and pink marble and topped with a magnificent bronze eagle, wings outstretched, as if it were poised to swoop on any recalcitrant envoys from the provinces. As I clambered out of the car and caught its eye, high above me, I felt a sense of foreboding, shared, I suspect by many of us in the delegation that morning. †

To honour us esteemed guests, the Germans had hung a huge Union Jack and a French tricolour over the tall columns at the entranceway with a red carpet leading up the steps. Once inside the building we found ourselves in a large central hall with a grand double staircase heading up and corridors leading off in all directions. With 30 million supporters the Nazis clearly had some Deutschmarks to throw around and as far as this building was concerned, they hadn't been reluctant to do so. There was shining brasswork, plush carpets, paintings and elegant plaster busts everywhere.

---

* The book burning was not confined to Munich but took place all over Germany, on 10th May 1933, to the accompaniment of a passionate address by Goebbels. Apart from the obvious targets of Communist or Jewish writings, anything deemed decadent, pacifist, liberal or licentious was ceremonially thrown on the fire and subsequently banned from schools, libraries and so on. This was not confined to just German writers but authors such as H G Wells, Hemingway, Dostoyevsky, Tolstoy and many others were black-listed. Many of the banned German writers went into exile while most of the remainder subsequently died in concentration camps.

† The Führerbau still stands. It now houses the Academy of Music and Performing Arts. http://tinyurl.com/Kilroy049.

We were ushered up the stairs and along a corridor lined with stony-faced SS men, standing rigidly to attention, each saluting with a loud 'Heil Hitler' as we passed. Most of our party breezed past them with barely a nod, but I responded to each with a cheery wave.

We were shown into an upstairs drawing room and, to our surprise, found we were the first to arrive. There was a buffet laid out, attended by silent footmen, looking like they had just arrived from the court of Louis XIV. Someone had thoughtfully stuck little flags on each platter. Heading for the Union Jacks I helped myself to a cucumber sandwich, no crust and a pork pie, no jelly. Apart from me, Jock McK-A, seemed to be the only one who was hungry but then he had to make a huge fuss when he spotted that the Union Jacks marking the sausage rolls were upside down. This was a terrible insult, according to him, so one of the poor footmen had the devil of a job rethreading the little flags on their cocktail sticks before he'd deign to try anything.*

We didn't have long to wait. The Italians and the French were not far behind and, finally, the man himself. And if you have a feeling that something was missing you would be right. There were no representatives of the Czechoslovakian government. About the only thing everyone was in agreement on was that the weighty business of deciding how, when and why their country was to be dismembered was best done without the messy complication of listening to any Czech moans and grumbles about the matter.

The Führerbau, flying the flags of the four nations on the day of the conference.

From time to time I'd wondered how our rulers conduct themselves at occasions like this. Do they snarl and attempt to outstare each other from across the room? Beat their chests and shout? Send in their champions to do battle in the middle of the carpet? The answer is they do all of this and more, but if you want a master class in how to manage things look no further than the Reichskanzler. From the moment we had arrived we'd been made to feel within his grip – the wealth and opulence of the venue,

* When flown correctly the larger white band of the upper arm of the diagonal cross on the Union Flag should be at the top on the side near the flag pole. It is possible to fly it upside down, with the smaller white band uppermost and this can be considered an insult on parades and so on, but not usually when identifying canapés.

the massed ranks of sullen SS outside, the death mask of Frederick the Great hanging over the fireplace. I didn't quite feel we were under arrest but there was always the feeling that we might be if things didn't go the way Herr H wanted them to.

So, in the brown corner, there is the Führer, looking pale, tense and agitated, surrounded by his adjutants. In the black corner, we have Signor Mussolini, trying to look like Caesar but not quite managing it in a uniform a size too small for him. In the red, white and blue corner are Daladier and Chamberlain together, not actually holding hands but looking like they would very much like to. Hitler goes over and greets Mussolini warmly, embracing in the continental fashion. For Chamberlain and Daladier, each merely receives a cold handshake. Mussolini stays put and ignores them. Chamberlain makes his way over to him and attempts to exchange pleasantries but is snubbed. Language is an issue of course. Only Mussolini speaks all four languages. For the rest, interpreters are needed. Yes, it is promising all the fun of a maiden aunt's funeral with the heating broken down but, at last, Hitler snaps the deadlock and invites the principal participants into his private study.

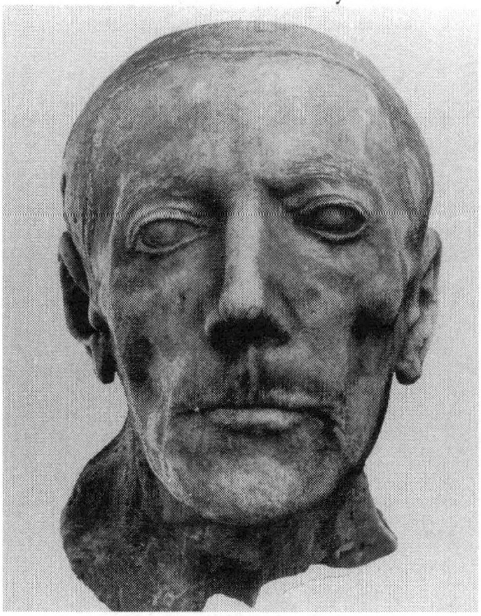

Death mask of Frederick the Great.

We'd all have liked a ringside seat at the meeting but this first session was heavyweights only. One of the Italian delegation tried to sneak in but was firmly blocked by an SS guard, standing rigidly to attention in front of the door. So it was just the four leaders with their closest advisers plus Schmidt, Hitler's interpreter, who had the joyous task of making sure they all understood each other.

The mood in the anteroom lightened with the main players gone. I'd not been a keen student of foreign affairs so couldn't put a name to many of those who were left, but even I recognised the ample form of Reichsminister Göring, bedecked with braid and decorations and with a happy red glow to his face as he helped himself to the refreshments. Alongside him was the diminutive Doctor Goebbels, quietly watching everyone with eyes like a cobra.

Our contingent had been reinforced by the arrival of the diplomats from Berlin and I spotted somebody I recognised, Nevile Henderson with a red nose and a carnation to match – 'one 'ell of an ambassador,' as McNulty insisted on telling everyone. I watched as he strode up to Göring and asked a question. Göring reluctantly put down what little was left of a pork pie, before carefully wiping the crumbs from his mouth. He commenced an animated series of gestures with his arms twisting and turning, one behind the other, with an accompanying explanation and Henderson just nodding all the while. I caught Henderson trying unsuccessfully to stifle a yawn, although in truth he might as well have been asleep for all the contribution he made to the proceedings that day. A year or so later, when I was on operations over France I realised that Göring had been demonstrating the "finger four" fighter formation. It was a pity that Henderson, or at least somebody, hadn't paid more attention that day, as it was a Luftwaffe tactic that sent plenty of our boys to their doom in the early stages of the war.

Other than that we had a rabble of Italians. I've no idea who any of them were, but by golly they knew how to turn up in force, dress for show and make a hell of a racket. One of them had an umbrella which he kept waving in the air to the accompaniment of much hilarity. I saw McNulty go over and remonstrate with them but he was easily beaten back by a barrage of what I imagined was full, frank and ribald Italian, overlaid with ironic cheers.

'Cheeky blighter that Capello. God help us if that daft bugger gets involved with negotiations,' was all he could say as he rejoined us, back in the safety of our compound.

And I nearly forgot the French. Well, that would be me and the rest of Britain for the next several years I might say. I found out later that the weedy and glum individual in the corner, suspiciously poking a baguette, was their ambassador, no doubt miffed that he had been denied entry into the holy of holies.

So we all stood around watching each other and wondering what to do while our lords and masters battled it out in Hitler's study. With the Italians in full flight (and not for the last time come to think of it) I did wonder when the bread rolls were going to start flying but the dignity of the occasion prevailed and everybody just stood around in small groups, chatting and exchanging pleasantries.

There was no obvious belowstairs brigade to mingle with and what with striving to avoid the likes of Goebbels and Göring and, more particularly McNulty, I found myself left to my own devices and wondering what to do with myself. I've since found that diplomatic missions are usually like this. You might have the fate of the world hanging in the balance but mostly you are just standing around checking your watch and trying not to yawn. It looked like being a long day I thought, so decided to busy myself at the buffet. Five minutes later, I had the sausage rolls arranged into a rather natty swastika. I was just contemplating the possibility of a Spitfire crafted from vol-au-vents when I heard the first major confrontation of the day.

It wasn't the heavyweights next door. It was our Dr Jenkins – the PM had brought his physician along – arguing with a rather squat piggy looking man, with a bald head and owl-like glasses. The man was perspiring heavily and squeezed into what looked like a rather odd variant of an SS uniform, with all the usual deaths head regalia but in grey of all colours.

'No, my good man,' said our good doctor loudly and slowly, in the manner Englishmen often adopt when addressing a non-comprehending Johnnie Foreigner, 'You German doctors may do it that way but we British... no – not – at – all. It's – *not* – possible.' He was waving a small bottle in front of Herr Doktor Piggie. Herr P made a lunge for it but Jenkins smartly pulled it away.

'Sie *müssen* dies nutzen,' cried the fat Aryan. This means 'you must use this,' and to make his point he waved a lethal looking syringe in the air.

Jenkins persisted with his cut-glass lecture. 'It's only a health drink, my man. A – health – drink, comprendez?' When it was clear that Herr P didn't comprendez he merely shrugged and turned his back on him with a sigh. And that was when he spotted me. 'I say old chap, could you possibly get me a glass of water?'

I nodded, found a clean glass and poured some water into it from a jug. As I put it down on the table in front of him, Jenkins unscrewed the cap on the bottle he was holding and tipped a couple of pills into his palm which he then dropped into the glass. The water foamed slightly and took on a pale grey colour. I noticed that everyone in the room had stopped what they were doing and were watching us.

'Bloody Kraut doctors,' he muttered between his teeth as he stirred the brew with his fountain pen. 'The PM's fighting his corner to try and save the world. Won't thank me for getting him to drop his unmentionables and sticking a needle in his backside, will he?' He winked at me as he said it, picked up the glass as he headed towards the study.

I picked up the bottle he'd left on the table. "Meth-amphetamine", it said on the label. The name meant nothing to me at the time although I was to see it often while serving in Bomber Command a few years later.

'Herr Chamberlain,' said Dr Jenkins, waving the glass at the two SS.

'Nein,' said one of them firmly, barring his way.

'My – prime – minister – needs – a – pick – me – up,' started the good doctor pointing at the glass as he continued his language lesson.

It occurred to me he might need some help. I walked over, took the glass from his hand and addressed the guard in German. 'Our prime minister urgently needs his medicine,' I said pointing at the glass.

'Ach, so,' said the guard as he stepped aside and swung open the door. The other ushered me through.

'But...' I replied, but it was too late. The door closed firmly behind me.

I had expected to see the participants seated around a conference table, all respectfully upright and rigid, with the usual paraphernalia, that is the water jugs, tumblers, agendas and so on conveniently to hand. Actually there was no table in the room at all, other than Hitler's enormous desk and instead everyone was seated any which way and each engulfed in voluminous armchairs and settees. Baron Strang, who turned up later in the day, wrote after the war that it had been a hugger-mugger affair. He must have gone to a better school than me as I had to look up the word. At any event, he was right, it was all disorder and concealment, with everyone awkwardly balancing cups and saucers on their knees with their notes, if any, strewn around on coffee tables or whatever surface came to hand.

There was one animated figure in the room. Inevitably it was Herr Hitler, standing silhouetted in the window, holding forth. As I crept across the carpet I gathered that things weren't going too well that day for Czech sovereignty nor for world peace for that matter, nor indeed for anyone bar the Nazis.

Chamberlain raised his hand, in a forlorn attempt to placate him. 'Herr Reich Chancellor,' he said, 'we understand the German grievances should be righted but, I say, in all circumstances, the use of force must be excluded.' He glanced at Daladier, who nodded back at him.

There was a sudden silence. Looking at Hitler, you'd have thought that Chamberlain had just waved his member at him, not made a quietly spoken and honest proposal. He fastened him with a long stare while he drew breath. 'Force?' The word popped out suddenly, muttered through clenched teeth. 'Who speaks of force!?' His cheeks were turning red and his eyes looked like they were going to pop out of their sockets. 'Herr Beneš applies force against my countrymen. *He* mobilised in May, not I.'

He was stabbing the air in Chamberlain's direction as he spoke. The PM looked as if a revolver were pointed at him and not just a Nazi digit. Bravely, I thought, he opened his mouth to speak but that was as far as he got.

'Hundreds of thousands of *my* people are driven from their homes, tens of thousands are thrown into prison and *your* brave democracies are not moved in the least,' Hitler spat out, pointing at Chamberlain and Daladier in turn.

They exchanged looks. Both seemed lost for words. Not so, Herr H.

'So, what can *I* do?' he asked and without waiting for a reply he answered his own question. 'I will tell you what I will do. I will settle this matter one way or another. I will take matters into my own hands.' Now he was pointing at himself as he spoke, his chest puffed up, head thrust back as his hair flopped over his forehead. 'I will march *before* my Volk as the first of its soldiers,' he continued, thumping the palm of one hand with the fist of the other. He certainly could command the room's full attention when he wanted to and I could see he was enjoying himself. 'And, be warned... behind me,' he wagged his finger at the audience, 'let it be known to the world, marches a Volk, a Volk that is *very* different from that of 1918.'

It's not often you get to hear a great orator at close quarters and it was a pretty impressive performance I thought even if he had, I suspected, practised it rather too many times in front of a mirror. And we had heard much of it before in any case, when he had announced his intentions in these terms to the German people and the world at large a few days earlier from the Sport Palast in Berlin.*

'I say...' started Chamberlain but the Reich Chancellor was not to be deflected.

'I have made the Czechs an offer,' Hitler continued, 'an offer on my carpet.'

He stopped and I could see his audience all doing a double-take. Daladier and Chamberlain exchanged a puzzled look then turned to look at me. Suddenly I realised everyone else was staring at me as well.

I have often wondered if we would have gone to war that week had our prime minister been sitting near the door. The problem for me that day was that he was on the other side of the room, between the fireplace and Hitler's desk and the only way I could reach him was to walk directly in front of the Reichskanzler as he was in full flight. Just as he was introducing the topic of carpet prices I was attempting to creep discreetly past his desk and, evidently, I had spectacularly failed to pass him unnoticed. 'I am sorry sire...' I started, wondering what I had done to incur his wrath.

'An Ardabil carpet from Tabriz, procured from the shah's palace. An *Ardabil* no less.' He stared pointedly at me, his moustache twitching. 'Finest silk, 26 *million* knots, all hand-tied by the twelve score virgins.' He was a natural orator of course and couldn't resist the opportunity to work himself into a lather, even on the subject of middle eastern floor covering. 'Hundreds of years old, 50 years in the making and now look...'

This didn't seem to have much to do with Czechoslovakia that was for sure and, along with everyone else in the room I suspect, I had no idea what he was talking about. That is, until he pointed behind me. I turned around, half expecting to see a rug with signs of severe dental damage, but no. It

* The translation of Hitler's famous speech was printed in its entirety in *The Times* a few days before the Munich meeting – on Tuesday 27th Sept 1938. It was also broadcast on radio so it is possible that Kilroy, a German speaker, had listened to it live the previous evening. By Kilroy's account here we note that Hitler repeated many of the key points from the speech at the Munich conference.

was my earlier shortcut at the airport that was my undoing, but also, as it turned out, Europe's salvation. There was a trail of mud leading from the doorway to where I was standing. 'I apologise, sire, I...'*

'And what brings you here with your filthy footwear, interrupting our conference?' he rasped.

He was speaking in German of course, with his coarse rural accent and angry words making him sound like some inflamed pig farmer whose neighbour's sheep had wandered into his herb garden. I wanted to explain that I was merely delivering a pick-me-up to our prime minister but, what with the stress of the occasion and the belligerence of my interrogator, I couldn't recall the German for "pick-me-up". 'I have this glass of water, sire...' I began.

He snapped his finger and motioned me to bring it to him. 'Danke,' he said as he plucked it from my hand. He sniffed it, then put it to his lips and, before I could intervene, took a good long draught. I'm sure it must have tasted strange and was expecting him to shriek that he had been poisoned but he didn't. He merely looked surprised, wiped his moustache and looked carefully at the glass. 'Englisch wasser?' he asked.

There didn't seem much point in enlightening him. 'Yes, sire. Brought with us today. From our ancient city of Bath...'

'It is good. Very good.' He put the glass to his lips again and this time drained it.

I'm not sure what I expected to happen next but he swayed slightly then closed his eyes, before putting down the glass and gripping the side of the desk top. I could see his knuckles turning white and took the opportunity while his attention was elsewhere to turn around and see what Chamberlain thought of it all. We exchanged looks and he pointed at the glass and then at himself, with a questioning look. I nodded my head and he stared back at me, looking worried.

Meanwhile a small dribble of foam had appeared at the side of the Reich Chancellor's mouth, slithering slowly down his chin. I was staring at this and wondering whether or not to summon medical aid when his eyes opened.

I'd never seen it before but have seen it several times since, latterly at 25,000 feet over Berlin. It was like staring into Hell's inferno. His eyes were unfocussed and the pupils appeared to be spinning in opposite directions, which you would have thought to be impossible, but it's not. He still had a

* There are two famous Persian carpets known as Ardabils, one residing in the Victoria and Albert museum in London and the other in Los Angeles County Museum of Art. The carpet in Munich was unlikely to be an original, as Hitler claimed, but several copies have been made over the years. One ended up in the UK prime minister's residence at 10, Downing Street, another in Hitler's office in Berlin and, by Kilroy's account, yet another was in Hitler's study at the Führerbau. http://tinyurl.com/Kilroy050.

tight grip on his desk. 'Englisch wasser,' he repeated in a hoarse voice. 'Sehr gut. Very good I think.'

He wiped his mouth, shook his head and smiled for what I guessed was the first time that morning. His eyes were returning to normal. 'Very good,' he said again, then turned to the others in the room, clearing his throat. 'Now, where was I?'

Nobody answered.

'Er, where was...?' He hesitated and shook his head again. 'Ah, yes, I know, I know,' he said in a quietly measured tone, pausing to take a deep breath. 'Gentlemen, I think I can see a simple solution to our little problem.' He paused to hold the empty glass up to the window and squint at it in the light. Nobody said anything. 'Very good,' he muttered again then continued. 'I apologise for my earlier outburst. I see a solution based on friendship. Our mutual friendship – that is the key.' He smiled dreamily in the direction of Chamberlain and Daladier.

Pervitin – the Wehrmacht's name for methamphetamine, distributed especially to air and tank crews.

They both nodded and I could see they looked relieved.*

'Signor Mussolini has a proposal with him. We should all look at it carefully and I think we will see a way that our great Nordic nations can stay friends.'

And that was all there was to it. I was ushered out of the room soon after so didn't catch the rest of the morning session but I heard about it afterwards and, from that moment on, it was all plain sailing easy-peasy child's play on a downhill ride. Mussolini had with him something called a five point memorandum. Essentially it said that Germany could have the lion's share of Czechoslovakia, but any Czechs who didn't like it would be allowed five days to get out, taking only the clothes they stood up in. And all the allies had to do was to agree that this was alright. If you had been following the news over the previous couple of weeks you might have thought that this sounded depressingly familiar and you'd be right. The

* There is no other record of Prime Minister Chamberlain being prescribed methamphetamine, although it would not have been thought remarkable at the time. The drug, a psycho-stimulant discovered in 1893, was widely employed by the military on all sides in WWII and, for many decades, was also used in civilian medicine. Today Methaphetamine is more commonly manufactured and supplied illegally as the recreational drug "crystal meth". See *End Note (5)*.

allies had rejected a very similar proposal made at the previous summit meeting only a few days earlier. This one, dressed up Italian style, seemed acceptable, to Chamberlain and Daladier that is, and so that was the Munich agreement delivered on a platter and the Czechs could go to hell. We found out much later that it hadn't been written by the Italians anyway. It had all been concocted in Berlin the previous day and sent to Rome, so Il Duce could present it as his. Such are the ways of international politics.*

* Kilroy's account of the morning session at Munich broadly tallies with other writers, although none of the others mentions the incident with the medication. From Kilroy's description it is likely that Chamberlain's doctor was arguing with Doktor Morell, Hitler's personal physician, who was much favoured by the Reich Chancellor and widely disliked by the rest of his entourage. Morell had treated the prime minister (for flu) at the earlier Bad Godesberg meeting and that is possibly why he brought his own physician on this last Munich trip. By the end of the war Morell was regularly injecting Hitler with complex (and unspecified) cocktails of substances, possibly including methamphetamine, morphine and cocaine, and it is commonly supposed that this treatment was at least partly responsible for Hitler's decline in health and decision-making capabilities as the war came to a close. In the late 1930s his medication intake was still comparatively light and so, possibly, the incident Kilroy describes was his first ever encounter with methamphetamine. Wikipedia on Theodor Morell: http://tinyurl.com/Kilroy051.

CHAPTER 9

Lunch was a miserable affair. It had been planned for us all to dine in style with Hitler at the Führerbau but our PM presumably felt more comfortable as far away as possible from the Nazis and so we had to be content with dried up sandwiches at the hotel. He invited the French to join us but in the long tradition of the *entente cordiale*, or possibly because they had got wind of our chef's capabilities, they decided to dine at their own hotel.

For the rest of the day events moved quickly. Once back from lunch, we found that the morning scheme of leaders-only went by the board when Capello slipped past the guards, the rest of the Italian contingent piled in behind him and everyone else just sort of followed them. This meant that for the next few hours it was a matter of everyone poring over maps and drawing up timetables and shouting at each other.

Postcard image of the Regina Palast Hotel, Munich, where the British delegation stayed.

Of course there were still a few matters to be discussed. I remember Chamberlain, ever the accountant, questioning how the books would be balanced if some Czech farmers had to leave their sheep behind. Even I could see this was small change alongside the other matter of a nation's dismemberment so wasn't surprised when Hitler delivered his full and earnest view on the subject of time-wasting. The prime minister sniffed and coloured a little, but otherwise let the matter drop. But Herr H didn't have everything his own way either. I found out later that he deeply regretted agreeing to the treaty at all because it lost him the chance of a triumphant entry into Prague at the head of his troops. Apparently that was what he had really been wanting all those weeks while the Great Appeaser had been earnestly shuttling backwards and forwards to Germany. In the end and thanks to the "Bath spa waters" he was denied it, well, denied it that day anyway.

I quickly tired of the petty wrangling and slipped out to the makeshift beer hall in the cellar. With a brief to explore the gutters and serving wenches that seemed as good a place as any to start my mission and this is where I met Rudi. He was an SS lieutenant, immaculate in his black uniform with the lightning flash trimmings and death's head badges, but slightly the worse for wear after a bierstein or two too many. I sat down with him and asked some innocuous question about how he thought the day was faring.

'You,' he said, pointing at me. 'You should go to war.'

This was said in excellent, if slightly slurred English, which took me a little by surprise. I was about to ask whether he meant me personally or our nation as a whole, but fortunately he didn't wait for my reply.

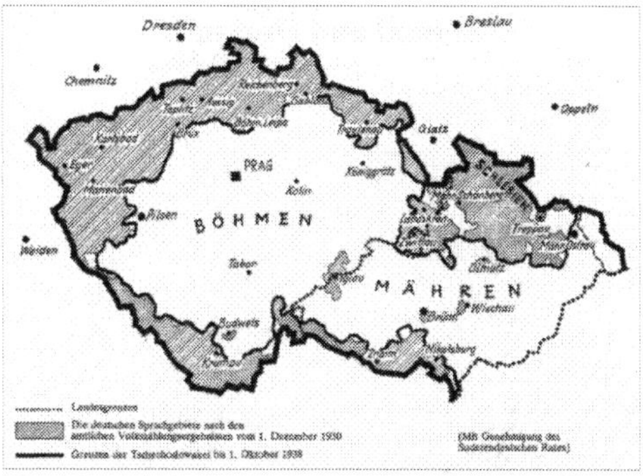

The Munich Agreement permitted the Nazis to occupy most of Czechoslovakia's borders (shaded). A few months later the Nazis seized the rest.

'See here,' he added, reaching for a box of matches and emptying it on the table. 'These,' he said, as he organised some of them into a line, 'are *our* army divisions.' He broke the heads of some of the others and arranged them in another line. 'And these,' he pointed at the appropriately headless ones, 'are the French.'

I forget now how he denoted the British army and navy and all the other European forces besides, but the long and short of it was that in no time at all we had the entire line-up for world war two laid out on the gingham table cloth. 'Now look here,' he pointed at the armies to one side of the overflowing ashtray – Switzerland. 'We are easily strong enough to take Czechoslovakia but,' he paused, 'while nice and busy there we have nothing to defend ourselves from this.' He stabbed his finger in a veritable forest of headless matches and bent cigarettes. He sighed and got up to replenish his glass, leaving me to study the form.

When he returned he placed his chair close to mine and sat down. He first took a good look around and then whispered, 'That is why, my friend, there are some in the military who feel, how should I say?' He paused. 'We have the wrong man at the top.' He pointed upwards then drew his finger across his throat.

This was all very interesting but he was being so terribly indiscreet that I found myself wondering how soon it would be before he had his very own express ticket to Dachau. But now Rudi was on the subject it was hard to stop him. He went on to confide that his uncle was some high-up in the Wehrmacht and *he* knew somebody, who knew somebody and...

He looked hopefully at me but I was unsure how to respond. It was all news to me and I realised it might also be of interest to McNulty. So, after Rudi had further laid bare how the next Reichskanzler would be democratically chosen I made some excuses and went back upstairs to seek him out.

McNulty knew where I was heading before I'd even got halfway though my whispered briefing. 'Yes, it's pretty damned obvious that the generals will get rid of Herr Hitler as soon as the war goes badly,' he glanced over at the man himself, who was busy jabbing at a map of central Europe, 'but there ain't going to be a war, is there?' He looked at our PM who was scratching away in his notebook, eyes half closed. 'And God help any of those Wehrmacht wallies if their security is so poor that any old Tom, Dick or Harry,' he looked down his nose at me, 'can pick up this sort of barrack room gossip after a few minutes chat in a bar.'*

We were standing in Hitler's study as we had this conversation, to a backdrop of all the noise and chaos that only the many diplomats of four countries can bring to such an occasion. The maps were still spread out all around the room, each with its own group of people crowded around and pushing each other out of the way in their efforts to give their own take on the ideal shape of bite to be taken out of Czechoslovakia. It occurred to me that it would save a lot of argument if we just said Herr H could have the whole of it, a view he also took about six months later when he did just that, helping himself to Prague and the rest of Bohemia.

With so many cooks and only the one small bramboračka to be spoiled, I thought that we would never see daylight on the matter, but miraculously our mini League of Nations *did* come up with something acceptable to all. It wasn't until late in the evening but, at last, the four copies in the four languages were spread out on Hitler's desk, alongside an ornate marble ink-well. Hitler, the first to make his mark, dipped his pen and it was dry. Ribbentrop, I think it was, had to be dispatched to get replenishments from the stationery cupboard. At least no dead eagle fell at anyone's feet.

Most of us missed that little drama. The junior diplomats and other hangers-on had been expelled from the study for the solemn moment so we were all crowded outside again, in the ante room. Shortly afterwards the leaders came filing out, looking tired but each clutching his copy of the precious document. The British one is still around for anyone who wants to read it, but it is hardly worth the bother as, according to the events that followed, it seems that the signatories barely looked at it again either.†

---

* After the war General Franz Halder, chief of the army general staff at the time of Munich, claimed that had Chamberlain not intervened with Hitler there would have been a military coup to overthrow him, as the Wehrmacht fully expected to lose in a confrontation with the other European powers. This may possibly have happened although there were many Nazis claiming retrospective opposition to Hitler in the war's aftermath. http://tinyurl.com/Kilroy052.

† The Munich Agreement is one short eight point document, timetabling the German invasion in four easy stages in just one week, allowing for plebiscites and international

And that should have been that, as far as our trip to Munich was concerned, but it wasn't, because there was to be an unscheduled Final Act to the drama. This was when Chamberlain met with Hitler the following morning and secured the famous "joint declaration" – the "piece of paper" – waved by the him to the newsreel cameras and cheering crowds after he landed back at Heston. It all meant nothing in the end of course but it most probably saved his career and it would never have happened had I had the good sense to keep my mouth shut.

I had my back to the door of Hitler's study so didn't notice, at first, the signatories filing out. Rudi had made his way up from the bar and I was standing with him, draining my glass of Moselle, when he asked me, in English, 'How do you think the British at home will react to this?'

He was pretty much the worse for wear by then and was getting a little repetitive. In fact he'd asked me the very same question only a few minutes earlier. Recalling my intensive education in the works of Livy and Plutarch back in the spring, courtesy of Matron, I thought I might put it to some use here. Without much reflection, I replied, 'Well you know what happened to Caius Martius don't you?'

I was reckoning that he wouldn't know and, at the very least, that might stop him asking me the question for a third time. Rudi paused to fill his glass and offer me some. 'Ah, Livy's account or Plutarch's? An interesting story either way. What of it?'

That put me in a fix. I think Matron and I had been covering this ground on the day lessons were postponed in favour of a romp on old Mungo Clark's desk and I was struggling to remember what, if anything, she had told me afterwards about it. 'I thought your schools didn't do the Classics much these days?' I replied, playing for time. 'All racial theories and Nordism, what?'

Rudi just glared at me. 'Yes, but what about the story, then?' he repeated, his glass tilting alarmingly. Herr H brushed past us at that moment and glanced around, frowning at him.

Then I remembered. 'Ah, yes, of course. Er, well, you know, he was the Roman general who concluded a peace treaty with their enemies?'

Rudi nodded.

'Yes? So when he came back to his people they didn't think much of it at all and assassinated him.' I stood back and awaited his answering chuckle.

'So?' Rudi looked at his watch.

---

commissions after the event, all of which came to nothing once the Germans had what they wanted. The full text is available online at: http://tinyurl.com/Kilroy053.

I could hear the clipped voice of our prime minister right behind me, mentioning something about bed time. People say the Germans have no sense of humour but that's not true. Then again it wasn't the funniest joke ever told so I realised that to get any reaction from Rudi I'd have to ram home the point with a pile driver. 'Yes, Rudi, but that was when someone called Vincent Ville of Mons Templi got hold of him.' I was making this up. 'He was a brute of a man and tore off Martius' testicles with his bare hands

At the Führerbau in Munich. In front row, the main participants, left to right: Chamberlain, Daladier, Hitler, Mussolini and Graf Ciano (Italian Foreign Minister). In the background: Henri Fromageot, Joachim von Ribbentrop, Alexis Leger, Ernst von Weiszäcker.

and fed them to the dogs.'

We must have been talking more loudly than I thought as suddenly I noticed everyone else in the room had stopped what they were doing and were looking at us. Rudi was oblivious but at least I was now getting a reaction from him. 'Oh I get it,' he said, as I tried in vain to shut him up. 'Vincent Ville of Mons Templi – Wins-town Church-Hill, yes? Will serve your PM right if Churchill does tear off his testicles after this shameful business, eh? Ha ha.'

I couldn't see the prime minister as he was still behind me but I heard later that when he heard these words he stopped in his tracks, turning very pale. He had to momentarily lean on an aide for support. The first I knew about it was when I heard him faintly wheeze, 'Get on to Herr Hitler's office,' as he walked past me, without acknowledgment. I heard him add some further instructions, something about a 7 a.m. start, then he was gone, out the door and down to the waiting car.*

'Künstlerhaus?' asked Rudi as he put down his empty glass.

I nodded and followed him out.

* The story of Caius Martius is told by several Roman historians, including Livy and Plutarch, but he is better known nowadays as the protagonist in Shakespeare's Coriolanus. He was indeed assassinated when he returned with a peace treaty but the incident with Vincent Ville of Mons Templi is not mentioned in any of these accounts. http://tinyurl.com/Kilroy054 (Shakespeare's Coriolanus).

CHAPTER 10

The Künstlerhaus, the Artists House, was a five minute drive away. On the way over Rudi explained that it was Munich's top night spot for up and coming young Nazis and that we could look forward to plenty of "distractions" there after our hard day saving Europe.[*] After we had been dropped off, while we were making our way to an entrance around the back my evening almost came to a premature end as I stumbled into a deep trench. Rudi pulled me out and, after finding me to be unhurt, he started muttering sharp words on the subject of certain racial minorities as he dusted me down. I asked what he was on about and he told me that I had just fallen on the site of a recently demolished synagogue. Apparently Herr H had taken exception to the view on retiring from his favourite night spot so he had invented some pretext for knocking it down. Rudi seemed to see my fall as a sort of Rabbi's revenge but I managed to get him to shut up about it eventually.[†]

Once inside, and with the day's business successfully concluded at the Führerbau, there was a lively atmosphere. There were several young SS, ties loosened and biersteins afore them, some of the French delegation at their own table examining their wine, while the Italians sat nearby playing some game with the beer mats and laughing uproariously. Also, something that had been absent all day, some womenfolk had found their way in. They were sitting with the SS and delicately sipping from champagne glasses.

As I waited while Rudi ordered the drinks I realised that I'd had Mac's camera in my pocket with me all day and hadn't used it since we arrived. I pulled it out and slid open the case, fiddling with the dials to make what I hoped would be the right settings for a good shot. With everyone in a celebratory mood I thought it would be a reasonable moment to try it out.

---

[*] The Künstlerhaus (the Artists House) still stands in central Munich. It was built in 1900, to be a meeting place between art and society. It was commandeered by the Nazis and used as a night club in the 1930s and 40s then subsequently taken over as an officers club by the Americans. In the post-war era it has reverted to its original function and today it is the venue for a wide variety of cultural events. http://tinyurl.com/Kilroy055 and http://tinyurl.com/Kilroy056 (for non-German speakers – your web browser should be able to make rough translations).

[†] Munich's Great Synagogue stood immediately behind the Artists House. It was the first synagogue in Nazi Germany to be demolished when it was knocked down, on Hitler's orders, in June 1938. Today there is a memorial stone in the street near the site of the original building. *Traces of War* article: http://tinyurl.com/Kilroy057.

One of the women noticed what I was doing and came up to me and introduced herself. 'Eva Braun,' she said, holding out her hand.

Of course the name meant nothing to me then, in fact meant nothing to anyone outside Hitler's immediate circle. All I could see was a slim, well poised young woman with mischievous greeny blue eyes. I politely took her hand and introduced myself.

'Can I see?' she asked, pointing at the camera.

I handed it to her and watched as she frowned and fiddled with the controls. 'What speed film is in here?' she asked.

Of course I didn't know.

Munich's Künstlerhaus still stands. The synagogue behind was demolished in 1938.

'We'd better assume it's not especially fast, which would mean, for these light conditions,' she looked around her, 'you would need a slower shutter speed I think.' She called to the barman, 'Frans, hey Frans.' Frans was busy chatting to one of the other ladies. 'Hey Frans.' Eva sighed, put the camera down and placed the fingers of both hands in her mouth before delivering a piercing whistle.

All noise stopped. Frans looked across. 'Hey Frans,' she waved, 'Turn up the lights. We need to take a photograph.'

She turned and winked at me. 'Look, I will show you how to take a good photo. She fiddled with one of the dials, pointed the camera at me and took a snap. 'Now,' she said, 'How about that bear's head?' There was a stuffed bear's head hanging over the bar and it was indeed a good picture she took as I still have it in my family album. 'Now you try.'

She handed me the camera. I said something about looking for the big picture before pointing it at her, making sure to take in her cleavage before slowly pressing the shutter. She merely raised her eyes heavenward and took the camera back. 'I think there will be too much camera shake in that one,' she said. 'Let's try a group photo.'

She called to the SS and got them to face the camera. 'Now stand close behind me,' she said and I will show you the correct way to take this shot. She had the camera to her eye and was facing her comrades in arms. 'See, nicely relaxed, eye to viewfinder, make sure it's level and...'

I should mention that Eva was very elegantly attired in a long silk evening dress with, well, nothing much at all at the back. She had pale skin, although there was some evidence of a tan, I thought, from the Bavarian sun. And the last thing I remembered was her bottom wiggling in a rather delightful fashion as she called me to stand closer behind her.

I have what is known in boxing circles as a "lantern jaw". A lantern jaw is basically a major weakness for a pugilist, when the lightest of taps on the chin will send him careering ever downwards and into oblivion. Some would say this is a handicap to carry through life but on balance I think it has served me well. For example, on one occasion I was glad of the insensibility in a Gestapo dungeon and there have been several times when an irate husband has hit the spot. Being unconscious does rule out a quick getaway it's true but the thing is, no matter how angry the cuckold is, there is not much he can do to vent his spleen on a deadweight recumbent body. I know, I've tried it myself in other circumstances and after a few desultory kicks you soon tire. Then there's the effect your demise can have on the good Lady Guinevere. I generally seem to come round fairly quickly and on more than one occasion I have found myself clasped to her bosom as she berates her hubbie for his loutish behaviour.

On this occasion I had fallen foul of Rudi, who had felt it incumbent to be the moral guardian of the Führer's moll* when he considered I was getting too fruity with her. This was all explained to me as I came to, happily clasped to fair bosom, but not Eva Braun's. I was with somebody called Helena in the back of a car and we were on the way back to my hotel.

It was only a short drive to the hotel and Helena helped me out of the car as I was still a little shaky on my feet. I had to lean on her on our way up to the room and it was then I caught our reflection in one of the full length mirrors on the stairway. It struck me that there was something vaguely familiar about her but I couldn't quite place it. When I asked she muttered something about August in Venice, but as I had never even been to Italy at that time it didn't make a great deal of sense to me.

I couldn't find my room key but the door was unlocked anyway and we both sort of crashed into the room when it opened unexpectedly. Helena parked me on the bed and stood in front of me. She had a briefcase with her and after fumbling around inside it she pulled out a bottle, which she waved triumphantly overhead. 'Night-cap?'

I nodded and watched as she fussed around the room looking for glasses. She was wearing trousers, a fashion that hadn't really caught on back home at that time. The glasses weren't clean enough for Helena's liking so there was a delay while she found a towel to wipe them. She had

* Hitler's relationship with Eva Braun from 1932 was largely unknown outside his immediate circle, until their marriage and joint suicide at the end of the war. Late in the war British Intelligence thought she was one of Hitler's secretaries. Presumably nobody had read the September 1936 issue of *Paris Soir*, where their relationship was spelled out. http://tinyurl.com/Kilroy058.

the air of confidence, lacking in girls my own age. I guessed that she must be in her mid thirties. Her hair was cropped short, which also struck me as unusual but overall I remember thinking how well the look suited her.

There was a loud pop and I just caught sight of the cork as it zipped overhead towards a picture on the chimney breast, where it ricocheted off Bismarck's left ear. Then she sat beside me, with each of us clutching a foaming beaker of France's finest. 'To der union off our great nations,' she said with a smile as we clinked glasses.

I nodded and smiled back. 'And to you, Helena,' I added, catching the full force of her velvet brown eyes for the first time. She put down her glass and leaned back. 'Und vot now, Englishman?' she asked.

I remember I had some difficulty undoing her blouse. The recent belting from Rudi on top of a bierstein or two too many hadn't done much for my coordination. Also I was dealing with a moving target, what with her chest heaving up and down in a rather bewitching fashion. After rather too much inept fumbling from yours truly she sighed, took my hands and pushed them away. I thought she was going to get up and leave but I needn't have worried. She briefly turned away from me and I could see the blouse slacken across her back before she came around to face me again. 'Englishman,' she said with a smile, 'for you, der bra is open.'

Eva Braun.

And, by golly, it was. I didn't know which one to go for first so decided to be greedy and have both at once. What a marvellous bosom Helena had. I still get a little aerated thinking of it now. At any rate I became so engaged with both her charms that it took me a while to notice that she wasn't thrashing around with much enthusiasm herself. Clearly I wasn't doing things quite right. I hadn't had much to do with German womenfolk at this stage in my career and found myself wondering if, perhaps, they did things differently in the Third Reich. So, what was it our weapons instructor had told us during my brief and undistinguished sojourn at Cranwell? 'To engage the enemy, left hand on the throttle, right hand on the stick, press the tittie and...'

'Gott im himmel,' she cried.

That was more like it, I thought, as I struggled to remove her undergarments. Then, at last, it was time to let rip with the eight inch Howitzer. 'Achtung, fraulein,' I shouted.

'Ahhhhh,' she cried, as I jumped aboard.

Five minutes later, I drained my glass and took a last drag of my cigarette before stubbing it out. Helena was snuggled up beside still breathing heavily. I was feeling pretty pleased with myself. Job done, mission accomplished, I thought. What next? It had certainly been a long day and not without its stressful moments but it seemed to have ended on a high note and I was feeling pretty drowsy. All that remained was for the lovely lady to gather her garments from all four corners of the room, make her excuses and I could get some much needed kip. I could feel her idly stroking my chest, her fingernail gently raking my chest hair. 'Englishman,' she asked, 'Haf you known many women?'

Well, there was a question. The short answer was 'a few but still counting.' I recall thinking that apart from the expensive young Hayley my encounters had usually ended in a disaster for yours truly in one form or other. 'Lost count, actually,' I answered.

'Well,' she drawled, 'can vee try zat again only a beet more slowly?'

I must have nodded off at that point as the next thing I remember was her fingernail digging into my chest. 'Ow, what was that?' I blurted out, then trying to sound enthusiastic, 'Er, yes, good-oh, give it another bash, what?'

I could feel her hand gliding down my chest, pausing briefly over my stomach then reaching below.

'I see,' she said.

It was clear to both of us that the mighty Howitzer was in need of some rearmament.

Helena sighed, propping herself on one elbow as she turned to face me. 'Englishman,' she said slowly, 'vee haf vays of making you stiff.'

'Really?' I replied, stifling a yawn.

Then she whispered in my ear.

'Oh, I see,' I said brightening at the idea, 'well that certainly sounds like a jolly good notion. Give it your best shot, eh?' and I lay back and awaited developments.

I could feel her tongue, all warm, wet and silky, gliding down my chest and slithering over my stomach. Her hands grabbed my thighs. I shut my eyes and awaited the arrival of paradise.

Nothing happened. What the devil was she up to? Surely she hadn't got lost?

I opened my eyes, to see that she had. Her head was hovering somewhere over my knees and with no sign of it moving in on target. 'Donner und blitzen,' she blurted out. 'You haf shaved your legs.' She grabbed the bedside light and waved it over me, scrutinising them closely. 'You English, so strange. Hey, no, you hafn't – you haf shaved only one leg. Heh heh, I like it.'

That was, of course, the result of the botched session I'd had a few days earlier with Mac's malfunctioning electric shaver. Helena carried on waving the light around, poking my legs here and there, examining both my shins, stroking the smooth one all the while. I was feeling a little foolish by then and about to suggest that she put the damned light down and return to the task in hand, when she cried out, 'Your camera!' Before I could stop her she had jumped off the bed, picked up my jacket and was rummaging through its pockets.

An eight inch Howitzer.

Of course, she found it easily enough and walked slowly back to the bed, fiddling with the controls. ''What speed film is in here?' she asked.

Blimey, not another one, I found myself thinking. 'No idea my lovely. Why don't you come back on the bed? I've just had a splendid idea.'

'We will need light,' she announced, as she flicked on the overhead light, frowning as she squinted at the bulb. 'Not enough.' She looked around. 'The bed,' she said. Before I could stop her she had grabbed it, with me still on it, and, grunting with the exertion, dragged it into the middle of the room. 'Now, you lie like so... and so,' she directed, positioning my limbs as she checked me through the viewfinder.

She still wasn't satisfied and scanned the room. 'The mirror. Ja, the mirror.' This was attached to the dressing table, a massive and ancient oak fixture that looked like it had once bridged the Rhine. Of course she couldn't move it on her own, so I had to get up and help her, then was pushed back on the bed and repositioned again.

'Head up, now. Face the camera.' She moved one of my arms to one side.

'Don't smile now. Scowl pliz. Yes, scowl.'

I had no difficulty complying with that instruction.

'And see. How you say? Look, your Hor-whistler, he iz koming back.'

And it was too. She was clicking away with the camera and climbing on top of me, using the mirror to get unusual angles. I don't know if it was the novelty of being in the eye of the lens or her smooth skin brushing up against me but something was most definitely putting me in the mood. I tried to grab her and return to the business in hand but she absentmindedly swatted me away and continued taking pictures. At some point she dropped the camera on my back and foolishly I made a remark about it feeling cold.

'Yes, it iz cold,' she said. 'But I know how to warm it up,' she added with a wicked smile, as she waved it under my nose.

The Minox camera, as Mac had lectured me, was a masterpiece of miniaturisation. A fully functioning camera, with a precision shutter and focussing with superb optics, and all crammed into a package no bigger than a finger of toast.

'Would you like me to warm it up?' she asked again. 'There is a special way.' She licked her lips and I could see her eyes looking downwards.

'Go ahead,' I muttered absentmindedly, as she pulled the bedclothes over us. I was thinking that these Kraut womenfolk had some odd ways, but if this one wanted to pleasure herself at the risk voiding the warranty of Mac's latest acquisition...

'Yarrooo,' I shrieked. 'Stop that.'

'Vot eez wrong my handsome Englishman?'

I had felt a sharp pain where I least expected it. 'Ow, I said stop it.' Crikey I hadn't suffered such an indignity since back in the third year when Randall and his chums had caught me alone in the shower block.

She looked disappointed. 'You no like?' Then a thought struck her. 'I know,' she said brightly and bounded off the bed and started rummaging in her briefcase. 'Iz a German invention,' she told me as she proudly brandished a large jar of Vaseline.

Fortunately she didn't have a very firm grip of it, so it was last seen sailing out of the bedroom window in the general direction of the Führerbau. 'Let him bloody well use it then,' I think I said.*

I strode around the room, switching off the lights. 'Now then, my little apfelstrudel, where were we?' I returned to the bed and found that at last she was in the mood.

We quickly got into what I might call a regular rhythm with her thrashing around with great ardour and with me at times hanging on as if my life depended on it. She was breathing more and more heavily all the while. Suddenly she started gasping, 'Hey, hey, hey,' over and over again.

* Helena must have allowed national pride to overtake the truth in this instance. Vaseline, petroleum jelly, was invented in the nineteenth century by Robert Cheseborough, an Anglo-American. The name however comes from the German word "wasser" (pronounced 'vasser'), meaning water.

I stopped.

'Don't stop,' she whispered.

'Are you sure?'

There was no reply.

'Are you sure?' I repeated. I realised I'd rather been stoking the furnace like a demented Jutland boilerman and was genuinely worried I might have broken something. 'Everything tickety-boo down there, darling?'

A groan was her only reply, which I took as a "yes".

And so we carried on, with Helena's hey-hey-heys getting louder all the while, until suddenly she let go with a 'Heil Hitler' screamed at the top of her voice.* Fortunately I was just about finished too and, taking my cue from her, I concluded the night's activities with a 'Nev-ille Cham-ber-lain' that really had the windows rattling.

---

* In the 1930s, to many Germans (and some British, like Unity Mitford), Hitler was, what would be described nowadays, a "sex symbol". To young German women he had considerable sex appeal, engendering the sort of hysteria seen a generation later with pop idols such as Elvis Presley and the Beatles. Several writers have remarked upon the sexual tension in his oratory, experienced both by the audience and in the speaker himself, for example: 'Women certainly found him attractive and schoolgirls were reported to have painted swastikas on their fingernails. "Heil Hitler" was the expletive one group of blonder Valkyries uttered when they reached orgasm.' See *Richard and Adolf* by Christopher Nicholson, http://tinyurl.com/Kilroy059 (Amazon).

This adulation wasn't confined to women alone. Many German men gave their lives to the cause with Hitler's name on their lips. For example "Heil Hitler" were the last words uttered by the prominent Nazi, Karl Ernst, executed during the 'Night of the Long Knives' on Hitler's orders. See *Unholy Alliance* by Peter Levenda, http://tinyurl.com/Kilroy060 (Google Books).

CHAPTER 11

When I awoke the next morning I found only an indentation in the pillow and the faint smell of Helena's perfume to indicate that she had ever been there. I got up and went to draw back the curtains. The day had started without me. The sun was already high in the sky and there was the hum of traffic from below. I was still feeling pleasantly woozy from the after-effects of the previous night so I took my time padding around the room, looking for my various items of apparel and getting dressed in easy stages.

There was no packing to be done of course, so a few minutes later I was ready to go. Then I remembered the camera. I patted my jacket pockets and checked through the bedding. A further search under the bed and in the wardrobe and cupboards failed to locate it. I noticed my door was wide open and I did momentarily wonder if someone had broken in and stolen it but then I saw something on the writing desk. It was a small cartridge and, underneath, on the crisp hotel stationery a note from Helena. When I read it I realised there was no further point in looking for the camera. It would seem she had "borrowed" it, as they say, but thoughtfully left me the film. Wondering how I'd explain the loss to Mac I went downstairs with thoughts of breakfast on my mind. I absent-mindedly stuffed Helena's message and the film cartridge in my pocket. If I had only known what trouble they were going to cause me I would have chucked them on the fire.

I arrived in reception to find my erstwhile colleagues had left without me. The manager was impressively apologetic, waving a clipboard and berating one of his underlings. He would see what he could do, he said and, as he reached for a telephone, he gestured at a box of cigars on the desk. They were large Havanas, nestling side by side and looking like dusky brown torpedoes. The underling, who seemed only too eager to get out of his range, helped me clip one of them then proffered a desk lighter as I puffed inexpertly, trying to get it alight. After that all I could do was wait, so I sat down in one of the reception armchairs, idly musing on the possibility of a rematch with Helena as I attempted to blow smoke rings through the open door.*

---

* Kilroy doesn't further identify Helena and possibly never knew any more than her first name but there is the intriguing possibility that the lady in question was Helene "Leni" Riefenstahl. At this time Riefenstahl was famous throughout Germany and the rest of the world as a dancer, actress, mountaineer, photographer and, especially, as a film maker – arguably the best of her generation. Kilroy only gives a few clues to Helena's

A few minutes later a car screeched to a halt outside. It was a ceremonial Mercedes, like the one we had used the day before. This time I was the only passenger so I sat in the front, alongside the driver. These cars show German engineering at its finest – purpose built for state occasions, open topped with seating for six, but instead of the usual cramped arrangements of a normal car, they are very, very roomy. You can stand in the footwell and wave to the adoring masses as you cruise past.*

There had evidently been a huge turnout for Chamberlain's triumphant return to the airport and many of them were still on the streets, slowly dispersing as they headed off to start their daily business. Seeing another car coming their way, some of the crowd stopped to cheer and wave their flags anew.

A Mercedes–Benz 770 with the newly elected Reichskanzler.

Of course they had no idea who I was but it seemed a shame to disappoint them, so I stood up, balancing myself against the dashboard as I waved in regal fashion as we cruised by. This caused them to cheer all the more and others rushed to the barriers to see what was going on.

---

identity but Riefenstahl certainly matches all of them. At the time of the Munich conference she was in her thirties and had recently been in Venice, where she collected the Venice International Film Festival 'Best Film' award for *Olympia*, her acclaimed film of the 1936 Berlin Olympics.

Despite being popular within the Nazi inner circle, Riefenstahl never joined the party. Post-war, she was tried four times by various authorities and each time was exonerated. Nonetheless her Nazi associations virtually finished her film career. She must have been a formidable woman. In the 1930s, when it was rumoured (wrongly) that she was being courted by Hitler, there was a popular joke: What would happen if Hitler married her?.... then Germany would have two Führers. In a long life (she lived to be over a hundred) she had two husbands and many lovers. http://tinyurl.com/Kilroy061.

*The car Kilroy describes was most likely a Mercedes–Benz 770, popularly known as the Großer Mercedes. It was widely used by high-ranking Nazis, including Hitler, throughout the 1930s and during the war. The convertible was the popular option for ceremonial occasions and features in much archival film footage. Only around 200 were ever made and some were exported. Emperor Hirohito and Pope Pius XI both took delivery of 770s. There are surviving models in Canada, Portugal and Germany, and also in private collections. http://tinyurl.com/Kilroy062.

I noticed we were taking the same route as the previous day and I even recognised some of the crowd. First there was the party of bierstein swillers in leather shorts, looking like they had stuck to their post for the duration of our visit, then the Boy Scout troop all dib-dib-dibbing and dobbing with their woggles. I had managed a couple of weeks in the Scouts myself, before I was thrown out, but remembered some of their strange ways and in particular the funny little two fingered "wolf ears" salute they use. So I saluted them in their fashion as we drove past and they saluted, cheered and hallooed back, some of them throwing their hats in the air. This caught on with the crowd further along, so I jammed the cigar in my mouth and repeated the salute for them, only with my hand high in the air, a touch they seemed to particularly appreciate.

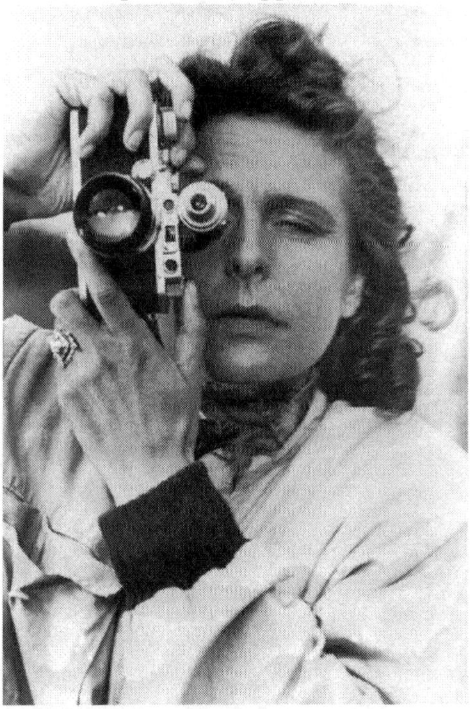

Leni Riefenstahl (1902-2003).

Many, many years later, I was sitting in the waiting room of a veterinary practice, just outside Westerham in Kent, when a doddery old man came shuffling in, accompanied by a nurse carrying a cat basket. I knew who he was immediately. We'd met a few times in the thirties and forties but, more particularly, I'd seen plenty of him in the news over the years, right up to his recent retirement. He looked much older in the flesh as he sat down heavily alongside me, puffing on a large cigar while he fussed over his animal. I was about to make a gentle quip about him being in the wrong place, what with him needing a doctor rather than a vet, when our eyes met and I could see he recognised me. 'Kilroy,' he growled.

I was about to reply, but Heinrich started bating at that moment, madly flapping his wings, with his talons sinking into my glove as he shrieked loudly. It was the devil of a job to calm him. 'Your cigar...' I started and he frowned at me, but removed it from his mouth and stubbed it out on the sole of his shoe.

'D'you know,' he said, waving the smouldering Havana at me, 'we used to have a television set in the Strangers Bar at Parliament back in the thirties? One of only a handful in the whole of London.'

I'd heard the old fellow's mind had started to go in latter years so I just nodded as I fed Heinrich a chunk of rabbit. The bird seemed to be calming by the minute and in fact was looking rather hopefully at the cat basket.

'I remember once, one evening during the Munich crisis, there on the screen was this cheeky young blighter, bold as brass and looking downright daft with a huge cigar, giving the "V" sign to those damned Nazis. "See? That's the way to treat the Jerries," I said to Baldwin and Halifax, although I could see that they didn't think much of it.' He paused and smiled. 'Certainly gave *me* an idea though. Always wondered what happened to that young fellow...' he said, with a wink at me.[*]

Two months later he was gone. Aspergillosis it was, which is deadly to hawks.[†]

Back in Munich, we drew up at the airport and I could see that one of the aeroplanes had already left and the other had both its engines running. Clearly there was no time for formalities but my driver rose to the occasion splendidly and drove up onto the pavement and then straight across the grass, parking in front of the plane and blocking its path. I could see the pilot gesturing for him to get out the way but he ignored him. I had no time for thank yous but instead clapped him on the back, thrust the cigar into his hand and leapt out. In my haste I only just remembered to run around the wing, but still caught the full blast of the propeller slipstream as I approached the rear of the plane, where I waited for somebody to open the passenger door.

---

[*] If Kilroy had managed to stay in the Scouts a little longer he would have known that their salute uses *three* fingers. It is the junior Scouts, the Wolf Cubs who use only two, supposedly to represent the ears of a wolf, although it is identical to the "V" for victory gesture. It is the Wolf Cubs too, and not the Scouts, who engage in the dib-dib-dib chanting that Kilroy mentions.

There is no record of a television in the Houses of Parliament at that time, although Westminster was within range of the Alexandra Palace transmitter. Outside broadcasts were virtually unknown before the war but the Movietone newsreel organisation was in Munich for the conference so it is possible that Kilroy's journey was filmed by them and subsequently transmitted by the BBC. No record of it exists today.

[†] Winston Churchill stood down from parliament in 1964, retiring to his home at Chartwell, near Westerham in Kent. He died on the 14th January 1965 and was given a state funeral. His old home is now open to the public, administered by the National Trust: http://tinyurl.com/Kilroy063. Churchill was very fond of cats and was given a ginger cat, called Jock, in 1962. There has been a ginger cat of that name kept at Chartwell ever since. The current incumbent is Jock VI. He has a Facebook page: http://tinyurl.com/Kilroy064.

A few moments later I was aboard. There were two things I noticed immediately. One: angry stares from my fellow passengers for holding them up and two: I was on the wrong aeroplane. There was no sign of McNulty and his merry gang, merely a sour-faced group of politicians.

There was only one free seat and it was at the front so I muttered good mornings to one and all as I clambered forward. The prime minister was sitting in the seat behind mine and, as I settled into it, I thought to ask if he'd had a good night's sleep.

'Yes, very well until some fool started moving furniture around and hollering my name,' was his tart reply.

Fortunately there was a loud engine roar at that point, as the pilot started his take-off run. Further conversation was impossible.

A quarter of an hour later and when we had levelled off into the cruise, I realized that the sour looks and glum faces were not my doing but that everyone had other things on their mind. Yes, we had averted war, but you wouldn't know it to look at them – they all looked so miserable. Our German hosts had stocked the plane with the best the Fatherland could offer but Chamberlain said he wasn't going to touch that "German muck" and everyone else followed suit, everyone except me that is.

The PM's advisor, Wilson, was sitting across the aisle from him and, from what I could gather, they were preparing a speech, with Wilson writing it out in long-hand in a notebook. Wilson kept muttering about what a bad business the trip had been and how it was best not to think about the dive bombers and the Czech women and their babies and so on until eventually Chamberlain told him to shut up about it. Of course none of that found its way into the final draft.

And this was when I first heard about the PM's impromptu meeting with Hitler early that morning, when they had signed a further agreement promising peace and goodwill between our nations for ever more. Both the PM and Wilson seemed to think it was quite a coup, arguing like an old married couple as to whose idea it had been to set up the meeting in the first place. Wilson kept saying, 'But Neville, I suggested it to you'. In answer the PM repeated how *he* had realised, as *he* was leaving the Führerbau, that *he*'d be eaten alive by the British public if he didn't come back with something like this. I felt the solid thrust of a knee in my back as he itemised each point.

At any rate, with all of this and the war itself now to look back on, it is this second agreement the public remembers best, not the earlier one that sold the Czechs down the Danube, but that's hardly surprising given the prominence Chamberlain gave it when he came back. Of course the one person who didn't remember it, or indeed either agreement, was a certain Herr A. Hitler, but that was all in the future then.

Meanwhile I was enjoying a fine German breakfast. Their breakfasts are made for airline travel, I thought, as I tucked into the Viennese sausage with delicate slices of cheese on Pumpernickel black bread. Washed down with a fine glass of Hock and finished off with a modest serving of sauerkraut, I reflected that there was no finer way to travel.

The PM and Wilson were still droning on and on and fiddling with sentence structure and suchlike and I think I must have nodded off at this point because the next thing I recall they had gone quiet and, looking out of the window, I could see the sky was a great deal darker. We seemed to have hit a bumpy patch too as every few seconds the plane lurched, recovered then lurched again. I noticed a tightening knot in my stomach and a salty taste in my mouth and realised, with some dismay, that this is what had awoken me – the return of Captain Queasy.

What was that Cranwell doctor's advice? Keep your eyes fixed on the horizon and think of something else, anything. But there was no horizon, dammit, only thick black clouds in every direction. Try and think of Helena, then, I thought, but all I could recall were all those glasses of champagne we'd quaffed and how they must now be sloshing around inside me along with that Viennese sausage.

Suddenly I knew exactly where this was going and frantically hunted around for something I could deploy – a bag, newspaper or magazine, or even a copy of *Mein Kampf* if it came to it. There was nothing to hand and I realised that the only thing for it was to try to make it to the facilities, situated what seemed to me like five and half miles away at the back of the plane. I levered myself out of my seat and turned towards the rear, holding a hand over my mouth and feeling giddy and light headed. It was difficult to stand as the plane was pitching and rolling so much. I took a step but almost immediately I stumbled and nearly fell headfirst into Wilson's lap.

There was a pause as I blearily gazed at him and I think Wilson knew what was coming as I saw him throw his hands up and heard him shout 'No!'

I turned my head away just in time and – I still have nightmares about this – how was I to know the prime minister was, at that very moment, rising from his seat alongside and so imperfectly placed?

It was all over in an instant. He was so startled that all he could do was flop back down again. I just sort of stood there and gaped at him, while hanging on to the back of a seat with drool running down my chin.

'You bloody fool,' he shouted at me, as Wilson handed him a handkerchief. 'You bloody disgusting fool.'

I tried to say something but the words wouldn't come out. Its not often you see your prime minister with a piece of sauerkraut dangling from his nose. He looked so helpless. He was just sitting there and I could see he wasn't sure what to do. I tried to pick a piece of sausage off his shoulder.

'Leave me alone, damn you,' he muttered as he swiped my hand away.

Meanwhile others had seen the affray and were rushing to attend. I was soon crowded out and was somewhat relieved to slink back into my seat, trying to make myself as inconspicuous as possible. As I sat down I found that, now that I'd voided my breakfast, I felt a whole lot better, almost with a sense of inner calm and well-being. Which is more than everyone else felt, as they gathered around trying to rescue the situation. The PM's jacket was removed and Syers made busy sponging it with a napkin. Others were trying to tidy up the man himself.

After a while I gathered that Operation Clean-up wasn't going too well. 'Christ, what the hell was that incontinent idiot eating?' I heard someone ask. Another questioned, 'Who invited him along anyway?' but he was quickly shushed when it was remembered that that little balls-up was down to the PM himself.

Eventually Wilson came up to me. 'We need your jacket.'

I blinked.

'The eyes of the world will be on the PM when we land and he can't turn up looking like he's been rolling around in a Munich beer hall.'

I blinked again, wondering what he was on about.

He obviously thought he was addressing an idiot and I suppose, at that moment, he was, so he spelled it out for me in monosyllables. 'You,' he pointed at me, 'are – the – same – size – as – him,' he pointed at the PM. 'You – must – swap,' he pointed at both of us. And just to make sure I got the message he thrust the PM's mucky jacket into my arms.

I had no alternative other than to stand up and remove my own much prized Saville Row acquisition. Wilson took it from me, removed my wallet and other bits and pieces and plonked them into my outstretched hands. 'He *will* look after it?' I asked as he made his way back up the aisle but received only an answering snort.

CHAPTER 12

There was pandemonium when we landed. The good news had preceded us back home and there were newsreel cameras, radio broadcasters and people, people, people. People everywhere. They crowded around as we climbed down the steps from the plane, cheering and singing and making it difficult to move away. I had my bottom pinched twice and got poked in the ear too but also received not a few pats and hugs.

Chamberlain approaching the microphone to make his first speech on returning from Munich, at Heston aerodrome.

Eventually a space was cleared and Chamberlain stood before the crowd, alongside the aeroplane and gave an impromptu speech, one of the most famous moments in our history. It was filmed* and has been shown many, many times since but you won't see me anywhere because I was in the least advantageous position on the entire aerodrome. I was close at hand, that's true, but was out of sight, kneeling in the mud just in front of the microphones.

This was my short, involuntary and, if I say so myself, largely successful period of secondment to the Movietone organisation (unpaid). A few minutes earlier a rather rattled gentleman, who I took to be a sound

* Chamberlain's speech at Heston, filmed by Movietone, can be found on YouTube: *Mr Chamberlain returns from Munich (3rd visit)*, http://tinyurl.com/Kilroy065. There are several other newsreels, covering all three of Chamberlain's visits to Germany that year, and they can be found by searching YouTube for "Chamberlain 1938."

engineer, had pushed his way through the crush and handed me a brace of cables with the instruction to hold them clamped tightly together while he found a screwdriver.

As is quite common in the ritzy world of the media, I've since learned, my newfound friend disappeared off somewhere, never to be seen again. Meanwhile I could see Chamberlain was about to speak. The cables were making an ominous crackling sound in my hands and I was wondering if I might shortly be adding prime ministerial electrocution to my earlier disasters, when I noticed that I was holding two halves of what is called a bayonet connector. Salvation! A simple twist of the hands, the two cables snapped together and the fizzing sound stopped.

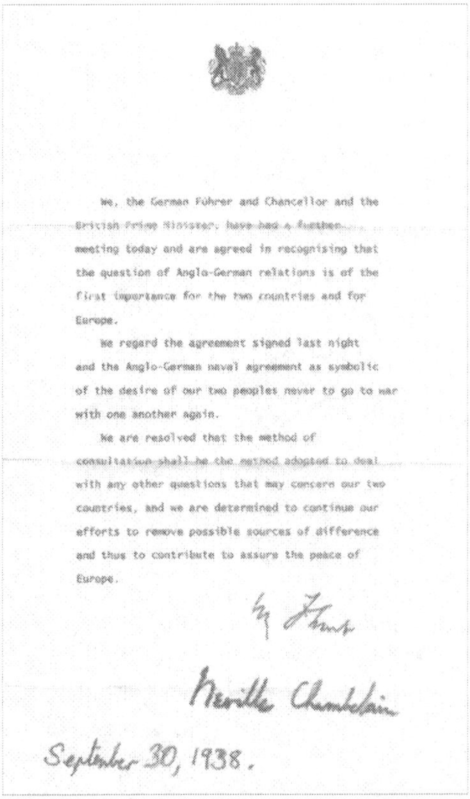

We, the German Führer and Chancellor and the British Prime Minister, have had a further meeting today and are agreed in recognising that the question of Anglo-German relations is of the first importance for the two countries and for Europe.

We regard the agreement signed last night and the Anglo-German naval agreement as symbolic of the desire of our two peoples never to go to war with one another again.

We are resolved that the method of consultation shall be the method adopted to deal with any other questions that may concern our two countries, and we are determined to continue our efforts to remove possible sources of difference and thus to contribute to assure the peace of Europe.

Neville Chamberlain

September 30, 1938.

Chamberlain's "Piece of Paper" – the Anglo-German Declaration.

It was too late for me to stand up. Chamberlain was discreetly clearing his throat, the crowd had gone quiet and I was only inches away, on the ground in front of him. I guessed the cameras would already be rolling, so decided to stay kneeling where I was.

I knew that this was history in the making and, caught in the excitement of the moment, I thought it wouldn't hurt if I made some notes. Whilst heroically handling the Great Heston Cable Crisis I'd been obliged to don the PM's soiled garment so I found myself rummaging in the unfamiliar territory of its pockets, looking for pen and paper. In one pocket there were some fly fishing lures and a pipe – Chamberlain's of course.* In another there was my wallet and a pen, one of Mac's new-fangled Biro ball-points. Then I remembered Helena's note and realised that that would do for paper. I eventually located it in an inner liner.

* Chamberlain was noted as a keen outdoorsman and fly-fisher.

To this very day, at school reunions, I am often reminded of how I saved a production of Romeo and Juliet one Parents Night. Now stay with me – this is relevant – I promise you. You see Juliet, who had been off colour ever since his voice started to break in dress rehearsal, completely froze for the last act. He just stood there, mouth agape, with ne'er a word coming out. And to make things worse, Widdly Wiggins, our drama teacher and chief prompter, had fallen asleep. So, instead of building up to the well-known tragic Shakespearian climax we just had a good old fashioned British balls-up. The audience was tittering and I could see Old Man Blenkinsop was about to intervene and send us all off for a thrashing when I grabbed the script from under the dripping nose of Rip van Wiggins. We were at the point where Juliet was supposed to deliver "her" famous soliloquy which starts with 'I will be brief, for my short date of breath' and then isn't brief at all but goes droning on for about 40 lines. But I managed to prompt the poor chap through the whole of it. Afterwards everyone congratulated me and said that Juliet had delivered his lines so well that it brought a tear to the eye.*

Meanwhile the prime minister was rolling along nicely with his speech. 'This morning I had another talk with the German Chancellor,' he intoned and I could see he was holding a piece of crisp stationery. 'And here is the paper which bears his name upon it, as well as mine.' By then I was frantically tugging his trouser leg.

It is very risky trying to distract a statesman in this fashion, when he is in full flow and you are in such a disadvantageous position. You risk a good solid boot in the solar plexus, which is exactly what happened to me as he smoothly continued. 'Some of you perhaps have already heard what it contains.'

Gasping for breath I renewed my assault on his trouser leg, as he waved the paper again, this time informing the world at large he would like to read it. He brought it down in front of him and cleared his throat before delivering the momentous message from our new ally. 'My dear Englishman,' he said, pausing momentarily for effect. 'My dear Englishman it says here.' He pointed at the document. 'Next time you are in Munich it will be your turn to stick it up *my* arse.'

Well, of course the PM didn't say that at all, but that is what he *would* have said had he really read the page before him. You see, and you are probably ahead of me on this one, Helena's loving note to me and Hitler's statement of peace and goodwill to Chamberlain had been mixed up in the earlier prime ministerial jacket debacle.

---

* This must certainly have been a memorable night. In the standard production of Romeo and Juliet the lines Kilroy mentions are delivered by Friar Laurence, *after* Juliet is dead. http://tinyurl.com/Kilroy066.

Fortunately for world peace and unusually for me, I was a little ahead of events that day. A few seconds before I had glanced down at my own piece of paper. That's strange, I thought, I don't remember Helena's note being typewritten. And I don't remember her telling me 'We the German Führer and Chancellor and the British Prime Minister...' That's when I started tugging the PM's trouser leg. 'You've got the wrong page,' I hissed, waving the correct one at him.

Prime Minister Chamberlain waves the Anglo-German declaration to the crowd at Heston aerodrome.

This is when I found out that I had foolishly underestimated Chamberlain earlier. I realised that he was, if not our greatest statesman ever, at least a master actor and (I'd maintain to this day) probably the best. Like an Olivier in his prime he was not to be deflected one jot by some demented young idiot distractingly tugging his trouser leg and, even when the penny dropped, with Helena's smutty words before him, his mouth gaped only slightly and his cheeks coloured just a little.

At that moment the PM caught my eye just briefly and I could sense his despair. I was still gasping for breath but could just find wind to prompt him though the whole of it. So, unlikely as it may sound, our prime minister did indeed read out the real Anglo-German agreement that day, which is more than Mr Hitler ever did come to think of it.

If you ever have the chance to see a film of his performance you might spot a slight stumble when he reached the bit about the Anglo-German naval agreement, which was when I nearly lost my place. Overall I thought we made a pretty good team. And just to show what a consummate performer he was he even had the brass neck at the end to smile and wave Helena's naughty note again to the cheering crowd – just as well he folded it first.

Once he had finished I got to my feet. This might sound naïve but I was rather expecting him to congratulate me on bailing him out. I even had the idiotic notion that he might be mildly interested to hear about my earlier success in the Shakespearian arena and that we could share a chuckle over the whole business. I pulled myself up to my full height and just as we were eye to eye I smiled at him. All I got back was a long stare. Suddenly he reached out and snatched the agreement from my hand, quickly stuffing it in his pocket. I reached to retrieve Helena's note but it was out of reach.

Instead he screwed it into a ball and threw it at my feet, before turning on his heel and stomping off.

I heard one of the Cabinet say, 'Crikey. What will Hitler do if he sees that?'

Someone answered, 'Invade Poland, I shouldn't wonder.'

Almost immediately there was a shout, from the Movietone director to a cameraman, I guessed. 'I hope you got that last bit, David? Absolute dynamite.'

'Sorry, Skipper. The power's just gone.'

I looked down and the bayonet connector had broken loose.*

* When Chamberlain returned from Munich it was widely believed that he had resolved the Czechoslovakian Crisis and secured peace but, as it turned out, he had merely delayed war by a year. On the one hand these extra months gave the Allies time in which to rearm but, had the agreement not been signed, it is possible that Hitler would have been toppled by his own generals, who thought Germany did not have the military strength to move on Czechoslovakia and simultaneously withstand a concerted attack by the Allies. Also, the Soviet Union had an interest in the region but was excluded from the Munich negotiations, and this was instrumental in it making its own deal with Hitler (the Molotov-Ribbentrop pact) which resulted in the invasion of Poland the following year, the event which triggered the war.

Nowadays it is the Anglo-German Declaration, the "piece of paper" signed by Chamberlain and Hitler alone, that is popularly recalled as the outcome of the Munich conference. The document was made famous by Chamberlain waving it to the crowds in London on his return, along with the message 'peace for our time' which he delivered shortly after the Heston speech, when he returned to Downing Street. The other document, the Munich Agreement, permitting the dismemberment of Czechoslovakia, was the real and embarrassing outcome of the conference, but this was brushed aside by nearly everyone from Chamberlain downwards. http://tinyurl.com/Kilroy067.

The Anglo-German Declaration resides in the Imperial War Museum in Kennington in London and can be viewed online at http://tinyurl.com/Kilroy068. The text of the Munich Agreement can be read online at http://tinyurl.com/Kilroy053.

CHAPTER 13

An hour or so later I was back in Claremont. It took a while to get back to normal after that, as the whole country went bonkers for a few days. Straight from Heston, Chamberlain had been invited onto the balcony at Buckingham Palace and thereafter was given a hero's welcome wherever he went. Closer to home there were parties and celebrations in every house and garden. I noticed that strangers were hailing each other in the street, or shaking hands at the bus stop. People even started filling in the trenches they had so recently dug. It was like the King's Jubilee, winning the Ashes and victory in the Schneider Trophy all rolled into one.[*] Everyone was just so very happy.

Winston Churchill in 1941.

There were a few dissenters and Mac was one of them. 'We haven't seen an end to it,' he told me one evening. 'That mad Austrian will want appeasing forever and God help us when we stop.' More significantly Chamberlain didn't have it all his own way in Parliament. Duff Cooper[†] resigned from the cabinet and Churchill, as ever, had the right words for the moment. While I was in the middle of an argument over the bill at the dry cleaner, he was at the despatch box, telling Chamberlain, 'We have suffered a total and unmitigated defeat.' adding prophetically, 'You were given the choice between war and dishonour. You chose dishonour and you will have war.' When I read of this and, having overheard the prime minister on the aeroplane, I knew that *he* knew that Churchill was right – it *had* been a shabby business, but he was never going to admit that when he was being fêted as David after Goliath. Why, there was even talk of calling an election.

After a week or so everyone calmed down. I was back to cabin boy duties at Heston and that would have been that for me on the Munich

[*] All three of these events did indeed happen in the 1930s, but not on the same day.

[†] Duff Cooper, Viscount Norwich, had been Secretary of War. He was First Lord of the Admiralty, a cabinet post, at the time of his resignation. http://tinyurl.com/Kilroy069.

front, except for some rather nasty surprises that came my way, each following the other in quick succession.

The first was over breakfast one morning. Mac dropped an envelope in front of me and said, 'I've had your photos printed. Open it up and let's have a look at them.' I was just supping some cornflakes at the time and almost broke a tooth on the spoon. Of course I'd meant to throw away the film but it had slipped my mind and presumably Mac had come across it, so now the evidence of my misdeeds in Munich was lying by the toast rack. I tried to fob him off, telling him how boring they were and how I'd sort through them later but he was not to be deflected.

'Nonsense. That was an historic trip. Exciting stuff,' he said rubbing his hands together as he sat down. With a feeling of mounting dread, I watched as he pulled out the prints and started looking at each in turn. Apart from one out of focus shot with Chamberlain's ear in the foreground there wasn't much to excite interest in the beginning but I knew that once we reached the bear's head in the bar shortly before I got clobbered by Rudi that the trouble would start.

Hitler passes through Graslitz in the Sudetenland.

Interestingly Mac barely blinked once we got there and just carried on handing the prints over to me one by one. In the first one I was Couchant Solo, as you might say, and at least I still had my socks on. Then we were two. Next a fascinating knot of arms and legs with Helena's face poking out from within. Then we had an intriguing view of what I can best describe as Nelson's column as it was about to bravely venture into the Black Forest. 'Fear naught boys,' the intrepid hero seemed to be saying to the cannonballs dancing along behind, 'Follow me to paradise or glory.'

I made some remark about the superb photography – how there had been such challenging light conditions and awkward angles but that every picture was perfect and with no sign of camera shake.

'And who is the lucky lady?' he asked.

'Er Heather, no Hayley. I mean er...'

'Well she certainly made a lasting impression on you. Still...' He looked at his watch. 'They should do well at Berwick Street market.' He yawned. 'I know someone there who'll give you a good price. And you'll certainly need the money to pay me back for the camera.'

I must have looked a bit crestfallen.

'Chin up old boy.' He slapped me on the back. 'Glad to see the family jewels are in safe hands, eh what?' And he wandered out the door chuckling to himself.

Once Mac had gone off to work I flicked through the photos once again. He hadn't even been bothered to look at them all earlier and that was when I had my second surprise. I came across a rather natty action shot of me hurling the Vaseline, stark naked and, I liked to think, looking like a Greek Olympian hurling the discus. I expected that to be the last but it wasn't. The next one showed Helena again in a tangle of limbs. I remembered that after our little Vaseline disagreement I had switched the lights off so this was a bit of a puzzle. I couldn't work out how we would have had any pictures then at all. I looked closely at the picture and realised with a jolt that, although I don't know my own backside any better than most chaps, I do know it's not covered in hair. Unlike this one. And I knew it couldn't be Helena's either, God forbid. So whose was it? The answer came about three shots later when I saw the leering face of Capello, our lively Italian delegate, sandwiched twixt breast and thigh.

The devious minx I thought, as I flicked through the remaining photos, wondering how she had the energy after our little tussle and why she then brought back the film and left me the note with it – but there lies the mystery of women I mused, something I still struggle with.

The last photo caught my interest, not because of the usual bedroom athletics which were becoming all too familiar but because of what lay on the bedside table in the background – a sheaf of papers held by a large paperclip and the words "*Streng Geheim*", which means "Top secret" visible on the top sheet. I took out a magnifying glass and could make out "Stufenplan", meaning stage-by-stage plan, some words that were too blurred to make out, but there, at the bottom, the name: "Adolf Hitler".

I found a more powerful magnifier and spent some more time studying the picture but couldn't make much sense of it. All I could conclude was that it must be important and presumably written by the Führer, but how it came to be propped up on Capello's bedside table in Munich was anybody's guess. Then I remembered that Jock McKnowall had given me his card at the airport so, on a whim I dug it out, stuck the picture in an envelope and posted it to him, with my compliments.

The next day I'd forgotten all about it, but who should turn up at the house? 'You bloody fool,' he rasped as I'd barely opened the door. 'What do you mean by sending that in the post?'

I blinked.

'We don't want any old Tom, Fritz or Herman to know our business do we?'

I invited him in. 'But...'

He sat down at the dining room table and pulled out the photo. 'Okay, laddie, now tell me how you came by this?'

'Well, sir, at Munich I, er, I er recruited somebody to take this picture for me and I thought...'

'Don't give me that bollocks. I know who she is, no question, now where's the negative?'

My heart sank. I realised I should have thought of this before. The negatives for a Minox camera are contained on one long strip of film, with all the pictures on it, side by side. I realised I should have separated them, then I could just give him the one or, preferably just not have sent him the bloody picture in the first place.

'Oh, I think Mac, er I mean Mr McKenzie, threw it out.' It was worth a try.

'Stop your nonsense laddie. Just go and get it or I can have Scotland Yard here in five minutes and they'll tear the place apart.' He glared at me.

'I went up to my room, thinking I'd have to go through the whole Nelson's column routine again. There didn't seem any other choice, apart from jumping out the window, so a few minutes later I was back downstairs with the envelope with both negative and prints.

McNulty was, if anything, even less fazed than Mac had been. After flicking through the first few pictures without comment, he lingered over one, featuring, as it happened, yours truly in rampant flagrante. When he whipped out a ruler and magnifying glass I couldn't resist a snigger, venturing, 'Surely you don't need any magnification for that one, eh, what?'

He grunted. 'Couldn't care less about the size of your apparatus, laddie, which I imagine is highly unreliable in any case.' He sniffed. 'Calibration, that's what this is about.' And he appeared to be measuring the bedside table.

And so he continued, fiddling around with the photos, magnifying glass and ruler. After a while I was getting bored and so went to make some tea. By the time I returned he appeared to have finished. The pictures were spread before him, arranged neatly in a rectangle.

'Sit down, sit down.' He gestured at the chair opposite him.

I did as he bid and waited as he stared long and hard at me. He appeared to be trying to make up his mind about something and eventually he decided. 'Right,' he said, 'First, tell me what you know about this woman, this...'

'Helena,' I said.

'Yes, er, Helena, if you like.'

So I told him the little I did know and the even less I knew of Capello.

He picked up the picture I'd sent him. 'I'll get our forensics to take a proper look at this but I'm pretty sure I know what it is.' He tapped the area showing the manuscript, poised as it was, just above Capello's hairy posterior.

I looked questioningly.

'God knows how that Italian idiot came by it, but it's a political treatise,' he said. 'The Führer's memoir if you like.'

'*Mein Kampf*?' I said. 'Why...'

'Not *Mein Kampf* you eejit,' he rasped. 'You can go to Foyles and buy that any day of the week. This is different.' He stabbed with his finger at the picture as he spoke. 'This is another memoir. Unpublished. And we've been trying to get hold of it for some time.' He stopped to eyeball me. 'Now tell me again everything you can.'

And so it went on. In the end I had to go and report to him the next day at his office in Whitehall. I certainly got a knowing smirk from his secretary as she showed me in. I told him again everything I could and if it helped him at all, he wasn't letting on. All I could gather was that the manuscript in the picture was the work of Herr H, that it had been of some considerable interest to our intelligence people and that I, or rather Helena, had just got as close to it as anyone other than the Reich Chancellor himself.*

Just when we seemed to be finishing, his secretary brought in a tray. 'Tea?' he asked, and poured me a cup. We went through the usual ritual with 'one lump or two?' biscuits and so on and as I stretched my legs out in front of his desk I reflected that he could be quite a decent old cove when he relaxed a bit.

He must have been having similar thoughts about me as suddenly he ventured, 'You've done well, laddie.'

'Well thank you, sir,' I said.

'You see, you might be a young eejit but things certainly happen when you are around.'

There didn't seem to be any answer to that.

'And we might have further use for you.' He was idly stirring his cup and looked up questioningly at me.

'Well, sir it depends I guess.' I was half tempted to say that if there were any more fair maids needing attention then I was his man, but as for being

---

* The manuscript Kilroy describes here is almost certainly the mysterious *Zweites Buch*, Hitler's second book of political theory and the sequel to *Mein Kampf*, written in the late 1920s. Hitler never sought to publish it and there were only two copies of the manuscript, only one of which survived the war (it has since been published and translated). Kilroy raises the interesting possibility here that the other copy was doing the rounds in Munich during the conference. See *End Note (6)*.

shot at, boiled alive or whatever other ghastly fates he might have in mind, well, I was perhaps a little less keen.

'We are looking for a youngster with aviation experience after the last one er...' He spluttered in his cup. 'Well, we are looking for a replacement. Let's just say that.'

'A cabin boy?' I asked.

'No, man, of course not.' He replenished our cups. 'An R.A.F. chap.'

Which of course I wasn't. I stared back blankly at him.

'I can get you into the Reserves and all trained up. How does that sound?'

The R.A.F.V.R., that is the R.A.F. reserves, wasn't quite a top notch berth like Cranwell, but then I thought that I didn't want to be stuck at Heston for the rest of my days. 'Well, thank you sir. Thank you kindly.'

According to McNulty I'd have to complete my training and get some experience under my belt and only then would they be able to use me. 'That fiasco in Munich,' he said. 'It means nothing. There will be war soon enough.' He looked at his watch. 'So get on with it and we'll keep tabs on you laddie. It may be a year, maybe longer, and when we're ready you'll get the call.'

I thanked him and was making to leave. 'Just one thing.' He looked slyly at me as I stood at the door, 'That incident with the PM on the plane back. You don't have any problem with airsickness do you?'

'No, sir, not at all.' And I spoke the truth. Candice had been right and I had stumbled (literally) on the perfect cure for my condition. I was never airsick again.

PART TWO: PHONEY WAR

1939-40

We'll meet again,
Don't know where,
Don't know when
But I know we'll meet again some sunny day

First performed by Vera Lynn (1939)
Words and Music by Ross Parker and Hughie Charles
http://tinyurl.com/Kilroy002

CHAPTER 1

If you ever have the misfortune to be called to arms I can heartily recommend phoney war. The French term for it is *drôle de guerre* and the German *sitzkrieg*, meaning "strange war" and "sitting war" respectively, but it all boils down to the same thing – that is loafing around while being paid for *not* getting killed, maimed or otherwise abused. I reckon the army has it best in a phoney conflict: tucked up in nice snug billets polishing their rifles by day and hard at it in the fleshpots and bars by night. We, in the air force, had to fly those hazardous war machines of course, and there was the possibility of bumping into Fritz upstairs, but if the Hun didn't want to mix it (not then he didn't anyway) and you happen to have the worst winter on record (we did), you have abundant leisure time for boozing and carousing in the local town and generally impressing the womenfolk with your snazzy uniform.

So that's how it was in France in that first winter of the war. Nice and safe. If you look in the history books you will see that our dear misguided Prime Minister Chamberlain had rushed us into the defence of the poor Poles in the autumn of 1939, and not by sending an army anywhere near Poland note, but by getting us to take the short hop across the Channel to a land where the champagne was cheap, the women immoral and where our French allies already had an invincible army in any case. At least that's what we thought at the time and if only two of those assumptions were right and the other sadly wrong I'll leave you to work out which for yourself.

At war's outbreak my own phoney berth was in the depths of wildest Leicestershire, some hundreds of miles from the slumbering front line in France and as safe a place as you could wish for in times of strife.* There

---

* Britain and France declared war on Germany on 3rd September 1939, with much of the British Empire following suit within hours. Future combatants, Japan, Italy and the USA remained neutral at that time. This was the start of the Phoney War, which continued until the German invasion of the West on May 10th 1940.

On the outbreak of war the French already had a considerable army in the field, defending the Maginot line, and the British soon added to it with the BEF (British Expeditionary Force) and a substantial air force, the AASF (Advanced Air Strike Force) but then, along with their French allies, they did very little. There were no major engagements on the ground while, in the air, bombers were only allowed to attack major military installations such as naval bases while being restricted to dropping leaflets on civilian populations. There was some significant action at sea, notably the sinking of the HMS Royal Oak at Scapa Flow, with a loss of over 800 lives, and the Battle of the River Plate, but for most of the military on both sides of Germany's western front it was a case of sitting and waiting. http://tinyurl.com/Kilroy075.

were plenty in my squadron who were eager to get to France right away and have a pop at Jerry, as they put it, but I wasn't in any tearing hurry. We didn't know back then that it was all phooey and phoney over there and my feeling (kept to myself) was that the war wouldn't in fact be all over by Christmas and that it might be pleasant to get through some or even all of it without getting my head blown off, or whatever other dastardly fate might await me. But then, newly qualified and with my pilot's wings still bright and pristine on my battledress I managed to achieve what all the others said they wanted and with no real effort at all on my part.

It was the day after "the incident", as it became known and there I was, at attention, before my squadron leader's desk. 'Enid Blyton,' he kept saying over and over, like it was a euphemism. 'My children read her stories, for Christ's sake. How could you?'

The answer to that was 'very easily,' in the first instance and she was a grown woman in the second, but I didn't think that was what he wanted to hear. 'We were exploring an idea for one of her books, sir – Nobby flying over Toy Town in a Miles Magister...'

'Correct me if I'm wrong, Pilot Officer, but the characters in Blyton's books are generally fully clothed and aren't often pursued across an airfield by a jealous husband?'*

'Yes, but...'

'This isn't funny, dammit.' He frowned. 'I've half a mind to have you court-martialled...'

I said nothing. He was no doubt thinking that the country was desperately short of pilots. I watched as he gazed out of the window, fingers drumming on his desk.

At last he seemed to reach a decision. 'Pilot Officer,' he said, pointing across the airfield, 'you see that kite over there?'

Our squadron had recently converted to the Hurricane. All the old Gloster Gladiators were supposed to be gone and good riddance too but actually just one had been left behind – the one he was pointing at. 'Sir?'

'Cannons,' he said.

'Pardon, sir?'

'"Cannons," I said.' He sighed and looked at his watch. 'That is it's just been kitted out with a battery of Hispano cannons instead of our more usual Jerry welcoming party.'

---

* At this time Enid Blyton was already a successful children's writer and on the brink of a messy divorce from her first husband. She introduced the immensely successful Noddy character (not Nobby as mentioned by Kilroy) after the war. Incidentally, Noddy *was* naked in the first story (before Big Ears gave him some clothes). Her last Noddy story was *Noddy and the Aeroplane* and, in the accompanying illustrations, the plane does indeed look similar to a Miles Magister. http://tinyurl.com/Kilroy070.

I squinted at the plane in the distance, saying nothing in reply. At that time most of our fighters were equipped with machine guns and I knew little about the heavyweight and slower firing cannon, apart from the fact that the Luftwaffe were using them extensively.

'God knows why, but the boffins think it's worth trying out on ops over in France. Personally, I think they're nuts, but then you're just the sort of chap to take this on, so off you go, what?'

'Yes, sir. Very good sir.'

'That'll be all, Kilroy. And try and keep your grubby mitts off the madamoiselles. It'll only stir up trouble with the locals.'

'Thank you sir. When would you like me back, sir?'

'Back?' He looked me up and down. 'I didn't say I wanted you back, did I? This is a permanent posting, Kilroy. Now off you buzz and see Adj. He'll give you all the paperwork. And goodbye.' He rose from his chair, brushed past me and stalked off.

An hour later I was sitting in the Gladiator cockpit with my kitbag jammed on my knee, peering around the side of it while I weaved the plane across the field. As I checked the engine Ts and Ps* I was reflecting that fixed undercarriage biplanes belonged to the Somme of 1917, not the Marne in 1939 and cursing my stupidity for ending up in one. I reached the downwind boundary, turned the plane into wind and gently dabbed the brakes before opening the throttle. The Gladiator felt ponderous. After the Hurricane it had a lumbering feel to it but (as I'd been warned many times) it also had a slippery eagerness to turn-turtle in a stall – not a good combination. So, with the engine roaring and the plane bouncing across the field, I found I was holding my breath, until at last we lifted off, just clearing the hedge at the far boundary and slowly climbing away to set course for Reims.

* Ts and Ps – engine oil temperature and pressure.

The trip would have taken maybe 25 minutes in a Hurricane but with a strong headwind it was all of an hour and a half before I saw the French coastline glide by beneath me, 10,000 feet below. 15 minutes later I was trundling and bumping across my new home base.

I had no idea where to park. Frontline operational airfields were an unknown to me and this one seemed to be just tents and sandbags. I took a guess that one particular cluster of tents might be serving as Squadron Admin, taxied in that general direction and gently braked nearby, before swinging into wind and cutting the engine. Some erks* came running up to attend as I undid my harness. I could see them looking curiously at the cannons as I stepped onto the wing and jumped down onto the ground, dragging my kitbag behind me.

***

Group Captain Belfrey was the name on the door. I'd been told to report to him first, at Group HQ, in a rather elegant chateau just up the road from the airfield. I'd come across such elevated rank only once previously, at the Wings parade at the end of my training, so I was rather wondering what this might be about as I knocked firmly and waited.

A Gloster Gladiator serving the Luftwaffe.

After knocking again and still hearing nothing from within, I pushed open the door and entered. The room had blackout curtains drawn down, so it took some time for my eyes to adjust. At last I made out a large marble topped table across from the door and standing on it, facing me, an enormous dog. There didn't seem to be any sign of my superior but just as I was about to turn around and walk out I heard his voice. 'Hold still, Tungsten.' It came from somewhere behind the dog. 'Hold still.'

Tungsten, who I subsequently discovered was three quarters Wolfhound, was staring hard at me. You might think it's not possible for a dog to look worried but this one certainly did. A mixture of worry with an expression that seemed to be pleading with me to do something. '"Hold still," I said, dammit,' repeated the CO and at that moment I could see Tungsten tense and both eyes bulge so I could see the whites all around.

That's when he noticed me. 'Ah, you must be Kingston?'

* R.A.F. slang for ground crew.

'Kilroy, sir.' I wasn't sure whether to salute or not. The Kings Regulations spell out all the whys and wherefores of greeting a superior officer but don't cover the scenario where his saluting hand is stuck up a dog's bottom.

He gestured at me with his free hand to sit down. 'I knew it, I knew it. Prolapsed haemerrhoids,' he announced triumphantly. 'Have you got that Reggie?' he shouted through a doorway to the side. 'Coal tar cream. Get onto Doc Maple for some and the old hound'll be right as ninepence in no time.'

There was a distinct plop, the dog's eyes widened once more and then Belfrey was extending his business hand in my direction. For one ghastly moment I thought he was offering to shake it with me but then I saw it was encased in a rubber glove. He expertly peeled it off, dropped it in the waste paper bin and plopped himself down on the chair behind the table. Tungsten, meanwhile, had taken the opportunity to jump down and take to a neutral corner, glaring at me as he minced past. 'Well, well, Kingsland. So you're our cannon expert I gather.' He looked me up and down carefully and shouted again through the doorway, 'Reggie, are you sure the Ministry has got it right? He looks a bit young for this sort of caper.'

There was a muffled reply which I didn't catch. This seemed like the moment to make my case, 'Well sir...'

'Never mind, we'll soon have you blasting away with it at those damned Jerries. Better than those damned pea shooters they've got now – they couldn't bring down a dead duck if you ask me.'

'But sir...'

'So, Kissedoff, I'll think we'll put you with the Bustards.'

'Pardon, sir?'

'"Bustards," I said. A-K-A Useless Bustards – har har. Been called that since the last show – no idea why. And with your cannon skills we'd better give you a flight.' He looked at the single slim ring on my sleeve. 'Why the devil you still a pilot officer?' He left no time for me to answer. 'Soon put that right anyway.' He looked at his watch. 'Reg,' he shouted again, 'Make this Piltdown fellow up to flight lieutenant. Acting that is.'

'Er, thank you sir.'

'And Felldown?'

'Er, yes, sir?'

'I hope you can knit.'

He produced a pair of needles stuck in a ball of wool and threw them at me.

'A pair of socks per week should do for starters. All got to do that extra bit for the war effort, what?' He waved a perfectly turned pair of hose at me.

CHAPTER 2

My new squadron leader, Stiffy Barnes was, if anything, even less pleased with me than my previous one. It took me a while to track him down but I eventually found him, in the bar in the officers mess, where he was quaffing a pint. 'He did what?' he spat out when I told him, the beer sputtering down his battledress.

'A flight lieutenant, sir.'

'Jesus Christ.' He whispered something to one of the men standing with him, who nodded sagely and glared at me. 'Er... how many hours on ops?'

'Well, none sir, but willing to give it a go, what?'

'Good God.' He turned again to the man next to him. 'Crikey, Tucker, where'd they find them?' Tucker shrugged and renewed his glare at me. Barnes put his glass down, all the better to jab at me with his finger as he spoke. 'Listen, young man, you might be some sort of fiend of the firing range back in bloody Leicestershire but it's another story in a Hurri at 20,000 feet with a 109 up your arse. Cannon or no cannon.'

'Hurri?' I asked.

'Yes, the Hawker Hurricane,' my new line manager told me. 'You have heard of them I trust?'

'Er, yes sir, but that's not what I've brought with me.' I pointed through the window towards the airfield in the distance. The light was fading outside and the Gladiator was some way away but you could still just make it out as the ground crew were wheeling it tail-first into a dispersal pen.

I'll spare you the rest. Suffice to say I'd just experienced my first good old fashioned service balls-up. And, for once, it wasn't my fault. Well, apart from the Enid Blyton bit it wasn't. Everything got sorted out in the end but it was a good couple of weeks before they got the cannons mounted in a spare Hurricane (I never did have to fly a Gladiator on operations, thank God), then another week before the ammunition turned up.*

---

* The Hurricane was the R.A.F.'s mainstay fighter in France at this time, alongside the hopelessly outdated Gladiator, which was being phased out. The Spitfire was only gradually introduced into the R.A.F. in the first year of the war, being dogged with early production difficulties and it was never based in France at all. Another fighter, the Boulton-Paul Defiant was being introduced at the same time as the Spitfire but its turret armoury proved to be ineffective in combat and it played little part in the war. http://tinyurl.com/Kilroy071 (Gladiator), http://tinyurl.com/Kilroy072 (Hurricane), http://tinyurl.com/Kilroy073 (Spitfire), http://tinyurl.com/Kilroy074 (Defiant).

My newly elevated rank didn't last long either. One evening, about a week after my arrival, a flight lieutenant, who I later discovered was Reggie Richards, Belfrey's P.A., came into the mess bar. He was carrying a clipboard and a rusty and dented bucket, which he placed at his feet. Every now and then one or other of the junior pilots would go over to him, drop something into it and have his name checked off. After a while Richards cocked an eyebrow at me and as I had no idea what this was about I just shrugged back at him. 'Socks,' he hissed, 'where are they?' Well, of course I hadn't taken seriously Belfrey's nonsense about knitting the damn things but it appears I should have done because the next day I was up before him. He didn't like my attitude, 'didn't like the fact that I'd arrived in the wrong damned aeroplane,' 'didn't like pilots who tied their ties with a Windsor knot' and, moreover, he 'didn't like his pilots looking like blue-arsed Basutolanders.'

This last remark was a reference to my sharing out of some of Mac's peculiar ball-point pens. Mac had been hoping the R.A.F. would adopt them instead of the pencil, normally used at altitude, but they soon proved to be even worse than the fountain pen and, with a sticky and highly indelible ink, most of the mess was now sporting stained fingers with ugly splodges on breast pockets.

So there I was, back to plain old Pilot Officer Kilroy again. Later that day I bemoaned my rapid demotion to my room mate, Sticky Stevens, but he told me I'd been lucky. When he'd transgressed, a few weeks earlier, he'd found himself nominated for the squadron boxing team. 'Up against the pongoes,* we were. I thought I was quite useful as a noble pugilist but *they* fielded some hand-picked gorillas from Plaistow and I can tell you, when those boys are not AWOL and knocking seven bells out of each other back in the East End, they are sure keeping the MPs busy over here. You don't want to mess with them, that much is certain,' he said pointing at his cheek, which still bore a dark yellow mark.

Other than my great sock-up there was little enough to worry about those first few weeks in France. The airfield was at a place called Condé-Vraux,† about half way between Reims and Chalons and about 100 miles

* The army.

† Condé-Vraux was indeed an R.A.F. airfield at this time, located roughly halfway between Reims and Chalons. It was the base for 114 Squadron, which operated

from the front line. It was home to two squadrons, one of them mine. Without notice the French had had to arrange accommodation for 20 odd R.A.F. squadrons in this corner of France and had dealt with the problem by requisitioning some boggy fields for us, while keeping all the plum aerodromes for themselves. So that was Condé-Vraux – no hangars, no control tower, no purpose-built premises for briefing rooms and so on – just a field with some moth-eaten British Army tents, trenches zig-zagging every which way, with sandbags piled up all around the parked aircraft and anti-aircraft guns and so on.

In those first few days, with nothing to fly, I was both new boy *and* Supernumerary Uno, which meant I could be lumbered with all the tedious admin duties that no one else wanted to do. Censoring the airmen's mail was one such task I remember but rather more interesting was my assignment as "Voodoo" – that's a service abbreviation for Venereal Disease Orderly Officer. This duty was Belfrey's invention and was quite possibly the only good idea he had in the entire war. If I say so myself I think I was an inspired choice for the job. I like nothing better than instructing others to do what I've no intention of doing myself so I rather took to lecturing the men on the perils of promiscuity, occasionally pinging a prophylactic at anyone not paying attention and generally terrifying one and all with gruesome pictures, borrowed from Doc Maple, of putrid peckers and the like. After a few days of my sterling efforts the consensus in the mess was that if we weren't destined to be the least clapped out unit in France then it wouldn't be for lack of trying on my part.

And then there was the ludicrous sock detail. Clearly Belfrey was mad and I wasn't the first in the squadron to come up with the idea of having him sacked, sectioned or just plain blown up but it seemed he was too well placed with the Air Commodore and so we just had to put up with him. I would be blowed if I'd knit the blasted things myself, wasn't enthused by the idea of paying LAC* Stanley, the junior officer batman, to do it for me

---

Blenheim bombers. There is a mystery here because no sources record any Hurricanes at Condé-Vraux in 1939-40 (apart from 1 Squadron, which was based there for just 24 hours on 17th May 1940). Kilroy certainly seems familiar with the area so the most likely explanation is that he was actually based somewhere nearby but chose not to reveal exactly where in order to mask the identity of the "Bustards" squadron, possibly in anticipation of litigation from its survivors.

On the second day of the German offensive (in May 1940) 114 was all but destroyed on the ground by Dornier bombers and thereafter played no part in the Battle of France.

There is no longer an airfield at Condé-Vraux but there is a museum on the site: http://tinyurl.com/Kilroy076. Chateau de Juvigny is near the Condé-Vraux airfield. It is now a hotel: http://tinyurl.com/Kilroy077.

and so in desperation I wrote to my mother. Her lone offering, when it eventually arrived, might have served a one-legged elephant but didn't look like it would get past the gimlet eye of Belfrey, so that left me rather stuck until I had the bright idea of writing to Hayley.

I'd last seen Hayley, at the Curzon Maison de Ill Fame, just before my posting to Leicestershire, when the sight of me in my new officer's uniform and with pilot's wings stitched on the breast had filled her with such patriotic fervour that she gave me one for free, as she put it. Well, not one actually, but several and I was so enthused by the whole business that she then had trouble booting me out. 'Chamberlain has recalled Parliament, don't you know?' she said and when I looked puzzled she explained that it was always frantic after the recall and she couldn't leave half the cabinet all kicking their heels downstairs while I had a wobbly and, anyway, didn't I have a train to catch?* I missed it, of course but there I was, a few weeks later in France and writing to her with the suggestion that the girls at the Mayfair Mollery might care to "knit for victory" when they had those odd spare moments and were not on the job so as to speak. And I struck gold with that idea, well wool anyway. A few days later a parcel arrived with enough hosiery to keep Belfrey off my back for many a long week. He was particularly taken with one pair, courtesy of Yvette apparently, which featured R.A.F. roundels around the heels. 'Splendid effort young man,' he said, patting me on the back, when I handed them to him in the mess bar. He even bought me a drink and then insisted on displaying them to everyone as they came in. 'Produced by England's finest,' he announced, pointing at the expertly turned heels. Most simply smiled politely at him while glaring at me.

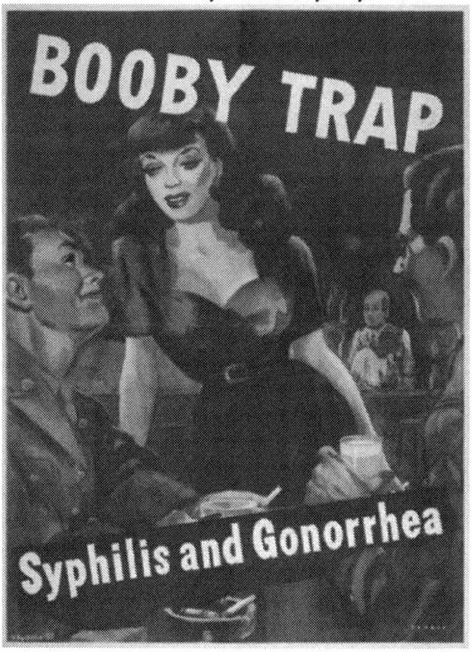

* Leading Aircraftman

* Prime Minister Chamberlain recalled Parliament early, on 24th August 1939, when details of the Molotov-Ribbentrop pact became public.

In contrast to the airfield, the officer accommodation, our mess and the all important mess bar were very passable. We were housed in Chateau Juvigny, a short hop from the airfield in the outskirts of Chalon. I gathered le Grand Haut Comte de Juvigny, or whatever he was called, had obligingly swanned off to the Cote d'Azur for the duration and rather foolishly, some might say, entrusted his magnificent spread to the officers and gentlemen of the Royal Air Force. The only downside to this arrangement was that we had to share the accommodation with Group HQ, in the shape of "Bags" Belfrey and his merry men. This was rather unusual as most of the squadrons in France at that time had some distance from what you might call the senior management and, as you've no doubt noticed, the Group Captain did have a tendency rather to interfere in our internal affairs. Additionally, his presence in the mess bar of an evening could put a damper on things although, as you will see, there were unexpected compensations for some in having him around.

At last my Hurricane, all cannoned up *and* with the right ammunition, was ready. In the short time I'd been with the squadron I'd heard plenty of talk in the mess about what a poor lot the Luftwaffe were and how they didn't want to fight, so I didn't expect anything much to happen on my first operational flight. As I was only too aware operations at Condé-Vraux had thus far been boringly routine, which is to say that several times a day we'd been sending up a section of three aircraft to stooge around the frontier looking for trouble and after an hour or so of nothing happening, they'd come back and land.

Mark 1 Hawker Hurricanes in France, inspected by King George VI, with the Duke of Gloucester and Viscount Lord Gort. Note the two bladed propellors.

As the new boy I was assigned to Flight Lieutenant Tucker, flying the first detail of the day. Turkey Tucker was the snotty one who was with the squadron leader in the bar on my first day. 'Okay, Kilroy, make sure you stick with me throughout. You're flying Green three,' was the extent of his briefing.

"Green three" meant I was in his "Green" section of three aircraft and as number three I was expected to fly immediately behind him and to the left, with the Hurricane's nose tucked tightly in behind his wing. Sticky Stevens, was his number two, with the same deal for him but on Tucker's right. And that was it for our little combat group.

A few minutes after take off we were at 10,000 feet and climbing steadily towards the western front. At this stage in the war R.A.F. fighters flew in tight formation. "Good true men who stick like glue will shoot the damned Hun right out the blue." This was Squadron Leader Barnes' little mantra – drummed into us at briefings and indeed repeated at any time there might be a lull in the conversation. It wasn't Barnes' fault that the tactic turned out to be utter tosh once Jerry did come out and fight, but no one in the R.A.F. knew this back then and so, in the absence of any greater wisdom, all I could do that morning was to stick my plane's whirling propeller as close to Tucker's left aileron as I dared and concentrate on not tearing lumps out of it.

It was hard work. You have to concentrate like buggery in close formation, anticipating every little twitch the leader might make and jockeying the throttle backwards and forwards all the time. It was a beautiful clear sunny day too, but I had no time to admire the view or, indeed, look for the enemy. Stevens and I were both reliant on Tucker to do this for us.

Suddenly over the R/T* I heard the controller's voice, calm, clear and unemotional. 'Fido to Green leader. Bandit, angels two zero. Vector one five zero.'

Tucker replied with a laconic 'Roger, wilco,' as simultaneously he turned on to the new heading, his plane's nose rotating upwards into what we called a "Battle Climb". The gobbledygook on the radio boiled down to a lone enemy plane that had been cheeky enough to come sneaking over France. It was up there somewhere and it was our job to sort it out.

Three of us and one of him may not sound that risky to anyone comfortably reading this by the fireside but I knew the Luftwaffe's larger planes were all bristling with gun turrets and could turn pretty nasty if they saw you coming. Not terribly heroic of me I guess and no doubt other pilots at the time didn't think that way but then they didn't survive the war and I did. I swallowed hard, forcing myself to remain calm and concentrate on staying in formation. "Angels two zero" meant the enemy was at 20,000 feet so we still had a way to climb to reach it and then... well Christ knows where it was or even what it was. A French bomber that had got lost would be the best outcome I thought. And I was in no position to look for it anyway, just keeping my nose snugly tucked into Tucker's armpit and hoping that he knew what he was about.

There were further exchanges between Tucker and Control and then, at last, Tucker to us, his voice raised with excitement. 'Green section. Bandit at twelve o' clock. It's a Dornier. A 17.'

This was some sort of good news. The Dornier 17 was a

* Receiver/transmitter.

reconnaissance aircraft, built for speed, specifically so it could run away from the likes of ourselves and, although it was well armed, its first instinct would be to put as much distance as it could between us and it. And unless we caught it napping, this close to the frontier we'd never catch it. It would be back over Deutschland in no time and at this stage of the war we were not allowed to pursue over enemy territory.

A Dornier 17 – the "flying pencil."

'Green section. Attack pattern three.' Attack. I realised that this was what all that training and zipping around in fancy military hardware had been about, but at that moment the word sounded like a death knell. Hopefully not mine. My mouth felt dry. I was on oxygen and there was a sweet rubbery smell coming from the mask. I tried to swallow, but no saliva came.

Stuck behind Tucker I still couldn't see anything but I guessed we had indeed caught the Dornier napping. The R.A.F. attack patterns at that time were a sort of aerial ballet, much rehearsed, all based on the shaky assumption that the enemy kept flying blithely in a straight line so that conveniently you could each home in on him in turn and blast him out of the sky. Number three attack was intended to deal with a target above and ahead of you. I risked a quick glance beyond Tucker but couldn't see anything. The sun was beating down into the cockpit and I could feel a trickle of sweat rolling down my cheek.

Time to unleash the dreaded cannons, I thought. A key point for all our various manoeuvres was to give Jerry a good blast with our weaponry before we were within range of his, something which definitely had my vote. I flicked over the safety catch on the firing button and quickly scanned the engine gauges. All systems normal. The Merlin was thrumming reliably and the plane felt reassuringly solid around me.

The belief had persisted in the squadron that I was some sort of expert with this new weapon and I'd even acquired the nickname "Cannonball Kilroy" but in truth I'd never fired them, even once. Shouldn't be much different from the 303s, I reasoned. With luck I'd get in a quick squirt at Jerry without too much hazard to yours truly and, who knows, if the blasted cannons were any blasted use at blasting and possibly with the wind in the right direction perhaps the new boy would distinguish himself with the squadron's first kill?

At last I saw the Dornier, just beyond Tucker's nose, slightly above and heading away from us and, I guessed, about half a mile away. The Flying

Pencil was its nickname – a long thin fuselage built for speed and with no room for a tail turret but with upper *and* lower gun stations just behind the pilot, specifically to deal with anyone sneaking up behind it, as indeed we were trying to do at that very moment. He must have woken up just as I saw him because suddenly I saw some pretty lines of fireworks streaming backwards and towards us from the lower turret. This was tracer of course, special rounds of ammunition intended to show the firer where his bullets were actually going and not for the entertainment of novice pilots. But it was still fascinating to watch as it seemed to move slowly to begin with and then suddenly it would speed up and zip past as (mercifully) it flew over the top of us.

From then on everything happened in a rush. Stevens and I peeled away from Tucker to let his attack go in first. The Dornier started weaving all over the place and I could see that Tucker had missed, as he rolled over and dived downwards. Next it was Stevens turn with the same result and then it was over to me. I squirmed down low in the cockpit hoping my engine would protect me from any stray rounds that might come my way and tried just to concentrate on the job in hand.

The tracer stream suddenly seemed less entertaining as it moved closer and closer to me, zipping over my head. I instinctively nudged the stick forward to get away from it but of course that pointed me away from the target and I had to make a conscious effort to force the nose back up. Never mind about any fancy deflection shooting I decided – I'd just get the bastard in the middle of the gunsight any old how and hope for the best, or if things started to look a bit hot, I'd stamp full on the rudder, pull the stick back hard and left and in an instant I'd either be heading down and away at full throttle or have torn the bloody wings off.

And, suddenly, there he was. I hadn't realised I'd been gaining on him so quickly – a sitting duck, filling my view. Quack quack. I think I even said it out loud as I pressed the firing button.

All hell broke loose. Pom-pom-pom pumped the cannons – so different from the rattle of machine guns – but the target had disappeared and the plane was twisting and swivelling all over the place. My first thought was that I'd been hit but I hadn't. I just couldn't control the plane. It was pitching, twisting and wriggling like, like, a French tart on Bastille Day.

All the while the cannons were keeping up their rhythmic pounding as I fought for control, all thought of the enemy forgotten. I've often wondered afterwards why it didn't occur to me to release the firing button but there it is, I didn't. Then there was a Hurricane, side on and right in front of me – so close I could see Tucker's terrified face. I wrenched the stick back, the plane bucked upwards and I was just about to sigh with relief as I passed over the top of him when there was a sickening crunch.

We landed in the same field, with Tucker just ahead of me. I could see him gathering his parachute in the gentle breeze as I floated over him. When you land by parachute you come down with the same force as if you had jumped off a ten foot wall so it's easy to break a leg if you mess up. Fortunately I had already accumulated some experience with leaps from first floor windows and so braced myself in good time in the prescribed manner, touching down with practised ease, rolling over and over as the parachute billowed all around me. I had landed no more than 50 yards from Tucker and had just punched the release on my harness and was stepping out of the straps, when he came up to me.

'Glad to see...' I started but that was as far as I got.

'You fucking idiot,' he exclaimed.

'But...' Suddenly I saw some colourful little stars wobbling around before me. They looked quite pretty I thought but then I noticed that my cheek was hot and that a front tooth seemed to have come loose. I guessed he must have punched me but couldn't recall it happening. 'Now th-teddy on,' I think I said.

'You nearly killed me, you moron.'

'Ow.' This time I did see the blow coming, a kick in the groin and managed to twist away just in time.

Fortunately the farmer turned up at that moment. He had a shotgun and it was pointed at us. 'Hände hoch, Nazi schweine,' he said in half-decent German but with a heavy French accent.

CHAPTER 3

It didn't take long to put the farmer straight but, on reflection, I'd have been better off sticking with him rather than returning to the squadron. I was grounded of course, pending a full investigation. And while I was grounded, as Belfrey put it, 'the silly bastard might as well actually make himself actually useful on the actual ground.' Thus, I was made captain of the cross country team – ten miles daily before breakfast, latrines orderly officer – not cleaning them thank God, but bad enough and was otherwise generally hauled off at short notice on any other unpleasant task that no one else wanted to do.

As it turned out my being grounded didn't make much difference as, in effect, the whole squadron was grounded anyway, by the weather. The autumn rains came and turned our field into a quagmire and you just can't operate a Hurricane with its wheels up to the axles in a mud bath. We had the men out digging drainage ditches (supervised by me of course – getting soaked while the other officers dozed in the mess) but still the airfield was awash. Perhaps someone from the Royal Engineers would have known what to do but all that my ditches achieved was to move the mud around, not get rid of it. Then, another task came up that no one wanted – press liaison officer. It was Barnes, our Squadron Leader, who came up with that one. *Picture Post*[*] was sending out a photographer and, he told me, like it or lump it we'd have to accommodate him as the Air Commodore had decreed it. So it would be my job to stick with him at all times and 'avoid all fuck-ups,' specifically making sure 'said press wally' took plenty of the right snaps – men looking busy and/or heroic and none of the wrong ones – same men whoring around and/or getting drunk.

Morgan Super Sports, 1937.

The next morning a rather natty Morgan three wheeler came screeching to a halt on the chateau forecourt. To my surprise there was a young

[*] *Picture Post* was a fortnightly newsstand title, endeavouring to offer the highest standards of photo journalism and published throughout the war. Many classic photos from the period first appeared in *Picture Post*. It folded in 1957. http://tinyurl.com/Kilroy078.

woman at the wheel, elegantly attired in what they called a "day dress" back then, all silk and figure hugging with its occupant not afraid to show her stocking tops as I helped her clamber out. I was about to ask the whereabouts of the photographer, when she handed me a camera. 'Lady Pamela,' she said. 'You can call me ma'am.' She extended her gloved hand to me and I wasn't sure whether to kiss it or shake it.

Meanwhile the investigation into my recent debacle was gathering pace and the fate of the "Maginot Mauler" as I'd become known, hung in the balance. My contention that there was something seriously wrong with the plane was widely disbelieved but the R.A.F. does occasionally play fair and so on this occasion our ground crew chief, Sergeant Oliver T. Oliver – known to one and all as Ollie – was dispatched to find the crashed plane and see what he could make of it. He returned with a lorry laden with bits of wing, cockpit and engine, which were unloaded in the only dry place on the entire airfield – an old barn which we grandiosely referred to as "the workshop". I'd no idea what he was doing in there but it was taking a while and seemed to involve regular visits to Squadron Leader Barnes to report on progress.

While this was ongoing I was kept busy by my press liaison role. Lady Pamela might have come from the top drawer but she knew how to work alright and it was my job to keep up with her, navigate between locations and lug her weighty cameras around. Thus in short order we visited a succession of farm cottages where the men were billeted, the last resting place of Tucker's plane, all corners of our boggy field of course, and also all over our wonderful chateau, which she referred to as 'the squadron nerve centre.' All the while it was bucketing down outside and, diverting as our photographer might be, roaring up and down muddy lanes in a drafty sports car with a leaky roof wasn't doing much for my good humour. I think it was on the second day – I was driving and had just mistaken the good lady's knee for the gear lever – when she swatted my hand away and abruptly asked, 'And where's my darling husband now?'

It seemed a strange question to pose and I think I muttered something about how I imagined he would no doubt be keeping the ship afloat back home but she replied, 'No, silly, I mean the Group Captain.'

That set me aback. Belfrey. 'You mean you and he?' I asked.

She must have noticed my mouth agape. I took another look at her. No doubt about it, a bright young thing, mid twenties at most, very pretty in a sort of bossy way and it was hard to imagine her spliced to a crusty old bag of bones like Belfrey.

'Didn't you realise?' she asked. 'You don't think I do this for a living, do you?' She pointed at the camera she was holding.

I shrugged. I'd no idea what to think.

'I talked Stefan* into giving me the assignment. Now I get to see the war zone for myself, catch up with the lord and master and even get paid at the end of it. I'm here until Saturday by the way.'

Saturday was all of four days away and, having already photographed every air force installation within 50 miles of the Marne I found myself wondering if we might find some alternative endeavour. She must have seen the way my mind was working as she firmly removed my hand from her knee (again) and asked, 'Don't you have a court-martial to worry about?'

As it turned out I didn't. Ollie knew his stuff alright and he established that the armourers had screwed up with the cannons and this was at the root of my troubles. There were two mounted on each wing, with the intention of delivering a broadside worthy of a Napoleonic battleship, but the right hand armament had jammed as soon as I touched the firing button.

I'd already been told I was off the hook at this point but Ollie had wanted to see me in the workshop. We were standing in the barn, alone, with bits of broken aeroplane all around. 'So you see, sir,' said Ollie, 'the recoil from the left hand guns, unmatched on the right, would have caused the plane to swivel around out of control – something that would have stopped as soon as you stopped firing, so why didn't you?'

I shrugged. There was no answer other than the fact I was in such a funk I didn't think to stop.

'I'll tell you why, sir,' he said. 'The firing button return spring was missing and once pressed that beast just wouldn't stop firing until it ran out of ammo.' He lowered his voice. 'Couldn't find it anywhere,' he said, 'and so that's why you are in the clear.' He turned to walk away and as he did so he dropped something into my hand.

I looked down at it. It was a small steel spring. 'Just take that as a thank you from me, sir,' he whispered as he walked out the door.

---

* Stefan Laurent, *Picture Post* editor and founder.

So that's what comes of officers and men fraternising I thought. One good turn deserves another and all that. In the course of my Venereal Disease duties earlier, Ollie had come to me, having copped a dose from an ill-judged night at *le Toit Rouge*.* He was desperate to keep this off his service record and all I did was to put him in touch with a French quack. I think he'd been struck off but he knew his stuff and soon enough Ollie was up and running again, with no one but ourselves any the wiser. I hadn't thought much about it at the time but it shows that, in life, you need friends in the right places and not always at the top.

And Lady P didn't depart on the Saturday as promised. The weather had perked up and with the sunshine I think we both rather started to enjoy our explorations of the countryside – the dainty picnics, with a glass too many of champagne and then a mad tumble on the blanket whilst still dizzy with its after-effects – these were all things we *didn't* get up to on those balmy autumn expeditions. Instead we were zipping up and down country lanes in, I recall, a mad quest to get a vital snap of some French cow that had valiantly succumbed to a Nazi sharp-shooter. Everyone knew about it but no one knew where it was. My suggestion that I use my service revolver to dispatch the first *vache* that came to hand was not approved and that is why, late one afternoon, we were roaring along a narrow lane on our way to Haut-le-Zip Fastener or whatever. 'Hang onto your hat,' I shouted as we rounded a particularly sharp bend on only two of our three wheels, swerving at the last second to avoid an oncoming tractor. I suppose, in the heat of the moment, I must have stuck the Morgan in the wrong gear or something as there was a loud bang, followed by what sounded like half the engine evacuating into the exhaust pipe. Lady P took it rather well. 'Darling Nigel will get one of the men to fix it,' she said, stifling a yawn.

It turned out that the innards of a Morgan V-twin were too much even for Ollie and so some vital bit had to be sent out from England. As Lady P wouldn't even con-sid-er going back without her precious vehicle, we had the benefit of her company for a few days more. By then she'd become quite a fixture of an evening in our mess bar. On one of her early appearances, I recall, she had given our barman, LAC Gardner, quite the run-around when she found what she said was the wrong kind of ice in her Highball. He told me later he'd had to go all the way to the fishmonger to get some more.

And she certainly kept old man Belfrey on his toes. I could see his eyes following her everywhere. Of course Bovington had to home in on her ASAP. I don't think I've mentioned him before but he and his cronies were the air force careerists, joined up before the current emergency and more

* The infamous "*Red Roof*" establishment in Chalons.

than happy to look down on us reservists at any opportunity. I'm not sure what Lady P made of them. All I could see was a gang of over-hormoned ex-public school boys, all haw-hawing away as they tried to outmanoeuvre each other for a glimpse down her cleavage. Not that any of them ever got anywhere with her, any more than I had. Once things looked like they were getting a little too raucous, Belfrey would sidle up and take her arm with a 'Think it's time to hit the hangar darling. Beddy-byes and all that, what?' And off they'd trot into the night.

Sometimes I almost felt sorry for Belfrey at morning briefings, seeing him arrive all hollow-eyed and unshaven. He was a Great War veteran and therefore a little old for lengthy night ops in the boudoir. God knows what she did to him back at his little cottage nearby but most days he came in looking like he'd done ten rounds with the Manassa Mauler.* Well that's what happens when a dry old claret encounters a fruity Beajoulais Nouveau I thought.

Meanwhile the ground had dried enough for operations to resume. I was off the black-list but still not flying as my replacement Hurricane had yet to arrive, but I was at the airfield one morning, merely to watch the squadron being put through its paces. It was a bright and sunny day but with a winter chill and I was glad to be in my flying gear, with my Irvin zipped to the neck to keep out a very fresh northerly. Lady Pamela, was there too, camera at the ready, along with a collection of fellow idlers and loafers, all shivering in the cold breeze as we stood there ready to enjoy the show.

They had taken off half an hour earlier and we were all craning our necks and looking eastwards into the pale morning sun, where we expected to see the boys return. I think I saw them first – twelve black dots, high up but getting larger by the minute. Suddenly they were over us, keeping perfect formation. A squadron of Hurricanes makes an unmistakable noise, a sort of low buzz, with all those Merlin engines turning over in harmony but looking above as they flew over I thought I detected a wrong note and, sure enough, I could see one of the planes, the one flown by Sticky Stevens, pulling out of the formation while the rest swept on into the distance. I could see he was in trouble with the engine making a noise like a flatulent French marshal. Finally it coughed and went quiet, with the propeller windmilling in the slipstream.

We practised forced landings as part of our training and an engine failure at altitude over the airfield is a textbook exercise that any competent R.A.F. pilot should be able to handle in his sleep. That's the theory anyway, but in practice it's not so easy when you are wrestling with four tons of

* Jack Dempsey was world heavyweight boxing champion in the 1920s. Born in Manassa in the USA he was nicknamed the "Manassa Mauler".

dead metal, a cockpit canopy covered in oil and you are trying to thread your Hurricane through the air and line it up in just the right place at just the right height and speed and so on. And what Stevens hadn't noticed was that the wind had changed direction while he was aloft.

We all stood and watched as he manoeuvred the plane nicely in line with the field and Stevens no doubt thinking he was as good as home and dry and buying drinks in the bar. I glanced at the windsock, which was flapping vigorously in the wind, from the other direction of course, and reaching out to the horizontal at times. I remember thinking that that was one hell of a stiff breeze for a downwind landing. Surely Stevens would notice that instead of the usual steady and controlled approach to land he was coming in like Jesse Owens on Benzedrine? I thought of dashing out in front of him and pointing at the windsock but by then I realised it was too late. Without an engine and on final approach he was committed.

We all watched silently as the undercarriage clunked down as the aeroplane cleared some trees at the edge of the field. When it was just a few feet above the runway he gently pulled up its nose, no doubt still thinking in terms of a classy three point landing. I held my breath. Nothing happened. Instead of a gentle touchdown the plane careered onwards, almost as if it were weightless. And on it went. I could imagine the panic in the cockpit. If he had approached the other way, by this time Stevens would have been casually unplugging his headset, listening to the gyros running down and waving to the crowd as his erks ran up to help pull him out. Instead, he was serenely sailing across the airfield, ten feet up at 150 miles an hour and wishing he'd taken a good look at that windsock when he had the chance.

My advice would be that if ever you should find yourself in that situation, well, don't be, as there is not much you can do. A little sideslip to lose some height perhaps? It's too low to parachute. Just sit tight is what it boils down to and hope and pray there is nothing very solid on the other side of the boundary hedge. Like a church.

I guess Stevens must have realised at the same time as us that that was where he was heading. He never was a one for church parade and clearly didn't feel like attending this establishment on this occasion either as, suddenly, the nose of the plane reared up in the air. It was as if by pointing the plane skywards he thought he could make it go that way. The plane hung in that position, like a crucifix, for what seemed an age, but was really only a couple of seconds. Then a wing dropped and the nose with it and it fell to earth.

I've seen others make the same mistake as Stevens, ending up with aeroplane and themselves in a thousand pieces, but Sticky was lucky. There was a loud crump as his plane hit the ground and it rolled onto its back but the God of all pilots must have taken over then as it didn't cartwheel but just smoothly went on its way, upside down and skidding across the grass before gently coming to rest. There was hardly any noise – only a long scream from Lady Pamela. Once the plane stopped the rest of us started towards it but two of the ground crew, armed with fire axes, got there first and had the hatch smashed open and Stevens out in an instant, dragging him away. I could see him shaking his head as someone asked him something so knew he was still alive.

'Well, that's that,' I thought. I was just turning back to head for the mess, thinking of the restorative powers of a glass of Napoleon Five Star, for me that was, when I heard a shriek from Pamela. 'Oscar,' she cried and pointed at the wreckage. 'Oscar.'

We all stopped and looked but I could see nothing other than a wrecked Hurricane. Just then I caught a whiff of petrol and heard a gentle whooshing sound as something caught light. There wasn't much to see but I could just make out some tiny flames licking around the cowling. I was about to reassure her that Hurricanes are single seaters and that there couldn't possibly be anybody, Oscar or otherwise, left aboard when she clutched my arm and pointed again. 'Oscar. He's in there. Do something.'

I looked again and this time I thought I could just see some movement at the back of the cockpit. I was in the middle of explaining that this Oscar chap that she was wailing over must be a midget as there really is no room at all in the rear of a Hurricane when Ollie came up and put me straight. 'It's the cat, sir. Been hanging around the workshop and fuck, I mean Christ knows how it got in the plane but it would seem she's rather taken with it.'

As if to emphasise his point Lady P turned around to the others. 'Won't somebody help me save him, please?'

I am allergic to cats. Give me 20 minutes in a house with felines and I start sneezing. It doesn't seem to matter what size, type or colour they are, whether moggie or pedigree, the effect is always the same, although I once had an encounter with a Blue Burmese that also brought me out in a rash. And I really don't like that sort of simpering, preening way they have, like they own not just the house but the whole bloody planet. The strange thing is, *they* always seem to like me. For example there's yours truly at some tedious dinner party and in will come bloody Felix, smugly swaggering into the room. After demonstrating to all and sundry how he can lick his own backside he'll head immediately in my direction, jump in my lap and stick his sandpaper tongue in my ear. 'Oh look,' goes the hostess, 'Mr F has really taken to you, hasn't he?' And, I'll grin inanely and pretend to pet the damn thing while desperately trying to shove it away.

So there I was with an hysterical female on one side and a detestable but distressed feline on the other. The flames had started to take a hold by then. Pamela was desperately trying to get to the plane herself but someone was holding her back. To this day I don't know why I did what I did next but you will see, in due course, it had an impact on all of us, and not least on the damned cat, who was destined to have a long and highly eventful life, but I'm running ahead of things here. I knew nothing about this at the time. All I knew was that the plane could blow at any moment. I could feel the heat of the flames from where we were standing, about 50 yards away. I noticed that Pamela was wearing a cardigan draped over her shoulders. I grabbed it, threw it to the ground and unbuttoned my flies. 'Avert your eyes ma'am while I unleash Armageddon,' I cried.

She didn't follow my instruction I noticed but just stood gaping at me. I think she thought I was going to attempt to dowse the flames from where I stood, but of course I didn't have the range and in any case that wasn't my intention at all. Once her cardigan was thoroughly soaked I hurriedly readjusted my dress, took a deep breath and wrapped the damned thing around my head. The flames had really taken hold by then and I could hear the odd loud crack as a round of "303" ignited. There was no time to waste so, now fully masked, I set out at a brisk trot for the blazing wreck. Just when I felt I should be there I felt a shove and some whispered advice. It was Ollie. 'That way, sir. You'll end up in the NAAFI if you carry on in this direction.'

No doubt you are thinking 'What an idiot,' and so on and all I can say is that thus encumbered it is surprisingly difficult to navigate, even over short distances. Try it yourself sometime and see if you can do any better. Anyway, with the benefit of my new heading I quickly made it to within a few yards of the plane. Peering through a slit in my improvised helmet I could see that the flames had spread along one of the wings but were still, mercifully, more or less clear of the cockpit. There were more loud cracks as the ammunition went off and I thought it prudent to crawl for the last leg of my journey.

I lay for a moment, panting, alongside the inverted cockpit, deciding what to do next. The hatch was open of course, from where Stevens had been pulled out. I cautiously reached in, feeling the compass on the dashboard, the lifeless joystick behind it and the pilot's seat. But there was no sign of the wretched moggie. 'Mostyn, Mostyn, where are you, you little fucker?' I cried. The heat was becoming intense now and so I found myself sort of half wriggling in through the canopy, headfirst that is, as much for shelter as anything. Once positioned, I renewed my search, frantically rummaging around just anywhere I could reach. I felt sure the plane was about to blow up and was thinking I really should get out and quick. There was a lot of noise from outside with the fire crackling and ammo going off but I swear to God I heard a miaow, plain as day. This inspired me to make one final effort and, stretching forward as far as I could, I found I could reach into the footwell. There, by the rudder pedals, I felt something furry. Praying that Stevens hadn't been flying in his slippers or some other such idiocy I grabbed at it and pulled it towards me. With one motion I squirmed back out, got to my feet and started to run back towards the control tower. I had only covered a few yards when I felt a tremendous blow in my back and I guess I must have blacked out for a few seconds because the next thing I knew I was on my hands and knees with bits of Hurricane raining around me. A couple of erks rushed up and they helped me to my feet. Pamela arrived just as I was being ushered away, looking all anxious and fetching at the same time. Our eyes met. 'Where is he?' she asked.

I stared back and felt a strange quiver in my chest as I tried to collect my thoughts. God, she looked the goods with that worried little frown she was wearing.

'Where is he?' she repeated.

Feeling rather stupid I looked down at my empty hands. The cat. Where was the little blighter?

We were walking side by side during this little exchange and by then we were some distance away from the blaze. Pamela stopped, turned and stood in front of me, coming up close and looking me square in the face. I could see streaks on her cheeks left by her recent tears and I caught a whiff of her perfume. I felt the flutter in my chest turn to a heavy regular drumbeat as she smiled, reaching out to just below my chin and unzipped my jacket. I stood there passively as she put her hand inside and I was wondering what she was going to do next, what with everyone watching us and everything when I felt a sudden and intense pain. I cried out loud but it didn't seem to bother her. She dug her hand in deeper and the pain got worse if anything. I found myself thinking what a little vixen she was and how it was no wonder Tucker looked so washed out most mornings when the thumping in my chest changed to a peculiar wriggling and a squirming and then it dawned on me. 'Stop, stop, stop.' I cried. I grabbed her hand firmly, removed it and reached in myself. 'Let me do it. You won't get him out with his claws sunk into my tit.'

That's how I had my first proper look at the beast. He was just an ordinary moggie really and unharmed by his recent adventure. He was coloured black with a white bib and had a smart leather collar proclaiming his name on a polished silver tag, but he had unusual eyes, one iris being green and the other brown, as they stared up at me with what I can only describe as a look of glazed adoration.

Not so his adoptive owner. 'Heterochromatism,' she said tartly as she snatched him away. 'It's very rare but they say such cats are destined for greatness.'

I nodded blankly. It was all one to me and I could feel a sneezing fit starting in any case. I noticed the source of my allergy was reaching out a playful paw in my direction. She batted it away and I could see her nose wrinkle. 'Better have a bath pilot,' she said, turning around to walk away. 'And you can keep the cardigan.'

CHAPTER 4

You know the verdict as soon as you enter the room. The sword lies in front of the President and if it points to one side you are in the clear. If it points at you, you are guilty. I marched through the doorway, stamped to a halt, saluted and glanced down. The sword was pointing at me.

I looked across at my counsel. Our eyes met and he shook his head. Behind the table sat Group Captain Belfrey and Squadron Leader Barnes, flanking the Air Chief Marshal – "Stuffy" Dowding, as we used to call him, the court president. None of them would catch my eye.

Dowding cleared his throat and pronounced sentence. 'Pilot Officer Kilroy you have been found guilty of gross negligence in combat and as a result of your folly one innocent non-combatant and, incidentally, eight animals have needlessly lost their lives. Have you anything to say?'

Air Marshal Hugh Dowding.

I raised my head and replied, 'Only how sorry I am sir. I know I should have correctly identified the target before shooting it down.'

He waited for me to continue and when it was clear I had finished Dowding reached for the black cap, which lay alongside the sword. 'For this offence, there is only one sentence that the court allows.' My mind was in overdrive and I didn't fully take in what he said next, only picking up fragments. 'Taken back to the place from whence you came.' He droned on. 'Firing squad to be drawn from your own squadron.' And on. 'Execution date two weeks from today.' Finally he snapped, 'Would you like to add anything?'

I gulped and said I had a final request. I was clutching at straws of course but thought that (for once) a spot of humility might be worth a try. 'Could you read out the names of the victims and could we have a minute's silence as a mark of respect for the fallen?'

Dowding's eyes widened, but he said nothing and flicked through the papers in front of him. 'Yes, I have the list here.' He cleared his throat. 'Er, yes. We will remember them. There's Dasher and Dancer, Prancer and Vixen.' There was a loud banging at the door. 'Comet and Cupid.' More banging at the door, then I heard a voice from outside.

'Mr Kilroy, sir. Good morning. I've got your tea here.' I opened one eye and could see Smudge, our batman, shuffling across the floor. 'Crikey, sir. It don't 'arf pong in 'ere. Mind if I open the window?'

He pulled back the blind and wrestled with the catch. 'Good night was it last night, sir? Oh, yes sir and a Happy Christmas.'

I waved back at him, but then a thought occurred to me. 'Smudge, old boy. Santa Claus's reindeer. You know: Dasher and Dancer and all that. What were the last two called?'

I watched him as he silently counted on his fingers. 'Donner and Blitzen of course.'

I sat up so quickly that I spilled my tea. 'Too right Smudge. Donner and Blitzen. Bloody Krauts in other words. So I was innocent don't you see?'

'If you say so, sir.' And he shuffled out, closing the door quietly behind him.*

I put down my cup, lay back and exhaled, running my fingers over my smooth unpunctured chest. I didn't know then but this was only the first of many nightmares while serving King and country. I soon brightened up though. There was the pleasant thought that on this seasonal day, unlike the poor chaps in the last show, yours truly was in his nice warm bed and wouldn't be slithering out of a boggy trench for a spot of footie in no-man's land after breakfasting on soggy biscuit. In short, with all operations grounded by the weather I would have nothing more irksome to do that day than participate in the squadron tradition of officers serving the men their Christmas dinner before setting to at our own light celebration. I caught a preliminary waft of Monsieur Turkey and Madame Stuffing through the window and paused to savour the prospect of the bottle or two of France's finest with which we would undoubtedly be washing it down. I closed my eyes and pulled up the bed clothes, reflecting that after a couple

---

* *Rudolph the Red-nosed Reindeer* was first recorded in 1949, so would not have been known to Kilroy or his batman ten years earlier. The song was based on a children's story of the same name, by Robert L. May, which was first published in 1939. May borrowed most of the reindeer names in his story from the 1823 poem *A Visit from St Nicholas* (also known as *'Twas the Night Before Christmas*) by Henry Livingston Jr. The reindeer names "Donner" and "Blitzen" (German for thunder and lightning) that feature in the story and the song, were, in the original poem, "Dunder" and "Blixem", both Dutch names. http://tinyurl.com/Kilroy079 (*How Santa's Reindeer Got Their Names*) and http://tinyurl.com/Kilroy080.

of hours kip I would be making my acquaintance with that little lot in the officers mess.

Half an hour later I was out in the chateau's court-yard in my PE kit, shivering in the blast from an icy northerly. All the other junior officers were there too, all blowing into their hands, beating their chests and generally jumping up and down in a forlorn attempt to keep warm. It was Belfrey's idea of course. Something about being good for the men's morale to see some "can-do" and "will-do" from their young officers, even on a feast day. I can picture him now, as if it were yesterday, sheltering under his umbrella, in his immaculate uniform and the little bottle brush moustache quivering over his lip as he addressed us in his clipped Cranwell tone.

So it was to be eight miles before breakfast – the route was three times around the airfield, but, he emphasised, we *must* take in the local sports field for some press-ups en route. 'That'll impress the locals, what?' the old buffoon lectured us. 'Show them what we Brits are capable of.'

With the icy conditions underfoot I'm sure we would all have collected broken limbs and sprained ankles that day but, calculating that no one would be around to check what we were up to, we did the obvious thing, which was to trot briskly up the road then, as soon as we were out of sight, head for the only sheltered spot in the entire neighbourhood – the sports field pavilion.

It wasn't heated of course but it was out of the wind and a darned sight warmer than outside. As we sat on a changing room bench Bovington passed around a packet of cigarettes. And, yes, you can warm your hand slightly from a ciggie's glowing tip but it doesn't do much for the rest of you. However, on the plus side we calculated that we would only have to hang around there for an hour or so and then we could plausibly head back to base, taking care to look suitably flushed and exhausted at the finish.

There was a rusting old cast iron stove in the corner, which was stone cold and contained only ash, so I thought I might as well scout around the building and, who knows, maybe even find some fuel? Five minutes later I'd found nothing more combustible than a dried-up lemon, a broken rugby boot and a referee's whistle minus pea. I was about to give up and sit back down with the lads when through the frosted-up glass of the changing room window I spotted some movement outside.

I rubbed away the frost and looked out to see one of our armourers, Smithy. He was on his knees and apparently praying on the 25 yard line on the rugby pitch. Without saying anything to the others I went out to investigate.

'Smithy, what the blazes are you playing at?'

Smithy leapt to his feet and whirled around to face me. 'Stand back sir. For Christ's sake.' He was holding a stethoscope and, lying on the ground behind him, was what looked uncannily like a plump, unplucked turkey.

I raised an eyebrow. 'Parachuted in by Jerry this morning sir. No bombs. Just this.' He pointed at it.

'And so?' I was about to ask, but at that moment I caught a movement out of the corner of my eye.

'Quick, sir, grab him. Before he does us all a mischief.'

In my experience the British fighting man can be an evil opponent in foreign field but, off-duty, he always has a soft spot for locals with four legs, a wet nose and a wagging tail. And, in this case, we had Booster. I doubted there was much to worry about but grabbed his collar nonetheless – wondering whether he had been planning to eat or make love to Jerry's Christmas present – it was hard to tell. I'd seen Booster a few times before, hanging around the men's quarters mainly. He was a peculiar looking thing of unclear parentage with a matted coat jumping with fleas, but all that was hidden that morning as someone had bedecked him rather gloriously in a knitted coat in the squadron colours. 'And you think it's booby-trapped?' I asked doubtfully.

'Sappers are on their way sir.'

'Hear anything ticking?'

He shook his head.

'I thought so. Well I don't see why those bastards should have it. You just don't understand the Jerries, do you?' Being half German myself I knew they liked a joke as much as anyone, even if we rarely found any of them funny.

Smithy looked doubtful as he fiddled with the stethoscope.

'It's Christmas. Remember in the last show how they came out and played soccer with us in no mans land?' I asked. 'Now stand back. I know just how to deal with this.'

He edged away as I took a run up at the bird and booted it hard and square in the rump, taking care to give it maximum follow-through. All those years struggling to make it into the Herne Bay third fifteen weren't for nothing I thought. Mr T took off like, well, like he was after Mrs T, describing a perfect arc through the air, sailing neatly between the posts and landing with a dull thud behind. 'Three points to me I'd say. And that's tenderised it nicely so, Smithy, I suggest you gather it up, pluck it, stuff it and get one of the cooks to bung it in the pot.'

As I turned away I could hear barking behind me and cries of 'Heel Booster. Heel.' I was just about to tell Smithy to be quick or the hound would have it when I felt the breath sucked out of me and a giant hand shove me in the back. The next thing I knew I was on my hands and knees with my ears ringing and pellets of mud raining all around. A small object landed in front of me. It was a studded leather collar with green, white and red ribbons knotted around it.

CHAPTER 5

The history books will tell you that the 1939-40 winter was one of the coldest on record, with the whole of Northern Europe turned into an ice field. It would seem that modern armies need blue skies and solid ground afoot every bit as much as Napoleon did or, come to that, the Romans, so there was precious little for us pilots to do other than sit around in the mess and talk about the heroics of our ground crew, who had to work outdoors throughout in a vain attempt to keep our kit battle-ready.

I said earlier that much of our time in the air was in close formation but we junior pilots did sometimes manage to wangle a trip aloft on our own. The trick was to agree with your fitter[*] that your plane needed an "air test". Then, once safely out of sight of the airfield, you would have your own personal Hurricane to put through its paces and all the wide blue sky in which to do it. With Jerry safely skulking on the other side of the Maginot, a thousand horses up front and a sturdy chariot to carry you, you would really feel one hell of a lucky blighter.

My fitter was a surly old devil from Bermondsey by the name of Dunton, who would only communicate with grunts and nods and would never take the hint, but one day it turned out my plane actually *did* need an air test and so that was my chance. It was one of those bitterly cold January days and no fun to be on the ground, but I knew that with the cabin heater on full, a watery blue clear sky above and precious little wind, it would be a great day to be in the air.

In no time, I had the petrol bowser over and all tanks filled to the brim, the engine started and turning over smoothly. You can't afford to hang around with the Merlin. They are not really designed for working on the ground and even on a freezing cold winter's day they quickly overheat so, with minimum delay, I had the plane bumping and weaving across the airfield, over to the far corner, where I could get lined up for takeoff. Once the plane was pointed into wind, I took a last quick glance at the engine gauges, another look at the windsock and opened the throttle.

There is so much power in the Merlin that you can't give it the gun all at once. Too much power too quickly and you'll up-end the beast in no time, going sweet nowhere with your arse in the air and the propeller tearing great divots out of the ground. This in turn will inevitably lead to an

[*] Each aeroplane had a ground crew comprising a fitter, responsible for the engine, and a rigger (and sometimes other specialists) who maintained the air frame.

encounter with the CO chewing large lumps out of you, so it's always best to be easy with the throttle at the beginning of the takeoff run.

With these thoughts in mind I fed in the power gently as the plane gathered momentum, holding a straight line as it bumped and skipped over the grass. There was one last big bump and then that was that – a perfect takeoff, or at least that was what *I* thought, and if no one was around to see it that was just too bad.

With undercart up and full boost I was soon at altitude with what seemed like the whole of Europe beneath me. I had kept a good lookout the whole way and had the sky all to myself. Perfect! Far below and over in the east I noticed some cloud rolling in but that was nothing to trouble me, or so I thought at the time.

With aerobatics it's essential to have a delicate touch and a feeling for what the plane can do. 'Slip her on her back and only *then* waggle your stick,' my instructor would tell me. 'She won't thank you for full thrust when she's got her nose in the air,' was another of his little aphorisms. Done to perfection aerobatics is like an aerial ballet and, with a perfect day for it, I was rather relishing the opportunity to put the plane through its paces.

I started with some lazy chandelles* followed by gentle loops and rolls – nothing fancy, but warming up for the more challenging manoeuvres: the barrel roll, hammerhead and flick roll. You have to be careful with the latter – go into it too fast and the wings will tear off – but I had the speed nailed with the Hurri entering and exiting like it was on rails. Time for an Immelmann I thought – named after a German in the last war who used it as a sneaky trick to shoot down our chaps. Which reminded me – I'd rather been focussing on the aerobatics and hadn't been paying much attention to the world at large. I remember thinking with a jolt, 'Who knows what his successors might be up to right now?'

I immediately pulled the plane around into the tightest of tight turns, while screwing my head around in all directions. As I'd been continually reminded, I made an especial effort to squint into the sun, from where I knew trouble was most likely to come at me. Nothing. Then I looked below. I knew it would be difficult to pick out the naughty Hun against the ground of course, but after a long and careful look I concluded that it was all peaceful and innocent down there. The cloud I'd seen earlier seemed to be rolling in rather fast or, more likely, I realised, I'd been blown towards it, whilst prancing around upstairs, but there didn't seem much to worry about in either direction.

* A chandelle is a 180° turn with a climb and is not strictly speaking an aerobatic or combat manoeuvre.

The engine thrummed reliably throughout, but then I remembered I was supposed to be giving it an air test. What was it Dunton had told me? A possible flat spot at three thou? And was that three thousand feet as in altitude or three thousand RPM as in round and round? I was buggered if I could remember and I'd just decided I'd have to tell him it was absolutely spiffing whatever when I remembered to check the petrol situation. That gave me another jolt. Both mains were almost empty. Had I really been upstairs that long? I reached for the fuel cock and switched hastily to the reserve tank. That meant I had just under 30 gallons to get home. Now 30 gallons might sound like a lot if you are thinking of filling up the old jalopy for a Sunday picnic but will barely wet the whiskers on a Merlin. What it boiled down to was that I'd enough petrol left for 20 minutes powered flight and then I'd be on the ground one way or the other. I remember thinking, with some relief, that with 20 odd thousand feet in the bank and the prospect of an easy gliding descent this should be more than enough to get me back to base, but then that would depend on knowing where base was of course. Well I could always ask Control for a QDM?* Good idea! But what else had Dunton told me? Blimey he had been in a right chatty mood hadn't he? Oh yes, the radio was unserviceable.

I renewed my gaze below. Northern France is the perfect place for a lost aviator. The channel coast, with all its large ports, is never far away and then there all those mighty rivers which are conveniently criss-crossed by the neat straight roads and railway lines. There are so many easy navigational fixes. Even a rock ape with only a school atlas should be able to figure out where he is in the twinkling of a protractor. As long as he can see it all mapped out below for him. Which I couldn't. The innocent clouds which had seemed way over east an hour or so previously were now blanketing the land in all directions.

I squinted below and occasionally saw some green. Once I caught a fleeting glimpse of a stretch of river but then thought it may have been the coast. I was just weighing up my options, with baling out one possibility. I could always blame the dicky engine I thought, when I spotted something. There was a small dot just above the cloud and heading west – another plane, that was for sure. Now, you won't read this in any of the training manuals but here's a tip: if ever you are lost follow someone who isn't. It worked for me once on an advanced Navex when I was training at Kincardine and seemed worth a try now. I cut the throttle, put the nose down and headed his way, with speed quickly building in the dive.

---

* QDM – Query Direction Magnetic – is a "Q" code abbreviation, once widely used in aviation radio communications. It is a spoken request from the pilot to the ground station (which can detect from which direction he is transmitting) for a magnetic heading which will take him directly overhead the ground station.

A fair number of our idle days in that first winter of the war had been spent doing aircraft identification exercises in ground school. It all seemed a bit of a bore at the time. An instructor would pull a model out from behind a screen, giving you a fleeting glimpse of it, sometimes at an odd angle and then serve you a bollocking if you didn't know instantly what type and mark it was and a whole load of other stuff, like what the pilot had had for breakfast and who he'd had the night before. On our side we had our own Hurricanes and Spitfires and so on up to the larger Wellingtons and Blenheims and they were easy enough. Then there was the French stuff, although with hindsight I don't know why we concerned ourselves with them at all. And then there was the Me-109, of course, the German fighter. You wanted to be sure you knew when one of those was nearby, but there were plenty of other cards up the sleeve of the horrible Hun and I struggled to get to grips with them all. As I was wishing I'd paid more attention to this part of our classwork, the plane below started to appear bigger and I spotted the big black crosses on each of its wings.

You've probably twigged that my proposed revision of the R.A.F. Navex training manual needs a few caveats. Make sure the plane you are following isn't a Jerry for one and, if it is, make sure you know what it is. Of course I am here now to tell the tale, so we know I survived this little encounter. I had a few points in my favour. Speed and altitude for one. I was motoring at three hundred plus with the controls firm and rigid in my grasp as I flipped the safety catch off the firing button. Another point in my favour: the Jerry pilot was a bigger idiot than I was. He was trundling along oblivious to anyone and everyone. I subsequently discovered he was as lost as me.

I opened fire and felt the juddering of the Hurricane as it skewed from side to side while I attempted to keep him in my sights with some fancy footwork with the rudder. Of course I missed. In no time I was almost on top of him and yanked the stick back to pull up, climb away and have another go. Still he trundled on. I didn't know whether to be pleased about this or insulted that my shooting had been so inaccurate he hadn't even noticed me.

There was a last point in my favour. At the time I thought I was attacking a new type of German fighter but it was actually an Me-108. The 108 is a utility transport, unarmed, about as dangerous as a dead donkey and not much faster. From a distance and on a cloudy day I would claim it does look a bit like a 109, with its single engine up front, but that didn't stop me taking a fair bit of stick in the mess over it, that is once I got back there. Bovington and his pals had a right laugh. 'Tell us again about the flying carthorse, Kilroy. Get it in the balls did you? Clip, clop, old boy.' And they'd descend into roars of mirth.

I prefer not to dwell much longer on my hapless performance. Let's just say that after several further balls-ups I did at last wake up the pilot with a final burst that must have grazed the cockpit and that sent him scurrying into the cloud.

That was the last of my ammunition and also the last of my fuel. The engine cut out when I was just above the cloud and instantly I was in amongst it, only just able to see my propeller, idly winding down in the breeze as the wind and grey whipped by me. I did wonder about baling out but thought I was too low to risk it. The cockpit seemed so silent after the roar of the engine and the chatter of the machine guns. All I could hear was the buffeting of the wind past the canopy, which I slid back. I tightened my harness and held the stick firmly, trying to keep the plane level. When you are in that situation, and God help you if ever you are, all you can do is sit tight and hope for the best. In the worst case you will plough into a hilltop and be dead before you know what hit you, but what you hope and pray for, as you sit tight and peer straight ahead, is that you will pop out at the bottom of the cloud and see a nice flat field in front, perfectly positioned and upwind just waiting for you to plonk the plane down in it.

Messerschmitt Bf108 "Taifun."

And that is exactly what I did get. The cloud bottomed out at about five hundred feet and there was the field, conveniently laid to grass. I just had time to lower the undercarriage and round out for a perfect three pointer.

Without thinking I went through the standard shutdown drill, turning off all switches and putting the plane to bed as they say. I undid the harness, flipped open the canopy door and slid out onto the wing. Suddenly I felt I needed a cigarette. Back at base smoking anywhere near the aeroplane would see you scrubbing out septic tanks for the rest of the war, but I looked around and as there didn't seem to be any top brass nearby I thought it worth the risk. I reached in my pocket, pulled out a packet of John Player, removing my lighter, which was tucked inside. By then I was standing alongside the plane and I'd just lit up and was taking my first deep inhalation when I realised I was going to have some company.

The aeroplane I had rather ineptly been using for target practice had followed me down. As I said earlier it turned out that he had been in the same fix as me – almost out of petrol and lost over the cloud. My precision attack had been the final straw and so, like me, he'd put his fate in the hands of Thor and come out lucky with a nice flat field to put down in.

Unlike me he made a hash of things thereafter. I saw his wheels lock down for landing, which was fine, but he hadn't got his approach right and it was clear he was too low. Just as he fed in the power to clear the hedge his engine cut and his bad day suddenly became a whole lot worse. At about 30 feet up, one of his wings glanced a tree and that pushed him off course. Instead of pancaking down in a nice flat field the plane careered off in another direction. I watched as it disappeared into a thicket to the accompaniment of a screeching and grinding of metal, terminating in a noise that I can only describe as being like an Irish pub at closing time.

I rushed into the woods in the general direction of the uproar, expecting to find not very much aeroplane and even less of the occupants. It didn't take long to find the spot. I was right about the plane, which was in a crumpled mess at the bottom of a tree, but was very surprised to see, a few yards away from it, two of the Luftwaffe's finest, both very much sound in wind and limb and both old enough to know better but squaring up to each other. They were so intent on their own little drama that neither noticed my approach.

'Dummkopf,' said the taller one as he took a swing at what I took to be the pilot. 'Blockhead.'

The pilot managed to parry his blow with what looked uncannily like a large pillow case. 'Please Helmut. Be reasonable. I told you to turn the fuel cock to the *left*.' There was a loud thud and a pair of long johns flew up in the air.

Helmut didn't seem to want to be reasonable. 'Does this look like Köln airfield?' he shouted and when there was no reply delivered a hefty shove, neatly intercepted by what clearly was a pillow case. A cascade of socks and shirts fell to the ground. When the pilot offered no further reply he continued, 'No, Erich, it doesn't look like Köln much does it? It looks like a poxy wood in the middle, in the middle of fucking...'

'Belgium,' I added for him.

They both stopped and turned to face me. I guessed they were in their forties, one bald and the other well on the way. They were sporting identical insignia, with enough of it to make them up to something like the rank of major I guessed. 'Berlin?' said Helmut and breathed a sigh of relief as he relinquished his hold on Erich's somewhat depleted laundry bag.

I remember thinking that Berlin must have some pretty big parks if they could possibly believe that we had ended up there when Major Erich took a step towards me, speaking in imperfect English. 'English flyer. Your hands up, pliz.'

'Not Berlin. Belgium,' I repeated and I could see the doubt enter their faces. I reached down and picked up something I had spotted a moment earlier – the first positive navigation fix I'd had in quite a while. 'See here, gentlemen,' I said in German and pointed at the empty bottle in my hand. 'Duvel. I think you will find that that is a Belgian beer.'

I could see they were still doubtful so I looked carefully at the label before tossing it to Major Erich. '"Belgisch" it says. Read it.'

The pilot glanced at it, grimaced and tossed it over his shoulder. There was a faint crash as it wreaked yet more damage on the cockpit canopy. He was still holding the pillow case and bent down to pick up a sock. I could hear him muttering, 'Belgium,' over and over again, as he ignored me, busying himself with the important task of underwear retrieval. Eventually he stopped, after I had handed him his long johns. He sighed and sat down heavily on what was left of the wing. He didn't say anything more but I could just detect his breathing as he quietly sat there with his head in his hands.

His comrade, Major Helmut, had an entirely different reaction to the news. There was a briefcase lying at his feet and he picked it up and put it under his arm whilst he rummaged in his pockets. Eventually he found what he was looking for and pulled it out. A book of matches, which he flicked open. It was empty. His face fell and he threw it away as he approached me.

His hands were shaking and I could see he was nervous about something. At the time I thought his worries were much the same as mine. With Belgium being neutral at this stage in the war, internment beckoned all of us. Why, I thought, we might even become the best of chums as we shared some damp little Belgian cellar, divvying up stale waffles while Europe tore itself apart.

The beer bottle hadn't told me where in Belgium we were of course but as it's only slightly bigger than a tennis court I guessed the border couldn't be that far away. I was thinking of suggesting that they 'tak' the high road' and 'I tak' the low road' as Rabbie Burns would say* and we could all leg it home on the QT before Poirot or maybe even a real famous Belgian turned up. My thoughts were interrupted by Helmut who tapped me on the arm. 'Please. Do you have a cigarette?' he asked in clear English.

I found my packet, extracted one and handed it to him. I flicked the lighter and it lit first time, but there was a breeze blowing and it went out. I tried again, with my back to the wind and my hand cupped around it, but this time I found that Helmut's cigarette was waggling around so much that it still wouldn't light.

'Permit me please.' He held out his hand.

* A line from *the Bonnie Banks of Loch Lomond*, not written by Burns, but traditional with well known arrangements by Andrew Lang, Ralph Vaughan Williams and many others.

I handed him the lighter and he turned his back on me, I assumed to have another go. Suddenly he set off, like Errol Flynn on a schoolgirls' picnic, crashing through the bushes and hurdling low branches as if his very life depended upon it. I noticed the cigarette lying on the ground where he dropped it and was just thinking, 'Good riddance, Fritz,' when I realised he had my lighter.

The lighter was of no great monetary value, just a Great War souvenir made of polished steel and one of millions churned out by some anonymous light engineering works. This one was engraved with the words "Gott mit uns" and had a crudely scratched question mark alongside. Worth only pennies perhaps but it had some small significance to me as it was all I ever inherited from my natural father. I've told you a little already of my peculiar family but one mystery that I had to live with for many years was the identity of my sire. Mutti would just clam up on the rare occasions I broached the subject and so all I did know was that he'd left behind this battered old lighter on the dressing table 20 odd years before, after no doubt behaving like a beastly bounder with my dear mother.

I was buggered if some damned fool Jerry was going to head off with my family inheritance so set off in pursuit. Helmut had had a bit of a start on me and I couldn't see him but I could still hear him alright, crashing through the shrubbery and headed in the general direction of the noise. Suddenly it went quiet and I paused, trying to figure out which way to go. There was a clump of ferns that had been flattened a few yards ahead and I padded towards it, cocking an ear for further clues as to Helmut's whereabouts, but the wood had gone as quiet as the grave and there was no sign of him. I couldn't imagine why he had stopped but knew he must be somewhere nearby. I started a systematic search, just like they do in the Boy Scouts, pacing out 50 yards in a straight line, then coming back the other way a few yards to one side. I was trying to be as quiet as possible but occasionally a twig snapped beneath my feet. From Helmut I could hear nothing at all. I can't say now for how long this carried on, probably for no more than two or three minutes, but I was just about to give up on Pater's parting present and head for France when I smelt burning. I sniffed the air but I couldn't figure out where the smell was coming from. I hesitated for a few seconds, looking in all directions and at last I noticed a thin plume of smoke rising from behind a bush only 30 or 40 yards away from me.

Making an effort to be silent I headed in that direction. I rounded the bush and at last I came upon him. He had his back to me and seemed to be making a camp fire, kneeling on the ground and fanning the flames with his briefcase. I could see my lighter, lying on the ground beside him. I strode up and had grabbed it before he even knew I was there. I'm not sure what I had planned to do thereafter, probably kick sand in his face and head to

France without a by-your-leave, but at that moment we heard voices nearby and we both froze.

I couldn't make out what the voices were saying at first. Certainly they weren't speaking any sort of French or German I'd heard before. It sounded more like something in between, so it hardly took Albert Einstein to work out that they might just be our neutral hosts come to find us. I could see the fire would give us away in no time but that didn't seem to bother Helmut, who kneeled directly over it and started desperately fanning the flames anew. Frankly I cared little if he wanted to burn his codebooks or Erich's underpants or his own testicles for that matter but I didn't see why I should spend the next several years locked in a cell with him and his laundryman because of it, so I launched myself at him, trying to grab his briefcase to beat out the flames. Of course he wouldn't let go of it and so we ended up rolling over and over in the dirt each struggling to gain possession of it. I remember spotting an expanse of exposed flesh, checking to be sure it wasn't mine and was about to sink my teeth into it when I heard voices close behind me. There was a sharp bark of command and then it all went dark.

CHAPTER 6

Pamela smiled from the other side of the table, her bright red lips glistening in the candlelight. I could hear the fire crackling in the grate and a door banging far in the distance. She carefully picked the plumpest cherry from the cut glass bowl and bit into it. I watched her breathlessly as she delicately removed the stone, twirled it with her fingers and flicked it dextrously at the magnum of Dom Perignon. It struck half way up the neck, then bounced off to describe a neat arc across the room before landing with a dull thud on the tiger skin rug. 'Your turn.'

I reached across to the bowl, chose another plump offering and put it to my mouth, sucking the sweet juice from it. I removed the stone, taking my time to make careful aim. I could see Pamela bite her lip as she watched me. I extended my arm then without warning flicked the stone with some force. It shot upwards, ricocheted off the chandelier, pinged off the candelabra and landed exactly where I'd intended, in Pamela's cleavage.

'You wicked boy. Come and get that back.'

'Pamela, darling. I think I've lost my cherry,' I muttered drunkenly but she didn't laugh. I staggered to my feet, realising I'd had far too much to drink. With the room spinning around me I stumbled around the table to her. She leaned back and watched me, her lips pursed with suppressed amusement. So there I was, inches away and preparing to grapple and board when I slipped and stupidly knocked over the champagne. I watched in dismay as the bottle rolled off the table and exploded with a loud bang on the floor. A fountain of foaming liquid shot into the air.

'Give the lazy sweinhund another one.'

I watched with amazement as the bottle exploded again, but this time the liquid came straight at me. Some of it went into my mouth and it tasted of salt.

I opened my eyes.

'Ah, at last mein herr, welcome to Belgium.'

I closed my eyes again and was treated to another deluge.

'Come sir, that was just a gentle tap earlier from Sergeant Habets. We need you awake now.'

I opened my eyes and tried to focus them as I wiped my face dry with the back of my sleeve. I was sitting propped up in a chair in front of a large oak desk in some sort of office. Behind the desk there was a little man, dressed like a bank clerk, completely bald and polishing his glasses. Standing beside him was Johnny Weissmuller's ugly big brother, clad in a tight blue uniform, looking a bit like a British bobby with a funny pointed hat. 'Shall I give him another dose, Inspector Perdu, sir?' he asked.

The inspector looked quizzically at me and I shook my head. 'I don't think that will be necessary Habets. Let's hear what the gentleman has to say.'

'Wash am I do in fear?' was the best I could muster. I was feeling each of my teeth with my tongue. A couple of them felt loose but on an initial inspection they all seemed to be there. My jaw was another matter. I rather wished it *hadn't* been there and I didn't need a mirror to work out that it must be very badly bruised and swollen at best. It felt tender to my touch and I was hopeful that no bones were broken, but it still felt like I'd been soundly worked over by Joe Louis.* I realised Perdu hadn't answered me and looking up I could see he hadn't understood my earlier question. 'What am I doing here?' I repeated.

'That is just what I want to ask you, sir.' He pulled out some pieces of paper. 'Perhaps you can explain these?'

There were about dozen pages in all, typed on rough quality foolscap. I turned them one by one and studied them carefully. My overall feeling was that they looked pretty dull fare and didn't make a great deal of sense in any case. There seemed to be some sort of timetable, with numbered units written alongside some dates, all of which seemed to be in the next couple of weeks. Each page was dotted with map references which of course made no sense to me at all. Every now and then I could spot a place name. A few I recognised. 'Namur,' I said.

'Yes.' Perdu's face brightened.

'That's in Belgium, isn't it?'

His face fell.

'I've got it. It's on the Meuse, isn't it?'

'Look, sir, spare us the Geography lesson. Would you explain what these are about?'

'I've really no idea.'

Perdu glanced at Habets who took a deep breath. He clenched one of his considerable fists in the other and started cracking his knuckles.

'Let me have another look,' I said and picked up the pages again and perused them with a bit more enthusiasm and interest. On a second inspection they did seem to make a little more sense. I stroked my tender chin as I studied one page in particular. 'Well it seems to be some sort of plan I think.' Then I spotted it at the top. 'Plan Yellow, obviously.'

'Yes, yes.'

'And these are the assembly instructions I'd say.'

* Joe Louis was world heavyweight boxing champion at that time. He held the title for a record 12 years.

'Good, good.' He was getting excited now.

'Assembly Instructions Number Two in fact.'

His face fell again. 'Yes, we can read as well you know.'

I glanced nervously at Habets, who was now leaning against the wall picking his fingernails. I said, 'I'd love to help. What do you want me to tell you?'

Perdu didn't answer at once. He stared hard at me as he drummed his fingers on his desk. Then there was a long pause while we all waited as he stared at the ceiling. It seemed like hours at the time but in reality I suppose it was only a few seconds. At last he reached a decision, took a breath and looked back to catch me straight in the eye. 'I'll be candid with you.' He paused for effect. 'Some of my superiors think these papers may be a plant.' He tapped them as he said it. 'And they lie here on my desk this very day simply to mislead us.'

'And?'

'On the other hand they may not be a plant.' He smiled and looked at me. 'And we are looking at the real thing.'

'Yes?'

'And, you, my friend.' He pointed at me. 'You hold the answer.'

I didn't like the sound of this one bit but could think of nothing to say so just sat back, gulped and stared back at him.

'Let's start at the beginning then.' Suddenly he was all crisp efficiency. He pulled out some charred pages from an envelope and waved them at me. 'Following your, ahem, unscheduled arrival on our soil, it would seem Habets arrived just in time when you were attempting to burn some offending documents.'

I was beginning to realise with mounting horror, that he was under the most ghastly misapprehension, but he took my silence as acquiescence.

'We are having our experts check over the material and it all adds up.' I went to protest but he waved me down. 'There is no point in denying it,' he continued, brandishing the pages at me, 'We are not fools you know. These documents originated at Herr Hitler's OKW* and, if...,' he left the word hanging, '...if they are to be believed then an unprovoked and dastardly invasion of our neutral country is imminent.' He glanced at the red, black and gold flag, hanging over the mantelpiece, pausing to wipe his eye before turning back to me. 'Now, you...' he pointed at me, '...you are going to tell me what your role is in all this.'

---

* Oberkommando der Wehrmacht (Supreme Command of the Armed Forces) – the OKW – was part of the command structure of the Wehrmacht (armed forces) of Nazi Germany during World War II. Created in 1938, the OKW had nominal oversight over the German Army, the Kriegsmarine (German navy) and the Luftwaffe (German air force).

I took a deep breath. It would seem events had moved on rather while I had been dreaming about Pamela and it was hard to know where to start. 'Well sir. I think I might have shot the bastards down. That's why they are here in the first place. So why don't you ask them about this?' I pointed at the papers.

'Shot who down?'

'Well, perhaps I didn't exactly shoot them down, but I forced them into the cloud and I guess they got lost after that and ended up crashing here.'

For once Perdu was lost for words. He exchanged a look with Habets that said something like 'How hard did you hit him?'

I blundered on. 'I can understand how it might have looked like I was burning the documents but really I was trying to save them. Why that daft Kraut...'

'Stop, stop, stop.' He held up his hands. 'You are making no sense at all.' He sighed and turned to his colleague. 'Habets, please take Major Reinberger down to the cells.'

I relaxed at this point. Whoever this Major Reinberger might be, a spell in clink sounded like just the ticket for him and good riddance too, I thought.

Habets strode towards me, grabbed me by the arm and lifted me to my feet. 'Come on Reinberger, let's be going, sir.'

I froze. 'Wait.' Habets carried on. 'Please stop. Stop.' He hesitated and I turned to Perdu. 'Inspector. I fear there has been some terrible mistake. I'm not Reinberger. I'm Kilroy. I'm an R.A.F. pilot.'

Perdu started laughing. 'Oh come on Major, do you take me for a fool? If you are in the R.A.F. why are you wearing a Luftwaffe uniform?'

I looked down and sure enough – instead of the blue serge I was so familiar with I found I was clad in the dark garb of the Hun. I now realised that I had felt a bit uncomfortable in it earlier but what with all the other circumstances of the interview I hadn't had time to take stock of what I was wearing and strange as it may seem, I just hadn't noticed.

Then Perdu delivered the clincher. 'And why, Major, why are you speaking German?'

Scheisse, I thought. Of course. German. I was so familiar with the language that I wore it like a second skin and could just slip in and out of it, as easily as changing my socks. Which I noticed, as I glanced down, had not in fact been changed. 'Inspector. My socks,' I cried in desperation. He didn't even look up. 'That proves it. R.A.F. socks. Look. Please.' He was studying that blasted plan and just waved me away. Habets was hustling me out of the door and so I had one last desperate try. 'Wizard prang old chep. See, I can speak English. Bit of a pea souper, what?' but he was having none of it.

And so I was manhandled along the corridor and down the stairs. Down and down we went. We paused at the bottom for a party coming the other way. Two gentlemen in what I could see was Saville Row's finest finery, leading an R.A.F. pilot out. It was Helmut. He smiled at me, looking down his nose. 'You bastard,' I cried in German. 'Don't think you will get away with it you scheisse sweinhund.'

He stepped neatly around me and addressed one of his companions. 'I say, any idea what that chap is saying? He seems frightfully upset, what?'

As prison cells go, and I've been thrown into quite a few in my time, this one wasn't too bad. A faint smell of disinfectant, bare walls, a high window and a rickety bed where someone had thoughtfully left a blanket. There was even a latrine in the corner. So, I thought, we had en suite facilities, which made it one up on the Savoy at least although, sadly, I hadn't noticed any tarts in the lobby at Fort Flanders or wherever the hell I was.

I sat down on the bed and tried to figure out what was going on. Clearly I'd been clobbered by Habets when they'd caught me wrestling by the fireside with Helmut and no doubt we'd all been chucked in the back of a paddy-wagon and brought here. Presumably Helmut had taken advantage of my insensibility whilst en route and had swapped identities with me. That much seemed clear but the question was: why had he done it?

I sat forward and did what I always do when there is a problem on my mind – scratched my left buttock. So clearly Helmut fancied his chances more by being Kilroy rather than being Helmut but why? And did he really think he would get away with it forever?

I was still pondering this little puzzle when my thoughts were interrupted by some noise from just outside my cell. I stopped scratching and cocked an ear. There was a shuffling of feet and a whispered conversation. I heard somebody muttering, 'Fifteen minutes,' in German, as the door creaked open. I looked up to see Habets standing to one side as he ushered in the SS.

There were two of them, Germany's finest, or so they both thought, each looking immaculate from their polished black boots to the lightning flashes on their lapels. The door crashed shut behind them and I heard the bolts slide into place.

The taller one strode confidently across the cell and stood before me. 'Raus,' he said, and I did.

I don't know why but I felt compelled to stand to attention. As we stood eyeball to eyeball, with him only a few inches in front of me I had a chance to take him in. He had a sort of handsome chiselled face, with a smooth complexion and a long thin nose, almost Jewish I'd have said had it been sited anywhere else. And I was sure there was something familiar about him but I couldn't quite place it.

'Lice?'

I realised I was scratching my left buttock again and stopped. I'd been speculating that he might be a bit of a one with the ladies but then I saw into his eyes. They were a steely grey and sparkling with intelligence, but behind them, nothing, like a viper. And where had I seen him before? 'No, I don't think it's lice. It was...'

'You will address me as Herr Direktor.'

'Herr Direktor.'

'And I want a straight explanation,' he barked, then proceeded to pace back and forth before me, tossing his gloves from hand to hand.

Clearly he hadn't come to discuss prison vermin or the weather or Marlene Dietrich's underwear and as there weren't any other subjects in my head at that time I kept quiet.

'Well?' He stopped pacing and stared at me.

I gulped. 'What do you want to know, sir?' This just didn't seem like a good moment to trot out my little yarn about me and Uncle Tom Cobbley and how it was all a terrible mistake and that I wasn't a damned Jerry at all but was plain old Pilot Officer Kilroy and rather partial to best bully beef and cricket.

He stopped and sighed. 'The plans, you fool, where are the plans?' This came out as a whisper and I noticed SS Herr Henchman moving to the door and pressing his ear to it as he spoke.

'I burnt them,' I whispered back. I was sure this was what he wanted to hear and I figured the sooner he heard it the sooner he'd be banging on the door to be let out and I'd get some peace. He had that lethal unhinged quality that always gets me rattled, but I figured he couldn't do me any harm with us all safely tucked up in darkest Belgium and dear old Habets patrolling up and down in the corridor outside.

It was as if he had been reading my thoughts. 'Don't think you are beyond our reach here, Major. I advise you to speak the truth.' He looked at his watch.

'I burnt them. All of them.' I repeated and fixed him with my innocent, truthful look that had served me so well on occasions in the past.

I could see him studying me and after a pause he nodded, then looked again at his watch. 'Good. Two hours from now I will be in Berlin, standing in the Reichsführer's office and he...'

'Reichsführer?'

'Himmler, you fool. Herr Himmler. This little fiasco of yours has gone right to the top. That's why I'm here. The Führer is livid.'

That's when I realised where I had seen him before. Back in the mess someone had pasted some press cuttings of our foreign foe near the dartboard and we used them for target practice between games. In one of the cuttings there was a picture of Hitler and Himmler, both looking smug after they had been busy jackbooting over some unfortunate European country or other. And standing just behind Himmler was my friendly prison visitor. I looked at the real thing across my cell and I was sure of it. I think we decided on 15 points for his nose and ten for his ear although I'd suggested just five for the schnoz as it was such an easy target. "Hangdog" we called him because we didn't have anything else to go on other than his hangdog expression. Later I found that our nickname wasn't that far off, when half of Europe came to know him as "the hangman".

Herr Direktor Hangdog swivelled his 15 pointer towards me. 'Just think, Major,' and he lowered his voice, 'with the plans still secret,' and he tapped his magnificent proboscis, 'we will be back here next week and it won't just be the two of us.' He gestured at Herr Henchman. 'Why...,' he smiled like a pointer shark as he patted me on the back, 'you and I will have more time to get to know each other then. You know, after the...' His voiced tailed off.

I could see they were making to leave and that is when it all fell into place for me. Helmut didn't want to be in Helmut's shoes because he knew after his recent balls-up he wasn't exactly up for promotion back home and he also knew that his internment would only last as long as Belgium, which, according to the plan, was not much more than a few days. They had both turned towards the door and were about to leave when I shouted, 'Herr Dartboard. Wait.'

He turned around. 'Dartboard?'

'I mean Direktor, sir. There might have been a few pages I didn't burn.'

He clicked his fingers and smiled as he turned to Henchman. 'See, I told you I'd get the truth out of him before we left.'

So I told him about the stuff that hadn't been destroyed. He didn't seem angry, just pleased with himself for getting to the truth and it wasn't difficult for me to tell it because I had really seen the pages with my own eyes and it really was the truth this time and he didn't seem to have any difficulty believing me.

At last it was time for them to go. 'You realise what this means?' he asked no one in particular as they waited for Habets to open up. 'They'll call off the invasion.' Then he turned to me. 'Well done, Major. It was wise to be truthful. Be assured we will look after your family well for you while you are staying here.'*

---

* It is clear from Kilroy's description that his interrogator was SS-Obergruppenführer Reinhard Heydrich, Himmler's deputy and chief of the SD, Gestapo and Kripo at the time of this encounter. Early in the war Heydrich was not widely known outside Germany but later became infamous throughout Europe when he was appointed Protector of Bohemia and Moravia, where he enjoyed the title 'Butcher of Prague' and 'The Hangman'. He was assassinated by Czech partisans in 1942. http://tinyurl.com/Kilroy081.

After the door banged shut I sat back down on the bed and heaved a sigh of relief. Fortunately for them, my family were tucked up safely back in Blighty, but I did briefly wonder what might happen to Helmut's nearest and dearest. In the meantime, of course, I was still stuck in this grubby Belgian hidey-hole, but the thought of *not* seeing my SS friend and his hooter back this time next week certainly raised my spirits.

A few minutes later I heard a voice outside my cell. 'I say, steady on old boy. Mind my gammy leg, what?' This was followed by a dull thump, a gasp and the sound of bolts crashing shut. I gathered Pilot Officer Helmut had been returned to our block and took some satisfaction that, rather than whoring around Brussels with our Embassy bods, he was back in clink and twiddling his thumbs along with me. Later I had cause to regret that thought. It was a few hours on, when we'd been brought some food and I heard him at it again. 'Excuse me, old chap. Any chance of a spot of custard?' The next morning it was 'Jam for breakfast? Really should be marmalade old boy,' followed by some loud clucking and tutting. And so it went on through the next day. Finally I'd had enough. I think it was when he started complaining about the wrong kind of "loo roll" that I ran to my cell door and started kicking and banging it and shouting. 'Why don't you fucking shut up you damned Kraut swine?'

Of course all I got back from him was 'Can't understand you old boy. You Jerries – no speaka da lingo, comprendo?' and I realised it was best to gnash my teeth, clench my fists and stay quiet.

I realise now that I haven't mentioned anything about the other member of our little triumvirate, Erich the pilot. I guess he was there with us in the lock-up but, after my encounter with him and his laundry in the woods, I never saw him again. I was pretty sure my SS friends had paid him a visit after they'd seen me but presumably he hadn't had much to add. Certainly no one came rushing in to let me out in a hurry. I guessed he hadn't even known about the invasion plans or whatever the hell they were and I don't suppose it bothered him one jot about my plight and his fellow countryman's shenanigans, so there the three of us sat for the next several days, staring at the walls, trying to stomach their infernal food, whilst Europe turned itself inside out.

The dartboard picture Kilroy refers to could be the one published in *The Times* on March 17th 1939. It shows Hitler and Himmler at the Hradschin Castle, Prague, after Hitler had proclaimed a German protectorate over much of Czechoslovakia. Towering over both and to one side there stands a figure not identified in the caption, but it is clearly Heydrich. Students of irony would appreciate the picture below it, of a Covent Garden performance put on for the French president, Lebrun, aptly titled *The Sleeping Beauty*. Alongside is an advertisement caption 'Your system wants a real rest and holiday.'

I only found out afterwards what had been happening on the outside. At the time I guessed that those plans must have been pretty important but had no idea that I'd landed in the middle of the biggest intelligence coup since the Zimmermann telegram.* No wonder Helmut had been so desperate to burn the papers. They showed the full story of a planned invasion of the west that was only a week ahead. But the funny thing was that the allies failed to make anything much of their windfall. For a kick-off they let it leak out pretty well immediately that they had the gen and, once he knew they knew, Hitler wasn't the sort of chap to hang around. First he kicked Göring's backside good and hard, as he saw the whole thing as being the Luftwaffe's fault, then within the hour he had his top investigators, my friends Hangdog and Honcho, under a diplomatic flag and over the border to find out what was what.

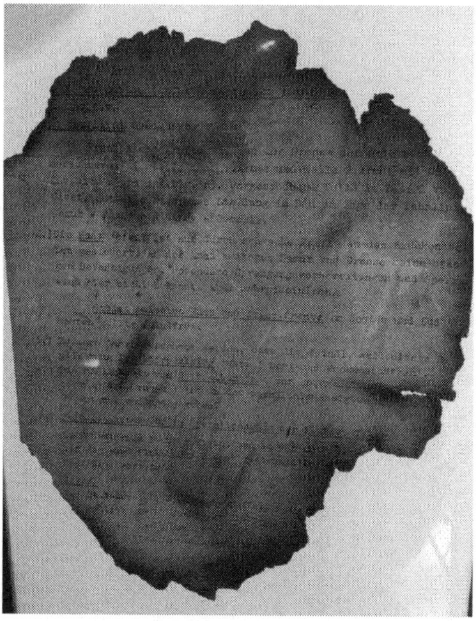

Remains of the German plans captured at Mechelen, now in the collection of the Royal Museum of the Armed Forces and Military History in Brussels.

Meanwhile the allies did what they always do best, which was to fall out with each other and panic. Gamelin, the allied Supreme Commander wanted the French and British armies to march into Belgium immediately, but the Belgians, predictably, wouldn't have it and even sacked their chief of staff for suggesting it. This was all in January, mind, and if you consult your history books you will find that the actual invasion didn't happen until May. This was because Hitler called the whole thing off, allowing us all to settle down for a few more months of phoney war. At the time this must

* The Zimmermann Telegram (or Zimmermann Note) was an internal diplomatic communication issued from the German Foreign Office in 1917 that proposed a military alliance between Germany and Mexico in the event of the United States entering World War I against Germany. The proposal was intercepted and decoded by British intelligence. Revelation of the contents enraged American public opinion, especially after the German Foreign Secretary Arthur Zimmermann publicly admitted the telegram was genuine, and ultimately led to the United States declaration of war on Germany. http://tinyurl.com/Kilroy216.

have seemed like a set-back for him but with hindsight it changed the course of the war. The earlier plan was pretty much a repeat of the German WWI strategy which would have no doubt led to similar stagnation, but once Hitler realised it had been compromised he changed it, coming up with the Blitzkrieg instead, with the result we all know.

My role in these great affairs of State was to sit on my cot staring at the four walls, twiddling my thumbs and railing at my nouveau R.A.F. chum in the cell opposite. Of course I was hauled out in front of Perdu several times but he got no further with me and I no further with him. I suppose you might just say that we didn't see eye to eye, and I don't suppose the powers that be were ever sure on the basis of my unreliable and erratic testimony that the plans weren't an elaborate Kraut hoax.

I think about five days must have gone by and I was beginning to wonder if I would ever see Piccadilly again when I heard voices in the corridor outside, English voices and not Helmut for once. I was on the brink of salvation and from an unlikely direction.

My cell door swung open and in strode Bovington. I think this was the only time in our acquaintance I was glad to see him. I sprung to my feet and was possibly even about to embrace him when I saw him take a step back and say, 'Who's this? Never seen him before in my life.'

Fortunately Stevens was just behind him. 'Stop acting the idiot, Bovvers. Of course it's Kilroy. Don't you think there've been enough fuck-ups already?'

I recall I really did embrace Stevens. All I could hear from him was a muffled 'Steady on old boy. Don't go giving Johnny Foreigner the wrong idea.'

And that was it really. It turned out that Belfrey had rather kicked off when he had heard about me being incarcerated in Castle Brussels. 'Whose side are these bloody Belgians on, holding on to England's finest?' he roared. Someone pointed out that that was the point – they weren't on our side, they were neutral but once the old boy had a gnat up his chuff he was not to be lightly deflected. So Bovington and Stevens were delegated to nip over the border, sort out our foreign office wallies, knock a few Belgians on the head, even give good King Leopold a right royal rogering if it came to it but whatever the cost bring me back, alive preferably. As it turned out Helmut's daft shenanigans had made things easier for them. The Belgians were so embarrassed by the balls-up they had made that they were glad to see the back of me.

A couple of hours later the three of us were in the back of a Belgian army lorry on the way to the border, rolling over the plains of Flanders, singing filthy songs and throwing empty Kriek bottles at *les Vaches* and *des Boers* as we sped past their boggy farmsteads. Some dull-witted border guard firmly stamped Stevens and Bovington's passports, pointedly turning a blind eye as I walked through, and we were back in France.*

---

* Kilroy's story sheds new light on what came to be called the Mechelen incident, as hitherto there has been no suggestion that an allied pilot had any involvement in it.

All sources agree that the German plans for a forthcoming attack in the west were compromised when a transport plane, carrying two Luftwaffe majors, Erich Hoenemanns and Helmuth Reinberger, crashed near Mechelen in Belgium in January 1940. Reinberger was carrying the plans in a case, although this was unknown to Hoenemanns at the time.

Kilroy's account concurs with all the important details of the incident, even down to the presence of the pilot's laundry which was in the aeroplane, for Hoenemann's wife in Cologne to wash. Reinberger did indeed desperately try to destroy the plans and the Germans did arrange for the miscreants to be interviewed in captivity, under a diplomatic flag, not long after the crash. This meeting was evidently bugged by the Belgians. In the end the Germans were unsure whether or not their plans had been compromised, and the Allies were uncertain whether or not the whole affair was a German ruse. Not long after, Hitler called off the invasion. The Allies continued to do very little of any significance and Belgium remained strategically neutral up to the actual invasion later that year.

In the immediate aftermath, Hoenemans and Reinberger were interned by the Belgians and condemned to death in absentia by the Germans. Hoenemann's wife did not long survive an interrogation by the Gestapo but Hoenemanns and Reinberger both survived the war. Ahead of the Nazi invasion they were evacuated to Britain and then to Canada, from where they were ultimately repatriated to Germany and partially reprieved. http://tinyurl.com/Kilroy082.

CHAPTER 7

'You're talking bollocks, old boy. Absolute bollocks.'

Flight Lieutenant de Merit-Fanshawe had peaked several hours earlier and had moved on from being plain rat-arsed to being simply ratty. We were sitting alone in Dick's Cock – more properly the Café de Dix Coqs – and neither of us knew it at the time but there would be precious few further opportunities for shenanigans in Chalons. It was early May and the news was bad, what with the Hun giving our Navy a bloody nose over Norway, but in our worst nightmares we could never imagine that within a few days there would be Panzers racing through the Low Countries and then onwards and past the very establishment in which we were sitting. This was still in the future of course on that cool spring evening and at that moment I should have left Fanshawe to his drunken ramblings but I suppose I'd had a few too many glasses myself so didn't feel inclined to back down. 'Look, I'm telling you,' I said, 'the trainee fell out during an aerobatic sortie and thc instructor flew back and landed in one piece. Said the jolly old Tiger handled fine from the front seat.'

'No, you can't solo a Tiger Moth from the front. Centre of Gravity and all that. You're making it up, old chap.' He thumped the table for emphasis.

I found myself wondering if Fanshawe might have some unfinished business with me. There was the usual snobbery from his type about us reservists of course but there seemed to be more than that. I guessed he might have found out that I'd "borrowed" his mistress a couple of times whilst he was back in Blighty on a gunnery course but I didn't reckon she was his one true love in any case. Then there was the small matter of the 20 quid I'd just taken off him at bridge but even allowing for that he seemed pretty riled. 'Look, I was there, I'm telling you,' I said persistently. I wasn't making it up either, but when someone wants to pick a fight they want to pick a fight.

'Well, what about Bertie Beetleston?' he asked.

'Who? What about him?'

'Tried to take off from the front seat. Went howling off down the field and straight into a farmhouse.' His hand swooped low across the table, re-enacting the crash by slamming into my glass and shoving it onto the floor.

'Probably pissed.' I extracted my handkerchief to wipe my shoes.

'Well, of course he was pissed or he wouldn't have tried a stunt like that. But he told me himself, once they'd patched him up, there's just not enough elevator authority to get the old bird up in the air.' He mimed somebody frantically tugging back with both hands on the joystick. I couldn't help thinking he looked like he was doing something else.

'Do you really need two hands for that?'

He frowned and looked puzzled.

I could see his cheeks reddening and decided it might be wise to return to our discussion. 'What I'm saying is I think we agree then.'

'What?' he exclaimed.

God, he might be four hundred and twenty seventh in line to the throne, I remember thinking, but he seemed a bit lacking in brain power. 'I didn't say you could *take off* from the front seat. I merely said that you could fly and land from there.' Actually I had rather underestimated him, as you will see.

'So, prove it.'

'What?'

'We've got an old Tiger Moth at the back of the barn. Squadron's on a 24 hourer and the top brass are all in Reims tomorrow. Get the beast all dusted off and then take off from the rear seat and come back and land it from the front.'

'What?'

'You heard me. Just change seats in mid-air. A clever chap such as yourself should be able to manage it. Here's a little wager just to make it more interesting.' He pulled out a bundle of notes and counted out 50 pounds.

'You're on.' I regretted it as soon as the words were out. If I hadn't been caning the sauce myself I would have been a bit more careful.

'Did you hear me say "No parachute?"'

Well I hadn't, but bravado took hold. 'Makes no difference to me.' I glared at him as he knocked back his glass. 'Old boy.'

'Where's your money then?' He patted his pile of fivers on the table.

'You'll get it tomorrow, if you win.' Of course I didn't have that sort of money, but figured that if I lost, paying back Fanshawe would be the least of my worries.

The next day I roused a couple of erks, slipped them ten bob each and got them to prepare the Tiger Moth. It had been at the back of the barn for ages and was covered in bird shit but they got it going eventually.

After a very light breakfast – I was feeling a little fragile – I went out to inspect it. Fanshawe and his pals were already clustered around, waggling the elevators, pinging the wires and scrawling obscenities in the dust on the wings.

Ignoring their ironic cheers and greetings to "the intrepid aviator" I clambered into the rear seat, got one of the erks to swing the prop and within a minute I was bouncing across the field and climbing into the clear blue sky.

Now, it occurs to me that you might not know the layout of a Tiger Moth, so here's how it is. It's a lightweight two seater trainer, that is a biplane with dual control and the seats in tandem. Obviously it can be flown with two aboard, but for solo it must be the rear seat that is occupied, otherwise it's far too nose heavy and out of balance.

So my task that day was to take off whilst sitting in the rear seat, change seats in mid-air, specifically without departing company from my aerial steed, and come back in the front, hopefully without diving it straight into the French countryside. My plan was that, with both seats being open cockpit, I would hop out of one, clamber along the wing and hop into the other. Easy enough on the ground for sure, but a bit more tricky in the air when you've got to hang on in the slipstream and fly the plane at the same time.

A Tiger Moth. Note instructor to the front and trainee pilot to the rear.

I levelled out at five thousand feet and looked around me. It was a bright sunny morning and the French countryside was mapped out below, looking green and luscious now that that icy winter was behind us. It was obvious that the campaigning season was overdue and I remember wondering what Jerry would have in store, when the plane hit an air pocket and lurched alarmingly. I jerked hard with the stick, but over-compensated so then had to correct for that, then over-compensated again with the plane twitching and flicking like a dictator's moustache until at last things calmed down, flying smooth and level again. I'd not been in a Tiger Moth for a while, since the day I'd spectacularly taxied one into the side of my own Nissen hut at the Kincardine air show and I was finding it surprisingly skittish after the solid Hawker Hurricane. I decided it would be prudent to spend a few minutes getting familiar with it again, via some gentle aerobatics.

My plans for the trip hadn't reckoned with having a monster hangover. I soon realised that aerobatics didn't seem such a good idea after all so I straightened up and flew along gently on the level for a while. I loosened my harness a little and raised myself from my seat, hoping that an 80 mile an hour blast of wind full in the face, might do the trick. It didn't.

There didn't seem much point in delaying any further. I tightened the throttle friction and set the elevator trim for level flight. There is no automatic pilot on Tiger Moths, but set like this I would need only the one hand to hold the stick and the other would be free to hold onto the aeroplane. I undid my seatbelt and stood up. I was treated to an icy blast in the face and the plane lurched. Instinctively I snatched at the stick to bring it back on the level.

Getting out on the wing proved to be a lot more difficult than I expected. First my feet caught in the harness, then I discovered that shifting my own weight affected the balance of the plane and I had to compensate by shifting the stick. The plane nearly stalled at one point, which would have been curtains for yours truly but, just in time, I regained control.

Next came the really tricky bit. The plan was to shuffle along the wing and then make a quick change of hands to grab the front seat stick and let go the rear. I don't know what went wrong at this point but suddenly the engine was roaring, the nose was pointing in the air and I was grimly hanging on to a harness with both hands as my legs floundered and tried to get a grip back on the wing. Somehow I scrambled up and got everything under control, but I was pretty well back where I started, by the rear cockpit. I paused to regain my breath.

You know that feeling when you sense you are being watched? A sort of tingling in the back of the neck? Well at five thousand feet, soloing a Tiger Moth from the wing is a strange place to experience it. I cautiously turned my head and looked straight into the eyes of the Luftwaffe. A 109. No, I was wrong. Two 109s. The second was just to one side and slightly below, with both flying in close formation with me.

The pilot waved and did the universal mime for drinking from a bottle. Well he wasn't far wrong was he? I could see he was struggling to keep his plane on station with me. Flying a three hundred mile an hour fighter alongside an 80 mile an hour trainer is a bit like trying to control a galloping thoroughbred alongside a dawdling donkey. His wing flaps were down and his nose was high and I could see he was jockeying the throttle.

I forgot to mention that suffering from the after effects of the previous night I had loosened my belt in the cockpit. And of course I hadn't tightened it before I'd gone out on the wing and of course it chose this moment to come loose. I didn't know this at the time. All I knew was that my flies blew open, the wind tugged at my trousers and slowly they slid down. There was nothing I could do. Both my hands were busy elsewhere. But I could see my Luftwaffe friends guffawing at my plight.

There is something called the *esprit d'aire* and no doubt you've heard of heroics in the Great War when a noble aviator on one side let off some disadvantaged chap on the other. Clearly I was hoping for a similar spirit in the new war. Thus far I'd been lucky. The Tiger Moth has no armament at all and a brace of 109s could pick it off at leisure, even if I was sitting comfortably in the cockpit and not dancing *in flagrante* on the wing. It would seem that only my bizarre antics had saved me thus far.

I said the Tiger Moth had no armament, but I wasn't entirely weaponless. With the feeling that I had nothing to lose, I loosed one hand, lifted my shirt and gave them the full frontal treatment from my personal 303 repeater. The lead pilot covered his eyes in mock horror and banked away. It was an impressive piece of flying, given how close he was to the stall, but he had forgotten about his wingman who, clearly, was watching me rather than the leader.

I found myself shouting a warning although of course they would never have heard me. There was the shrieking sound of metal on metal as the two planes collided – the leader's propeller chewing into the other's canopy with fragments of glass flying in all directions. There was a loud bang as his propeller shattered and the engine screamed and blew up, erupting with a thick black pall of smoke. All I could do was watch in horror as the two planes, locked in a deadly embrace, fluttered slowly downwards, to land with a mighty splash in a river. There were no parachutes.

After that encounter with the Luftwaffe, the task of gaining the front cockpit didn't seem like much of a problem at all. A bit of juggling the stick, a quick shuffle forward and I was in there. I found, as I had claimed earlier, the plane didn't fly so badly from the front, so all that was left was to get back to base and claim my winnings.

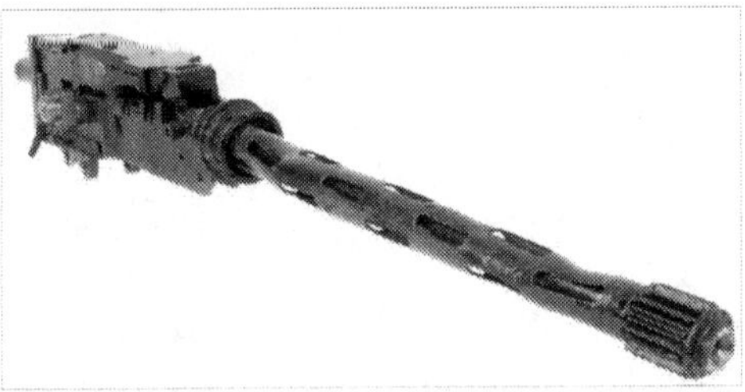
A Browning 303 machine gun with fighter mounts.

I soon got my bearings and ten minutes later, feeling pretty pleased with myself I was over our field. As I looked down to check on the windsock, I noticed there was rather more activity below than usual – some lorries drawing up and men running around in all directions. Then I noticed the Bentley parked on the perimeter road. This was Belfrey's, a pristine example of the famous 3.5 litre Cabriolet from 1935, in a gleaming British Racing Green finish. Very nice to behold it's true and I'd often admired it from afar but the bad news for me was that Belfrey must be with it and, not, as I'd been told, at some big-wig conference in Reims.

My first thought was to divert to another field – anywhere would do and at least it would give me time to think up some excuse for later – when my engine, sputtered, caught, sputtered again and then died. The Tiger Moth has the simplest fuel gauge possible – just a vertical stick attached to a float in the tank. Nothing to break, jam or wear out and it's cunningly positioned right in front of the windshield where the novice pilot can't ignore it. All you need to know is that when the stick has almost disappeared into the tank you are out of fuel. Idiot-proof really.

The propeller soon wound down to a standstill and in the unaccustomed silence I could hear the wind whistling through the rigging. I surveyed the field below and started to think about how I'd get the plane lined up for a nice safe dead-stick landing. We had practised this sort of thing often enough in training and on this very type too but I soon found that I had a problem that day as, along with no engine, the plane was also all out of balance in fulfilment of said wager conditions. In this unusual configuration and without any power up front to lift us I found that the plane just wanted to drop its nose, pick up speed and dive into the ground. When I tried to pull the nose up with the stick it slowed up, it's true, but then it wanted to stall and – trust me – you do not want to stall an engineless Tiger Moth just a few hundred feet above the field. So I ended up in a sort of compromise, swooping downwards, heaving frantically upwards until the wings started fluttering, and then back downwards again, over and over with the ground getting nearer by the second. I was in a right lather of course and it was taking all my concentration just to keep the plane in the air at all so I really couldn't give any thought to where I was positioned over the field, our height and the wind direction and so on. That became obvious when the ground and the boundary hedge appeared just where I didn't want them to be – looming large in the windshield. So there was to be no escape, I thought as I gripped the stick with both hands, wishing I'd remembered to really tighten my harness – tighten until the pips squeak and you'll walk away with a full set of teeth my instructor had told me. My approach had been way too fast and the plane bounced hard, swerved and bounced, came down hard again, lurched then careered through the hedge, speed undiminished, as if half the Luftwaffe were after us. I confess I just shut my eyes at this point, let go of the stick and covered my head. There was an almighty crump and then all hell broke loose. I was told later I managed six full cart-wheels but all I knew at the time was that I was being banged around in the cockpit like a pea in a tin can. My head must have hit something hard at some point and I suppose I blacked out as the next thing I recall was a splash of water hitting my face. I opened my eyes to see an erk hanging over me, wearing a concerned frown. I realised I was lying on the grass and I recall wondering who it was who had pulled me out of the wreck.

A crowd of curious faces were looking down at me. High ranking servicemen have a lot of gold braid on their uniforms – scrambled egg we call it. There seemed to be an awful lot of it on show here. Somewhere near the back, but coming nearer by the second, I spotted Belfrey. His cheeks were flushed and his pupils were like pinpoints as his face stopped and hovered only a few inches above me. 'You stupid bastard,' he hissed. 'I'll have your bollocks ripped off then I'll stop your wages until you've fucking paid it all off, you bloody oaf.'

I was in no position to argue of course but was thinking that this seemed a bit extreme. At this time the R.A.F. was pranging planes every day just about and this one was only a clapped-out old trainer – why, I thought, I was probably doing the service a favour by getting rid of it, but of course I didn't say that. We were some distance away from the beast, smouldering by the roadside as the fire crew hosed it down, when I spotted something beneath the crumpled and charred timber and canvas – it was a flash of highly polished steel, immaculately finished in British Racing Green.

'I'm sorry, sire,' I began to grovel but got no further.

'C'est magnifique,' I heard someone cry. 'C'est magnifique.' It was a voice from the back of the crowd, and the speaker was forcing his way forward. Belfrey turned his glare in this new direction as the man finally made it to the front. The newcomer gazed down at me, beaming. I saw a funny looking man, a Frenchman of course, and of such exalted rank I wasn't even sure what it was. Suddenly he knelt down beside me with a concerned look on his face and I thought he was going to kiss me. Then, to my horror, he did. On both cheeks. 'C'est magnifique,' he said, breathing garlic all over me.

I was all for that, I thought (well maybe without the garlic) but even I was inclined to think that my recent botched arrival hardly justified such superlatives when he grabbed my hand and clasped it to his breast. 'L'homme qui a abattu les Messchersmitts, n'est ce pas?' he asked.

Bentley 3.5 Litre Cabriolet.

I realised he was asking about my recent exploits with the Luftwaffe and nodded, wondering how he might know about them.

He fumbled in his breast pocket and pulled something out. 'A Teega Mort et deux Messerschmeets?' he asked and I nodded again. I guessed he must have seen me from the ground – my good luck it would seem.

'C'est magnifique,' he repeated as he reached out for my lapel. 'Mais ce n'est pas la guerre. C'est de la folie.'* He was still kneeling and sat back on his haunches as he said these words, only to gaze wonderingly at me.

* 'It is magnificent. But it is not war. It is madness.' Also uttered by General Pierre Bosquet when he witnessed the Charge of the Light Brigade in the Crimean War in 1854. http://tinyurl.com/Kilroy083.

Fortunately he didn't seem to expect much back as I couldn't think what to say anyway. I noticed his eyes had turned a little glassy and he looked down for a moment, composing himself, before he stood up sharply and saluted, holding the salute for what seemed like an age. There was a loud bang from a flash gun and a ripple of applause from the assembled crowd.

I felt sufficiently encouraged by this to attempt to stand and one of the erks helped me to my feet. Sticky Stevens was nearby and he came up and he patted me on the back. 'Well done, old boy,' he said. 'First Frog gong on the squadron, eh?' I looked down and saw something pinned to my jacket with red and green ribbons. Then suddenly the world started to spin and my legs gave way.

***

When I came to, I found I was sitting in the front seat of a car and we were rattling down a country lane at some speed. There was a weighty camera in my lap with flash gun attached. I turned to the driver and found it was Pamela.

'Ah – the patient awakes,' she said, patting me on the knee. 'How are you feeling, my brave young Icarus?'

I muttered something about being a little groggy and then asked, 'How did you get here?'

'Arrived in Reims this morning for the big pow-wow. On another assignment for the mag of course.' She double de-clutched and there was an answering roar from the engine as we surged up a hill. 'Catching your exploits on film was a bonus. Lucky I had the telephoto. And then the medal ceremony too. Kissed by Vuillemin – the air marshal, eh? Not many can say that – well not many men anyway.'* I grabbed the door strap as we swerved around a corner. 'All great theatre. Marvellous. I might get a bonus and you might even make the front cover.'

'What the, er, dog-fight or the medal ceremony?' I asked but she didn't answer. I was rather hoping for the medal ceremony. Heroic as my earlier action might have appeared to the uninitiated and, admiring as *I* was of my secret weapon, I couldn't quite see it being the lead story in the *Picture Post* but, I've since discovered, it's best to leave these sort of decisions to the editorial team.

We were in her little Morgan three wheeler, and, I could see we were on the outskirts of Chalons. 'Best to get you to the hospital, I think,' Pamela

* General Joseph Vuillemin was the Chief of the Air Staff, the Commander in Chief of the French airforce, from the outbreak of the war until the armistice. He had troubled relations with the British, continually arguing for many more fighter squadrons than they were prepared to give and (late in the Battle of France) he controversially thwarted an R.A.F. bombing raid on Italy by ordering lorries to be parked across the airfield. http://tinyurl.com/Kilroy084.

continued. 'Concussion. Can't be too careful. Your M.O. chappie wanted to check you over but Nigel wouldn't hear of it. Said something about keel-hauling being too good for you. He can be such a cross-patch at times.'

'The Bentley...?' I asked.

'Oh, don't worry about that,' she said. 'He'll soon get another. You should see what I did to his previous one.'

I was thinking that she might be better placed than me to soothe him after these little mishaps. We had slowed a little by then for the tight streets of Chalons. I recognised les Dix Coqs as we cruised by and then there were a couple more turnings before we screeched to a halt on the hospital forecourt. Pamela walked around the front of the car, opened my door and helped me out. I was no longer feeling woozy, but didn't resist her supporting arm as she led me through the entrance.

The hospital was a French civilian establishment but, surprisingly, Pamela seemed to know her way around and evidently knew some of the staff too. I found later there had been a cocktail party to end all cocktail parties there when she'd been over before Christmas. Her French was excellent too and thus, in no time, I found myself in the presence of Docteur Marcel Petiot who gave me the once-over. He tapped my knees with a rubber hammer, shone a light in my eyes and made me stick out my tongue. He was a man of few words it would seem – just indicating what he wanted from me by mime and the odd grunt. Yes, there was something odd about him I thought. I looked up at his face as he leaned over me. Staring into his eyes it felt like I was looking into two long dark tunnels. Or bottomless pits. He was an odd one alright and mercifully I never saw him again. You might wonder why I say "mercifully" and it's because, well it's another story and not mine but, if you are interested look him up. Marcel Petiot.* At any rate he gave me a clean bill of health that day and told Pamela to take me back to the squadron.

I affected a stumble as we walked back along the corridor and felt Pamela's arm around me again. She helped me back into the car and then got in alongside me. She was driving a lot more slowly as we cruised out of

* Marcel Petiot was a doctor in Paris during the German occupation. Under the codename Dr. Eugène he ran a bogus escape route to South America, at a price of 25,000 francs per person. He had three accomplices who directed would-be escapees to him – Jews, resistance fighters, ordinary criminals and others. Once they were under his control he murdered them, taking all their valuables and disposing of their bodies. Eventually the Gestapo got to hear about his "escape route" and sent an investigator. He also disappeared. After the war the remains of 23 people were discovered at Petiot's home in Paris and he was convicted of murder and guillotined. It is estimated there may have been as many as 60 victims. The war film, Seven Thunders (1957), features an identical character, Dr Martout, and there is also a film, Docteur Petiot, made in 1990. http://tinyurl.com/Kilroy085.

town and I could sense she had something on her mind. 'You are still looking a bit peaky,' she began. 'I've got some medicine back at home that will do you the world of good. Would you...?' Her voice tailed off.

'What a splendid idea,' I replied. 'Still feeling a bit wobbly. Spot of matron's jolly old jollop would be just the ticket.'

I smiled and tweaked Pamela's knee as she executed a smart U turn and we picked up speed again. A few minutes later we screeched to a halt outside a pretty little cottage standing alone beside some woodland – Chez Belfrey I presumed. I got out unaided and sauntered in behind her. I sat down on the settee as she went to organise my medication. A few minutes later she returned, carefully balancing two tumblers, each filled to the brim with a clear liquid. She handed one of them to me and told me to drink it. 'What is it?' I asked. Gin and Tonic she said, as she knocked back her own glass.

I don't recall finishing my drink. A few hours later I was lying on the bed upstairs with Pamela dozing beside me. I think I must have dropped off myself. The sun had gone down and it was a dark moonless night outside. It had been a tiring day. Demolishing several hundred pounds worth of government property, not to mention the Bentley rather takes it out of you, I thought. On top of that there had been a couple of low flying missions with the frisky Lady P, some lengthy post-coital chit-chat and now I was plum tuckered out, as our antipodean allies would say. I was just thinking of getting up and heading back to base when I heard the front door creak.

Be prepared. That's the Boy Scout motto. I didn't retain much else from my brief acquaintance with the movement but it's an excellent little axiom. You might suppose that in my haste to bed the delectable Pamela I'd disrobed with mad abandon, but no, my clothes were neatly placed in the right order across the room, making a pathway to the window, and, *being prepared*, I had earlier opened it.

It was the work of a few seconds to get dressed. Meanwhile the Group Captain was crashing around downstairs, howling for his supper. I haven't mentioned before that besides being our senior officer on station, he'd also once been the Interservice Boxing Champion (Welterweight Division), a title he'd held for five years in a row. This was not a few years previously of course but you never wholly lose those pugilist skills and, as I dressed in haste, I worried that, old prune he may be, the ability to land a hard right on a glass-like jaw was likely still with him.

The trick to making an exit in these extreme circumstances is to resist the temptation to leap too soon. You don't want to end up face to face with the lady's better half just as he's booting the cat out the back door, so you must resist all temptation to flee at once. Wait until you hear his tread on the stairs *then* make a bolt for it. I glanced over at Lady P. She was looking a little less perky than she'd been an hour earlier, but at least she had put on her dressing gown. I gestured at her to be silent as her husband's ranting drew nearer. I counted his first six steps up the staircase, then nimbly climbed up on the window ledge and leapt.

It was unfortunate the Scouts threw me out so soon. I gather there's a "Tracking and Woodcraft" section in *Scouting for Boys* that stresses the value of reconnaissance and I just didn't have the chance to pick up that little life lesson. But if I *had* taken the trouble to recce my escape route properly I would undoubtedly have noticed that the bunker, which was conveniently sited below the window, wasn't built for my weight and also noticed that it wasn't in fact a bunker.

Thus, my hopes of a stealthy exit were rather spoilt when I leapt down and the structure gave way and splintered beneath me, making enough noise to wake Napoleon in his Paris tomb. And Tungsten.

You might remember Tungsten from the day of my arrival in France, when he was having some problems with, ahem, his rear end. I think the horrible hound ever after thought I was in some way to blame for his predicament that day. Leastways he always gave me a wary look if we encountered each other in the mess. I've already mentioned he was three quarters Irish Wolfhound and the other quarter would be saltwater crocodile, or at least from his jaw size you'd think it was.

Being rather busy with Lady P earlier I was unaware that Tungsten had gone outside for a snooze in his much loved kennel and the first I knew of this was when I trod on a hairy mound as I pulled myself out of his shattered home. Fortunately for me I wasn't facing his sharp end and also fortunately for me, he was big, lumbering and not well blessed in the brains department, so there was a slight delay while he gathered his wits and made ready to draw blood.

Belfrey meanwhile had reversed direction and was howling for vengeance as he made his way back down the stairs. It was very dark outside and there was no time for feeling my way, so I just sprang in the most promising direction which proved to be the rose garden – again paying the price for my fleeting acquaintance with the Scout Movement. I tore through that, as it tore through me then, at last, I came to a back wall. It was high but I reached the top with an athletic leap and managed to scramble over, leaving man and beast howling in my wake. I sprinted up the lane and into the woods where I paused for breath, heart pounding. Mercifully there was no further sound of pursuit.

CHAPTER 8

The next day I weighed up the possibility that old man Belfrey had recognised me in what my mad matron had once described as a *braccis descendit*[*] state. I was pretty sure he had only caught a brief rearward view, in poor light and retreating rapidly of course, so thought, on balance, he probably hadn't. Also in my favour, after my hasty and unscheduled departure from our steamy *nid d'amour*,[†] I'd managed the long yomp back to the Chateau without bumping into anyone and had then got lucky as I made it past both the gate guard and my recumbent room-mate without waking either. The torn trousers I quickly binned and, fortunately, my only injuries from wood splinters, dog and rose were a few superficial scratches and grazes so I figured there was little hard evidence against me. I guessed the lovely Lady P would most probably have concocted some story about a French fifth columnist or something – God knows there were plenty of those around – so I thought the odds were that we'd got away with it.

With all the other shenanigans it was only while I was getting dressed that I remembered the bet. Some might carp that my grand arrival had left something to be desired but there is a saying in aviation circles that any landing you can walk away from is a good one so, by my reckoning, de Merit-Fanshawe should stump up. I mentioned this to roommate Sticky, who was yawning and stretching on the bed alongside and it was then I discovered that old money aristocratic de Merit-Fanshawe wasn't as dopey as I'd imagined. 'Didn't you know, old chap?' asked Stevens.

'Know what?' I asked

'Fanshawe's got his own squadron now. In Edinburgh. Flew off to join it just after you set off on that mad endeavour.'

So that was that then. I reckoned up the grand tally for yesterday's endeavours. There had been rather a lot of broken hardware and zero improvement in the Kilroy coffers on the one hand. But, on the other, I had the squadron's first *Croix de Guerre* and had enjoyed the undying love of the bountiful Lady P – well, for a few hours anyway. My thoughts strayed to Belfrey's badly broken Bentley, realising that Frog gong or no Frog gong, it would be prudent to give the old boy a wide berth for the time being. And I think I would have done a pretty good job of that had it not been for Albert Ball night.

---

[*] Schoolboy Latin for "trousers down".

[†] Love nest.

Albert Ball had been a WWI fighter ace and it was a tradition for the squadron to celebrate the anniversary of his passing with a few sundowners in the mess bar, followed by formal dinner. It was pretty well mandatory to show up for this sort of occasion and, unfortunately, it was that very evening.*

I made a point of getting there early, with Sticky in tow. We sat in a quiet corner and I had my back to the room. There was an empty chair near us, which was bad luck because, shortly after, it was occupied by Basher Bacon. Basher was another junior pilot, but noted more for his encyclopedic knowledge of the theory of flight rather than his meal time repartee.

I could hear things livening up behind me and sure enough, I soon discerned the booming voice of Belfrey, with his 'gin and it' and 'what you having, old boy?' I kept my head down, feigning indifference to what was going on behind and pretending to be listening intently to Basher's chat about some fancy new radiator that, he claimed, could make your plane go faster instead of slowing it down.† Stifling a yawn and trying to filter out Basher's mathematics I could only just catch the odd fragment from Belfrey. I gathered that joiners were a scarce resource these days in this neck of the woods and Lady P had been quite traumatised by the whole business. 'Our allies,' I heard Belfrey repeating over and over. 'Our bloody allies, and then as soon as my back's turned the bastards are up there going through my wife's drawers.'

This sounded very promising. Pamela had gone for the dastardly French Army line rather than the fifth columnist one but it was just as plausible. Then I heard Stiffy Barnes ask, 'Are you're sure it *was* a frog, sir?' then adding, 'I thought you mentioned a blue uniform or something? A lot of boys in blue all around here, sir. And some of our MT‡ chaps would rob

---

* Captain Albert Ball had 44 victories to his credit when he crashed to his death on 7th May 1917 whilst serving with R.F.C. 56 Squadron. He had been decorated with the VC and the DSO with two bars. Kilroy only ever gives his squadron nickname (the Bustards) and not its number but it can't have been 56. 56 Squadron operated Hurricanes in the Battle of France but was based in Essex throughout. http://tinyurl.com/Kilroy086.

† Sticky was probably talking about the Meredith effect, identified by F W Meredith in 1936. It proved only to be of use with the advent of high performance aeroplanes and was employed later in the war, with considerable success, in Spitfire and Mustang fighters. With careful design the Meredith effect allows the drag from a radiator hanging in an aeroplane's slipstream to be cancelled out by considerable thrust to the rear, produced by the heat energy removed from the radiator itself – in effect an early form of jet propulsion. http://tinyurl.com/Kilroy087.

‡ Motor Transport.

their own grandmother, shouldn't wonder. I could get one of my pilot officers to investigate?'

I held my breath at this point, elbows on the table and leaning towards Basher, who was earnestly drawing a maze of arrows and swirling lines on the back of a packet of John Players. 'Oh I don't know, perhaps you're right?' said Belfrey, 'but Pamela was *sure* it was a Frenchie. Says it has quite put her off garlic. Better leave it I think.'

Captain Albert Ball, VC, DSO and two bars, MC (14th August 1896 – 7th May 1917).

I cupped my hands over my face and exhaled. No, not a whiff of it, I thought. So feeling renewed confidence I suggested a top-up all round. I picked up our empties, nodding to one and all as I walked over to the bar, generally trying to effect a jaunty relaxed air. I was just standing patiently watching the barman pour a glass of Beaujolais and wondering what would be the chances of another tumble with Lady P when I heard a low throaty growl from behind. Next thing I felt a huge shove in the back which sent glasses, Beaujolais and my good self flying in all directions. I landed on the carpet, face down with a heavy weight pressing on me. My first thought was that Belfrey had suddenly seen the light and taken firm and decisive action, but screwing my head around I could see him standing just a few feet away from me with a look of puzzlement on his face.

It was Tungsten of course. I felt an agonizing pinch where he had my arm clamped in his jaws but with his great weight on top of me I was helpless to do anything about it. People came running from all directions and soon hauled him off. Eventually I managed to pick myself up and dust myself down as the barman dragged him growling behind the counter. 'No harm done, sir,' I said turning brightly to Belfrey, rubbing my arm. 'My, he's a lively fellow isn't he?'

There was another growl from behind the bar and Belfrey gave me a long look. He opened his mouth to say something but changed his mind, just grunting instead, as he turned his back on me to resume his conversation.

There was nothing else for it but to continue with my order. The barman meanwhile had locked Tungsten in the back room. 'Can't understand it, sir,' he said to me. 'Normally the Group Captain's dog is such a friendly fellow and I thought he liked you, sir.' He glanced at Belfrey standing some distance away. 'Mind you,' he said, lowering his voice, 'it's not the first time he's turned nasty, like. Do you remember that business with Pilot Officer Bovington? He needed 15 stitches I recall.'

I didn't remember it but I did remember Lady P's last visit to us and was wondering if Bovington's leering attendance on her in the mess bar might have gone a bit further than I had previously thought. I would have done anything to leave right away but of course I had to take the drinks back to the table and sit down again, shrugging off Sticky and Basher's concern. 'Didn't hurt a bit,' I lied. 'Now what was that about that aviator, Basher?'

'Radiator,' he sighed and pulled out his cigarette packet again.

I kept out of trouble for the rest of the evening. It was the typically riotous occasion that you'd expect in an officers mess populated with young men with nothing much to worry about apart from a million armed troops only a few miles away. Even Belfrey seemed quite jolly, if his loud laugh was anything to go by. He was at the far end of the table from us but I kept sensing his eyes boring into me. I risked a quick glance in his direction from time to time and, sure enough, whenever I looked at him he seemed to be staring back at me.

Someone had struck a deal with a local French Army unit to swap chefs for the evening so we had some exceptionally fine fare. I'm not sure what the French thought of the arrangement – and probably that's why they had no fight in them when the Germans turned up a few days later – but at least on Albert Ball night *we* were very well served. Later on, when our ties and tongues had been loosened by not a few bottles of the local produce, Basher demonstrated his expertise with the port by neatly removing the top of the bottle with the aid of hot tongs and an ice cube. According to him this was the only way to open a fine *Colheita* without disturbing the sediment and I suppose it would have been if some idiot (me) hadn't immediately grabbed the bottle and nearly dropped it. I've never been that fond of the stuff anyway so slopped out only a small measure for myself, passed the bottle to the right (to accompanying catcalls) and drained my glass with a single swig. I looked at my watch. 'Job done,' I thought with some relief. After all my recent shenanigans I was more than ready to hit the sack. I was just reckoning that at last it would be reasonable for me to slope off when I felt a tap on my shoulder.

It was Belfrey. 'Cordroy, isn't it?' he said.

'Kilroy, sir.'

'Yes, Kilfor. You might be interested to know that one of Sergeant Oliver's men used to work for Rolls Royce. And I mean on their cars – not the aero engines.'

'Yes, sir.'

'In the paint shop.'

'Yes, sir. Very good sir.' I wasn't sure where this was going but I had a feeling that, at the very least, I might be asked to pay for the paint.

He reached out to my lapel, with the Croix de Guerre still pinned there and stroked his chin. 'I think we should get to know each other better, young man. Dawn detail?' He looked at his watch. 'Shall we say zero eight may zero six hundred zulu?' This was service gobbledygook for six o' clock the next morning.* 'See you at Dispersal.'

'Why, yes sir. Zero six hundred sir? Thank you sir.' There didn't seem much else I could say. Under the circumstances it seemed like a let-off so I must have sounded genuinely grateful.

Once he had gone I took some joshing from Sticky and Basher. It was considered a great honour to accompany the station commander on these details. They had both been around longer than me but had yet to be asked.

'I wonder what plane you'll be in?' asked Basher. In peacetime Belfrey's outings were noted as much for the planes he got hold of as for what went on in the air. A de Haviland Comet was still spoken of in hushed tones in the mess. I guessed he must have very good contacts at the Air Ministry but, even so, I thought something exotic like a Comet† would be pretty unlikely so near the front line. More likely we'd be flying one of the planes already around and the choice was limited.

'It won't be a Hurricane, that's for sure,' ventured Sticky

It couldn't be the Hurricane because, we all knew, it would have to be a two seater. 'And it won't be the Tiger Moth either,' I ventured, slapping the table to applaud my own joke. Neither laughed and I could see Sticky glancing quickly towards the other end of the room.

Whatever other idiocies Belfrey might be guilty of, he was a superb aerobatic pilot. Legend had it that he'd put on the display of the tournament at a World Championship in Paris back in the thirties, in an

* "Zero eight may" means (Wednesday) 8th May, which was just two days before the German Blitzkrieg started on the 10th.

† The DH88 Comet was an experimental twin engine two seater all-wood aeroplane built by de Haviland in the mid thirties. Only five were ever built, one of which, "Grosvenor House", set several records in international air races. The Comet was influential in the design of the highly successful Mosquito, which saw much service for the allied air forces later in the war. http://tinyurl.com/Kilroy088.

Avro Tutor of all things.[*] I'd also heard that he would likely have won an Olympic medal at the 1936 Berlin Olympics had Hitler had his way and aerobatics been allowed as an Olympic sport.[†] 'Not one of those awful Fairey Battles?' I asked.

'God, I hope not for your sake,' muttered Sticky. We'd recently had a flight of Battles transferred to our airfield – poor sods. The Battle was the R.A.F.'s latest single engine bomber, at that time doing nothing more deadly than dropping bombs on the bombing range and leaflets on Cologne. It certainly wasn't noted for any aerobatic capability but was fast gaining a reputation for being shot down all too easily. In the end we had to conclude we'd no idea what Belfrey would wheel out next day but we had a pretty good idea what it would not be.

The next morning I was up before the dawn, flying boots polished, kit gleaming and everything (including me) bright and ready much earlier than needed. Standing outside in the courtyard was Florrie the Flatnose, an old Morris Oxford we'd recently acquired as officer transport.[‡] She was already loaded with 20 souls or more but I managed to squeeze myself onto the running board and cling on for the short trip to the airfield. As we passed the scene of my recent triumph and tragedy, I noticed that someone had cleared away the remains of the Tiger Moth but the bent Bentley was still there, looking like, well, like some idiot had landed an aeroplane on top of it. There were a few low whistles as we drove by and a couple of ribald remarks which I ignored and then the heavily laden Florrie rumbled to a stop and I stepped down.

The base was already abuzz, with one of our Hurricane flights taking off for a dawn patrol and the Fairey Battles being readied to be shot down God knows where. I found a parachute pack in the Dispersal hut and

---

[*] The first Aerobatics World Cup was held at Vincennes, Paris, in June 1934. Berhhard Fieseler won the event in a plane of his own design. There were also two fatalities and one near fatal crash. An Avro Tutor, an early R.A.F. trainer, *was* flown by Placido d'Abreu. There is no record of anyone by the name of Belfrey competing although it is possible his routine, mentioned by Kilroy, was a non-competitive display. Fieseler was the owner of the German aircraft manufacturer of the same name, which subsequently built several WWII aeroplanes and also the infamous V-1 "doodlebug", an early cruise missile. http://tinyurl.com/Kilroy089.

[†] There was an Olympic Air Display at Berlin's Tempelhof aerodrome immediately prior to the 1936 Olympics, which featured an international aerobatic contest but there were no flying competitions in the Olympics proper. Gliding was included as a "demonstration" sport – the only time it has featured in the Olympics.

[‡] The Morris Oxford "flat-nose" saloon car dates from the late 1920s. The nickname came from its flat-nose radiator which replaced the distinctive earlier "bull-nose" design. http://tinyurl.com/Kilroy090.

clipped it on, while wondering where Belfrey was. Some ground crew were wrestling with a tarpaulin over an aeroplane nearby. It was a Miles Magister.

You might recall that the Miles Magister figured briefly in my little encounter with Enid Blyton. As I stood looking at it that morning I was thinking that I'd been right – it really was a natural for a children's story as from a distance it looked just like a toddler's toy plane anyway – a little low wing monoplane, painted bright yellow, a single underpowered engine and two open cockpits in tandem, each with its own dinky little windscreen. I'd never actually flown in one but could see it offered much improved visibility over the R.A.F.'s other trainer, the Tiger Moth – no wings or rigging or anything at all overhead the cockpits, just pure open air.*

So there was the Maggie, gleaming in the morning sun with the faint smell of petrol wafting towards me. I turned my head to look at the sky above. It was a beautiful clear day dawning. I screwed up my eyes and stared hard into the sun, now making itself felt, just above the horizon. There was a voice behind me. 'No need to worry about Jerry,' I heard.

Miles Magister.

I turned around and there was Belfrey, making quite a sight. I'd been warned to expect something like this but even so it was hard not to let my jaw drop. From the waist up he looked like someone who had just popped out of the billiard room, resplendent in a maroon smoking jacket. Down below he had on some ridiculously baggy flannel trousers, flapping around in the gentle breeze. I'd been told he'd been a naval pilot in the Great War, in the R.N.A.S.†, and had developed a liking for naval garb then – hence his "Bags" nickname – although quite honestly "Bats" would have suited him better as he'd clearly landed on his head rather too often over the years. At first I thought he was carrying a billiard cue but on closer inspection I realised it was a rifle. 'Too early for Jerry, I think.' He sniffed and looked up at the sky. 'But if he does show up we'll have this to sort him out.' And he threw the rifle to me.

* The Miles Magister was bought by the R.A.F. in attempt to modernise their training programme – teaching pilots to fly in an aeroplane approximating the sort of planes they would be flying on operations. It was also popular as unofficial transport for pilots going on leave. http://tinyurl.com/Kilroy091.

† Royal Naval Air Service.

He must have seen my puzzled look. 'Lee Enfield,' he said as he started some stretching exercises. 'In the last show my observer bagged a couple of tri-deckers before breakfast with one of these and we had a right old session in the bar that night, I can tell you.'

I started fiddling with the safety catch. Belfrey came up to me and I thought he was going to take it back but instead he punched my parachute clip. The chute slid off my shoulders and onto the ground. 'No room for that with the optional upholstery,' he barked, picking it up and throwing it to one of the airmen. 'Follow me. You'll soon get the idea.' He climbed onto the wing and I followed. I could see that instead of the usual bare metal seats the plane had been fitted out with bulky embroidered seat cushions.

'Lady Dorothy,' he said with a sigh.

I looked puzzled.

'My first wife.' He gestured at the rear seat. 'You can have "The Death of Richthofen". I could just make out what looked like a splintered red aeroplane with a speech bubble above containing the word "Arrgh". He pointed at the front cockpit. 'I will take "Mannock's Revenge".

I didn't answer as I was struggling to get into my seat. My intercom cable had become wound around the throttle control and I was trying not to drop the rifle as I untangled it.

'You've not been in one of these before?' Belfrey asked.

I shook my head.

'Well you don't have to make such a dog's dinner of it. Look,' he said, grabbing the rifle and showing me where to put my feet before shoving me hard down into the seat. I sat there, feeling bewildered as I tried to find the various harness straps. Belfrey sighed, reached over and located each of them, quickly getting me trussed and strapped in tight and handing me back the rifle as he climbed into the cockpit in front.

A few minutes later we were at five thousand feet. There were some light wisps of cirrus up high but otherwise it was all pale blue above with the chequerboard of northern France lying neatly below.

Of course the old boy was right. With the Phoney War still going full tilt we didn't have much to worry about on the Hermann front. Nonetheless I found myself wondering what we'd do with a downhill downwind flat-out speed of 150 mph if a 109 showed up. I certainly didn't think my party piece in the Tiger Moth would work a second time. I screwed my head around nervously to see if we had company but I couldn't see anything.

Suddenly the plane lurched upwards and twisted. The plane was dual control so I could feel exactly what Belfrey was up to as my control stick moved in unison with his. I guessed this must be the start of his aerobatics routine. It was an Immelman and very neatly executed. I could hear Belfrey over the intercom. 'You can keep your ruddy Hurricanes,' he said, as we executed a perfect loop. 'Anyone can aerobat with a thousand horse power up front.' We started a barrel roll. 'Whereas this... this is a challenge,' and I could hear the note of satisfaction in his voice.

My worries about the Hun were rather forgotten at this point. As I've already mentioned Belfrey was a superb pilot and I was rather enjoying myself. 'Let's try some negative G,' I heard him say and we half rolled and carried on in straight and level flight, only inverted.

The first thing you notice with negative G is that all the muck and rubbish on the floor comes floating up and this is where an open cockpit is advantageous, since it floats up to head height then just disappears forever out into the slipstream. It's strange looking "up" to see the ground and "down" to see the sky, but we'd done plenty of this sort of stuff in training so I just let him get on with it, hanging comfortably in my safety harness and remembering to push my feet lightly back onto the rudder pedals.

Suddenly the plane started lurching up and down. We were still upside down. I wondered if we were having engine problems as I wasn't aware of any aerobatics manoeuvre like that. 'Everything okay sir?' I asked.

There was no reply and all I could hear was his heavy breathing over the intercom. Eventually he came on. 'Still with me?' he asked.

'Yes, sir.'

'Okay, let's do a bunt then we'll have you back on the ground in a jiffy.' He righted the plane and applied full power for a gentle climb.

The bunt, or *outside* loop, takes the plane around a full circle of a vertical loop but unlike a normal loop your head is *away* from the centre. It sounds simple enough but with lots of negative gravity to contend with it's a very uncomfortable manoeuvre for both pilot and passenger. We started on it with the nose slowly dipping below the horizon, then with the engine roaring we went over into the vertical. I expected Belfrey to ease back on the throttle but he didn't. Even with a feeble old Magister it doesn't take long pointing downwards at full throttle to pile into the ground but of course the old boy knew what he was about and he just kept pushing us on and on around the loop. By the time we reached the halfway point I wasn't enjoying it at all. We were going like the clappers, upside down, with the blood rushing to my head and my body doing its level best to shoot out of the cockpit. I remember thinking how glad I was of my five point harness, what with my parachute being safely stowed back at Dispersal, then I felt something give.

When something like that happens you don't waste time investigating. You grab the nearest handhold you can and scream for help. 'Christ, Belfrey, pull out, pull out,' I yelled. There was no reaction. I was being catapulted out of my seat and scrambling frantically at the dashboard made no difference to anything. The next thing I knew my knees had banged on something and I was in the full blast of the slipstream and I was falling.

***

I don't suppose you've been wondering much about Oscar recently, have you? You might recall that the bountiful Lady P was somewhat besotted with Oscar the cat and his heterochromatism, or wall-eye as I called it, and that I'd rather foolishly rescued the wretched beast from a blazing Hurricane a few months back. I didn't know it at the time but this was a key moment in my life (and his). You've probably guessed that my noble rescue attempt inevitably led to Lady P's bedroom and you'd be right. At any rate she confessed later that her heart first went out to "her noble Hector" (me) on that day he had "fearlessly held the pass at Thermopylae"* (rescued the blinking moggie). But there's more to it than that. Some might even say that for a few short months in 1940 my destiny and Oscar's were entwined. You are no doubt thinking, 'What a load of old horse manure,' but hear me out. I don't normally believe in such tosh either but, call me superstitious, I can say that at least the cat and I both survived the war and each of us with not a few adventures along the way too.

Ollie, the ground crew chief, seemed to be almost as besotted with the cat as was Lady P. 'You see, sir,' he'd told me earlier on the day of the Albert Ball dinner, 'he might be a French cat but I don't think he likes the French very much.'

I liked Ollie and he knew his way around a Merlin better than any, but there were times he spouted the most amazing nonsense.

'As soon as we R.A.F. showed up he was here, sir.'

I tried to look impressed.

'And the noise. The bigger and noisier it is the more he likes it.'

This was true. I'd seen Oscar snoozing in the grass only yards away when the fitters were running a Merlin at full bore.

'But some of the locals, they think he's bewitched.'

'Oh, come on, Ollie, these country folk can be a right superstitious lot.'

'You ask them, sir. They all know him because of that funny eye. And what about the bus crash?'

'What about it?'

'He was on it.'

'What, a cat caught a bloody bus? Did he have a ticket? You'll be telling me next that goods train pile-up was his doing.'

---

* Lady Pamela's Greek history is a little awry here. Hector is a character from Homer's mythology, a prince who fought in the Trojan War – http://tinyurl.com/Kilroy093. The defence of the pass at Thermopylae is a real historical event that occurred in 480 BC, during the second Persian invasion of Greece. A tiny Greek force held out there for three days against the might of the Persian army – http://tinyurl.com/Kilroy092.

'No, not the train sir but I do know old man Duval said he'd throw him on the fire if he ever comes anywhere near his farm again.'

The Duvals' farm was the temporary home for most of our ground crews. 'Blimey, that's a bit much,' I said.

'That was after his tractor ran into the river on the day after young Marie fell off her bike.'

'What?'

'The cat was hiding in the saddlebag sir and her tyre burst suddenly.'

'And the next day the cat let the brake off on the tractor I suppose.'

'No sir, but he was in the trailer all the while. And, don't forget, it was Grandma Duval who broke her leg on the bus too. I said the cat didn't like the Frogs much. Well he'd do well to steer well clear of them now I'd say.'

'Oh, Lordy, Ollie, you've been having a bit too much Pernod, that's what you've been doing.'*

'And what about here, sir?' His eyes had taken on a slightly mad gleam. I made to walk away but he grabbed the cuff of my jacket.

'What?'

'Here. This station. There's the crash you rescued him from, sir, and then your little, er, incident yesterday with the Tiger Moth.'

'But he was nowhere near the wretched machine.'

'He was, sir. We found him sound asleep in the wreckage after you went to hospital.'

I sighed.

'Well sir. You can believe me or not but I'd watch out. That's *five* crashes I make it. He's a nice enough fellow on the ground but he loves hanging around the aeroplanes and, with his record, I wouldn't want to go up in an aeroplane with him if I were you, sir.'

Later that day Oscar was, as usual, hanging around the aeroplanes – sometimes chased away by the ground crews and at other times fed, photographed and petted by Pamela. One particular plane took his fancy. It had a heady smell of dope from its newly painted wings that made him pleasantly drowsy. He found a comfy spot well inside the fuselage where the control cables ran and he could sleep undisturbed, without the riggers and fitters even knowing he was there.

The next morning he was awoken when the tarpaulin covering was pulled off and the plane was shunted around on the grass. He was used to lots of hustle and bustle and didn't stir. Two men climbed aboard and the

* French farmers were highly superstitions of cats at one time. Although the practice had largely died out by the 1800s, cat persecution was widespread around Europe, and especially in France, for many centuries. The French have phrases like "cour à mioud" ("courimaud") meaning "cat chaser" and "faire le chat" – pass the cat, which all relate to past unpleasant rituals. For example see: http://tinyurl.com/Kilroy094.

engine started. The noise didn't bother him. In fact he liked the racket it made and all the bouncing and bumping as the plane roared across the airfield.

Then they were airborne. The bumping stopped but he could still hear the steady thrum of the engine – a nice smooth mechanical purring which he liked to listen to. As the plane climbed higher he could sense the air getting colder and a little thinner but he still felt comfortable. Some time after that he felt the plane twisting and turning and wrenching up and down. He'd been in planes before of course and there was that terrible flight that ended with the fire but he'd never been bucked around as badly as this. And he wasn't keen on it at all. He climbed through the fuselage hoping for a more comfortable spot, but if anything it was worse there. He'd wormed his way past the man at the rear, the one who had pulled him out of the burning plane, and was down at the feet of the other man, just by the rudder pedals, when it happened.

Suddenly the weight just came off his paws and he was helpless to do anything about it as he was thrown into the air. He was terrified. Evidently the man behind didn't like what was going on either because he had started hollering and shouting too. Oscar knew, instinctively, that as long as he could stay inside the cockpit he would be safe but he could feel some huge invisible force trying to throw him out. In his terror he had his claws fully extended and had managed to sink them into a cushion but he knew it wouldn't be enough to hold him for very long.

Then he spotted it. An expanse of leg, a hairy shin with a rather odd sort of baggy trouser leg flapping around it. Normally he wouldn't dream of taking such liberties but here, there seemed no alternative. He bunched up his hind legs and leapt, tensing his front paws so his claws would get maximum purchase on landing. After some frantic scrambling he reached comparative safety – some way up the trouser leg, hanging onto the man's knee and safe at last from being thrown out of the cockpit. Now the man started shouting and was trying to beat him through the trouser leg. Oscar knew his claws would be hurting him but what could he do? He tried to pull them in but the beating and thumping got more insistent and was becoming quite painful so in an attempt to escape he scampered even higher up. Then the beating stopped. He realised the man was trying to push him back down the trouser leg. Well there was no way he was going to succeed there. He just needed something soft and compliant to sink his claws into and then even Hell and her five kittens wouldn't shift him.*

***

* For an hilarious (and less painful) stowaway cat incident see the YouTube video: http://tinyurl.com/Kilroy095.

It was the intercom cable that saved me. This was the cable from my flying helmet which plugged into the dashboard. Fortunately it was a sturdy service issue arrangement designed to withstand the gormless machinations of generations of R.A.F. trainee pilots and was enough, just, to provide me a lifeline as I hung desperately clinging onto it, buffeted in the slipstream.

Belfrey still seemed oblivious to my plight. I'm sure I wouldn't have been able to hold onto the cable for very long but fortunately I didn't have to. I didn't know it at the time but this was thanks to the timely intervention of Oscar. Suddenly the plane righted itself and I could hear Belfrey roaring and shouting and see him beating at something in his lap. The plane was careering about, bucking and zig-zagging all over the place, but at least it was the right way up so I wasted no time in scrambling back in the cockpit, head-first as it happens, but any way up was good enough for me.

And there I stayed, arms tightly clamped around the seat bottom. I gathered that all was not well up front. Despite its recent traumas my intercom still worked and I could hear all Belfrey's yelps and cries as the plane seemed to be charging all over the sky At one stage I heard Belfrey command, 'You have control,' which was the signal for me to take over the flying but I was scarcely in any position to do so.

I heard afterwards that the entire airbase paused operations to watch our arrival. It was fresh eggs for breakfast that day but, no matter, Sticky, Basher and most of the squadron went without in order to watch the fun.

I never did manage to get myself right way up in the cockpit so had no idea what was going on but apparently the sight of my legs waving freely in the breeze certainly added to the overall theatre as the plane weaved and plunged on its way around the circuit. Sticky insisted I had been signalling 'Fuck off' in semaphore as we flew the downwind leg but I don't think anyone else noticed. In any case, all I knew at the time was that there was some sort of immense struggle going on in the front cockpit and I just hoped that good would prevail and we would make a safe return to Mother Earth.

We nearly didn't. Belfrey messed up the final approach and the plane stalled about 30 feet above the grass. 'Nosed down and dropped like a stone,' Sticky told me later, with some relish. The nose dug in and I was flung out of the cockpit, sailing over the propeller, landing some distance away and tumbling over and over in the grass.

I must have banged my head because I don't recall anything more until I awoke in hospital. I was still there the next day and had a visit from Ollie who told me Belfrey had fared rather better than me, with only minor bruising in evidence. I guess he must have also carried a laceration or two in the most unlikely of places but, if he did, he didn't seem in any hurry to tell anyone about it. There was something else that Ollie couldn't wait to tell me. 'You see sir, when we went to pick you up and get you on the stretcher, you'll never guess who we found nuzzling up and trying to poke his head into your flying suit?'

***

Shortly after we were in full retreat and, along with much else, Oscar was left behind at Condé-Vraux. That should have been the last I heard of him but it wasn't. Years after the war I met up with Ollie, who was by then in a wheelchair. During the hostilities Ollie and I had both qualified for the Goldfish Club* and we were attending their annual dinner which, that year, was in the National Maritime Museum in London. After the meal I was pushing him slowly through one of the galleries when he grabbed the wheelchair wheels to bring us to a stop and cried, 'Look.'

He was pointing at a painting. 'What?' I said.

'There.'

All I could see was a rather uninteresting watercolour.

'It's Oscar,' he said, all excited, like he'd just stumbled upon the crown jewels.

Oscar/Unsinkable Sam on gangplank – ship unknown.

'Who's he?' I replied. 'You don't mean that picture of a blinking cat, do you?' At that moment I didn't know what Ollie was on about. The picture was indeed a portrait of a cat and, I thought, a rather unlikely exhibit to find its way into the exalted company of Captain Cook, Lord Nelson, Jellicoe and so on. It might seem strange, as you've read the story here, but despite the pivotal role Oscar played in my life for those weeks in 1940 I'd rather forgotten about him in the intervening decades.

It didn't take long for Ollie to remind me.

I peered closely at the picture. I could see it was expertly drawn but in the end, I thought, it was just a picture of a mundane looking black and white cat. 'I suppose Oscar did look like that though,' I admitted. 'But what's wrong with his eye? It looks all sort of smudged.'

'That's the whole point. The eye,' said Ollie, getting all excited. 'Don't you remember, sir? Oscar's wonky eye?'

We'd both left the services many years before but Ollie still called me "sir" occasionally, usually in moments of high excitement. I'd forgotten all

---

* Goldfish Club membership is open to anybody whose life was saved after they "came down in the drink" – ditched or parachuted into the sea. Club website: http://tinyurl.com/Kilroy096.

about the eye until then, but then it came back to me – the heterochromatism that Pamela had always been faffing on about. I stared closely at the portrait. Viewed straight on it was unremarkable but, with the light reflecting on it at the right angle, you could see an odd smudge of blue and green colouring in the iris of one eye. 'By golly, I think you're right,' I declared, getting a little excited myself. 'There can't be many cats that would match that.' I looked it up later and found that complete heterochromatism, where one eye is a uniformly odd colour, is common in cats, but the partial condition, which Oscar had, was much, much, much rarer. 'Well I'll be damned,' I said, standing back to admire the picture more fully.

Ollie wheeled himself up close to examine the picture minutely. 'I just knew he was something special,' he said. 'Three crashes with the Frogs then three with us – the little rascal.' He turned to examine the placard alongside. 'Bloody hell, sir. The Bismarck!' he declared, punching his fist into his outstretched palm. He paused to read on. 'And the Cossack and then the Ark Royal! What a little star! Effing hell, sir, pardon my French.'*

* The picture Kilroy describes is "Oscar, the Bismarck's Cat", a pastel portrait by the artist Georgina Shaw-Baker which is in the possession of the National Maritime Museum at Greenwich in London. Oscar was famous for surviving three warship sinkings within a few months in 1941 – two Royal Navy ships and the Bismarck.

Hitherto there has been no information on Oscar's earlier life. If Kilroy's account is to be believed we have the extraordinary possibility that he had already had a distinguished, not to say extraordinarily destructive career in French agriculture and with the R.A.F. before he even started with the Kriegsmarine. See *End Note (7)*.

PART THREE: WAR

1940

There'll be bluebirds over
The white cliffs of Dover
Tomorrow, just you wait and see

There'll be love and laughter
And peace ever after
Tomorrow, when the world is free.

Written in 1940, recorded by Vera Lynn in 1942
Words and Music by Walter Kent and Nat Burton
http://tinyurl.com/Kilroy205

CHAPTER 1

I was sitting in the back of a car and I was puzzled. I felt warm and comfortable, snug even, but couldn't work out how long I'd been there or how I'd got there. And where was I anyway? The car's engine wasn't running and the front seats were both vacant so clearly we must be parked somewhere – that much was obvious. Then I noticed a curious drumming sound coming from the roof and, preposterously, had the feeling that we were floating gently through a grey dark cloud. I puzzled over this for some time, until it came to me that it might even be heavy rain that I was hearing and that, just possibly, the windows had steamed up. I wiped a patch clear and, sure enough, it was bucketing down outside.

The car was hardly fresh from the assembly line. There was a strong smell of stale wine and gauloises coming from the upholstery, some of the roof lining had come adrift and one of the seat covers was ripped. Then it came to me. It was our very own officers' carriage of many a celebratory evening – dear old Florrie the flat-nose.

I took a deep breath and stared through the clear patch in the window. We were parked on a narrow straight road and, stretching as far as I could see, was a miserable procession of humanity. There were cars, lorries and bikes, nose to tail, all the way to the horizon. Then, beside the road and on foot, were men and women, old and young, and children too. All of them had their heads down and their coats and jackets tightly buttoned as they trudged along, getting spattered as the vehicles crawled by. They were pushing prams, trolleys or in fact anything with wheels that could carry their suitcases, boxes and other paraphernalia.

'Ah, you're awake, sir?' This was Ollie, poking his head through the driver's window. 'It's no-go I'm afraid. Two of the valves have...'

'Ollie, where are we?'

Ollie looked puzzled. 'Why, just outside Wipers, sir.'

'Ypres?' I gave it the correct French pronunciation. 'But...'

'Where I picked you up, sir.' Ollie opened the door, climbed in and sat down in front of me. 'Any ideas what next, sir?'

I looked at my watch. The glass was broken and the second hand not moving.

'Well the car's kaput,' Ollie continued, 'And the Krauts are most probably having coffee and croissants in Amiens by now, sir. CO said he wanted me out and back ASAP, lest we got cut off.'

'Amiens?!' I exclaimed. Amiens was on the Somme, deep inside France and not that far from the coast. 'What a load of nonsense. They can't possibly have got there from Belgium overnight?'

There was a pause and I could see Ollie peering anxiously at me in the rear-view mirror. 'Look, er, are you alright sir?'

'Yes, of course I am, dammit.'

'It's just that the Jerries shot out of Belgium ages ago, sir. Cut through our lines at Sedan.' He paused and stroked his chin. 'Must have been ten days ago I'd say. Since then they've clobbered their way through... ooh,' he was counting on his fingers, 'St Quentin, Peronne, le Cateau, Cambrai and, er, I forget where else now, sir. Oh yes, and Reims too of course. The AVM* left there pretty sharpish a few days back I gather.'

It was my turn to pause for thought. 'Ollie, what date is it?'

'Why, Monday, sir.'

'No, the date Ollie, the date.'

'20th May, sir.' He glanced in the mirror again. 'Or it might be the 21st come to think of it – I haven't seen a newspaper for a while.'†

That gave me a jolt. The last thing I could remember was a forced landing at Reims airport just after the balloon went up and then being attacked by Stukas an hour or so later for my pains.‡ That would have been on the 10th or thereabouts I reckoned. 'Crikey, Ollie, what have I been doing for the last ten days?'

He wiped the windscreen and sighed as he looked up at the sky. 'Well you've been in the thick of it, sir. Several sorties a day. Look, do you not remember any of it?' I could see him frowning at me in the mirror. 'Came back with your kite full of holes a few times too. Cox and Dunton had a right old job keeping her airworthy. Shame she's gone now, sir, but at least you're still in one piece.'

This took some digesting. Me – in the thick of it? The thought of all that hostile jagged metal shrieking around my soft pink body made me feel quite queasy. Just as well I'd blacked it out. I'd never have thought I had the nerve. 'What about the others, Ollie? Are they all alright?'

'Well, I'm afraid Sergeant Stanley bought it on Friday, sir, and Officers Thomas and Welham are missing like you were but we're still hoping they'll

---

* Air Vice Marshal Playfair, Commander in Chief of the R.A.F.'s Advanced Air Striking Force – http://tinyurl.com/Kilroy097. His headquarters in Reims was abandoned on 15th May. It is now an hotel – Chateau les Crayeres: http://tinyurl.com/Kilroy098.

† The German forces took Amiens on 21st May.

‡ Reims airport, which was a key airbase for the R.A.F., was attacked by the Luftwaffe on the first day of the Blitzkrieg, 10th May. http://tinyurl.com/Kilroy099.

turn up. Made the Hun pay for it anyway, that's for sure, sir. Squadron's got 25 of the bast..., I mean Jerries, already sir.'

The casualties Ollie mentioned hadn't been with the squadron long enough for me to know them well. I'd once seen Stanley in a bar doing a trick with a glass of beer, drinking from the wrong side and emptying it down his throat without a drop spilled. When was that? Must have been all of two weeks ago. Strange to think he wouldn't be doing that ever again. 'Twenty five on the scorecard, you say Ollie? I don't suppose it's possible that I...?'

'Well, not exactly, sir.'

'What do you mean "not exactly" Ollie? Surely I either got one of the blighters or I didn't?'

'Oh, crikey, sir. Do you not remember? Last Wednesday, downed one good and proper.'

I nodded. 'And?'

'Turned out to be a Frog, sir. A Frog fighter.'

'No?!'

'He's okay though sir. In hospital in Paris. In fact both of them are.'

'Both?!'

'CO says you got another just before you got shot down over there, sir.' He pointed up at a dark cloud hanging over the town. 'That one's okay too. Last we heard is that he *will* walk again, so that's good and all's fair in love and war as they say, sir?'

Dewoitine D 520.

'I'm surprised the CO wants me anywhere near his squadron if that's the best I can do.'

'Well, sir, not for me to say, but he did seem especially keen to have you back.'

'Meaning what Ollie?'

'Well, sir, you know how he can go off on one at times? Well...' He paused and looked nervously at me in the mirror.

'What, Ollie?'

'Well, not for me to say, sir. But I don't think he was being fair anyway. Those Dewoitines of their's do look a lot like 109s and it's not as if their flak boys are on the ball is it? Always popping off at us too.'

I was about to question him further but at that moment a car rumbled to a stop alongside us. Our two cars, side by side were now blocking the road and, almost immediately, a cacophony of car horns started blasting from further back.

Ollie got out and a short while later he poked his head back through the window. 'Frenchies, sir. Army, and one of 'em's quite the *large fromage* I'd say. I can't really understand much of what they're saying but I think the gist of it is that they've run out of petrol.'

'And?'

'Well, they might as well have ours, sir, as we're not going anywhere? We've got a siphon in the back and, with your French perhaps you could ask them for a lift? They've plenty of room – only two of them in the car.'

A few minutes later and we were on our way. When I'd seen what was on offer I'd nearly refused to get in. It was a French army staff car – a Citroën and a well-known model called a *Traction Avant*, which means "front wheel drive". This may sound innocent to you and indeed it looked harmless enough as it stood there, black paintwork sparkling in the rain and little flags flapping on the bonnet, but I'd only ever been in one once before in my life. That was a few years previously, back in England, and after we were involved in a terrible accident I'd vowed never to go near another. But needs must in time of war so there I was, a few minutes later, sitting in the back of the wretched vehicle, with a five star Général d'Armée holding my hand.

'Mon ami,' he said, pausing to wipe his nose with his free hand, 'mon sauveur.'

I didn't know it at the time but I was cosying up with Général Gaston-Henri Billotte, the Commander-in-Chief of the British, French and Belgian armies – the man in charge of the whole caboodle, in short. 'Ah, merci, mon Général. Merci de nous transporter,' I replied in my politest French. I felt his grip tightening if anything. I'd been quite a while in France by then of course and had become used to some of their strange ways but couldn't recall anything in *The Field Service Pocket Book*[*] that would help me with this situation. I just rather weakly tried to disengage, but of course he wasn't having it.

He gestured at the heavens with his free hand and, as he turned to face me, I could see faint tracks running down each cheek. There was moisture welling up in both eyes. 'Ah, monsieur, après moi, le déluge,' he said with a grimace.

And the rain chose that moment to stop. The driver smartly flicked off the windscreen wipers and, as if on cue, the sun came out from behind a cloud. Ollie, sitting alongside the driver, made some silly remark about no wipers in Wipers.

[*] *The Field Service Pocket Book* was published by the War Office over many years and issued to British officers in both world wars. It contains instructions on how to organise billets, bivouacs, burial parties, and much else besides but, as Kilroy says, it offers nothing on soothing French generals. Amazon: http://tinyurl.com/Kilroy100.

I didn't reply. I was thinking back to when I was 14. Pater, Helga and I had been driving through the Dorset countryside in just such a car. Citroëns weren't that common in England then and I couldn't recall how Pater had come by it – most likely he'd taken it in part payment for some business deal that had gone wrong. He certainly got rid of it quickly enough, after the accident that is, so it only figured in our lives for a few days at most.

Meanwhile, on the road from Ypres, Monsieur le Général was rabbiting on about the *Entente Cordiale* and all those brave English airmen. I nodded politely, while doing my best to ignore him. I didn't know it at the time but he'd just been at a conference with the British. The war was going very badly for us by then and one of our generals became so exasperated with his spinelessness that he grabbed him by the lapels and shook him.* At last my friend, the Général, nodded off. I seized my opportunity to free myself from his grasp and sit forward on the edge of my seat where I could more easily see what was going on upfront. I've often wondered what would have happened in the Battle of France had I simply had some shut-eye too at that moment. Everyone, from Lord Gort† downwards would no doubt say that it would have made no difference and that we were destined to lose, come what may, but I do wonder at times.

In the mid-thirties, the Citroën was an acclaimed design. André-Gustave Citroën, the company founder, had done what no one else had done before – that is to connect the engine to the same wheels that did the steering, thus keeping all the important mechanical stuff at the front – hence the name *Traction Avant.* He also came up with a number of other innovations I won't bore you with but there was one feature particularly relevant to this account. The Citroën had unusual front doors which were hinged at the rear, not at the front as is more or less universal these days. Some would say this was further evidence of Monsieur Citroën's genius since this innovative arrangement allowed the chic lady passenger maximum opportunity to display her wares on entry and exit. Nowadays people in the car trade call this arrangement "suicide doors"

Citroën Traction Avant.

* This was General Edmund Ironside. He shook him by the button on his tunic. http://tinyurl.com/Kilroy101.

† Commander-in-chief of the British Expeditionary Force.

– not in front of the customers of course, but there are good reasons why they fell from favour.*

The Général was snoring gently and Ollie, in the front, was studying a map. I remember thinking that at least our French car was on a French road.

That day in Dorset, we were in a French car on an English road and that had some significance in what was to follow. I remembered it as a clear sunny morning with the car bowling along nicely, down a narrow country road with its gentle twists, turns and undulations. We were looking for a Post Office, which Pater claimed was in a village nearby. We zipped past a couple of lads, about my age, fooling around on bicycles on the other side of the road. I went to wind the window down and shout at them to watch out. That's when it happened.

Further out from Ypres the road had widened a little, the crowds of refugees had thinned and we had picked up speed. The sun was beating down on us. Ollie announced that he was feeling hot and went to wind down the window. I shouted a warning and lunged forward.

I only meant to shout a cheeky remark at the cyclists but, being in an unfamiliar car, I mixed up the door handle with the window winder. I realised my mistake almost at once but it was too late. The door opened just a fraction momentarily but was immediately caught in the slipstream. I felt a sharp tug and then it was wrenched from my grasp, flying wide open and crashing all the way back onto the rear passenger door.

I shouldn't have panicked. I should have just waited for Pater to come to a stop then gently closed the door but, eager to put things right immediately and, ever mindful of Pater's famous temper, I grabbed a handle on the dashboard with one hand, reaching through the open doorway and behind me with the other, feeling for some means to quickly pull it shut. I managed to locate the door's strap before we stopped and was just heaving it closed when we saw the motorcyclist. He was cresting the brow of a hill immediately in front of us and heading our way, fast.

As it happened, Ollie knew what he was doing in the car outside Ypres and *had* reached for the window winder. What he saw was some lunatic (yours truly) lunging for the door handle, and being well versed in the ways of suicide doors he fought to stop him.

Back in Dorset, Pater cried out and attempted to swerve in towards the kerb. A collision seemed unavoidable. The motorcyclist was going way too fast. It was a narrow

---

*The Citroën Traction Avant was produced from 1934 to 1956, but with considerable disruption during the war. It featured a number of innovations in addition to its front wheel drive – a "unibody chassis", independent suspension and a strong lightweight construction which meant it was fast and fuel efficient. At the time it was considered rakish and sporty, and is still sought after by classic car collectors today. http://tinyurl.com/Kilroy102.

The arrangement with the front doors was not so unusual at that time. They have since come to be known as "suicide doors". Rear doors that open this way are called "kidnap doors". http://tinyurl.com/Kilroy103.

road and, adding to the difficulties, my passenger door, which just happened to be wide open at that very moment, wasn't on the pavement side, as it would have been in an English car, but was on the road side and blocking most of the oncoming lane. I could hear the screech as the motorbike skidded and saw smoke coming from its tyres. The bike was still moving fast and by then was so near that I could see the rider's gritted teeth, and his terrified eyes behind his goggles. Just when I thought a crash was inevitable he must have swerved or something because there was a roar and a whoosh as he slipped past us.

We came to a stop, unscathed, but our motorcyclist's troubles were only just beginning. Having swerved to avoid us he was now heading straight for the young boys at the roadside. I swivelled around in my seat in time to see him clip one of their bikes, and then his own large machine crashed onto the road with a shriek of metal.

My fight with Ollie spilled over to the driver's side of the car. We each thought we were trying to stop the other from opening the door. By then I was more than halfway over and into the front and somehow my leg got stuck in the steering wheel. The driver jammed on the brakes and we started to skid into the oncoming traffic.

At first I thought the motorbike rider had been lucky. He wasn't tangled up in the wreckage of his bike but had been thrown over the handlebars and was sailing through the air, across the road with a nice flat grass verge to land on.

I couldn't dislodge my leg from the steering wheel and the driver was still braking hard. With the two in combination it was inevitable. The car rolled. I can't say how many times. Lots. I just covered my head with my arms, pulled myself into a ball and wished for it to stop.

The motorbike had slithered to a stop. We too were at a stop and the boys were lying still by the side of the road. Only the motorcyclist himself was still in motion, hurtling at some speed, headfirst with arms outstretched, towards the verge.

We were still rolling over and over when I caught a glimpse of a truck, just a split second before it ploughed into us. The impact felt like a punch. There was a deafening bang and the car crumpled all around me, but it was the screeching of metal I remember most. It seemed to last an eternity and then, at last, we were at rest. I opened my eyes. I felt breathless and stunned and was unsure whether I was hurt. Then I heard the hissing steam and smelt the petrol and I knew we all needed to get out and quickly. In the broken tangle of car and people I found I was lying near the Général. He was deathly pale, his eyes were closed and there was a stream of blood coming from his ear.

There was a rock in the verge. Just the one in an otherwise beautifully flat expanse of grass. I just knew what was going to happen and held my breath and shut my eyes. And, in the sudden silence, I plainly heard the noise as the poor man's head struck it – a loud thwack sounding like a direct hit in a coconut shy. I jumped out of the car and ran to him where he lay by the side of the road. He was deathly pale, his eyes were closed and there was a stream of blood coming from his ear.

Pater must have come up behind me because suddenly I felt myself being grabbed. 'Back in the car. Quick.' Helga was over with the boys and he grabbed her as well. 'Quickly, both of you.'

We looked at each other.

'Did you not see who that was?' Pater asked. 'Quickly now. In the car. We'll have to get help.'

I think it was Ollie who pulled us out of the wreckage. He and the driver managed to flag down an army lorry and the Général was carted off to hospital where, I subsequently heard, he died a couple of days later. His death wasn't much mourned by the allies although it certainly troubled me when I heard of it.*

Elsewhere, in Dorset, Pater gunned the engine and we raced up the road, away from the carnage. He was convinced there was a hospital nearby but, if there was, we never found it. After fruitlessly chasing up and down country lanes Helga at last made him stop by a phone box, where he made the call. 'Ambulance is on its way,' he announced, with a sigh of relief, as he climbed back in the car.

Helga suggested we should go back. 'Nothing we can do,' he answered as he shook his head. 'Did you not see who that was?' he repeated.

His death was widely reported. He was Leading Aircraftman T. E. Shaw, better known as Lawrence of Arabia. He suffered head injuries and died six days after the accident, without regaining consciousness. Unlike the Général, there was no doubt that he was a great man and he was much mourned.†

---

* Général Gaston Billotte was the chief coordinator for all operations of the French, Belgian and British armies in Belgium and must take much of the blame for the Allies' disastrous campaign there. The car crash followed a conference with the British in Ypres and he died, without regaining conciousness on 23rd May 1940. The British general, Henry Pownall, said 'With all respect, he's no loss to us in this emergency.' http://tinyurl.com/Kilroy104.

† An inquest held a few days after Lawrence's death returned a verdict of "accidental death". The two boys on bicycles had only superficial injuries and were exonerated. Some witnesses reported seeing a private black motor car heading in the opposite direction immediately before the crash. The owner of this car never came forward. See *End Note (8)*.

CHAPTER 2

Once the Général had been taken away, Ollie and I were left standing at the roadside, both somewhat shaken by recent events but otherwise unhurt. We still had the problem of getting back to the squadron, which had moved from Condé-Vraux while I'd been in hospital. It hadn't moved far and, on an uncluttered road in untroubled times, it would have been a simple three hour drive due south to get to it. The problem was that the road was very much cluttered and, worse still, two whole German armies lay across our path. According to Ollie our only hope was to go west, hugging the Channel coast for Abbeville, and hope to get there before the Germans.

Belgian refugees.

At last we managed to flag down a French army lorry. 'Où allez-vous?' I asked the driver.

'Abbeville,' came the reply.

We climbed into the back of the lorry, which was occupied by a dozen or so poilus.* I sat down on a kit bag beside their officer, Lieutenant Leclabart. Conversation was limited. I was fagged out and although he was happy enough to talk about the weather and other irrelevances he was none too eager to explain what he was up to. Having recently seen the quality of French leadership it was hard to know whether the foot sloggers like him were acting under orders or if they even had any orders or, if they did, whether they understood them or were just making it all up as they went along.

We arrived in Abbeville a few hours later. The tailgate crashed down and we clambered out. It was obvious the town was about to fall. There was the crash of gunfire, sounding uncomfortably close, with a pall of smoke

* An affectionate WWI term for French infantrymen.

hung over everything, with the air smelling of brick dust and cordite. We had stopped in a park, which in normal times would have been a pleasant enough place for a stroll but, on that day, all I noticed were sandbags and shallow trenches, hastily dug, with hollow-eyed French army men crouching within.

Incongruously there was a brightly painted bandstand nearby, undamaged and just waiting for a sunny Sunday and a brass band to turn up. I walked up to it and climbed the steps to the circular platform, the better to see what was going on around me. I know now that that is just the way to win you a sniper's bullet but, on that morning my daftness went unpunished and, as it turned out, I was well placed to see what was about to befall.

I heard a kerfuffle coming from down below on the opposite side of the bandstand and walked across and looked down. All I could make out was a disorderly crowd of French soldiers standing over an open trapdoor which, I guessed, must lead to a cellar which would be right beneath me. Some were shouting down through the opening, whilst others stood alongside, grimly pointing their rifles down into it and a few, further back, were shouting encouragement as they passed a bottle around. There was a smell of stale sweat and booze and if it hadn't been for the rifles you'd have thought it was a bunch of revellers out on a Saturday night. With everyone crowded around I couldn't see what was happening until it became apparent that some people had come up from the cellar. I could just make out three men and a woman in the throng, civilians, holding their hands up to protect themselves as they were jostled and pushed by the crowd all around. A voice rang out from the rear. I noticed for the first time that one of the drinkers at the back had an officer's stripe. The men stopped the pushing and shoving and the civilians let down their guard and looked in his direction to see what was up. The officer pushed his way to the front. He had a rope in one hand and a bottle in the other, which he carefully put down on the ground. The rope he tied tightly around each of the civilian's waists, before giving each free end of it to two of his men who coiled it around *their* waists. He picked up the bottle and barked an order. Those with rifles fixed their bayonets and prodded the prisoners, none too gently, with them. Soon this strange party was marching away in a ragged line, towards a latrine, just a short distance away.

I had a pretty good idea who, or rather what, the prisoners might be. In those days there was a lot of talk about "fifth columnists" spying on the allies and communicating by washing lines, smoke signals or whatever, to feed useful information back to the enemy. Such people did exist – we know that now – but most of the people detained at the time were the product of over-fanciful imagination or the victims of score-settling following a petty rivalry. I figured that I was witnessing four recent detainees being marched away for a "comfort" break. I wondered what they might have done to deserve their irregular incarceration but concluded that they wouldn't be detained for much longer as the Germans would be in town soon enough.

I noticed the sight at the same time as the woman – a pile of bodies alongside the latrine. There must have been 20 or more, lying one on top of the other, blood-stained and lifeless where they had been thrown in a rude heap. The woman started screaming and tried to run but of course she was bound by the rope to the three men. Then they saw what she was about and attempted to run too but the two free ends of the rope were firmly held by their escorts who roughly dragged them towards the latrine and then forced them to stand before the wall. Meanwhile the rest of the escort were lining up, ceremoniously pulling the bolts on their rifles as their officer barked an order.

I'm not sure what I would have done next but, fortunately, I didn't have to do anything. The surly Lieutenant Leclabart had climbed onto the bandstand alongside me and had seen the scene unfold just as I have described it. I heard him gasp with amazement, as he drew his pistol. He jumped down and rushed towards his fellow officer, shouting all the while.

'Êtes-vous imbeciles?' he roared.

The other officer, blinked, took a swig from his bottle and raised it high above his head. It was obvious he was about to give the order to fire. Leclabart fired his pistol in the air. 'Are you mad?' he shouted again.

There ensued a furious argument. The gist of it was that Leclabart wanted to see a written order for the executions whereas his fellow officer, who clearly didn't have such a thing, argued that it was unnecessary in these straitened times. He paused for refreshment once or twice I noticed, and it was clear this wasn't his first bottle of the day. His speech was slurred and he was swaying a little as he argued his case. Some of his men were gathering behind Leclabart as the argument progressed and I don't know how things would have gone had Leclabart been alone but of course he had *his* men nearby and they were all sober. Unbidden they formed into a square by the bandstand and, under a barked command from their sergeant, they marched up, standing rigidly to attention in front of him.

The other officer capitulated. He shouted an order and his men with the rifles shouldered their arms while the others dropped the rope. They didn't march away but just sloped off in dribs and drabs. Some, once they were behind him, spat on the ground while others gave him the French equivalent of the V-sign – the *bras d'honneur* as it's called. All had sullen expressions but soon they were gone, melted away into the parkland.

Leclabart untied the captives and gestured for them to return to the bandstand. None of them was in any hurry to run off, I noticed. Up to that point I'd merely stood on my vantage point and watched but, deciding at last to become involved, I jumped to the ground, walked over to the trap door and levered it open. I imagined Leclabart would want to return his charges there, but there was a surprise waiting below – a sea of faces blinking up at me. Leclabart ordered them all up on parade. It took some time for them to file up the steps and, in the end there must have been 40 or 50 of them, standing awkwardly on the grass with Leclabart's men encircling them.

And that was the end of the Abbeville massacre. 20 odd dead indecently piled up by the latrine and 50 or so survivors. Old and young, men and women. I found out later that they had been brought in from Belgium only the day before and that there were hardly any genuine fifth columnists amongst them. One of the dead was the driver who had brought them there, another casualty was a Canadian ice hockey coach. Both just caught up in a drunken nightmare. In a strange twist of history the drunken officer ended up being honoured as a war hero. The Germans in those days might have been happy to go clobbering all over Europe, but were also sticklers for fair-play when the mood took them. After the occupation they had a full criminal investigation into the affair and the drunken officer ended up being executed. After the war the French named a street after him. It still bears his name today and passes near where the latrine once stood.*

Abbeville's "kiosque" still stands.

Meanwhile the Battle of Abbeville was gaining momentum. We were under mortar fire and I was crouching behind the bandstand for cover. I was thinking that it wasn't my place to fight it and that it would be better all round, for me especially, if I could get out. Ollie came scampering up at that moment. 'Good news, sir. There are some British army here.' He

---

* 21 detainees were summarily executed in what became known as the Abbeville Massacre, just before the town fell to the German army on 20th May 1940. After the occupation the Germans condemned Lieutenant René Caron to death for his part in the massacre and he was executed at Mont Valerian in Paris. Mont Valerian is infamous as the place of execution of many French resistance fighters and as such Lieutenant Caron was honoured as a war hero after the war. There is a street named after him, very near the site of the massacre.

The bandstand still stands. It is at the junction of Allée du 8 Mai 1945 and Alle du 11 Novembre 1918 in Abbeville's Jardin d'Argos (Google Streetview: http://tinyurl.com/Kilroy201). Rue du Lieutenant Caron is nearby. See *End Note (9).*

pointed at a trench nearby. 'They've got some wounded loaded up in a Leyland, over by the park gates.' He pointed into the middle distance. 'They are looking for a volunteer to drive it. Dieppe's just along the coast. What'd you say, sir?'

What Ollie didn't mention was that the previous two volunteer drivers had been blown up before they even reached the lorry but somehow we got there in one piece. From then on things got slightly easier. Dieppe was out of the battle zone so, as far as I was concerned, that was in the right direction. We had a close call with a Panzer along the way but our red cross markings were honoured and an hour later we were on the harbour-side laying everyone out on their stretchers and trying to find someone to take care of them.

CHAPTER 3

The rest of the journey back to the squadron must have taken at least another day, perhaps two. It's all rather sketchy to me now. Starting with my misguided bet in the Tiger Moth only a fortnight earlier I'd crashed, been blown up, shot at, shot down and crashed again too many times, and that had rather taken its toll. All I can recall about the journey now is a succession of lifts in motley vehicles, once waking up to find we were trundling along slowly in a train, and a vague recollection of a couple of bicycles, although Ollie denies that ever happened.

The blitzkrieg had forced just about every R.A.F. squadron to relocate at short notice, out of the firing line. Ours had moved about 50 miles south, to a similarly unserviceable field at a place called Anglure. The comfort of the chateau was behind us now and our new home-from-home was a primary school with the staff room reserved for officer accommodation and the school hall used to accommodate the men. I was directed to one of the classrooms, which was being used as a briefing room. I walked in to find Stiffy Barnes standing at the front with the blackboard behind him, facing the aircrew who were sitting on top of the little desks, trying their best not to look like eight year olds. Ollie was there too, balancing on top of a ladder as he attempted to pin an enormous map of France to the wall. 'Ah, Kilroy,' said Barnes, 'Thank you for joining us.' He looked at his watch. 'At last.'

Most of the aircrew hadn't noticed me until then. I nodded at them as I threaded my way between the desks towards a vacant one. They were all looking at me rather curiously I thought and some were sniggering, which seemed a little odd to me at the time. Sticky Stevens had patted me on the back and whispered a greeting as I passed but none of the others said anything. I looked to the front wondering what would come next. I'd no idea what Barnes had in mind and never did find out because he didn't get the chance to say anything more.

The door crashed open and in strode Belfrey. 'Where is he?' he barked, 'Where is he?'

I stood up. 'Good morning, sir.'

'Yes, for you, maybe,' he growled. 'Now pray tell me where have you been these last five days while these brave young men have been doing five, six, seven ops a day and getting blasted to kingdom come for their pains?' He waved in the general direction of the aircrew. 'Fannying about I suppose?'

'No sir. Shot down in Belg...' I began.

'And when did you last attend aircraft recognition classes, eh?'

'Er. Only two wee...' I think I said.

'Well you must have been drunk or fast asleep. Or both, I suppose. So what's the difference between a D-520 and an Me-109*, viewed from below?'

'Er, the undercarriage, sir?' He had me stumped there. I could remember very little of the previous ten days but, from what he was saying, I thought it likely that at least one of my "kills" had been a D-520. The French had only recently brought it into service and, at that moment, what with being rather flustered by Belfrey's interrogation, I couldn't for the life of me think what the damn thing looked like from any angle.

'I don't suppose you'd recognise one if you were sitting in its cockpit with the maker's name tattooed on your privates.'

There didn't seem any answer to that. The thought popped into my head that at least "Dewoitine" was quite a long word, but I calculated that this probably wasn't a good moment for manly banter.

Belfrey turned to the rest of the room. 'So here's how it is, chaps,' he said. 'There we are, day in day out, taking on the full might of the Luftwaffe and not a sniff of our noble allies pitching in to help us.' He paused for effect. 'And then, and then, at last, a couple of Frogs do show up and some nincompoop,' he gestured at me as he drew breath, 'sees fit to blast them out of the sky.'

Most of my colleagues were just sitting there straight-faced although I thought I could detect a few sniggers from the back row.

But Belfrey wasn't done yet. He turned back to me. 'And after loafing around in Bel-gium,' he said, stretching the name out as if it were a dirty word. 'In Belgium, you finally decide to head back and were no doubt further delayed because you were busy bumping off a few more Frogs along the way?'

That gave me a jolt. Ollie was still in the room, perched on top of his ladder and I think he nearly fell off. I looked up at him questioningly as he recovered and was relieved to see him shake his head. 'Oh no sir. Came here ASAP of course. Had to route by Abbeville.'

Belfrey seemed satisfied with that. He fell silent and I could see him looking around the room. I was beginning to hope that I might at last be off the hook and, in one sense, I was. After a while he asked,'Are Skinner and Sturt here?'

A couple of hands went up.

'Ah yes. Flight Lieutenant Skinner and Flying Officer Sturt, I think?'

They both nodded.

* The Dewoitine D-520 was the French fighter equivalent of the Hawker Hurricane and a good match for the German Me (or to be correct: Bf) 109.http://tinyurl.com/Kilroy105.

Belfrey pointed at me. 'Gentlemen, I give you Pilot Officer Kilroy.' He then turned to me and pointed back at them. 'These are your new crew. I suggest you go and see Flight Lieutenant Scroggins right now with a view to getting going ASAP.'

I didn't know what Belfrey was on about at the time. The Hurricane, being a single seater has a crew of one alone – that was just me of course and no room for any others. In fact the only crew I'd ever had up to that point in my career were my ground crew, Dunton and Cox, but ground crew were always the more lowly ranks and not flying officers or flight lieutenants.

I found Scroggins easily enough and he was only too keen to put me in the picture. He issued a chit for me to draw some more kit from stores and dropped a small tattered booklet down on his desk in front of me. 'You'll need this,' he said.

I picked it up. I still have it as a matter of fact and it lies before me as I

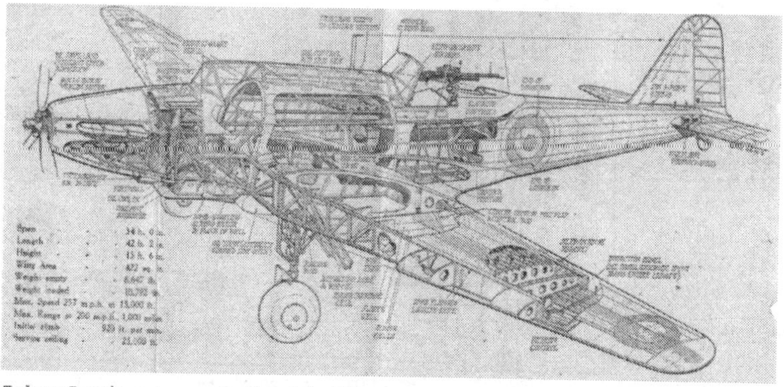

Fairey Battle cutaway in R.A.F.'s *Pilots Notes.*

write these words, although I still tremble when I look at it. At that time the Air Ministry produced concise publications for the pilots of all the R.A.F.'s operational aircraft – *Pilots Notes* they were called. This one was *Pilots Notes – Fairey I Battle/Merlin I Engine.*

'Fairey Battle?' I asked, trying not to sound alarmed, although my heart had started thumping so loudly I was sure he could hear it.

'What's wrong, old boy?' he asked. 'It's single engine, exactly the same as your late lamented Hurricane – a Merlin I right?[*] Everyone says they are veritable pussy cats to fly and it's not as if they'll be asking you to fly it upside down or anything.'

'But why me?'

[*] There were several marks of Fairey Battle, most commonly marks I, II and III, which followed the mark of Merlin engine with which they were fitted. http://tinyurl.com/Kilroy106.

'I think you know "why you?"' he answered, giving me a funny look. 'But in answer to the more general question of "why?" it's because it's here – got lost a couple of days back and it's been with us ever since. Now we've only got two thirds of the crew.'

'So, where's the pilot?'

'No one knows. Shacked up with his mistress or drunk in a ditch I shouldn't wonder. Their squadron leader is raising merry hell with us – says he's desperately short of kites *and* crew come to think of it, and wants this infernal sitting duck back. He's absolutely quackers if you ask me, eh?' He chortled heartily at his own joke.

Tact clearly wasn't Scroggins' strongpoint. He'd reminded me, as if I needed reminding, that the Battle was a *dreadful* aeroplane. It's true it had a great engine up front, the fabulous Rolls Royce Merlin, but everything behind that engine was, well, *awful.* It was what they called a light bomber – a single-engined light bomber – which, put simply, meant it did nothing at all very well. Firstly it had only a small bomb load, with all the punch of a Christmas cracker – well I could put up with that – but much worse, it had neither the speed, height nor the defensive capability to withstand the fighters or the murderous ground-fire. If ten went out on a mission and two came back this was thought to be pretty good.*

Fairey Battles (and Bristol Blenheims) for scrap.

I must have been looking so glum that even Scroggins noticed and he took it upon himself to cheer me up. 'Look, old chap, this is only a temporary secondment. If you should... er, I mean *when* this little show is over you'll be back with us, eh? And you've got a first rate crew there. Flew with them myself back in '36. Skinner and Sturt. Skinner had a double first from Aberdeen University as I recall.'

'A Scotsman?' I asked.

Scroggins nodded.

'So that'll be fun,' I said, 'Probably be drunk as a skunk half the time and in the unlikely event he's sober it will be all "Hoots mon," "Moon-licht nicht" and "kilts awa" no doubt?'

Scroggins didn't answer. He was looking past me, over my shoulder, with an amused look on his face. Suddenly I heard a booming and very

* See http://tinyurl.com/Kilroy106) for the aeroplane itself or see *End Note (10)* for its disastrous combat record.

plummy voice coming from behind. 'Very good, I say, very good accent. But we're not all descended from Rob Roy, old chap.'

I turned around and it was Skinner. 'Oh, I didn't mean...'

'No offence taken, old boy. I'm quite used to it... *e*ctually.'

He extended his hand and I shook it.

***

Half an hour later we were at 1,000 feet and leveling off. Scroggins was right. There wasn't much to flying the Battle, especially after the Hurricane. It was a bit like riding a lumbering elephant after you've been used to a skittish thoroughbred. It was very easy to handle and nice and stable but, dear oh dear, was it ponderous. It would be fine in peace-time or as a trainer, I thought, but not quite what you want when you are in the middle of the Battle of France. "Beware the Hun in the sun" – the thought came to me and immediately I swivelled my head around and upwards to see if Fritz was lurking up there anywhere, but then I remembered there were another two pairs of eyes aboard to look out for such hazards and I should just concentrate on flying the beast.

I didn't have to worry about navigation either. This was a relief as there was a fair bit of haze that day and ground features were hard to see. It's hard work in a single seater where you have to do everything – fly the plane, monitor the fuel and engine, keep a lookout *and* navigate. In the jolly old Battle you have others to share the workload.

Scroggins had been right about Skinner too. 'Fly zero six five, skipper. At cruise on flight level three zero ETA Chartres at two seven,' came his confident ringing voice over the intercom.

He was bang on, too. At 13:26 GMT precisely I heard him again on the intercom. 'Two o' clock low, skipper. Our field is just behind those trees.'

Sure enough I could see an expanse of green with a row of Battles lined up to one side, glinting in the afternoon sun. At "two seven" as he'd predicted we were overhead and five minutes later I had us on the ground and bumping over the newly mown grass to park. Skinner knew what was what of course and he directed me to a stand alongside a heavily sandbagged dispersal pen.

CHAPTER 4

As soon as we stopped the ground crew came running up, helped us out and ushered us into a waiting lorry that whisked us off to the briefing room. There was no time to get my bearings or stow my kitbag or even visit the latrine. Such is the glamorous and exciting life on a front-line bomber squadron, I thought.

The briefing room turned out to be a red and white marquee on a patch of grass beside a rather grand manor house in the corner of the field. I did wonder if the war had interrupted someone's wedding but never did find out what the story was. The place certainly wasn't designed for the comfort of the aircrew as it was hot and steamy in there, with the afternoon sun beating down on the canvas, made worse by the thick pall of cigarette smoke hanging over everyone, all crowded together. Heads turned as we entered. A wing commander was standing at the front. I guessed he knew Skinner and Sturt already but he didn't seem bothered as to who, what or where I was – presumably my pilot officer's stripe was enough for him. 'Thank you for joining us,' were his opening words, as he looked at his watch. 'At last.'

That was the second time that day I had been greeted in such fashion and I found myself wondering if I would ever catch up with events to the satisfaction of senior management. All I could think was that it would be nice to live long enough to have the chance.

Wingco started the briefing. I guess it must have been only too familiar to anyone on the squadron who had been lucky enough to survive the last couple of weeks. The mission was to attack some bridges just behind the German front in a bid to disrupt their supply line. We were to keep a tight formation at low level. The weather forecast was for clear skies now the earlier haze had lifted. This meant we would have no trouble locating our targets and the German fighters and flak* would have no trouble locating us.

I looked around at my newfound comrades in arms. Their faces were pinched and drawn. One of the pilots put up his hand and asked if there was any chance we could have a fighter escort. The Wingco frowned, tweaked his moustache and muttered something about "wanting a bloody nursemaid next." There was an answering rumble from the floor, which I

* *Flak* was absorbed into English about this time, from the German abbreviation for *Fliegerabwehrkanone*, meaning "aircraft-defence gun".

think must have alerted him to the fact that a few motivational words might be in order.

Having casually knocked back any chance of a fighter escort the Wingco sat down on a table, removed his hat and calmly waited for the hubbub to die down. 'Now listen here, chaps,' he said. 'I've brought the padre along to have a few words with you, but before he speaks I would like to say something myself.'

He paused for effect and I could hear someone coughing nearby.

'Some of you will know that I was a church warden before the balloon went up so I think I'm qualified to speak on behalf of that great air marshal who guides all our destinies.'

There was a muttered "Jesus" from Skinner, standing alongside me.

'Yes you are right to say "Jesus" because some of you, who knows, even many of you, will be in his arms in the next few hours.' He glanced at his watch again. 'Now I know we are sending you out on a bit of a sticky wicket but someone has got to do the job, what?'

No one answered.

'I ask you not to dwell on the unfairness of being struck down in your prime, but to reflect on the fact that you are doing God's work in fighting this evil monster called Adolf Hitler.' His voice was rising as he warmed to the theme. 'You should fear not the flames of an exploding fuel tank or the bullets of a Messerschmitt cannon.'

Somebody farted loudly. It may even have been me.

'What are a few moments of excruciating pain in a blazing aeroplane when you are saved an eternity of agony at the hands of Satan?' He was really getting in a lather now and closed his eyes for the next bit. 'Yes, I say to all of you: you should not fear these earthly things because they will lead you to the great architect who holds all our destinies most dear, and you will be able to sit at his right hand.'

Somebody raised a hand. 'So will we be angels at six o' clock then, sir?'

There was a hush and the CO blinked. At first I thought he was going to bawl the man out but, suddenly, his face crumpled. I was wondering if he was going to cry and then, to my astonishment, he did – the tears streaming down his face. He buried his face in his handkerchief and all we could hear was a muffled cry of 'such brave boys.'

We all stood around awkwardly until the padre put his arm around him and led him away. When he got him to the back, the padre turned to us and announced, 'I think what the CO is saying is that our thoughts are with you all. Er... good luck, chaps.' And with that he put on his hat and they were gone.

There didn't seem much more we could do. We picked up our gear in silence and headed out to our aircraft.

R.A.F. bomber crews in those days had a tradition of, er, watering the tail wheel of their mount before going on an operation – a custom I was more than ready to uphold on this occasion, while the ground crew stood back at a safe distance, and upwind of us of course. Afterwards, we paused by the wing, looking awkwardly at each other. I thought Sturt and Skinner both seemed pale and drawn and I guessed that I must be looking pretty much the same. Sturt muttered something like 'Let's give 'em hell,' and then, without another word, he and I climbed onto the wing to board, while Skinner ducked under it to his own entry hatch.

R.A.F. bomber crews in the Briefing Room.

The ground crew went with us to ensure everything was battened down properly and we were all securely strapped in. I thought then that the Battle was an odd-ball and I certainly think so now, although there are few enough to see these days. Instead of the more comradely arrangement of everyone boarding through the same hatch and then clambering around inside the fuselage to individual battle stations, we each had our own entry point. Once in place, there we stayed for the rest of the mission, out of sight of each other and with only the intercom to remind us anyone else was aboard. So while I clambered into the front cockpit, pretty much like I was boarding a Hurricane, Sturt climbed in similar fashion into his position, about halfway to the tail. He was in charge of our main defensive armament – a solitary Vickers 303 – and was seated facing the rear. Since it's not done to shoot off bits of your own aircraft his field of fire was limited – mainly upwards and backwards – a design defect that the Luftwaffe had quickly clocked onto. Meanwhile, Skinner boarded into the space between us, through his personal floor hatch, leading into a cramped area where he could navigate and, with luck, later aim the bombs.

The first part of the mission was uneventful. The weather was perfect – for peacetime flying anyway – all gauges were showing normal, the Merlin was purring nicely and we had plenty of petrol. The squadron had taken some knocks over the last couple of weeks and could muster only six planes on this occasion. The other five were flying in a tidy "V" formation, while yours truly was the odd one out, stuck in the most vulnerable position, at the back – "tail-end Charlie" as it was known. In line with the standing instructions of the time the squadron was holding tight formation at low level. With German flak batteries all over the Low Countries this might seem a lunatic idea but the alternative was worse. By keeping low, at least their fighters couldn't get below us, where we had no defence at all. Also, once over the target and, if by happy circumstance we didn't get blasted to kingdom come by the ground fire, at least we had some sort of chance of getting our bombs in the right place.

Until we neared the target our main worry would be the Luftwaffe, but I had no time to look out for enemy fighters in any case. It took me all my concentration to avoid piling into the ground or colliding with the planes in front as we swooped and soared over the undulating countryside at nearly 250 mph. At regular intervals, over the intercom, I'd hear Skinner's calm voice giving me a navigational fix. I still recall the last one. 'Flying zero five six, Skipper. ETA target four seven.' We were on course and but ten minutes away from the target.

We cruised on. The sky was eerily empty – a beautiful blue from horizon to horizon and I was beginning to hope that, for this mission, we might even get away with it. But just as I had that thought, Skinner broke in again, his voice high-pitched and shrill. 'Twa bass-turds abeen at sex o' clock.'

'What...?' I begun, but was interrupted by Sturt. 'Spotted, Jock. Here goes.' Simultaneously there was a ripping sound from the rear. This was Sturt earning his keep with the Vickers. In reply, our attackers' tracer came streaking past us, looking pretty and harmless although it's anything but of course. I found my hands twitching involuntarily on the controls. My fighter boy instinct was to take instant and violent evasive action but we'd been ordered to hold formation, come what may, so I had to will myself to keep the plane on station and fly straight and level.

The rest of the squadron, all ahead of me of course, took their cue from Sturt and opened up on the fighters as well. 'Fit a stramash,' Skinner bawled to the sound of gunfire all around. At first I felt some comfort from this collective fire but then I could see it getting closer and closer to us. Just when I was wondering if we were going to get blasted away by our own squadron it stopped. A second or so later there was a "whumph", the controls bucked and I caught a glimpse of a 109 passing only inches above the cockpit, then streaking ahead into the distance. I watched it bank hard and curve back to get ready for another go at us, but by then we were under fire again.

There was a mirror on the dashboard and, risking an occasional glance, I could get some idea of what was going on behind, which was just as well as I couldn't understand anything Skinner was telling me. We were lucky, if you can call it that, in that these attackers were rookies and there were only two of them. They should have attacked in unison and they should have kept low, where our guns couldn't get to them, but they didn't, and they paid the price.

'Got the bastard,' was Sturt's comment as one of them blew up in mid-air. 'Tell him to pit a stookie on't,' added Skinner. A few seconds later the other pitched down suddenly and piled into the ground. 'At least he's nae fae Torry though. Heh, heh?' added Skinner, chortling at his own incomprehensible joke.

There was no time to congratulate ourselves. 'Bandits at seven o' clock low,' came a mercifully understandable message from Sturt, even if it was bad news. I looked in the mirror and nearly bit my tongue. Half the Luftwaffe were upon us. At least, that's what it seemed like at the time. And this lot were no Dieter Dummkopfs like the last lot. They attacked in unison, from behind, and stayed low, where it was difficult to bring our guns to bear. Even now I can't bring myself to recall it in any detail. I just have a memory of murderous hails of bullets that seemed to last for ever, followed by all too short moments of respite as the fighters regrouped for another go at us. Over and over.

I saw first one then another two of our squadron go down. As tail-end Charlie we should have been the first casualty. We certainly had some close calls and took some damage but, miraculously, the plane kept flying. With the battle still raging my crew and I were still very much alive and well, and Skinner especially so. 'Crivvens, a foggy bummer, Skipper. A foggy bummer,' he cried out during one of our rare moments of respite.

Had the planes of that era had ejector seats I'm sure I'd have pulled his at that moment. Instead I found myself scanning the skies for what I surmised must be some alarming weather event.

'Haud still, Skipper, I can just see it. Haud still.'

I saw a hand snaking around my seat coming from behind. It delivered a solid thwack on my arm. 'Got the bass-turd, Skipper. One less fifth columnist, eh? Heh, heh.'

'Speak English, you idiot,' came Sturt's voice. 'It's a bumble bee, Skipper. Plague of them back at the airfield.'

I looked down at my arm to see what I can happily report was the only blood to be spilled on our plane that day – a dark red splodge with bits of black and yellow mixed in.

Just then another wave of fighters came in and downed our flight leader. There was a flash of light and an explosion, uncomfortably close, in front of us. Our plane bucked and dipped alarmingly and when the smoke cleared he was gone. There was nothing left but fragments that seemed to be hanging in the air. I flinched as we flew through them. There were some bangs and clatters as we hit bits of R.A.F. hardware, bomb and, who knows, personnel but all our vital systems remained intact through it all.

That left just us and one other Battle, plodding along towards the target like we were doing a royal flypast. The fighters were having such an easy time of it I knew there was nothing we could do to survive another attack but, as you often find in a survivor's memoir, luck played its part for us that day. The fighters wheeled away at that moment, not to return. No doubt they were out of petrol or ammo, or both possibly.

But our troubles weren't over. We still had the bombs to deliver and it occurred to me we should be upon the target by now, if we had held our course. I asked Skinner for a direction and an ETA and he replied with more gibberish. 'Dogs MacBollocks, Auchtermuchty, Auchtermuchty,' he said, or something that sounded pretty much like that.

I think you'll agree it had been a trying afternoon for me, what with the full and undivided attention of the Luftwaffe on top of having to endure Skinner and his gobbledygook. I knew it wouldn't help but I decided that if I answered in kind it might at least make me feel a little better. 'Ballater, Ballater,' I said, knowing that Ballater was a village in the heart of his homeland.

'Say again, Skipper?'

'Ball-att-ere, Ball-att-ere,' I replied rather mischievously.

'Wilco, Skipper. Right away, old chap,' came the reply, back in Skinner's best plummy English.

I heard a loud crash behind me and then felt a gale blowing around my feet. I was about to ask what was up when Sturt's voice came on the intercom. 'Christ, Skipper, I can't get the canopy open. I'm stuck in here.'

'What do you mean?'

'I can't bail out. I'm stuck,' he shouted.

'What? Who said to bail out?'

'You did, Skipper. Told us to bail out here. Several times.'

'I said "Ballater," Sturt. It's a place. Jesus Christ. No one's abandoning ship just yet.' Well, there I was wrong. I looked in my mirror and caught sight of a parachute billowing in the middle of a field, with the figure of Skinner being dragged along behind it. And, lucky chap, that was his war over. I bumped into him at a reunion many years later. Time is a great healer so I suppose I'd just about forgiven him by then. And I managed to understand much of what he said too, until he'd had a few whiskies anyway. He was a POW for five years and then came back to become a Mathematics Professor at his old seat of learning. I hope his students understood him better than me or they'll all be thinking that one plus one is 37.*

---

* Skinner was speaking Doric, a dialect from the North East of Scotland, centred on Aberdeen... abeen – above; stramash – brawl/uproar; stookie – plaster cast; foggy bummer – bumble bee; "At least he's nae fae Torry" – at least he's not from Torry

So, there I was, over the battle zone with absolutely no idea where the target was. The plane had plenty of charts aboard, stacked on the navigator's table, but with our navigator busy ploughing a Flanders field we had nobody to read them. I was kicking myself for not taking a chart with me but there it was, I hadn't. With the Battle so compartmentalised it wasn't on for me to nip back and grab one of Skinner's but there was one other plane left with us so, in the absence of any better plan, I followed it.

Everything seemed eerily quiet. It was a relief after the hell of the last quarter hour, but then a horrible thought occurred to me. Perhaps the other chap was lost too? He certainly didn't seem to be flying very accurately. As I followed him my compass kept drifting from side to side. I'd already tried to raise him on the radio but had had no response. Now I edged slightly ahead and waved at him. Still no response. I tried semaphore, slowly mouthing the words, 'Where the fuck are we?' Nothing. I waggled the wings but got nothing back from that. Then I noticed it. A neat round mark in the middle of his forehead and a thin red line tracing its way around his eyebrow and down his cheek. His glazed eyes stared defiantly heavenwards. Where were his crew? Well Christ knows what had happened to them – they were nowhere to be seen. I suppose the plane had been flying on luck and a prayer, but my manoeuvres so close to it broke the spell. The delicate balance was lost and it started to bank and turn away from me. I watched as the turn got tighter, all the way to the ground. Nobody got out.

Queen Elizabeth and George VI's arrival, with Princesses Elizabeth and Margaret and corgis, at Ballater station in Deeside in Aberdeenshire, in 1938.

So that left just me and Sturt. Somewhere over northern France. Or Belgium. We crossed a road. I could see a column advancing along it in the distance and when I turned to investigate I found it was German artillery on the move. The guns were horse drawn, with the troops on foot and with the only mechanisation in the shape of a couple of lorries in the rear. That's the way it was in those days. The mighty Panzers had certainly caught us Allies out over the last couple of weeks but coming up behind them the main weight of the German army blitzkrieged on Shanks's pony or Herr von Hors, just like the Romans.

(traditionally one of the poorer parts of Aberdeen), meaning things could be much worse for him. http://tinyurl.com/Kilroy107.

At last I'd found something safe to do battle with and I called to Sturt to get ready for a bombing run. Without Skinner this meant that he'd have to do the bomb aimer duties and, as we cruised towards the column, I caught sight of him in the mirror, climbing over the back of his seat into the middle position. By then there was some small arms fire coming our way but after the nightmare of the fighters this was of little concern. I remembered there was a forward mounted gun in the wing. Mess gossip was that it was useless but as I had its firing button right there, under my thumb, it seemed a shame not to use it. And, predictably, I don't think I achieved anything much, although it certainly let the Jerries know we were coming their way.

Sturt had disappeared from view so I guessed he must now be crouched down on the floor with the bombsight. There was a solid clunk, which could only be the bomb doors opening. And I had us nicely lined up on the road. The column was only a short distance ahead and the enemy were all running for cover, leaving livestock, wagons and their cargo to their fate. 'Okay,' I said, 'No second run, Sturt. At the first sight of anything at all press the tittie and then let's eff off ASAP.'

'Wilco, Skipper.'

By then we were overhead the column and there, in the middle of it, I saw a big, big gun. I guessed it was some sort of Howitzer and, right on cue, as we passed over it, I felt the plane shudder upwards. I banked hard to turn away from the blast. The bombs didn't have far to fall so, almost immediately, I heard the explosions and felt the plane rock in the shockwave. There seemed to be a lot of earth being thrown up from the fields near the road and I also caught a glimpse of a horse spiralling upwards, winging its way heavenwards, like a modern day Pegasus, but there was disappointingly little damage on the road itself.

Sure enough, as the dust and debris settled, I could see that we hadn't hit anything of consequence but I was past caring at this point. The main thing was that we'd completed our mission, survived, and it was time for home. I calculated that, with a South West heading, a firewalled throttle and a saucer of help from Lady Luck, we'd be tucking into ham and eggs in half an hour or so.

At that moment Sturt came on over the intercom. 'Let's go around again,' the idiot suggested. 'The fighters have gone. They're looking pretty shaken up down there and we've still got some ammo.'

This was the last thing I wanted to hear right then. Sturt outranked me but there's a protocol in the R.A.F. that the pilot is always the commander in the air, even if he's a lowly flight sergeant and there's an air chief marshal in the back. So I didn't really have to take any nonsense from him at all but, stupidly, I took time out to argue.

I stared hard at him in the mirror. 'Now see here,' I said, fixing him with what I hoped was an authoritative look. 'Now see here.' I was about to tell him we were low on petrol (which we weren't) but I didn't get the chance to tell him anything. I caught a glimpse of something out of the corner of my eye and the next instant this object filled my windshield and there was a sickening crump.

Of course I should have been keeping a proper lookout and not engaging in bus queue banter with Sturt. I found out later that we had collided with a Fiesler Storch, a German reconnaissance and communications aircraft that looks not unlike its namesake, with the fixed undercarriage hanging down like the legs of a stork in flight. If I'd been looking where we were going I'd have avoided it which would have been good for its crew that's for sure and especially good for Sturt too.

At the time all I knew was that we had hit something big, but luckily with a glancing blow. Now, if nothing else, the Fairey Battle is a solid piece of machinery and would ordinarily have some sort of chance of limping home after a collision like that but, unfortunately, the Storch had mangled our prop. And, with only one prop in the first place, there is only one way you are going to go when that happens.

I was too low to bail out. There was a big dent in the left wing and the cowling had torn loose from the engine, which was screaming and vibrating, making a hell of a racket. There was every chance it would tear loose from its mountings, so I cut the petrol to it and all went quiet. Now all I could hear was the air rushing past. It was a relief to experience some peace and tranquillity after the clamour of battle.

For all its faults, the Battle seemed to manage quite well without an engine. Those who have never flown one often suggest that without a motor it must fly like a brick, but this isn't true. All I had to do was to wind back the trim wheel to hold the nose up and with everything under control and the plane in a nice steady descent I could start planning for an orderly meeting with *terra firma*. We were very low of course so I had to be quick about it, but luckily there was a nice flat field right in front. I pointed the nose at it, opted to keep the undercarriage up and pancaked into the middle of it, with the plane gently slewing around as we ground to a stop. Considering the almighty hash I have so often made of things while at the controls of an aeroplane I couldn't help congratulating myself on this occasion that it was as expert a dead-stick landing as any you are likely to see.

CHAPTER 5

I sat there, collecting my thoughts and listening to the whirring of the gyros as they wound down. The sun was streaming in through the cockpit roof and it felt so pleasantly warm and comfortable that I didn't want to get out, but then I caught a whiff of petrol and that brought me to my senses. I undid my harness and pulled back the canopy, to be met by Sturt.

As we jumped down there was a sharp crack over our heads. I turned around to see a lorry pulling to a halt at one end of the field. There were some soldiers tumbling out of it, while a couple of others were taking pot-shots at us. We had landed near the road so I guessed that these must be our friends the Howitzer Huns. We crouched down and ran in the opposite direction, leaping over a fence and crashing into a woodland.

No doubt you have heard of the Geneva Convention, which lays down the rules for dealing with prisoners of war and captured combatants. It is all well and good in theory but, in practice, if you have just been strafing and bombing Jerry then have the misfortune to prang your kite in the field right next to him, don't bet on him coming up to you with brandy and cigars. And to make things worse I'd noticed that our pursuers were in the grey-green combat wear of the Waffen SS, not the Wehrmacht, which is to say we were dealing with lunatics and fanatics rather than the regulars.*

With these thoughts in my mind we legged it, crashing through the bushes, hoping to put a good distance between us and our pursuers. I've already remarked on how flat the country was but I can tell you that there was at least one ravine around because I fell into it. One minute Sturt and I were careering through the bushes, jumping over tree stumps and ducking under branches and the next I was flying through the air, with an impressive amount of open space beneath me. I remember thinking, 'Christ this is going to hurt,' and rolling myself into a ball and shutting my eyes. Ninety nine times out of 100 when you take a fall like that you are going to end up dead or in a wheelchair but in this case the ground must have fallen below me at just the right angle because, instead of splatting hard into it, my first contact was a glancing blow. It flung me head over heels of course and I continued to tumble, over and over and ever downwards, but was

* The earlier and infamous SS (Shutzstaffel) black uniform was discontinued on the outbreak of hostilities in favour of a grey-green, which was only subtly different from the regular army Wehrmacht colours. Kilroy must have had very good vision to spot the difference at what must have been a considerable distance, but then he was a fighter pilot.

unchecked until one final almighty great thump in my back which knocked the wind out of me.

I may have lost consciousness briefly because the next thing I remember was looking up at the ridge I had fallen from, at least a couple of hundred feet above. I could see Sturt staring down anxiously and the soldiers coming up behind and grabbing him. One of them levelled his rifle at me and started firing. He would only have been 60 or 70 yards away but he was a poor shot. I rolled over behind a rock, kept my head down and crawled away into the undergrowth.

None of the Jerries seemed too keen to follow me down the steep slope so I was safe for the time being. Not so, for Sturt. A few minutes later I heard his cries of 'What are you doing?' over and over again, getting louder and more urgent with each utterance. Then he was shouting, 'I've surrendered you bastards. You can't do that.' Then there was a 'My God.' And after that the shrieking started. I covered my ears to blot it out and stumbled off down the ravine.

It didn't take me long to realise I was trapped. There was a small stream running along the bottom of the ravine with a rough track alongside. Looking behind me I could see the path winding its way up to the plateau from whence I came and a platoon heading down it already. Looking the other way, the ravine widened out into a valley and not far beyond into flat open grassland with a line of soldiers sweeping along it, like grouse beaters on a moor. I headed off the path into the undergrowth and found salvation.

Fiesler Fi156 Storch.

In front of me was the mangled wreck of the reconnaissance plane we had collided with, its two occupants still inside, hanging by their harnesses. I scrambled up to it and wrenched open the door. I'm not sure what I had in mind at this point, perhaps a forlorn hope that I might be able to surrender to the Luftwaffe instead of my friends in the SS, or perhaps the occupants wouldn't notice me if I just sort of hid inside. In the cabin was the silence of the grave. No, not quite. There was a wasp buzzing around, mindlessly trying to escape through the plexi-glass. And from overhead I could hear the steady drip, drip of petrol leaking onto the instrument panel.

I studied the two occupants and realised that neither was in a fit state to take my surrender. One of them, the passenger and the older of the two, was clearly dead, his head lolling at a very unnatural angle. I guessed that he must have been a general or some such senior rank, to judge by the grandeur of his uniform, and he certainly looked like a well fed general too. The other occupant was much younger, seated at the controls. He too had expired. His brains spread around the cockpit left no doubt about that.

So with the Hunds of Hell hot on my heels and a dead German aviator of about my size and age in front of me it didn't take Albert Einstein to work out what to do next. I undid the pilot's harness and he slumped into my arms. No doubt you have heard how heavy and awkward a corpse can be and it's all true, but when you are desperate it's amazing what can be achieved. First I removed all my clothing and once naked started on the pilot. I was still struggling with his belt when I heard the sound of dogs barking. I looked up and could see them and their handlers, but still some distance away up the slope.

His uniform was not a perfect fit, but not bad. The boots were a bit tight. Of course being in German uniform meant that, if captured, I would be executed as a spy rather than sent off to a POW camp, but having heard poor old Sturt's screams I didn't think the Geneva Convention was going to help me much with these Krauts in any case.

I removed my identity disc and took the pilot's from around his neck, throwing all my discarded clothing into the cabin. I glanced at the new disc and discovered that I had become OberLeutenant Hans von Stauss. The barking sounded much nearer now. I reached into the Oberleutenant's pockets and found what I was hoping for. A lighter. I was just about to apply it to the pool of petrol on the dashboard when I spotted something alongside General von Fatty – a leather briefcase with a gold Swastika and Eagle embossed on the side. I grabbed it, lit blue touch paper and retired to a safe distance.

The plane was going at a merry blaze as my newly found comrades in arms came up to join me. 'Save him somebody can't you!?' I cried. Christ, I nearly said it in English. And, fortunately for me, it was just too late for anyone to get near.

It is amazing what a uniform can do for you. Ten minutes earlier they would have set the dogs on me at best. Now I was suitably attired I didn't have to do anything much, other than appear dazed and shocked, which I was anyway and the troops solicitously led me away back up the ravine.

Which is how I met SS Hauptsturmführer Fritz Knöchlein. He clicked his heels, saluted and introduced himself as I was led up to him. I could just manage a groan. 'Ah OberLeutenant, you had a lucky escape. Let me take you to my vehicle and get you away from here.'

As we walked to his car I spotted to one side a blackened object hanging from the branch of a tree, with a fire crackling beneath it. The wind blew an unfamiliar smell in my direction and when I had worked out what it was I had to stop myself from retching. The captain waved nonchalantly at the scene. 'Ah, you see the welcome we give our R.A.F. friends. That's our revenge for what they did to Boris.'

I thought some reply was in order but was struggling to blot the scene from my mind. 'Boris? Was he a close friend of yours?'

He laughed. 'Friend? No, Lieutenant. Boris was the regimental mascot. A beautiful wolfhound, which I raised from a puppy.' I could swear his eyes became a little glassy at that moment, but then his face hardened. 'Such a dear sweet natured puppy. To think he was blown to pieces by those filth, but we will avenge him. Be assured of that. That schweinhund on the tree is only the beginning. When we find his pilot, down in that ravine somewhere, he will be joining him on that branch there.'

I was just digesting this piece of news when a corporal came running up, saluted and handed him a piece of paper. I stood silently as he read it. He frowned and turned to me. 'But, Lieutenant, you should have told me you were on an urgent mission.'

I stuttered something about being a little overwrought following the demise of my aeroplane. 'But with your assistance, I hope to fulfil my orders sir,' I added, hoping that his assistance would also tell me what my urgent mission was.

He took the bait. 'Yes, of course, we will get you to Charleville as quickly as possible.' He handed me the paper. It was in German of course but, translated, it read as follows:

> To: *All stations*
> From: *Generaloberst Keitel, OKW*
>
> *Imperative you locate Fiesler Storch, crashed approx 20 kms west of Lille. Provide General von Schleicher with all assistance to attend HQ Army Group A*

He watched me read the note then added, 'I don't think old von Schleicher* will be going anywhere now but at least you have his dispatches. I imagine that is what HQ wants anyway.' He eyed the case I was carrying.

I almost dropped it in horror, but just recovered in time. 'Yes, sir, it was imperative that they be preserved. How fortunate I got them out in time. Perhaps one of your men could deliver them on behalf of our late lamented general?'

I held the case out for him, but he wasn't having that. No, his officers were far too busy and the contents of the case far too important to be entrusted to a rating. I would have to deliver it in person.

* Not to be confused with General Kurt von Schleicher, who was at one time Hitler's Defence Minister and was murdered in the Night of the Long Knives in 1934.

I felt like a fish being played on a line. I could only try to wriggle some more. 'Of course Herr Captain. Just give me the direction and I will head there immediately.' And, I thought, as soon as I am around that corner it will be hey ho, gay Paree I go.

He gave me a funny look. 'No need to go on your own. I think with a little assistance from us we can get you there quickly.' He paused to consider, rubbing his chin and muttering how he couldn't spare his only half track, whereupon I thought it incumbent to repeat my kind offer of my own merry way, but he just ignored me.

We were standing by a roadway and as ill luck would have it an elderly Renault sedan came careering around the corner at that very moment. Knöchlein stood in the middle of the road and it screeched to a halt. His men surrounded the vehicle and gestured for the occupants to get out. Four nuns. Christ knows what they were doing in the middle of a battlefield. Well I suppose he does know come to think of it. Mother Superior quickly took charge of the situation. She was an elderly old crone, but by gum, she was game. How dare these common soldiers interrupt God's work. Now they were going to be late for Vespers. The Abbot would be furious – it was his car apparently. And so on.

All this was lost on Knöchlein as it became apparent that he didn't speak a word of French. He stood there rubbing his chin and then came to a decision. He motioned to one of his troopers and whispered something to him, then turned to me. 'Take the car. Corporal Weber will go with you. He will make sure you don't get lost.' Knöchlein gave me a long stare when he said that and then just turned and strode off. I would like to say that that was the last I saw of him, but sadly not.

We jumped in the car, Weber in the driving seat, me alongside, and when it started this initiated further hysterics from the reverend M.S. I could still hear her berating all and sundry as we turned onto the main road.

Progress was slow. We were trying to head south, but crossing our path was the weight of two whole German army groups streaming west across the Belgium border. There was a fair bit of civilian traffic on the by-roads too – Belgians who wanted to be in France, French who wanted to be in Belgium and, in short, it seemed that everyone had to be somewhere else and everyone was in our way.

I tried engaging Corporal Weber in conversation but was treated to monosyllabic grunts. It occurred to me that I could avoid the whole HQ debacle by making a run for it, but thought that unless a clear opportunity arose I didn't fancy my chances much. That Weber came across as a wily old fox, one of those seen-it-all done-it-all NCO types, who'd doubtless have no trouble tracking me down and *that* would leave me with a whole lot of explaining to do.

I think I must have fallen asleep because the next thing I recall was a clear road and a signpost as we flashed by. It was ten kilometres to Charleville, meaning we would be there in about 20 minutes. Then the thought of having to humbug it with a bunch of top Nazis on arrival determined me to make some escape attempt, however hapless.

A few minutes later we came to a village and, as we drove through the market square, I yelled out, 'Stop!' There was no doubt Weber heard me but the car careered onwards. When it came to dumb insolence, I thought, our men were pretty bad but that Weber really took the pfefferkuchen. It was time to remind him of his lowly position in the grand military hierarchy. 'Scharführer, I order you to halt,' I rasped in what I hoped was my most authoritative Kriegsakademie voice.

He turned and scowled at me, but the car slowed and trundled to a stop at the roadside, beside a café. Perfect. 'Wait there Corporal. I need a leak.' I did too. It had been a long and taxing day.

I climbed out of the car and headed across the pavement. I just caught the name of my destination in tired lettering above the door as I strode through below it. Café de la Belle Epoque.* As I glanced around the gloom within, I spotted a signed picture of Victor Hugo on the wall. How appropriate. I could see that the place hadn't been swept since he'd been there.

Reflecting that it was a pity that a few more literary giants hadn't popped by in the meantime, I looked up, to be confronted by the wide eyes of Madame and Madamoiselle poking out from behind Monsieur. 'Why so afraid?' was my first thought. It took me a few seconds to adjust to the idea that this wasn't jaunty jolly old Pilot Officer Keelroy and his squadron of brave peelottes making a grand entrance at "Dick's Cocks" in Condé-Vraux but was instead a dastardly Blitzkrieger crashing into their world with but one thing on his mind. In my best French I asked them where it was.

He pointed to a door at the end of the counter and I was about to head that way when I spotted that the counter itself was labouring under the weight of what could very well be the best cheeses in the whole of the Ardennes. In such an unlikely place too, I thought, as it hit me how hungry I was. Now, some would say I should have spent more of my time in France on aircraft recognition rather than cheese familiarisation but at least, on this occasion, I could easily identify a Morbier, a Picodon de l'Ardeche and even a Vacherin Mont d'Or, and that was just from the ones closest to me.

I pointed at one that wasn't familiar and looked enquiringly at my reluctant host.

---

* Belle Epoque – Beautiful Era, commonly said to have lasted from c1870-1914.

'Limburger.' The womenfolk were still clustered behind him. 'Made by *les Trappistes*. German Trappistes,' he added with a sneer.

I asked how he came by a German cheese, but he just tapped the side of his nose and added nothing. I looked outside and could see that my comrade in arms was busy manoeuvring the car out of the path of a lorry. 'Deux baguettes, s'il vous plait.'

Monsieur reluctantly prepared the rolls for me, a task made more difficult as his household had to follow closely behind him at each stage. At last he was finished and handed them to me. I grabbed them and headed off on the next stage of my mission.

I think I have told you enough of the unkempt nature of the café so I will spare you the detail on the next five minutes. As I had hoped, the convenience at least had a convenient window leading to the rear. I had to smash the glass but just managed to scramble through it without injury. Then I made my way through the orchard at the back and over a wall into a lane.

Which way *wasn't* Germany? West of course. I glanced up to take a bearing from the sun and headed off in the best general direction. I was in a narrow lane with a stone wall on one side and a hedge on the other. I had only gone a few yards when I heard the clatter of metal on cobbles and from around the corner swung a tank, its commander with his head poking through the turret and smoking a large cigar. His eyes widened and he smiled but it was pretty clear he wasn't going to stop.

I had no choice but to run back "à toute vitesse". Fortunately there was an alleyway a few yards up the lane and I dived down it just in time. I stood there regaining my breath and watched as a succession of half tracks, lorries and more tanks roared by. It occurred to me that another route might be in order. I smoothed back my hair, paused for breath then strode the other way up the alleyway, affecting a confident gait that I was far from feeling. At the end of the alley there was a roadway with a large statue in the middle. I paused to admire it whilst wondering what to do next. It was a magnificent edifice for such a small village, the gleaming bronze life-size figures atop a solid marble plinth. I noticed a tarnished brass plaque on the side with a list of names. No Kilroys of course but there were four Lavals. Poor old Madame Laval I thought. As I was reading it I became aware of a gushing sound from nearby, as if someone had left a tap running.

I slowly walked around the side of the memorial. The gushing sound stopped just I came face to face with Corporal Weber. He glared at me as he buttoned his flys. 'Ah, there you are,' he said. 'Sir.'

I could see the Renault a few yards away, still parked where I had left it. He hitched his rifle over his shoulder and headed back to it. There didn't seem anything else I could do but follow him.

CHAPTER 6

It took a while to explain our way past the guard post but at last we were waved through. We trundled up a short driveway and onto the forecourt of a respectable looking town house. The name *Maison de l'Ardenne* was etched on a brass plate outside – for the time being the General Headquarters for around half the German Army.[*] I was marvelling at how modest the place looked, compared with, for example, Les Crayères – our own AVM's recent magnificent hidey-hole at Reims. Mind you, *that* got bombed on the very first day of the Blitzkrieg, so there might be something to be said for *not* having your HQ in the most prominent building for miles around.[†]

I climbed out of the car and headed to the main entrance, where I briskly mounted the steps and breezed through the door, affecting an air of efficiency and enthusiasm I scarcely felt. My faithful corporal was dogging my footsteps. 'Thank you Corporal. I think I can manage from here.'

He handed me the case.

'Oh, thank you Corporal. That will be all.' But he wouldn't take the hint and continued to follow me. I spotted an army uniform, sitting at an improvised reception desk. I squinted at the nameplate in front of him. Major Fokker didn't look up, but carried on writing something in a ledger.

I coughed. 'Urgent despatch for the field marshal, sir.'

'No field marshal here.' he said crisply and carried on writing.

This required a bit of thought. I would have given anything to just tippy toe out of there at that point but with Corporal Wedlock and I so well spliced it didn't seem possible. I could hear the lout's heavy breathing just behind me so, clearly, there was to be no easy exit for me at that exact moment. Then I recalled the *All Stations* message Knöchlein had shown me. Wasn't it somebody called General Shyster who had got the chop in the plane? Christ, I'd seen it only a few hours ago, but it felt like weeks. Bugger, what was his name? Sidecar, Shiteman, Slighthand? Then I remembered. 'I

---

[*] The Maison de l'Ardenne still stands at 18bis Avenue Georges-Corneau, 08000 Charleville-Mezieres, France – French Historic Monuments website: http://tinyurl.com/Kilroy108. At this stage of the war it was the headquarters of German Army Group A, under the command of Generaloberst Gerd von Rundstedt, which was a substantial part of the German invasion force but not quite half.There was also Army Groups B to the North and C to the South.

[†] This was Air Vice Marshal Playfair's HQ, mentioned earlier. Les Crayères was raided by Luftwaffe bombers on the first day of the Blitzkrieg but they missed their target.

carry General von Schleicher's urgent despatch. Please direct me to the High Command.'

The major sat up then all right. 'Why didn't you say so? I will take you to Colonel General von Rundstedt[*] immediately.'

As the major rose, I seized my opportunity to bid farewell to my chauffeur. 'Thank you, Corporal, you can return to your unit now.'

He hesitated and I could see his mind working overtime. He glanced at the major then, reluctantly, he saluted, turned and sauntered out.

The major led me down a long corridor. I couldn't get over how quiet it was. There I was, at the height of the Battle of France with the Germans winning ten nil, and rather expecting a building abuzz with phones ringing and underlings scurrying backwards and forwards but, instead we just passed a succession of rooms with little or nothing ongoing. I remember thinking they must have been doing something right to enjoy their recent spectacular successes but I've seen more life in Whites' club lounge after a steak and kidney pudding lunch than I witnessed that afternoon on my way to the general.[†]

Maison de l'Ardenne. Von Rundstedt's 1940 HQ.

At last we came to some double doors and the major swung one of them open to reveal a large room. From the chandeliers I guessed it had been a ballroom before the war had descended upon Charleville, but now there was little trace of its former grandeur. All the drapes had been pulled down and lay in bundles in the corners. There were several large tables

[*] Gerd von Rundstedt was a Generaloberst, a Colonel General, at the time of the Battle of France. A few weeks later, following the fall of France, he was promoted (along with 11 others) to Generalfeldmarschall, Field Marshal. He was old-style Prussian military, and of retirement age in 1940, but was still serving Hitler at the end of the war, having declined any involvement in the various plots against him. After the war there was pressure to have him tried at Nuremberg, for war crimes on the Eastern Front, but in the end it was decided that no serving army officers would be put in the dock. He was eventually released from British custody and died in poverty in Hannover in 1953. http://tinyurl.com/Kilroy109.

[†] White's is the oldest and most exclusive of London's gentleman's clubs, being founded in 1693 and still in operation to the present day. Prince Charles is one of many, many aristocratic members. Former Prime Minister David Cameron was a member until 2008, when he resigned over the club's refusal to admit women. His father had previously been the club's chairman. http://tinyurl.com/Kilroy110.

scattered around and charts everywhere, on the tables, on the walls and even on the floor in one corner. There was a large map of North America pinned up behind what looked like a small stage. I couldn't see any pins in it so it didn't look like Roosevelt had much to worry about for the time being. At a table in a far corner there was an elderly French couple arguing furiously over a pile of photographs. But everywhere else there were Wehrmacht uniforms. Plenty of scrambled egg too. I counted four colonels and two brigadiers. And the Colonel General.

After the war much nonsense was written about what took place in this room over the few hours I was there. The problem was that the participants, those who lived to tell the tale anyway, weren't inclined to tell the truth, while the historians – William Shirer, A J P Taylor, Liddell Hart, Churchill and the like – weren't around at the time to see what really happened. Worse, they weren't interested in hearing from me so they all missed the mark in the end. But truth is stranger than fiction, as they say...

No one noticed us as we walked in. Von Rundstedt was bent over a table with the rest of them gathered around in rapt attention. On the table was a map of Northern France and the Colonel General was jabbing his finger at what looked suspiciously like Dieppe. 'Where is that fool heading now?' he asked the wise heads around him. 'We need to be turning the screw on the British, not Frog walloping on the Somme. We must stick the jackboot in here, here and here.' He jabbed three spots in a line on the French coast – Boulogne, Calais and the last one, near the Belgian border – Dunkirk.

'But sir, I think we need to take care. That counter attack at Arras...' interrupted one of the colonels.

'Diesel fuel, von Sodenstern. Diesel fuel,' spat out von Rundstedt.*

The others looked back at him, with a measure of puzzlement.

'The British are nearly out of it and I know what their little game is. They've only enough to get them to the coast and that's *exactly* where they are heading so that their Royal Navy can rescue them.'

'But...'

'Cut them off, here, here and here,' he pointed at the three channel ports again, 'and they've nowhere to go but our prison camps. And *that*, my friends, will be Britain out of the war.' He rubbed his hands as he eyed his audience.

'But...'

'And only *then*, we'll deal with the Frenchies, that is if they haven't all run off to Algeria in the meantime.'

---

* Generalleutnant Georg von Sodenstern was von Rundstedt's chief-of-staff, ranking higher than a colonel. http://tinyurl.com/Kilroy111.

The major and I were waiting patiently by the door while this exchange took place but, at that moment, von Rundstedt looked up and caught my eye. His eyes widened and his face erupted into a huge grin. 'My God. Hans.' He spread his arms, took a pace towards me and embraced me. 'Hans, Hans.' It fair took the wind out of me. Then he was pounding my back. His whiskers rasped against my cheek and I could detect a faint smell of cabbage.

At last he took a pace back. 'But, Hans, do you not remember me?'

I nodded noncommittally. There didn't seem much else I could do.

'Thank God, you are safe. Your mother would never have forgiven me.' He gazed fondly at me.

I thought it was time to say something. 'It was nothing, sir. And she sends her regards.'

He looked stern. 'You told her you were coming here? I hope not.'

Generalfeldmarschall Gerd von Rundstedt.

'Well, no sir. I meant she often speaks of you, of course.'

He seemed relieved. 'Let me look at you. Yes, your mother's eyes that's for sure, but your father's nose I reckon. Always was an ugly old devil, God rest his soul, but I fancy you have your mother's looks overall, you lucky old dog.' He held me at arm's length. 'But you don't remember me, do you?'

There didn't seem much point in denying it. 'Not to look at, sir.'

The assorted colonels, brigadiers and majors were watching our little family reunion with some amusement. He turned to them and said, 'Meet Oberleutenant von Stauss. The last time I saw him was, ooh, 15 years ago when his father and I were in the old Third.* I remember it well. A chubby cheeked little boy in a sailor suit.' He turned

* Von Rundstedt commanded the 3rd Division (Reichswehr) in 1932. It ceased to exist in October 1934, when the army was restructured.

back to me and dabbed his eye. 'But the Kriegsmarine wasn't for you, eh Hans? See the handsome Luftwaffe pilot before us.'

I waved nonchalantly and could see the assorted colonels, brigadiers and majors scowling back at me behind forced smiles. One of them muttered something, which I only just caught, along the lines of 'pain in the backside.'[*]

At that moment a corporal appeared and served us from a tray of coffees. The general glanced at him then nudged me in the ribs. 'But, say, Hans, I bet you can't wait to get into Emile.' He slapped me on the back.

I nearly choked. Fortunately most of the coffee landed back in my mug. Agreement seemed the best option. 'Of course, Herr General.' I grinned back at him whilst looking doubtfully at the corporal. I was wondering how the Germans could be doing so well on the battlefield while their High Command was up to God knows what at HQ.

The general must have sensed my puzzlement. 'But Hans, surely you don't want to be flying one of those crane things for the rest of the war?'

It was a relief to have a question I could answer. 'You mean the Fiesler Storch, Herr General?'

'Yes, yes, the Storch. Would you not rather be piloting a 109?'[†]

The pfennig dropped. 'Oh I see. The 109. Emile? Yes, of course, Herr General.'

There was a pause as we sipped our coffee and I could hear the French couple's debate getting more animated. 'See here, woman, that is Pont Neuf. And the swamp is in the field alongside.'

But she wasn't having that. 'The only swamp is in your brains you pig-head. That is Pont d'Avigney. Look.' She picked up some of the photographs and rearranged them on the table.

The general drained his coffee. The man was just about to answer his wife but the general interrupted him. 'Enough.' They both fell silent. He nodded at a sergeant standing by the door. 'Get rid of them.'

The sergeant unslung his rifle and advanced towards the couple, who turned towards him, their faces white. The woman started crying while the man stuttered, trying to say something.

The general's voice boomed out. 'I don't mean get rid of them. I mean get rid of them. Throw them out.' He turned back towards me. I could see two very relieved Frenchies being prodded out. 'And, you.' He pointed at a major nearby, 'Get rid of that photographic crap. We'll not be needing it

---

[*] *Stauss* is the Middle High German word for buttocks.

[†] In 1940 the latest Messerschmitt 109 was the 109E, known throughout the Luftwaffe as "Emil" from the German phonetic alphabet word for "E". http://tinyurl.com/Kilroy112.

now the Luftwaffe is here.' He slapped me on the back, to the accompaniment of more glares from the Wehrmacht.

The general put his arm around me and guided me towards a large table. 'Now let's have a look in that briefcase shall we?'

For reasons that will soon be apparent I'd been rather hoping that the briefcase had been forgotten. It was daft of me really, as the whole point of my being at GHQ was to deliver it to the Colonel General, so he was hardly likely to forget it. And there he was, smiling warmly at his nephew as said nephew was looking for a hole in the floor he could jump into. 'Oh dear, I seem to have mislaid it. Allow me to look for it outside,' I think I said. Not very imaginative, I know, but it was all I could come up with at the time.

'Don't trouble yourself young man. It's over there.' He pointed to a chair by the door and snapped his fingers. A major picked it up and brought it over to him. The others clustered around us as von Rundstedt flicked open the catch. He smiled at me and added, 'Now my fine friend. With the timely arrival of this missing jigsaw piece, wir werden die Briten wie eine Weihnachtsgans ausnemen.'*

I knew what was going to happen next and didn't anticipate many more smiles from my new found uncle. Von Rundstedt reached in and I could see a puzzled frown cross his face. He withdrew his arm and held the case open as wide as it would go, as he looked in, his eyes flicking from side to side. 'Wo ist es?'

'Where is what, sir?'

'The map of course. General von Schleicher's map. Where is it?'

You need a poker face for these situations. Luckily I have one. 'What map sir? I know nothing about that.'

'The map you fool. Von Schleicher was ordered to bring a hundred mil map for Dunkirk's western approaches. We have urgent need of it.'

I thought it best not to reply. I could hardly tell him his precious map was at that very moment not 20 miles away, neatly folded into a padded strip and pressed firmly into the broken shards of what had once been a lavatory window.

He passed the briefcase to a major alongside him, who continued what I knew would be a fruitless search for it. 'Herr General, I am sure we can manage without. We do have the map here,' he said.

I could see the general's cheeks taking a reddish tinge. 'Yes, von Muck, but you would say that. You are the one who lost the original. Don't forget all the marshes around here.' He pointed at the map we did have. 'But where's the detail? Where are all those damned swamps and creeks? Do you want our tanks to get stuck in them?' He sighed and waved at the table. 'How can we work with this crap?'

---

* We will gut the British like a Christmas goose.

I stared down at the map and studied it more closely. I could just make out the legend – "Camping Guide to Flanders".

Someone said, 'The photo reconnaissance. The photos!'

Von Rundstedt brightened at this. He turned to the major 'Yes you, Major Fokker. Get those two Frogs back and let's see if we can make anything of those photos.'

The major looked worried. 'You said get rid of them, sir. I put them on the stove. Security and all that.'

Have you ever seen a man who is about to burst? Well, that is what my Uncle General looked like at that moment. He swallowed several times whilst loudly tapping the table. And I was sure I could hear him grinding his teeth. Everyone else froze and watched him, as if waiting for a grenade to go off, and in the end it did. 'Attack,' he cried.

'Pardon, sir?' said von Sodenstern.

'I said "Attack." As discussed earlier. Boulogne and Calais are as good as ours. So let's attack, attack, attack. One firm push on Dunkirk and the British, as they themselves might say, "will be all at sea", except, of course that's the one place they won't be.' He sniggered quietly at his own joke.

'But...'

'If you think losing that blasted map is going to change anything, it isn't...' He wagged his finger at me and von Muck. 'This is war, not a sunday school picnic. I'm tired of mollycoddling that bunch of hosenscheissers in their Panzers. Ficken sie – fuck 'em. It's only 15 kilometres to Dunkirk. The price is high but the rewards are great. Advance, advance, advance, I say.' He banged the table to keep time. 'Tell them to take snorkels if they are worried about falling in a ditch.'

Someone asked how to spell snorkel and was met with a withering glare. Then there was silence. Von Muck resumed his search of the briefcase, unzipping an inner compartment and, to my great surprise, he found something. It was a single piece of paper.

Von Rundstedt snatched it away from him, glanced at it and smacked his forehead. 'Ich glaub mein Schwein pfeift.* Why didn't you tell me about this?' He was waving the paper at me.

'Well, sir, you see...'

'A Führer directive. To be delivered by hand, it says here. Why didn't you mention you'd been to his headquarters?'

Always blame the dead I thought. 'Well General von Schleicher thought that...'

'Never mind. Let's see what our Supreme Commander wants this time.' He put on spectacles and started to read aloud.

---

* I think my pig whistles – an expression of great surprise.

'From the Führer and Supreme Commander of the Armed Forces. Directive 12A for the conduct of the war – 22nd May at 13:30.' He looked at his watch. 'That is, er, just over 24 hours ago.'

'It is intended that OKH,* at the earliest opportunity should continue the attack on the enemy forces north of the Somme while continuing its destruction of the Belgian army.' He looked up from the page and glared at von Muck, who was still fiddling with the briefcase. 'Our air, sea and land forces must coordinate fully...'

Von Rundstedt was starting to lose me around about then. All I recall is that he laboriously went through the Führer's orders, unit by unit for the Luftwaffe and then the Kriegsmarine before he came to the army's role. 'Now, at last, Army Group A,' announced von Rundstedt with a sigh. 'Let's see what the Führer wants from us.' He turned over the page.

It was blank.

Everyone turned to look at me. 'Where's the rest of it?' barked von Rundstedt.

Well I did say earlier that I had been rather dreading the grand opening of the briefcase. I was hardly likely to come out with it, but the truth in this case was that... well, let's just say that the facilities at the Belle Epoque had been sadly lacking and that I'd had to improvise with the materials to hand. 'I suppose von Schleicher must have mislaid it, sir,' was the best I could come up with.

'Christ, how'd that pig's testicle ever get a general command? And this is no damned use at all.' He screwed the directive into a ball and tossed it to me.† 'Here, give me that briefcase.' He snatched it away from von Muck. 'Surely there must be *something* in there somewhere,' he mused. 'Otherwise we have one map – missing; one Führer Directive – half missing.' He started rummaging inside and brightened momentarily. 'See, there's another compartment here.' He fiddled around some more then turned the briefcase upside down and shook it. Something fell out, landing with a plop on the table in front of us. It was a baguette.

---

* Oberkommando des Heeres (Supreme High Command of the German Army) – the OKH.

† Hitler issued many directives throughout the war. Most were circulated to only a handful of generals in the High Command. Führer Directives 11 to 15 cover the six week French campaign with *Directive 12A* issued on May 22nd 1940 by Kilroy's account, sandwiched between *Directive 12: Prosecution of the Attack in the West* on May 18th and *Directive 13: Next Object in the West*, on May 24th.

Many of Hitler's directives have been preserved and are available to the interested reader. Hugh Trevor-Roper's *Hitler's War Directives 1939-1945* is comprehensive, and translated (Amazon: http://tinyurl.com/Kilroy113), but contains no mention of *12A*, which was presumably an amendment to *12*. http://tinyurl.com/Kilroy114.

The general turned to me. 'What the hell is that? And don't tell me that damned fool von Schleicher was hiding his lunch in there? An explanation please, young man, and it had better be a good one.'

Well I'd had a pretty trying day and sheer exhaustion got the better of me at that moment. Stupidly I just said the first thing that came into my head. 'It is a present from the Führer, sir.'

With such a lunatic response I expected him to have me clapped in irons immediately, but to my surprise he seemed to be inclined to believe me. 'The Führer sent this? Herr Hitler?'

I nodded, while I found myself wondering what he would have said had I told him it had been delivered to me by a troop of one-legged bare breasted Amazons. Probably he would have wanted to know which legs they were hopping on.

'He gave it to von Schleicher along with the Directive?'

I nodded again. I'd no idea where this was going but didn't really have much option other than to go along with it and hope for the best.

'So, I ask von Schleicher for a hundred mil map for sector 27 and he gets hold of half a directive and a ham roll?'

'Cheese.'

'What?'

'It's a cheese roll.' I picked it up and took a bite out of it, before pointing at a lump of cheese within.

'But what can it mean?'

'The Führer shed you'd undershtand, shur.' I took another lump out of it. Christ I was peckish.

'Stop that.' He snatched the roll away from me, opened it out and examined it carefully, prodding the contents with his finger. 'Isn't that Limburger?'

'I believe it is sir. Yes, German Limburger, sir. Nicely matured too.' I reached out for the roll again but the general whisked it out of my reach. The other officers gathered around him and I could only look over his shoulder as they poked and prodded my tasty snack. Their voices were low and I couldn't quite catch what they were saying. Somebody muttered something about a fucking corporal but was quickly hushed by the others. Von Sodenstern picked up the roll, sniffed at it and turned to me. 'What butter is that?'

'Danish of course. The Führer insisted on that.' A thought occurred to me. 'Those are Norfolk tomatoes by the way. The county of Norfolk in England. They were captured off the Brits in the Ardennes. The Führer said it had to have British tomatoes.'

They all exchanged glances. The major dug his pencil in and pulled out a piece of lettuce. They turned to me.

'Belgian.' Blimey, I thought, we might as well have the whole League of Nations in there.

The conference continued and then von Sodenstern had an inspiration. 'Our Führer has strange ways at times but I think I've got it sir. This is a German cheese in the tight grip of a massive French stick, peppered by a British tomato and slipping around in Danish butter. I think the Führer is telling us to be careful sir, or we will get a thrashing from the Frenchies.'

They all nodded wisely and turned to the general.

'Scarcely likely,' muttered von Rundstedt but I could see it had made him think. He scratched his head, staring long and hard at the baguette. He kept opening his mouth to speak but then said nothing. Then, at last he shook his head. 'Alright, alright. That's agreed. Caution first. We will consolidate and regroup. We don't want to get caught with our pants down like at Arras the other day.' He turned to Major Fokker. 'Get on to Guderian immediately. Any tanks over the canal line at the West of Dunkirk must withdraw. He won't like it but those are his orders. Tell him to consolidate and regroup, get his supplies in and get his vehicles repaired.'

A reconstruction of the famous cheese baguette, in the Imperial War Museum (cafeteria), London.

'But sir...' started Fokker.

'He'll be back on the move soon enough and the Tommies will still be there. After all, they can't escape that quickly, surely?' He guffawed and elbowed the major in the ribs.

There was an answering round of sycophantic chuckling and von Rundstedt turned to me. 'That von Schleicher set you a pretty poor example but, see, you have had your uses in the end, eh?'

This seemed like as good a time as any to make my little bid for freedom. 'Glad to be of help, sir. And, with your permission, may I return to my unit?'

'No laddie. You can stay right here for now. We're down a Luftwaffe liaison officer and you can cover for him until he returns. Major Fokker will show you what to do.' He and the major exchanged glances. 'Besides, we will have a little surprise for you tomorrow morning.' They grinned and nodded at each other.

I didn't like the sound of that but there was nothing I could do about it, and so had to sit up half the night with the major filling in forms. He was the most tedious bore, a stickler for detail, and insisted on checking everything over and over. He got in quite a tizz when I got a map reference wrong and we almost sent an SS division to Albania. I tried to slope off a few times, but there always seemed to be someone with me so in the end had to just put up with it and sit tight.

At last, around about three in the morning, we were finished and the general gave us permission to turn in. I've already mentioned that the premises were comparatively modest so the junior officers' sleeping accommodation was limited to what had once been the servant's quarters, a few scruffy rooms with army cots jammed together any old how. If I'd had a mind to escape at that moment I probably could have but frankly, I was just about done in and only too glad to stretch out and get some shut-eye.

CHAPTER 7

Next day dawned bright and sunny. I was awakened by the sound of hustle and bustle in the corridor outside as everyone sluiced off and spruced up. Full dress uniform seemed to be the order of the day. As I'd arrived somewhat unprepared, so as to speak, I had to make do with yesterday's flying attire, as kindly lent to me by the late Oberleutenant von Stauss.

I hardly recognised the operations room when I returned there. Everything that could be tidied away was tidied away and everything else was cleaned and polished. Somebody had thoughtfully placed a display of flowers on a table by the door. I spotted von Sodenstern in the corner carefully arranging some military banners while Major von Muck bawled out an orderly who had left a broom standing by one of the windows. The Battle of France seemed to be on hold for the time being.

I didn't have long to wonder what all the fuss was about. I could sense a buzz coming from the corridor outside, then the door was flung open and in he strutted, the face that adorned a thousand postage stamps, a man on the brink of his greatest triumph. He strode in, pulled off his gloves and threw them to an aide.

As one we stiffened and saluted.

The Führer brushed past me and stood at the map table. 'Right. Situation report,' he barked out with barely a pause for breath. He was accompanied by two men I didn't recognise but knew by name – Generals Keitel and Jodl.* They stood on one side of him while von Rundstedt and von Sodenstern were on the other. Us lesser ranks kept at a respectful distance. In particular I made sure I was right at the back, recalling that Hitler and I had already been acquainted in rather different circumstances, 18 months previously at Munich.

The Colonel General started to point out the troop dispositions on the map, delivering with some pride. An explanation was scarcely needed, I thought. There were neat lines of numbered black markers, representing German units, all over north eastern France and the low countries. The blue markers, the French, were out in force and evidently preparing to defend Bordeaux to the last man. Then, in a wide area encompassing much of Flanders, it looked as if someone had dropped his breakfast. The British

---

* Generaloberst Wilhelm Keitel was Chief of the OKW throughout the war, in effect Germany's War Minister – http://tinyurl.com/Kilroy115. Generaloberst Alfred Jodl was his Chief of the Operations Staff – http://tinyurl.com/Kilroy116. Both were tried at Nuremberg after the war, found guilty on multiple counts and hanged.

Army. Von Rundstedt turned to Hitler and said, 'So you see, mein Führer, we have the situation under control, thanks to your timely message.' He glanced up and caught my eye. 'It took time to work out the meaning but I'm sure we are doing the right thing.'

'Time?' Hitler barked. 'You took time? Surely not? I was very clear. Very clear indeed.' His clear blue eyes flashed like Krupp steel as he directed his gaze at the Colonel General.

Hitler's arrival at von Rundstedt's HQ.

Von Rundstedt tugged at his collar. 'Yes of course, sire. What I meant of course was it took not long at all but, the main thing is, as you wished, that we are *now* consolidating our considerable gains and proceeding with caution.'

'Caution?'

Von Rundstedt nodded, looking worried.

'Caution? You said "caution"?'

'Jawohl mein Führer.' He gulped and continued to fiddle with his collar.

'Is your shirt too tight, Oberstgeneral?'

'Nein, mein Führer. It is just a little hot in here.'

'Exactly! Exactly!' Hitler stabbed at the table as he spoke and several of the counters fell over – all British of course. 'That was the whole point of my directive. Make it hot for the Tommies. Their head is in our noose and now we will slowly tighten it. *Not* with caution so much as slowly, slowly...' He had both hands in front of him, fingertip to fingertip, as if strangling somebody.'

'Your instructions were in the directive?' asked von Rundstedt, looking even more worried.

'Yes, yes, of course, where else would they be? Directive 12A, you must recall, sent just 36 hours ago?' He sighed. 'Sometimes I wonder if you generals can read. Next time, perhaps, I'll enclose a... a rice pudding. You like rice pudding I think? Yes, a big bowl of rice pudding. Ha ha. Perhaps you'll pay more attention then, hmm?'

There was a stunned silence. It would seem we'd all just witnessed a very rare event, a Führer joke, and no one knew how to react. Von Rundstedt looked puzzled and glanced at von Sodenstern. Von Sodenstern bore a thunderous expression while scanning the room – looking for me I presumed. Keitel and Jodl looked uncertainly at each other, trying to make up their minds whether or not to risk a sycophantic chuckle. In the end everyone decided to ignore it. Von Rundstedt carried on smoothly. 'Yes, of course mein Führer. Your directives are always our first priority and, accordingly, we are treating the British with slow caution and slowly-slowly as I think you said. In the north, Boulogne and Calais are besieged and will surely fall in the next 48 hours. The British counter-attack at Arras has failed and also, er, we have halted the advance on Dunkirk.'

'Dunkirk? Halted? Why?

'Well, mein Führer our supply lines...'

'You've halted the advance just ten kilometres out and with the British in disarray. Why?'

'Er, I...' Von Rundstedt was fingering his collar again. 'Er...' Then his eyes lit upon me in my slightly bedraggled, slightly ill-fitting flying gear. 'The Luftwaffe!' he cried suddenly.

'The Luftwaffe?' asked Hitler with a touch of incredulity, as if von Rundstedt had been calling upon the Lone Ranger*.

'Yes, mein Führer, we thought, perhaps the, er, Luftwaffe would be better placed to take on the British as, er, as er...

'We have captured most of their anti-aircraft guns,' von Sodenstern finished the sentence for him.

Hitler briefing his Generals.

'Yes, that's it, mein Führer. We have their guns. So the Luftwaffe, yes?' he asked.

Hitler paused, looking from von Sodenstern to von Rundstedt, with his mouth barely open as he quietly tapped one of his incisors with his fingernail. 'Hmmm,' he said. 'Hmmm.' Just as I was wondering if his incisors were shortly going to be sunk into von Rundstedt's neck he spoke. 'Gut. Sehr gut, very good Colonel General,' he said with something almost approaching a smile.

Von Rundstedt said nothing, but looked like an enormous weight had been lifted from his shoulders.

'Yes, Generaloberst. I like it,' Hitler continued. 'Göring is eager to play with his new toys. So let him have his way. The air bases are nearby so we'll leave Dunkirk to him and then, I assure you, the British will rue the day they ever set foot in France.'

The briefing continued but I can't recall much of it. We none of us knew it at the time but one of the most important decisions in the war had

* *The Lone Ranger*, a fictional American cowboy, first appeared on US radio in 1933, but is better known from a 1950s TV series of the same name. http://tinyurl.com/Kilroy117.

just been made. It was a wrong one, as it turned out, from the German viewpoint, and an enormous reprieve for the British. Over the next few days, a third of a million men were pulled out, the cream of the British Army, from those very Dunkirk beaches and pontoons that earlier the Germans could have captured in an afternoon. And the Luftwaffe? Well I suppose you could say God played his part there. The Luftwaffe had little say in matters as it was grounded by low cloud for much of the time.*

I like to think I played no small part in saving the British Army that day but thus far I had done little to save my own skin. I'd seen von Sodenstern stiffen as soon as Hitler mentioned the rice pudding. He must have been wondering what kind of madness had come over him when I'd come up with that nonsense about the cheese sandwich. I rather regretted my fatuous humour at that moment as I saw his scowl as he scanned the room for me, looking like a man who would like to ask some serious questions once the Führer had departed. Of course he spotted me soon enough and our eyes met – his savage glare and my affected innocence. There were some SS guards standing to attention by the door and he walked over to one of them, whispered something and pointed at me. The guard quietly paced across the room and came up to stand close behind me. I could sense his breath on the back of my neck.

At last the briefing ended and orderlies arrived with drinks. I walked over to a side table, closely followed by my new SS friend of course, and poured myself a coffee. Hitler, I noticed, was drinking tea. The atmosphere in the room had changed, with all the main participants seeming relaxed now the important decisions had been made. Hitler was treating von Rundstedt to a monologue on his diplomacy skills, with him nodding awhile and trying not to look at his watch.Von Sodenstern and von Muck were chatting about the ancient battle of Cannae of all things. I'd covered that ground between tumbles with Matron one memorable afternoon and knew all about Hannibal luring Varro into the jaws of his army, but was wondering what Corporal Hitler would make of it. Then I sensed something odd and I wasn't quite sure what it was. There was a curious odour in the room and I couldn't place it. It was not altogether unpleasant, more a sort of damp sweet smell, like a musty overcoat. I sniffed the air several times, but could determine nothing further.

The coffee had certainly sharpened my appetite and I was reminded that I hadn't eaten for some time. The high command had devoured all the

---

* Kilroy's account of the infamous Dunkirk "Halt Order" concurs with the known history but certainly sheds new light on the motivations of some of the participants. It was questioned by some German senior officers at the time and has been long debated by historians since. Hindsight says it was a colossal mistake but mistakes in war are common and, as they say, hindsight is an exact science. See *End Note (11)*.

biscuits so I cast around for something else. Then I spotted it. It was my old friend the baguette, all on its own, still half-eaten, on a side table on a bone china plate under a crystal cover. It would hardly be in the first flush of youth after being mauled by assorted colonels, followed by a night in the open at German GHQ, but at that moment it seemed like just the ticket for a hungry airman. I edged towards the table, removed the cover to pick it up and was just about to insert it in A1 Mouth, use for the eating with, when it slipped from my grasp and fell on the floor. I reached down to retrieve it but was beaten to it by a blur of hairy brown fur that leapt out from under the table with the speed of a Panzer division.

My mother's Onkel Otto in Bremen used to breed dogs, hunting dogs and cattle dogs mainly, so I'd acquired some familiarity with our larger canine friends on my various family visits. Onkel Otto had drummed into me that with large dogs there is only one top dog and it's not the dog. So I leapt into action. My cheese roll certainly wasn't going to go the way of Varro, and disappear into the jaws of hairy hound. Said hairy hound might have one end of it but I was determined it wasn't going to get the other. I had one arm around its throat and was gouging its eye with one hand whilst trying to prise its mouth open with the other when I heard a voice behind me.

'What *are* you doing?'

I looked up to see the unmistakable features of the conqueror of the western world. I was so surprised that I loosened my grip. Just a split second, that's all it took and I watched with dismay as the baguette disappeared with one gulp down the mangy mutt's throat. A gob of saliva dropped from its jaws and splashed me in the eye as I tried to extricate myself from the tangle of limbs and paws. 'My, he's a playful fellow, mein Führer, isn't he?'

Hitler clicked his fingers. The dog trotted towards him and sat at his feet. 'She.'

'I mean she's a friendly lass, sire. Looked a bit hungry so I thought I'd share my roll with her. Bit of rough and tumble. Dogs love it don't they?'

He scowled. 'Yes, in the right place.' I could see him sizing me up as I dusted myself down. 'I see the Luftwaffe has flown in. But you look familiar, Lieutenant. I've seen you before.'

This was not what I wanted to hear. Over 18 months had passed since the day I'd dosed him with methamphetamine in the Führerbau in Munich and this was certainly not a connection I wanted to see made at von Rundstedt's HQ in Charleville. In my favour was the sheer unlikelihood of a junior member of the British delegation and the Luftwaffe pilot before him being one and the same person. Also I'd filled out a little in the meantime and acquired a moustache. I just hoped that that would be enough to put him off the scent, but I could see he was puzzled.

'What unit do you serve with, Lieutenant?'

I hesitated.

'Come on Lieutenant no need to be tongue tied. What geschwader?'

'Two, sire.' A low number seemed a safe bet. At least it would exist and with any luck the Führer wouldn't know much about it.

'Two. Would that be Geschwader two – Fighters, or Geschwader two – Destroyers?'*

Damn. Neither sounded like they flew the Fiesler Storch. And other than diving under the table, which I might even have done had that bloody dog not gone back there I had nowhere to go. So I stiffened, looked the Führer straight in the eye and answered with a quiet hint of modesty. 'Fighters of course, mein Führer.'

I was feeling pretty uncomfortable at this juncture but it was almost worth it to see the look on von Rundstedt's face. Of course I was already in trouble with von Sodenstern and now it would seem my long lost Uncle had also cottoned on to me. He turned and stared hard at me with a deep frown, like a man wrestling with some complex inner problem. His mouth gaped and his eyes widened to dinner plates as the pfennig dropped. Well not a pfennig really, more like a whole Deutschmark's worth of them. The colour drained from his face and I thought he might faint, but you don't make it to High Command without considerable powers of recovery. Quickly he composed himself and I could see he was about to say something but the Führer beat him to it.

'What fine company you keep, Herr General. Von Richthofen's finest and heroes to a man.† But now I must be leaving you.' He found a broken biscuit lying on a table, tossed it in the air and watched it go straight down Field Marshal von Fido's throat. As he was doing this I could see von Rundstedt whispering to another of the SS guards who immediately moved towards me. So now I had two of the swine stationed right behind me.

The Führer shook von Rundstedt's hand, muttering his congratulations. He clicked his fingers and the dog obediently trotted behind as he made his way out the door‡ with Keitel and Jodl following. As soon as he was

---

* Destroyers. The Me 110 twin engined fighter bomber was known as the Destroyer. In the Luftwaffe at that time it was more prestigious than the 109 but was soon found to be a poor match for the R.A.F.'s single-engined fighters. Later in the war it was redeployed, very successfully, as a night fighter. http://tinyurl.com/Kilroy118.

† Kilroy was claiming to serve in Jagdgeschwader 2 ("Jagd" means fighter). JG 2 was nicknamed "Richthofen" in honour of WWI fighter ace Manfred von Richthofen. http://tinyurl.com/Kilroy119.

‡ Hitler had several pet dogs over the years, most famously Blondi, a German Shepherd bitch, acquired in 1941 and who died with him in the bunker in Berlin at the war's end. It

through the door I felt both my arms grabbed and pinned behind me. Von Rundstedt was heading towards me and it certainly didn't look like he was planning to give me a kiss on both cheeks. In sheer desperation I called out, 'Mein Führer.' He was just about to round a corner in the corridor, but he stopped and turned around. 'Mein Führer. Could I be so bold as to ask for your help?'

He said nothing but exchanged a look with Keitel.

'I am long overdue back at my unit and I am sure these gentlemen here have had enough of me.' I could see they didn't agree but went on anyway. 'Perhaps, mein Führer, if I could ride with your escort to the airport, I would then be able to secure a flight back?'

Hitler paused for a few seconds, while I wondered whether he was going to laugh out loud or have me hanged, drawn and quartered. In the event he did neither. 'No, you won't go with my escort.' His expression was unchanged, inscrutable even. 'You can come with me. You can tell me all about operations in the 109.'

I felt the grip on my arms loosen and wasted no time in heading for the door. As I passed von Rundstedt I couldn't resist a parting shot. 'I will pass on your regards to my mother, Uncle.' And then I was on my way.

There were crowds lining the streets of Charleville – a few sullen French faces, out to see their conqueror, but mainly German army, cheering and throwing flowers in our path. We were in a convoy of gleaming open-topped limousines, the Großer Mercedes 770s I'd already come across in Munich, while we were busy selling out on the Czechs. We were attended by BMW motorcycle combinations buzzing around us and followed up by the cleanest army lorry I'd ever seen, one of those three tonners lovingly crafted for the Nazis by Henry Ford. I seemed to have been given the role of dog handler in this triumphant procession, which meant I was in the middle row of seats in the first car with the hairy mutt alongside, while Hitler's personal bodyguard, three grim looking SS thugs were behind me. The man himself was in the front, standing alongside the driver and delivering his penguin flipper salute to one and all. Once we reached the outskirts and the crowds thinned he sat down in the front seat and turned around to speak with me.

'Munich,' he said.

In my entire life I can't think of a word uttered that I less wanted to hear. I opened my mouth to reply but nothing came out. My first thought was of the Gestapo dungeon that awaited me, but then the possibility of a surprise open-topped exit flashed through my mind. This had to be rejected

---

is possible that in 1940 another German Shepherd, called Blonda, was still alive. Otherwise the identity of the dog here is a mystery. http://tinyurl.com/Kilroy120.

as we had rather picked up speed in the open countryside. At any rate, before I could speak or act the Führer went on.

'Yes, I remember you now. The young man with that delicious English water, yes?'

He was so sure of himself there didn't seem much point in denying it. I nodded.

'How is your mother?' he asked.

It had certainly been a day of surprises. I had to remind myself that he couldn't be talking about von Stauss's mother since I was pretty sure he didn't know anything about my brief role impersonating him. He could only be referring to, well, to my real mother I supposed. She was at least German. I hadn't heard from Mutti for months, not since the Great Sock Debacle, but every question deserves an answer. 'She is fine, mein Führer. Fine.'

'One should always respect one's parents but especially you should respect *and love* your mother.'

His eyes were boring into me and demanding an answer. 'Why yes, mein Führer, my mother, er, of course I do, I do.'

I was mighty confused by this turn of conversation and thought my response a little weak but his face softened when he heard my answer and – it may have been the slipstream of course – I could swear his eyes turned a little glassy. And if I told you he started reciting poetry at that moment you wouldn't believe me, would you? But that's exactly what he did do. His eyes half closed and he took a deep breath.

> *'When your mother has grown older,*
> *When her dear, faithful eyes no longer see life as they once did,*
> *When her feet, grown tired,*
> *No longer want to carry her as she walks...'*

I can't say I've ever got on well with poetry and this occasion was no exception but I thought it prudent to utter a few words of praise. 'Very good mein Führer, very...'

'Silence you fool. I haven't finished.'

'Oh, er...'

> *'Then lend her your arm in support...'*

He went on in similar vein, while I maintained a dutiful silence. About midway I confess my mind started to wander. I was wondering if his own mother was still alive but thought it unlikely. Eventually he stopped and I waited a while just to be sure he'd actually finished. 'Excellent, mein Führer. Excellent. May I inquire who wrote those splendid words?'

He puffed up a little at this, turning both his thumbs up to point at his chest.

'*You*, mein Führer? How extraordinary. Such, er, emotion. I'd no idea...' I was lost for words of course but *you* try coming up with something succinct and praiseworthy when a Reichskanzler starts spouting this sort of nonsense. I was actually thinking along the lines of 'better not give up the day job' but with the Munich business hanging over me I felt I was in enough trouble already.*

I expected him to return to this line of enquiry but he had further surprises in store. 'Do you know I once lived in the same street as you?' he asked.

If this had been anyone other than the conqueror of the western world I'd have replied with a 'pull the other leg matey.' Instead I just gulped. 'In Mayfair, sire, in London?'

'Nein, in the English port of Liverpool, before the Great War.'

In the same street but not at the same time then. It occurred to me the Führer seemed to know an awful lot about me. You may recall I mentioned at the very beginning of this account that Pater, Helga and I had landed in Liverpool from New York, as we fled the mafia just after the Wall Street crash, but we hadn't stayed long. I was only eight at the time and barely remembered it but Helga occasionally spoke of a flat in one of the back streets there. I was surprised that anyone bar ourselves knew about it.

'In Upper Stanhope Street.' He struggled with the English pronunciation. 'You are wondering, how I know about you, yes?'

And I was wondering what the hell he'd been doing loafing around in Croxted but, by golly, I'd caught him in an affable mood. I nodded.†

'Let's just say my security people take an interest in... people... those who were at Munich, and at Berchtesgarden, Bad Godesberg and so on.

---

* Hitler was said to be devastated by the death of his mother in 1907. The poem seemingly really *was* written by him, authenticated (in 1923) by the Archiv des Instituts für Zeitgeschichte München, Findmittel [online], ED 416, p. 6 (http://tinyurl.com/Kilroy213). Both the German original and its English translation are widely available on the Internet, for example in Wikiquote at: http://tinyurl.com/Kilroy214.

† Hitler's elder half brother, Alois Hitler, married an Irish woman, Bridget Dowling, and lived at 102, Stanhope Street in Liverpool for several years, just before the outbreak of WWI. Bridget Dowling's memoirs record that Hitler lived with them there from 1912 to 1913, while he was on the run, avoiding conscription in his native Austro-Hungary. (Hitler later enlisted as a volunteer in the *Bavarian* army, in which he served throughout the war, being twice decorated.) Some historians discount Dowling's story, but for the period February 1908 to May 1913, often referred to as Hitler's Vienna years, he was a down and out and there is little hard information of any kind that can prove or disprove Dowling's assertion. Kilroy's account here provides new evidence which would appear to support it. The house itself was destroyed in the last German air-raid on Liverpool, on 10th December 1942. *Streets of Liverpool*: http://tinyurl.com/Kilroy121.

Even the small-fry like yourself, but what I see, I remember.' He tapped his head.*

I found out later that Hitler had a superb memory. He could devour whole volumes of briefing documents and remember pretty well everything right down to the inconsequential detail, often catching out his Generals on some minor nuance of troop manoeuvres.

He swung further around in his seat, reached behind and lightly touched my knee. He stared straight at me, with a look so penetrating that it was hard not to flinch. 'So your mother foolishly stayed in Britain while you did the right thing and came to fight for the Fatherland, yes? That is good. Very good. Germany has need of fine young men such as yourself.'

Well that was a relief. He looked away at that moment and muttered something to the driver and, at last, after a rather tense morning one way and another, I could see a small ray of hope. Clearly this world dominating lunatic with the photographic memory had not seen anything to indicate I had a recent acquaintanceship with the Royal Air Force. Well, I wasn't going to enlighten him.

Mutter

Wenn deine Mutter alt geworden
Und älter du geworden bist
Wenn ihr, was früher leicht und mühelos
Nunmehr zur Last geworden ist
Wenn ihre lieben, treuen Augen
Nicht mehr, wie einst, ins Leben seh'n
Wenn ihre müd' gewordenen Füsse
Sie nicht mehr tragen woll'n beim Geh'n
Dann reiche ihr den Arm zur Stütze
Geleite sie mit froher Lust
Die Stunde kommt, da du sie weinend
Zum letzten Gang begleiten mußt

Und fragt sie dich, so gib' ihr Antwort
Und fragt sie wieder, sprich auch du
Und fragt sie nochmals, steh' ihr Rede
Nicht ungestüm, in sanfter Ruhe
Und kann sie dich nicht recht verstehen
Erklär' ihr alles froh bewegt
Die Stunde kommt, die bitt're Stunde
Da dich ihr Mund nach nichts mehr frägt!

-- Adolf Hitler

"The Mother" by Adolf Hitler.

For the rest of the journey we spoke of my service in the Luftwaffe. After what I'd been through over the previous 24 hours, it was easy to make up enough of a yarn to keep him at bay. Then we were at the airport. Now, I'm calling it an airport, but it was just a large field with a couple of huts really. A few days earlier it had been in allied hands and I could see the remains of a couple of Dewoitine D 520s, lying crumpled and charred near

* Chamberlain visited Germany three times in the space of two weeks during the Czechoslovakian crisis: Berchtesgarden, Bad Godesberg and, lastly, Munich. http://tinyurl.com/Kilroy122.

the windsock. What I took to be Hitler's own chariot was standing ready, a lumbering Junkers Tri-motor, clean and shining in the morning sun. There was a squadron of Me-109s and assorted bombers, transports and what-not, adorned with that ugly black cross, Luftwaffe and Wehrmacht personnel all over the place, fussing with the planes and generally trying to create the right impression as the leader breezed by.

Our car pulled to a stop near the Tri-motor and Hitler got out. He paused to have a word with a Luftwaffe colonel, then turned back to me and said, 'There is a transport flight to Berlin leaving shortly, with room for you on it. Colonel Stark here will sign you onto it.'

He must have interpreted my look of horror as mere puzzlement. 'Berlin *is* where your unit is stationed if I remember correctly?'

'Of course, mein Führer.' I forced a look of gratitude and pleasure as he turned and strode towards his waiting aeroplane. We all stood and watched as it departed, along with its 109 escorts. I'd like to say that that was the last I saw of him but we were indeed destined to meet again before the war's end, under very different circumstances.*

---

* The *Visit Ardennes* website has a slideshow containing several photos of Hitler's historic visit to Charleville. See: http://tinyurl.com/Kilroy211.

CHAPTER 8

A few minutes after the Führer's departure I found myself on the flight deck of a Junkers 88. The pilot turned around to face me and we shook hands. 'Alen Balcker. Welcome aboard my friend.' He gestured at an ammunition box alongside him. 'Sit on that and watch. See how a real aeroplane is flown.'

The engines were idle, but there was a strange continuous screeching sound assaulting my ears, like a banshee howl. 'What is that racket, Captain?'

'Don't worry about it Lieutenant. That's our cargo. Two hundred cockerels, all bound for Carinhall.'

Christ, the Krauts had only been in France a couple of weeks and already they'd emasculated the place. 'Who would want two hundred cocks, then?' I asked.

'Fatty Göring, of course. I did say Carinhall, didn't you hear? I hope he wants them for their fighting prowess and not their meat. There are some tough old French birds out the back there.' He laughed at his own joke.

I squatted down and took stock of my surroundings. There was so much space compared with the cramped flight decks I'd been used to, but so much more to take in as well. And two of everything. Two throttle arms, a couple of mixture controls, pairs and pairs of dials, twinned levers of unknown purpose and, no doubt, a brace of flies in Balcker's trousers.

Balcker plugged in a helmet and handed it to me. I put it on and heard his voice over the intercom. 'Right then. Let us do the Führer's bidding and get you back to all those comely mädchen awaiting you in Berlin.'

Berlin. 500 miles east give or take an autobahn or two. Why did these damned Krauts keep taking me in the wrong direction? I could see Balcker's harness included a parachute pack. I gestured at it. 'Where's mine?'

Balcker laughed. 'No need for one. This is just for me to sit on. You are not in a 109 now. We have a spare engine, don't forget.'

Bugger. I watched as he flicked the switches above him and the starboard engine coughed, slowly turned and then caught. It was just getting up to speed when he slapped the side of his head, flicked a switch to off and we were back with the banshee howl. 'Scheisse. The livestock import permit.' He unbuckled his harness. 'I've left it at control. We should get the R.A.F. to deliver this lot for us. They can drop what they like without any paperwork,' he said with a smile. He climbed over me and headed down the hatch, calling over his shoulder that he would be back in a minute.

I watched him as he ambled towards one of the huts. On the roadway I saw a car screech to a halt and a Wehrmacht colonel jump out. von Sodenstern. He seemed to be in a hurry. Putting two and a brace together it didn't take much imagination to guess what would happen next if I just sat around and waited so I slipped into the pilot's seat and scanned the control panel. What had Balcker done to get the engine started? It was just a couple of overhead switches that had seemed to do the trick, wasn't it? After a bit of experimentation I hit the right combination and was treated to the steady thrum of the starboard engine turning over. Now for the other one. Same procedure only with the switches on the left presumably.

I glanced out and could see some activity at the control hut. To be specific Sodenstern, Balcker and a half dozen troopers were heading smartly in my direction. Then, at last, I had the port engine turning over. But it wasn't catching. Cough, cough, cough it went as it turned slowly. Cough, cough, cough, like a Victorian novelist. Why did this plane have to have so many bloody engines?

And that Balcker could certainly put on a turn of speed, I thought. I lost sight of him under the wing and guessed he must be near the ladder so, more in hope than expectation, I opened the starboard throttle. There was an answering roar and the plane surged forward. Of course a twin doesn't taxi too well on one engine. Specifically, you can kick the rudder all you like but it will keep going in circles whatever you try. Half way around my first loop I could see Balcker picking himself off the ground and preparing for a fresh assault. Still only me aboard then. Well me and two hundred cockerels. Behind Balcker, von Sodenstern was lining up the troopers and pointing in my direction.

Another loop and I still couldn't get the bloody engine started. There was a loud crack above my head and, instinctively, I ducked. I looked up and could see a neat hole in the windscreen. At last the port engine fired. I immediately opened up both throttles, leaned forward to deliver a "V" sign to Sodenstern and his gang, with hopes of departure very much on my mind.

I hadn't gone very far when I felt something pressing, cold and hard, into my right temple. I turned and looked into the dark brown eyes of Captain Alen Balcker. He drew his free hand sharply across his throat and nodded at the throttles. This didn't seem like a good time to ask for a flying lesson, so I eased them back and the engines slowed to idle. He reached above me towards the switches but, at that moment, there was another loud crack and he stopped, his hand hovering above my head. Neither of us moved. We must have been like that, frozen still, for only a couple of seconds but it seemed much longer. With a Luger pressed to my head I didn't feel any sudden movement was advisable but at last I turned to see what was up. It was only then that I noticed that someone had spilt what looked like porridge on the dashboard and it was dripping down over the instrument panel. Balcker's gun hand dropped to his side as I looked up at his face. Barring a small entry wound above his right eyebrow it seemed much as it had when I first met him, a few minutes earlier, but the back of his head was another matter. I watched silently as his other hand dropped to his side and he crumpled to the floor.

I didn't allow myself much time for mourning and quickly had the throttles open again. At last we were heading in a straight line. More or less. I should mention here that R.A.F. training, excellent as it is, does not include a lot of multi-engine time if you are destined to fly on single-engined hardware, as I had been. So apart from a few hours in a sedate old Anson this was pretty new to me, and flying on two engines is, well, twice as complicated as flying on one. But at least we were up and running and I was just congratulating myself on this when I noticed that Mr Ford's lorry had joined in the hunt and was going to block my exit if I went for an orderly departure. There was only one thing to do. I pointed the plane at the far corner of the field and pushed the throttles fully forward. This was our take-off run come what may. Downwind, upwind who cares? I didn't have time to think of such matters as there was a roar from the engines and I had to look pretty lively with the rudder to try to keep us on the straight and narrow. We missed the lorry by a whisker as the plane bounced and swung like a trapeze artist's unmentionables then, at last, we were airborne. I'm only glad I didn't own the house on the other side of the hedge as I am sure we took most of its roof tiles with us.

Have you ever been driving an unfamiliar car and been caught in a thunderstorm? You know – you can't see a thing and where the hell is the windscreen wiper switch? Well you multiply that by a thousand and that's how I felt. And, for me, there could be no slowing down or stopping by the roadside to read the manual. But it is a truism that once you are off the ground, most planes are easier to control if you don't try anything too adventurous. The Junkers 88 seemed to be no exception. I adjusted the trim for straight and level and took stock of my situation. At least the primary flight controls were familiar to me and even the pair of throttles weren't too much to worry about. Why, if you moved them in unison I could just about believe I was back in a single engine Hurricane or even the Fairey Battle, heaven forbid. So the best plan seemed to be to climb a few thousand feet and head north west, to what I hoped would be comfortably back over allied territory, although uncomfortably in a plane with black crosses on the wings. I would worry about landing the damned thing when I had to.

Whilst learning the ropes at Kincardine I'd been told that there are more ways of killing yourself flying an aeroplane than in any other of life's pursuits. And aviators just love to invent jargon to describe all these different ways of doing yourself in. For example you could fall foul of the stall, the flat spin or the ground loop. Or, if you think that these sound like too simple a way to die, try wake vortex, propeller icing or altimeter mismanagement, any of which can take you off to permanent repose just as surely.

I might add that you can avoid all these, if you keep your wits about you, but there's one hazard of the air that you can't do anything about. Birdstrike. It just comes up and hits you, so as to speak, and it's no joke. You would be amazed at the damage that can be done if you hit a pigeon when you are cruising along at a couple of hundred knots. And I'm not just referring to the fate of the poor old pigeon here. Your cockpit canopy can be shattered leaving yours truly with a minced face and chewing feathers. Alternatively your propeller, and I am talking about a finely honed piece of solid steel here, can be literally shredded by its chance encounter with little Percy Plumpster. And there is absolutely nothing you can do to prevent it happening, other than hope that the little blighters steer well clear of you.

For most people unlucky enough to encounter this hazard our fine feathered friend usually comes at him from *outside* the aeroplane. Ah. I expect you are ahead of me here. And, yes, the first I knew about the Gallic version of the Great Escape was when a fat brown feathery ball landed on the dashboard in front of me, stretched its wings and strutted back and forth, stopping to peck at the porridge which had until very recently resided in the cranium of Captain Balcker.

Swallowing bile, I swept the bird away, but he was back immediately, dancing up and down and resuming his feast. Then I noticed that he had changed colour, to a dappled black and white. Well, of course he hadn't really. I looked down and there was my old friend Fatty Brown, having a crap on poor old Balcker whilst it was his sparring partner who had replaced him, right in my way on the dashboard.

I was about to sweep off Black and White in the direction of his defecating chum, when he was joined by his twin brother. So then there were two of the blighters in my line of vision, and not much brotherly love either as they set about each other like a couple of Socialists at a hustings. It was easy enough to push them off, but not so easy to deal with the four Liberal activists who replaced them. Then things decidedly took a turn for the worse when the Tory front bench decided to join in the democratic process.

I remember one flying instructor telling me, 'Fly the aeroplane. Concentrate on that. Always fly the aeroplane.' This was uttered when I'd just dropped my map on the floor and put the plane into a spiral dive whilst I was scrambling around for it. Well, I'd like to see how he would have coped with two hundred cockerels on the rampage.

I thought I wasn't doing too badly under the circumstances, and who knows, maybe I would have got us safely back down but then things took a turn for the worse. I had managed to open a small window in the canopy and had just rammed a particularly bellicose Communist through it, when I noticed a change in the engine note. Specifically, where once there had been two Jumo Vee twelves reliably purring away now there was just the one doing what it should whilst the other was screaming and doing its best to shake itself to bits. It would seem that Trotsky* had taken exception to his expulsion and exacted his revenge on my port propeller. Fearing that the errant engine would tear the wing off there was nothing else I could do other than shut it down.

Opinion is divided in aviation circles about whether two engines are safer than one. Those in favour of two say that you can lose one engine and still make it home. The single engine lobby, and I'm definitely one of them, say that with two aboard you're twice as likely to have an engine failure and when you are down to your last engine the plane is well nigh uncontrollable anyway.

Junkers Ju 88.

Now, if I'd had several hundred hours in JU 88s in my log book and, incidentally, had no livestock to contend with, I would no doubt have coolly feathered the broken prop (no pun intended), adjusted the trim and had us serenely crabbing across the sky in no time. However with just my Hurricane skills to draw on, and in the middle of the Tolpuddle riots, I adopted a different strategy. I flapped. I flapped like, well I flapped like a couple of hundred cockerels. I urgently messed around with the fuel cocks, booted Chamberlain up the backside and paused to wipe the sweat from my brow. I half-strangled Halifax, frantically flicked switches, tapped gauges and wiped some more sweat from my brow. I discovered how to turn on the cabin light. Then I foolishly left the controls and attempted to get the little blighters back in their cages. I think I managed just two, whilst also managing to inflate the life raft and jettison the lavatory. Hey, take that Fritz.

Then I came to my senses. Fly the aeroplane. I struggled back to the cockpit, brushed aside a couple of hecklers and anxiously peered out the side window. I could see the engine windmilling idly in the slipstream and

* Coincidentally Leon Trotsky, one time Commander in Chief of the Red Army, was having a particularly bad day, whilst Kilroy was wrestling with the cockerels. It was 24th May 1940 and he was living in exile in Mexico, having been sentenced to death in absentia by Stalin. He just escaped an assassination attempt by a Soviet GPU unit led by Iosif Grigulevich. A few weeks later he was murdered when an NKVD agent, Ramon Mercader, drove the pick of an ice axe into his skull. http://tinyurl.com/Kilroy124.

somewhere, far far below it and not where it should be at all, the blue morning sky.

Fly the aeroplane. I pushed the stick hard over but nothing much happened. I put both feet on the right rudder pedal and stamped down as hard as I could. The horizon levelled just a little but it still wasn't where I wanted to see it. Then I tried both hands on the control stick and I forced it hard over and back. A small change, but not enough. I glanced at the altimeter and that was winding down like a Polish watch. Not long and it would soon be over. It would almost be a relief.

I can't recall what I did next. Waggled the stick around like I was stirring soup. Danced on the rudder pedals. Wrenched the throttles backwards and forwards. Involuntary aerobatics, my flying instructor would have called it, and it can be very amusing too, if you are watching it from your back garden.

Suddenly we were at ground level. We were still flying but with the tree tops above me and an enormous French oak looming in the windshield. I shut my eyes and wrenched back on the stick. You aren't supposed to manoeuvre a bomber like that so close to the ground and I paid the price. Anyone lucky enough to have a grandstand view of my arrival would no doubt have described it as "arse over tit" but all I knew was that I was being tossed around the cabin like a ping-pong ball, bouncing off the walls, floor, ceiling and everything else in quick succession. All the while there was a continuous screeching sound, like a train shunting and, finally, a loud crump as we came to rest, with the cabin filled by a haze of dust.

I expected to be in pain, as I lay bloody and battered in a bedraggled heap on the floor, but actually felt nothing much – just stunned. There was a light breeze blowing in from somewhere and a ticking sound, like a clock, but otherwise silence. The peace was most welcome but it didn't last long. There was a whoosh as one of the petrol tanks caught light. Of course I was desperate to scramble out but found I was too weak to move and so just lay there helplessly watching the fire and hoping for rescue. Luckily the wind was blowing the flames away from me or I'm sure I wouldn't be here now. The smoke was another matter though. I guess the fire must have been sucking all the oxygen out of the air and so all that was left were fumes, the dense black acrid smoke that I can taste even now. My eyes smarted, the back of my throat stung and my lungs choked as I breathed it in. I tried again to crawl away but still couldn't move a muscle and just lay there helpless and choking and coughing and wishing I would black out.

Then suddenly the smoke was gone. I looked around and could see the fire was still going and the smoke swirling everywhere but the air around me was clear and pure. I recall looking out and wondering how much longer the plane would burn and then thinking, 'Who cares?' I felt rather good. I thought I must be in a plane crash more often if it was going to be this pleasant, and then I caught sight of something odd through the broken windscreen. I had crashed in a field and striding across it, in an orderly fashion, a village procession was coming towards me. Some of them were carrying banners, one of them was banging a big bass drum and another was tooting on a trumpet.

I squinted at the trumpet player and realised with a jolt, that I knew him. Old Eric had been our gardener at the house in Mayfair until he'd retired a few years back. And one of the flag wavers looked strangely like Helga's great aunt. Christ, what was her name? Never did take to her. And what were they doing out here poncing around a field in Flanders? They came up to the plane and stopped, the drum still beating and the trumpet trilling. I realised with a start that I knew them all. Nearest was Grumps, that is Pater's father, who used to visit us in New York, now standing with his hat in his hand and a beaming smile on his face. 'Don't let him get you on your own,' Helga had repeatedly warned me. Just once I forgot her advice and wished I hadn't. Now he was standing before me with such a sweet and welcoming smile.

Then I heard a voice. It came from somewhere above and had such a strange quality, deep but mellow and soothing. It was a voice I'd known all my life and although I knew this for sure at that very moment, for the life of me I can't say now who it was. 'Welcome, welcome. It is time.'

That made me pause for thought. 'What on earth were they up to?' I wondered. No doubt you are thinking that I was a bit slow off the mark, but I say this to you: see how quick-witted you are with your backside stuck in a frying pan after you have been cart-wheeling over the French countryside. They were all smiling and gesturing to me to join them. Then the voice repeated, 'Come, it is time.'

I looked back at them and I remember thinking that I hadn't seen any of them for a long time. With a shock it dawned on me why and with that thought I decided it wasn't "time" at all. 'No, it bloody isn't. You can fuck off.' The drum stopped banging and they all exchanged looks. 'You heard me. Fuck off the lot of you.'

'Well, young man. We don't use language like that here. And I don't know if you have any say in the matter anyway.' This was Grumps' second wife, the one who ran off with his money, standing sweetly with a posy in one hand and Grumps' gnarled fist held firmly in the other.

'I'm telling you. I'm not interested in your poncey parade. Now bugger off.'

That got them thinking alright. They exchanged looks, shrugged, shook their heads, then turned and shambled back the way they came. Except for old Eric the gardener. He paused, slowly turned around and treated me to a two finger salute before ambling after the others.

CHAPTER 9

It was the cockerels that saved me. You see the fortunes of war had landed me, if you can call my arrival a landing, back with the British army, in the form of a detachment of the Royal Norfolks. Just before I showed up they had been in a fierce firefight with Jerry and, not surprisingly, were in no mood for plucking some idiot Kraut pilot, as they thought I was, from his burning aeroplane. But someone had spotted our French allies flapping around in the cockpit and, for squaddies on reduced rations, *there* was something that was certainly worth saving. Blinker, a platoon corporal, grabbed his trenching tool, ran up to the wreckage and smashed his way in. He grabbed the birds by the fistful and threw them outside. Of course I didn't know anything about this at the time. I heard about it later – years later as it happens. At any rate the flames were getting hotter and hotter all the while and Blinker was just about to make his exit when he heard a voice coming through the smoke. 'You can fuck off.'

That stopped him short. An English voice. Or was it some German trickery? Or perhaps there were prisoners aboard? He clambered along the fuselage to investigate. From outside, he could hear his mates urging him to get out but through the smoke there was another pathetic cry for help. 'Fuck off the lot of you.'

That settled it. He edged towards the voice and saw me lying in a crumpled heap. They breed them tough in Norfolk. I'm a big lad myself, but Blinker just grabbed me by the collar and the seat of the pants and swung me over his shoulder as if I weighed no more than one of the recently liberated chickens. He was further encouraged in his labours by yours truly announcing, 'I'm not interested in your poncey parade. Now bugger off.'

Fortunately he didn't take my advice and so that is how I came to find myself, when I regained consciousness, not in Paradise with my ghastly antecedents but in the village of le Paradis with the second Battalion of the Royal Norfolks.

'Hey Blinker, the Jerry's coming to I think.'

This was the first I knew of my survival. I opened my eyes to find myself on a bed in what I took to be a farmhouse bedroom. I shook my head and made to get up. I was still pretty woozy but discovered I couldn't stand up anyway. I was handcuffed to the bed frame. There was the sound of boots thundering up the stairs and a corporal came crashing in. 'Okay Stan. Leave this to me. I speaka da lingo. Listen to this.' He crouched down beside the mattress, looked me straight in the eye and slowly intoned, 'Mine hair. For yew the vore eez over.'

I just didn't know what to make of this and dumbly stared back at him. He mistook my hesitation for incomprehension and repeated himself. 'Look Fritz. Vore eez kaput. For yew that eez.'

Again I said nothing, which gave one of the other men a chance to help out. 'Perhaps he's Austrian, Corp?' He turned to me. 'Adolf-o, you speak-o Austrian-o?'

I decided it was time to put them out of their misery and replied in my best Home Counties voice, 'I say chaps. Do you mind awfully much speaking English? It will be a lot easier for communication, what?'

They exchanged looks and one of them asked where I learned to speak like that.

'Same place as you, old boy. Back in Blighty of course. I'm as English as you are. And an R.A.F. officer, to boot.'

That got them thinking. An officer was called. I never did find out his name. He clearly had more weighty matters on his mind so was less than overjoyed to be distracted by me. As I recall, we had the briefest of chit-chat about school ties and how Portsmouth beat Wolves in the 1939 Cup Final but when I moved on to the difference between brown ale and mild and bitter, he sighed and shook his head. 'Look old boy,' he said, 'I'd love to natter some more but we are rather busy at the moment. Can't raise Brigade HQ and we're surrounded. We've got Attila the Hun and his 50 legions in those woods.' He gestured out the window. 'And then there's Hermann's Horrible Hordes, Adolf's Personal Khazi Shovellers and God knows who everywhere else.' He waved vaguely at the four corners of the room.

'And so that's bad news for us, then?' I asked.

The officer glanced at the men around us. 'Hell no, if you're talking about surrender. At least we've got the Royal Scots alongside us and they're a pretty tasty lot in a fight. We'll give a good account of ourselves alright.'

'And?' I asked

'And then what? We'll see, I guess. And, as for you – you seem as English to me as burnt steak and kidney pud but the fact is you are in a Kraut uniform and arrived in a Kraut aeroplane, so let's just leave you tied up here for now. Once we've dealt with those bastards out there,' he nodded at the window, 'we'll figure out what's to be done with you. In the meantime, keep your head down. It's going to be pretty rough over the next hour or two.'

I thought he was exaggerating at the time but I was wrong of course. You see, at that moment, things didn't seem too bad. Although I was handcuffed to the bed I managed to drag it closer to the window, where I could see outside. The sun was just starting to rise on what promised to be a balmy May day in rural France and it was all peace and tranquillity out there. There was no sign of the enemy – just a faint indication of the grass being smoothly ruffled by the breeze and, over in the far corner of the field, a dim glow where my latest chariot was quietly smouldering. I wondered how long ago I'd crashed – it had been broad daylight then. And it was hard to imagine that, just out of our sight in the morning gloom, Hitler's worst were lining up to put us to bayonet and bullet.

Meanwhile, inside the farmhouse, the Norfolks had no time for daft musings. They were preparing for battle. I hadn't been privy to army exercises on Salisbury Plain so the niceties of what the British Army call house defence tactics were new to me. Sandbags were being dragged into the room and dumped in place, with furniture broken up and the pieces rammed into every opening and aperture. I heard some prolonged loud banging above followed by the sound of splintering timber, mixed with ripe Norfolk curses. Some tiles spattered down past the window. 'Ah good,' declared one of the officers. 'That will be our mortar emplacement nice and snug.' A squaddie came in, roughly shoved me and the bed back in the corner and started attacking the wall with a sledgehammer. I remember making a note to myself that if ever I got out of this mess then at all costs I must avoid having the Royal Norfolks as house guests.

Then all was quiet. The window was now blocked with sandbags and bits of broken furniture, with a couple of men positioned behind it, a pile of grenades and ammunition boxes behind them. I noticed one of the men spitting into both his palms before picking up his weapon, muttering something about 'giving 'em hell.' Others were lying on the floor with their 303s at the ready, poking through the recently hacked holes in the wall.

No one seemed bothered much by me, one way or the other, so I thought it prudent to get down from my bed and lie on the floor too. I was still handcuffed of course and remember feeling relieved, in a strange way, that with no weapon to hand I was to play no part in the proceedings. And as there was clearly going to be no opportunity for heroics from me I might as well do the sensible thing, I thought, and unheroically crawled under the bed.

The battle didn't start. It erupted. One moment all was quiet and the next the air was full of noise. The regimental history says the fight lasted all day but in my mind it seems like it took only a few minutes. Then, when I think again, there were times when it seemed like forever. I couldn't make out what we or the Germans were up to at any stage. Early on I remember one loud explosion, uncomfortably close and I felt the punch of the shock wave which knocked the breath out of me. And always there was the sound of our answering fire filling the room – the ripping of the Vickers and the irregular banging of the 303s mingling with curses from our men and the explosions outside.

We took casualties of course. I heard men cry out, some a short cry quickly cut off and others an endless terrifying shriek. It was obvious we were getting the worst of things. More and more I heard shouts for ammunition. Then the building started taking more and more hits and the air filled with choking dust from the falling masonry.

I don't know how long it had gone on when I looked up and saw Blinker standing over me. I'd no idea where he'd been after our earlier encounter but, suddenly, there he was, covered in grime with sweat streaming down his face and staining his battledress. 'Hold out your hands,' he shouted, grabbing them and placing them either side of the bed frame. 'Hold still.' There was a sledgehammer lying nearby. He picked it up and I flinched as I saw what he was about but with a swing worthy of a lumberjack he struck a precise blow. I felt my hands part and I was free. 'Now pick up Spud,' he shouted, pointing at one of the wounded as he grabbed one of the others. 'Pick him up and follow me.' I did as I was bid, only just managing to haul the body over my shoulder. We struggled down the stairs, each with our load, me expecting a bullet or worse at any minute, then careered through what was left of the kitchen and out into the yard. The sound of battle was all around, bullets zipping through the air and knocking chunks out of the masonry, but I had no time to be frightened. I just followed Blinker across the yard and after a short dash breathed a sigh of relief as we reached the comparative safety of another building – it must have been a cowshed.

The rest of the battle is a blur. I vaguely recall acting as number two to a Bren gun, feeding it with clips of ammunition. It was being operated by someone called Babbler, the Batallion cook of all people.* At some stage I must have burned my hand as we changed the barrel but noticed nothing at the time and still managed to keep up a steady supply, that is until there was no ammo left. Babbler cried out that he'd get some more. I could hear bullets zipping overhead and the burps of the German machine gun fire, more than enough to keep me fixed to the spot, but he leapt to his feet and rushed across the yard, disappearing around the corner. I never saw him again.

I seemed to be sitting there forever, beside the useless Bren gun, with the sound of battle all around, but gradually the noise and clamour quietened and then all was silent bar the groans of the wounded lying near me. I wasn't sure what to do so sat quietly, with an eye on the door. Suddenly a trooper appeared, in SS uniform, nervously edging through the doorway, with a Karabiner at the ready. 'Hände hoch,' he barked and those of us who could, raised our hands.

---

* "Babbling brook" is Cockney rhyming slang for "cook" and hence the nickname Babbler, which was more commonly used by the Australian infantry.

We were made to assemble in the yard. The unwounded helped our less fortunate comrades as we came out of the various corners of the farmstead in dribs and drabs. I was surprised at what a small party we made, having put up such a stout resistance. Perhaps there were 60 or 70 of us in all, some lying, some leaning and a few, like me, standing, with our SS captors standing back and scowling, weapons at the ready. I was just behind a Captain, the man who had interviewed me earlier. An SS lieutenant approached, with an ugly looking Mauser in his hand and the Captain went to ask him something. With barely a pause the lieutenant punched him hard in the mouth, walking straight past as he fell to earth. An SS corporal was just behind and I could see he was going to follow up with a kick to the stomach. I shouted a protest, stepped forward and made to push him away. He cried out, his face flushed with anger and raised his rifle, flicking off the safety catch. Our eyes met and we both froze. It was Corporal Weber. 'You!' I exclaimed as he roared, 'Sie sinds.'

A few minutes later I was standing before Hauptsturmführer Knöchlein. He was seated in the back of a half-track command truck, open-topped, with what I guessed must be his wireless operator and some assorted runners. It had been only a couple of days since I'd seen him, when poor old Sturt was being barbecued over an open fire and he'd sent me off to von Rundstedt's HQ, but a lot had happened in the meantime and it felt like weeks. I'd rather forgotten that I was still in my Luftwaffe guise so I'm not sure what I'd have said to explain myself had Knöchlein asked but, fortunately, he didn't. 'It would seem we've rescued you from those English swine,' he said with a cold smile as soon as he saw me.

'Er, yes, Major. Danke.'

'You delivered the message to HQ, yes?'

'Of course, Major, with Corporal Weber's help.

'And ended up a prisoner of the British?'

'Yes, Major, you see...' I pointed across the field to the smouldering Junkers. 'And then I...'

He held up his hand. 'No time. You can tell me about it later. But they tortured you, yes?'

'Nein, Hauptsturmführer. No.'

'Hmmm.' He reached for one of my hands, the wrist still circled by the broken handcuff and the palm red raw where I'd been burned by the Bren gun barrel. 'These are cigarette burns, yes?' he asked.

I hadn't been aware of the burn myself until that moment. 'No, Major. They treated me well. This is just the heat of battle, the, er, cross-fire I suppose.' I shrugged.

He whispered something to one of his men, who picked up his rifle and advanced on me. I flinched involuntarily but the man merely grabbed my arm, placed it on the tailgate of the truck and coolly shot off the handcuff lock.

'You seem nervous,' commented Knöchlein as the man shot off the other lock.

'Do I Major?' I replied, trying to sound calm when I felt anything but.

'Relax Lieutenant,' he said. 'You are among friends.' He reached for a pistol, on the seat beside him, a Luger. 'Take this. It belonged to one of my lieutenants but he won't be needing it where he's gone.' He slipped it into its holster and threw it to me. 'You can come and watch the fun.'

Le Paradis farmhouse where the survivors of the Royal Norfolks surrendered.

He rose and beckoned to me to follow. It was late afternoon and we were parked on a narrow country road, only a short distance from the farmhouse, now in ruins, and the yard where the prisoners were gathered. Behind our half-track were a couple of BMW motorcycle combinations, their crews standing nearby, and chatting to Weber, I noticed. Further up the road, away from the farmhouse, three lorries in a line, beside a barn. Knöchlein barked an order. Their tailgates dropped down and the men inside climbed down, SS troopers, uniforms stained with sweat and grime. From each of the lorries they carefully lowered a Spandau – a machine gun. Spandaus are heavy and need a crew of four – two for the gun itself and two to manhandle the ammunition. I watched as the men staggered under their loads, across the road and through a nearby gateway leading to a paddock flanked by a hedge at the side of the barn.

All along the road, troopers were gathering. They looked battle-worn but relieved to have survived. I sensed something more than that – an air of expectation perhaps, but about what I couldn't be sure.

Meanwhile more Norfolks had been found in some distant outpost and had joined their fellows. At last Knöchlein seemed satisfied that all that was left of the battalion had been mustered. He shouted an order. The gate to the yard was swung open and, after a pause, out came the British Army in defeat – a long file of them. They limped up the lane, past the SS troopers standing at intervals all along, clutching their carbines and looking sullen to a man. Some of the men were on improvised stretchers, some firmly on their feet, and others only just. Their heads were down and they were silent, the only sound the shuffling feet as they struggled to show pride and keep in line.

At last they reached the lorries. Their tailgates were still down and I expected the men to be loaded onto them, but when the column reached that point, Knöchlein barked an order, a sergeant ran up and shouted at the prisoners to pass around, through the gateway and into the paddock.

'What's happening?' I asked. I'd just noticed Blinker. He'd seen me too, first with a jolt of recognition and then a weary shake of his head.

'Do you know how many men we lost to these swine?' Knöchlein asked.

'But sir, there are wounded there. Some of them need urgent medical attention, sir. Surely to God we can be of some help?'

'You Luftwaffe types need to toughen up,' was all he replied as he turned his back on me.

The prisoners silently filed through the gateway in the hedge. As the last one turned off the road Knöchlein blew a whistle and it started. On the other side of the hedge I saw very little, but I certainly heard it – the rattling, tearing sound of three Spandaus unleashed on unarmed men, and the shrieks and cries as they were hit. It could only have been 20 or 30 seconds before the firing stopped but that wasn't an end to the business. There were feeble shouts and cries of pain coming from the paddock indicating that, miraculously, there were survivors. Knöchlein shouted an order and a sergeant rallied some nearby troopers who ran up the road, fixing bayonets as they went. He turned to me. 'Come on. No witnesses. No survivors.'

I hesitated.

'Come on. That's an order, Lieutenant. I said "no survivors."' He pulled my Luger from its holster and slapped it into my hand.

I looked at it, bemused. Corporal Weber joined us at that moment. He was fixing his bayonet to his rifle while studying me in my uncertainty, with a look I can only describe as bordering on amusement.

'Come with me. Now.' Knöchlein shoved me in the back, none too gently and half pushed, half guided me the short distance up the road and through the gateway.

It was a well-chosen killing ground. The only easy way out was the gate we had just come through but some of the poor devils had tried to scale the hedge. I could see their bodies piled up where they had fallen. The Spandau crews were dismantling their weapons, their job complete. One of them was whistling. Meanwhile Weber and the troopers had lit cigarettes. They were strolling around the paddock, laughing and joking like they were on a country ramble but pausing every now and then to dig deep with the bayonet.

Knöchlein was standing beside me, all puffed up and studying the scene with some pride. 'You see, Lieutenant, this is how wars are won. Not with your fancy aeroplanes but with bayonet and bullet. Dirty work but the Fatherland needs it and we do it well don't you think?'

I grunted a non-committal response.

Suddenly he started and tugged at my sleeve. 'But what's that?' He was pointing at something. It looked like a bloodied sack on the ground, only a few paces away from us.

I didn't answer.

'Over there. That man moved. Those fools have missed him.' He pointed again. 'Right, Lieutenant. You deal with him. Go on. Prove you're a man.' He shoved me in his direction.

I've often wondered what would have happened had I refused, but I didn't. I stumbled over and saw there was indeed somebody lying there, face down in the mud. I found I was still holding the pistol but with my free hand I turned him over. He groaned as I did this and our eyes met. It wasn't Blinker. It was someone much younger, only 17 perhaps and I could see the fear in his eyes.

I knelt beside him, raised my gun and pointed it at his head. 'Lie still. Play dead,' I hissed and pulled the trigger. He flinched of course. It's hard not to when a powerful firearm goes off at such close quarters, but at least he didn't cry out. 'Lie still,' I whispered again and stood up.

I stood up, only to collide with Knöchlein, who had been standing right behind me. 'I thought so,' he said, sounding almost triumphant. 'I knew it. I knew it. You Luftwaffe swine are all cowards and there's the proof.' He pointed at the young man. He was reaching for his pistol as he spoke, which was in a holster on his belt. 'Stand away. I'll show you how man's work is done.' He pushed me out of the way and I watched with mounting horror as he lowered his gun to point at the young man's head.

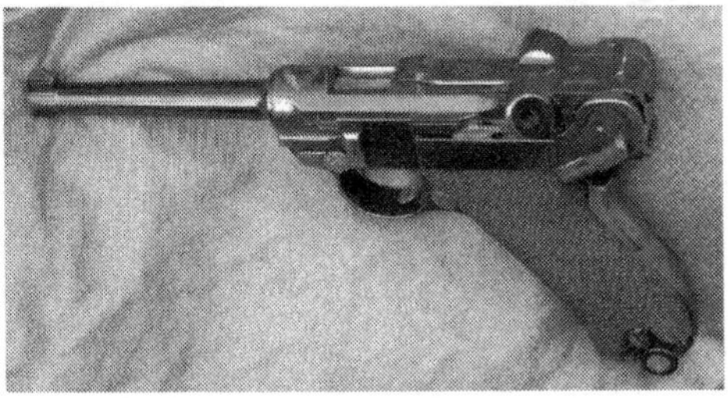

Luger P08 of the German Reichswehr.

My excuse for what happened next is that I had no time to think. I just acted instinctively. As Knöchlein's finger tensed to fire I found, almost unbidden, that I had raised my gun to his head. With no conscious effort someone, me obviously, squeezed the trigger. There was a loud click and then... nothing.

I have to say that, although he was quite possibly the most odious character I met in the entire war – and, remember, I'd been with Hitler only a few days earlier and was to encounter not a few Nazis later on – he certainly had guts. Where others would shout for help or cry out in shock, he merely started when he heard the click, then smiled. 'Touché, my friend. Touché,' he said as he raised his pistol to point at me.

At the end of our pilot training we did a short course called "Escape and Evasion". It was run by a grizzled ex-Commando and was supposed to give us some survival skills, should we ever be shot down over enemy territory. I can't say any of us took it very seriously at the time but one piece of advice had stuck in my mind. 'If you are ever at close quarters and in a tight spot,' our instructor had told us, 'try a jab to the solar plexus, here, just below the rib cage.' He pointed at the spot. 'Don't go for the head or balls because you'll most probably miss. With surprise, a soft tap on the spot is enough. Like this.' And it was a good 15 minutes before I was able to resume with our class work.

He might have recommended a soft tap but a hefty blow seemed a better idea, and with my untrusty Luger for good measure. There was no reaction from Knöchlein at first and for a moment I was cursing that ex-Commando, but then, at last, I heard the swine give out a single desperate gasp and to my immense relief he keeled over, hitting the ground like a sack of bricks.

I looked around. The Spandau crews had departed. Weber and his ramblers were at the far end of the field and as far as I could tell hadn't noticed anything untoward. Forcing myself not to run, I headed briskly to the gate but, when I was still some way from it, I heard a shout from behind. It would seem that Weber had spotted the recumbent Knöchlein and was now heading at a quick trot in my direction. Discretion no longer needed, I sprinted the rest of the way, through the gate and onto the road.

The three lorries were still parked outside, with the crews idly loading their machine guns in the back of them. One of the lorries, I noticed, had smoke billowing from its exhaust. The driver was at the wheel but not for long. I'd never driven a lorry before but I got lucky. By the time he'd picked himself off the ground and shouted a protest, I'd rammed it into gear, let slip the clutch and, engine roaring, was accelerating up the road.

I managed to find another gear and slowly picked up speed. I looked anxiously in the rear view mirror and could see some mightily perplexed Spandau crewmen standing in the road, but with no sign of purposeful activity. I can hardly say it was a clean getaway but, after the horrors of le Paradis it was some relief to have the chance to put me some yards and miles away from the ghastly place.

Things were still pretty desperate, of course, but I found myself formulating a plan – specifically get ten or 20 miles safely down the road and then turn north and somehow or other hook up with the British army, whatever might be left of it. When I think about it now it all sounds pretty hopeless – a German truck, driven by a Luftwaffe lieutenant in the middle of the German army with, no doubt, my details radioed to every unit in

Flanders but, in any case, I didn't get very far with my plan as, shortly after, I saw in my mirror a BMW combination. It was gaining on me, with my old friend, Corporal Weber, firmly in the driving seat, a rifle with bayonet propped up in the sidecar.

There was no way I could outrun a BMW but the road was narrow and windy and it was difficult for Weber to overtake. So we progressed in convoy across the French countryside, Weber trying to get past me all the time and me, in the manner of all good road chases, swerving from side to side to block him. By then the sun was setting. It was on my right, meaning we were heading south and, specifically, in the wrong direction.

I realised it was only a matter of time before Weber managed to get past or the road was blocked or I got to Berlin or something but there didn't seem much I could do but press on and hope. We must have driven along like this for at least half an hour, me swerving all over the place, hoping Weber would land in a ditch, occasionally terrifying oncoming traffic, but still keeping ahead of him – just. Miraculously there were no blockages but I could see we were nearing a large town and I couldn't see me blitzkrieging my way through there. We were in the outskirts when I saw the sign: Arras – scene of the previous week's British counter-attack but firmly in German hands now. The road was widening too and, inevitably, Weber at last managed to squeeze past me. At the last second I spotted a narrow lane to one side and, in desperation, swung down into it. It *was* narrow too, with the hedgerow closing in on me and tree branches hanging down and banging on the cabin roof. I saw that Weber had turned behind me and so was still there in my mirror. Then the tarmac surface ran out and few yards further my way was blocked by a gate. We crashed through it, into a boggy field.

BMW Motorcycle combination.

I knew the game was up at this point. The BMW combination was used for reconnaissance and this sort of rough ground was its natural home. I swerved and bumped and even threw the wretched lorry into reverse at one point but Weber followed my every move with ease. In the end we slithered into a ditch, nose down and I couldn't pull out. I watched as Weber parked nearby, dismounted and grabbed his firearm. He must have known I was unarmed so casually strolled up to me, taking his time to savour the moment, as I sat in the cabin, desperately fighting with the gears and accelerator, with wheels spinning beneath me. He wrenched open the door and stood back. I stared down the barrel of his rifle, wondering if he'd just shoot or perhaps ask questions first.

***

I've never been in an earthquake but I've a pretty good idea what it would be like because of what happened at that moment. The first I knew that anything was amiss was a cry from Weber. Simultaneously there was a loud creak and the lorry, already nose down in the ditch, lurched and dropped forward several feet. It stopped suddenly with a grinding, graunching sound, hanging in space, nearly vertical. At the time I had no idea what was happening. It felt like we had simply burrowed into the ground and, in a sense, we had. The world had turned pitch black and I could see nothing, not even my hands in front of me. All I could do was brace myself against the steering wheel in a desperate attempt to avoid falling through the windscreen. We hung, like that, for a few seconds then there was a roar, the lorry rolled on its side and we were falling.

CHAPTER 10

There was no furniture other than the chair to which I was tied. I was in a chamber or a cellar or a prison cell perhaps, or maybe something else. Whatever it was, it was carved out of solid rock. Light came from a single guttering Hurricane lamp, revealing only one way out – through a crudely hewn opening in the wall opposite me – leading to a narrow passageway. I could see a man walking briskly along it, stooping at intervals, under the overhanging rocks.

'You can call me Marcel,' he announced softly on arrival. 'Now tell me how that man on the motorbike came to be chasing you?'

He was speaking German, with a strong French accent. I answered in kind, 'He was a shit, ein Scheiß, and it's a long story mein Herr.'

Marcel paused and stroked his chin. I noticed he held a pistol in his other hand. He sighed. 'Unfortunately for you, you have chanced upon something here, something you shouldn't have found.' He looked at his watch. 'In a half hour you will leave this room, possibly on your feet but, more likely,' he coughed, 'dragged out by your heels.' He stretched and yawned. 'It has been a long day for us and my compatriots think I shouldn't waste even that time with you but I'm inclined to give you a small chance. I'm figuring that a man who is wanted by the SS may, perhaps, be of use to us?'

Well that little speech got my full and undivided attention, that was for sure. I wasted no time in answering. 'I see, sir. Well, the SS were massacring British prisoners of war at a village called, er, called, er, le Paradis I think it was. I tried to stop it.'

Marcel's eyes widened. 'A massacre?' Then he frowned. 'But why would a Luftwaffe pilot be there and why would he intervene?'

It was that damned Luftwaffe uniform again. It had been my salvation at the beginning but ever after it had been a curse. It might sound strange but what with the stress of my situation I'd forgotten I was wearing it and, with German being almost my mother tongue, it had passed me by that we had been speaking it. 'But I'm not Luftwaffe, don't you see?' I shouted in English, 'I'm English, a *bifstek, un Anglais*, that is an Englishman, matey poo. Listen: Tally ho, jolly hockeysticks, cor blimey strike a light, apples and pears... Er, have you clocked that my fine fellow-me-lad? English?'

This short exchange bought me a stay of execution at least, but I remained tied up and very much under suspicion until word filtered in, the next day, about the massacre. But that wasn't the end of it for me. I still had to prove my credentials and explain how I had been blundering around in the most unlikely places in the middle of the blitzkrieg. You know the story so I won't repeat it here. Marcel made it a hard graft but in the end the only remaining stumbling block was whether or not I was indeed an Englishman in the R.A.F. as I said I was, or perhaps a spy or a plant or something else. But at last my Alma Mater, the Herne Bay Academy for the Malnourished, proved of some use to me. Before the war, one of Marcel's accomplices, Pierre, had often holidayed in Herne Bay and was able to quiz me at length about the wretched place. So it was that I knew the length of the pier and where to find the clock tower and bandstand, and could trade anecdotes about the putrid ale and loose barmaid at the Four Fathoms whilst being fully conversant with the infamous "Brides in the Bath" murder.* All this meant that I had to be the real John Bull, n'est-ce-pas? And at last, after two whole days of confinement I was accepted as an ally.

'Come with me,' said Marcel, as he untied me. We were speaking in English now my nationality had been established. 'You can join the others.'

A few minutes later we were walking beside a narrow gauge railway track, in an airy tunnel, Marcel's flashlight pointing the way. After a quarter mile or so, the tunnel widened into what I took to be a cavern and it became apparent we were at some sort of junction, a crossroads. We stood and I watched as the light flicked all around us. In the far corner, I caught the crumpled remains of my lorry. 'The SS rat is still underneath it somewhere,' Marcel announced. 'But you, my friend, have Henri to thank for being here in one piece today. He was the only one of us strong enough to lift the cabin, and only by a few millimetres at that, but it was just enough for the others to pull you out.'

I shivered. There was a cold draught coming from somewhere and I could hear the tinkle of running water in the distance. Up until then I'd had only the haziest idea of what had happened to me after being caught by Weber but it was at last starting to fall into place. 'So, my lorry fell down a shaft? A ventilation shaft?' I ventured.

Marcel nodded.

'But what *is* this place?'

Marcel didn't answer immediately but played his flashlight around, illuminating scrawled place names and arrows etched into the walls. Auckland was further up the line, with Christchurch behind us and Wellington to our left. Elsewhere there were graffiti, soldiers names and their units, obscenities, jokes and even an image of a young woman,

---

* George Joseph Smith committed the first of his "Brides in the Bath" murders in Herne Bay in 1912. In 1915 he was convicted of this murder and two others, and hanged – http://tinyurl.com/Kilroy125.

The *Four Fathoms* pub is in the High Street, near the pier. It should be emphasised that it changed management and bar staff long ago.

expertly painted directly onto the chalky wall. 'From the Great War,' said Marcel. 'Dug by New Zealanders mainly. An enormous maze, 30 metres under the town of Arras, when the frontline was just there,' he pointed, 'one kilometre up that tunnel. Back here there was accommodation for 25 thousand men, all snug and safe below ground. And a railway, munitions, lighting, command posts and even a hospital. Certainly gave the *boche* a fright when all that lot appeared where he least expected.'

I peered up one of the tunnels trying to take it all in. 'But what of it now?' I asked.

'It's been sealed and forgotten about these many years, but now the Germans are back,' he spat, 'those of us in the know,' he tapped his nose, 'can make use of it. Who knows? Perhaps we will fight the Nazi scum from here? But come, you will meet some, how you say, *fugitives*? People we are sheltering from Nazi justice.'

Marcel led me off the main corridor into a cavern, which had once been a dormitory, to judge by the bunk beds crammed into it. He switched off his flashlight and it took a while for my eyes to adjust to the candle light. Someone had found an old settee, dragged it into the middle of the floor and incongruously draped a tiger skin rug over the back of it. I plonked myself down but immediately felt something strange. 'Christ, what's that?' I exclaimed as I leapt to my feet.

'Vlad-dee-mir,' said Marcel.

I turned to find myself face to face with the glaring eyes and rank breath of a tiger. 'Vladimir?' I repeated.

'No, no. Vlad-dee-mir. In Russian the second syllable...'

'Never mind about that. What the hell's he doing here?'

'Oh, don't mind him. He's a Siberian. Just a cub really and quite harmless.'

I found myself rather hoping that, er, Vlad-dee-mir knew this too, as he licked his chops and eyed me with interest. 'But...'

'Just ignore him,' Marcel replied, sounding a little too blasé for my liking. 'Here, let me introduce you to his family.'

His family – a human family I was relieved to see – must have been sleeping off monster hangovers to judge by all the empty wine bottles strewn around. Keeping a wary eye on my feline friend I waved a cheery hello to Monsieur Min and Madame Mum, 40 year olds, I guessed, but no taller than toddlers, and Hip and Hop, Siamese twins. I also recall Jingo the Gypsy and of course Henri, my recent saviour, standing seven foot six at least, as he crushed my hand with his cheerful handshake. There were others too, whose names I can't remember now – a bearded lady and a rather comely trapeze artiste who subsequently spent most of the night sitting happily in Henri's lap.

'Cirque Suprême chose the wrong time to visit Arras, that's for sure,' explained Marcel. 'So now we must find a way of getting these desperate fellows to the safety of Paris and keeping them out of Dachau.'

'But why would the Germans arrest a circus?' I asked, without thinking.

Marcel snorted. 'Well let's just say they fall short on a number of points of the Nazi's so-called racial purity,' he added in a matter-of-fact tone, glancing around at them as he spoke.

At that moment Pierre arrived, with a British army major, looking somewhat bedraggled, right behind him. 'Messieurs,' Pierre announced, 'we have another stray. Major, er, Major Blunder.'

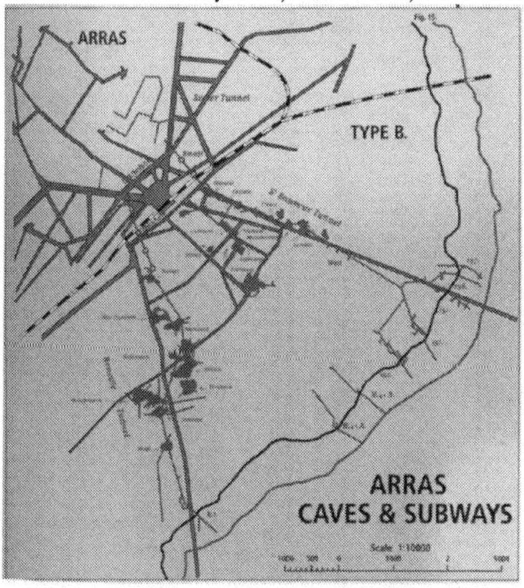

Map of the Arras tunnels. The outer wavy line, bottom middle to top right marks the WWI front line.

The major's face reddened and he leapt in quickly. 'Bloody Ell. How many times do I have to say it? *Blundel.* It's a bloody ell not an arr.'

Pierre frowned in puzzlement, glanced over at Marcel, delivered a classic Gallic shrug and sat down without comment. The major seemed somewhat deflated by this but he kept his thoughts to himself, well almost. I caught the occasional muttered 'bloody fools' as he stood in the middle of the room waiting for his eyes to adjust to the light. His cap, perched precariously on his head, looked like it had been run over by a Panzer division, but that was the smartest part of him. There was something worryingly odd about his manner, I thought, like he'd faced one or two too many Stukas in the past few days.* As his eyes alighted on me his face suddenly hardened and he took a sharp intake of breath. 'You've got a bloody Hun in here,' he cried out as he pointed at me. 'What a bally cheek,' he shouted at no one in particular. 'Get me a sabre. Quickly now. I'll run the bastard through.'

Fortunately there wasn't one, although he had to be restrained while Marcel explained my true loyalties. 'Raff you say? A bally old Brylcreem boy? God help us,' he said at last. 'Why's he wearing that Kraut gear then? Get him a proper uniform,' he clicked his fingers at Pierre, 'Pronto.'

* Stuka – nickname for the Junkers 87 dive bomber, famous at that time for its pin-point bombing that so effectively terrorised the infantry. http://tinyurl.com/Kilroy126.

To my surprise, Pierre meekly nodded at this and headed off.

Having wanted to put me to the sword a minute earlier the major was now all affability. 'Call me Vince, old fruit,' he said as he pumped my hand. 'Got separated from my regiment, somewhere around Béthune. Jolly old adjutant and two of my captains shot from under me, but needs must...' He waved vaguely around the cavern. 'Royal Norfolks, actually. What's your squadron?'

That set me aback. I decided that I would have to mention I'd recently been acquainted with the Norfolks and he brightened considerably at this. 'Le Paradis? The second battalion?' He plonked himself down on the settee, absentmindedly shoving Vladimir to one side. 'Wonderful chaps. I bet they showed you a good time,' he said as he slapped me on the knee.

I took a deep breath and delivered the bad news.

'Christ, those bastards. Those bloody Nazi scum. I'd like to get the swines who did that in a fair fight.' He sighed and dabbed his eye. 'But just you wait and see – one day we'll beat this cursed nation and bring them to justice.'

I nodded, whilst thinking that that seemed pretty unlikely, but there I was wrong. Knöchlein, at least, did pay for it in the end, although that was to be some years later.*

Pierre returned at that point, with a bundle under his arm. It represented a promotion for me, a flight lieutenant's battledress, with a blood stain on the arm, but I reckoned it was a considerable improvement on my Luftwaffe garb. The boots fitted well too. I asked after the previous owner.

Pierre and Marcel exchanged looks. 'Didn't make it I'm afraid,' said Marcel. 'Head injury and there was nothing could be done.' He handed me a glass of wine.

I looked at it, like he'd given me a measure of cough medicine. 'Red?'

'Bouzy Rouge,' replied Marcel. 'It's not all champagne around here. It's good. Drink it.'†

---

* In its essential details Kilroy's account of what came to be known as "Le Paradis Massacre" concurs with the known history. After the massacre French locals were made to bury the bodies and recorded that 97 had been murdered. Miraculously two of the Norfolks escaped the butchery to be recaptured shortly after, surviving the war as POWs. Their evidence subsequently secured the conviction of Knöchlein as a war criminal and he was hanged in 1949. See http://tinyurl.com/Kilroy127 (massacre) and http://tinyurl.com/Kilroy128 (Knöchlein).

† The Champagne region produces a small quantity of still wines, mainly red, called Coteaux-Champenois. They are not widely available outside France. Bouzy Rouge is one such label.

Those circus folks certainly knew how to enjoy themselves. A hundred feet above us, the Germans were happily jack-booting up and down the streets of Arras but you wouldn't know it down in our snug little cavern. Henri the Huge was a dab hand on the fiddle, with Heidi and Hester – his daughters apparently – on drums. That cute trapeze artiste – Christ I wish I could remember her name – treated us to some folk dance. I couldn't begin to describe it other than to say that it involved a lot of wobbling and wiggling.

Then, in a flash, it was time for Marcel to break open another case. He explained that the Comte de something or other had unwisely been using the caves for his wine cellar and even more unwisely fled to the South of France in the face of the German advance. 'Can't risk the Nazis getting their hands on this, can we?' commented Marcel, as he pulled a cork with practised ease.

And so it went on. Even the blundering major seemed to be relaxing a little, clapping along, with Madame Mum perched on the sofa on one side of him and Vladimir snoring quietly on the other. I remember, at one point, Jingo the Gypsy taking centre stage to play an odd looking instrument – a big-mouth guitar, I was told. It must have cost a fortune – spotless, highly polished wood with gleaming brass frets in a dark ebony fretboard. All around it was a beautiful piece of workmanship, which is more than I can say for his playing.

'Can't someone help him tune it?' I whispered to the bearded lady and she frowned and whispered me to be quiet. This was Beatrice. She could sing like an angel, swear in 18 different languages and had the body of a Venus. Without a hair anywhere. Except on her face of course. And all I can say is that although the whiskers take a bit of getting used to, if ever you get the chance, give it a go – I can heartily recommend it.

Then it was the morning after. Or to be more accurate it felt like it was the morning after. I'd lost my watch in the Great Uniform Swap with Oberleutenant von Stauss (deceased) and with no daylight it could have been any time. I was roughly shaken awake by the major. 'I have a plan,' he said, perching himself on the edge of the bed, doing his best to ignore the presence of Beatrice, entwined around me.

'What?'

'A plan. See here.' He produced a map. I gazed blearily at it and could just make out Arras at the bottom and the English Channel at the top.

In the years since, I've been privy to the plans for the Dieppe Raid and the R.A.F.'s Battle of Berlin, not to mention Operations Fustian and Market Garden, amongst many others. I know it's easy to be wise after the event but many would say they were all plain daft ideas in the first place and, not surprisingly, disasters when executed. But, having said that, I've never, ever, heard a dafter plan than that of the major.*

'What?!' I pronounced. 'You are off your tiny rocker.' I pulled up the bed clothes and snuggled back down with Beatrice. I'd been dreaming I'd joined a flying circus in Paris and, at that moment, even without the major's ludicrous scheme, the idea of rejoining the beleaguered British Expeditionary Force was seeming less and less attractive by the minute. And Beatrice was a game lass too. She felt so lovely and warm as she purred and wriggled in response to me, her whiskers rasping on my cheek. And we were just about to have another set-to when the covers were ripped off us.

'How dare you speak to a superior officer like that,' the major roared as we both blinked up at him. 'And you can stop that disgusting nonsense. Get up this instant and report to me in, in...' He looked at his wrist where there should have been a watch. 'In five minutes.'

---

* The Dieppe Raid, on 19th August 1942, was supposed to demonstrate the feasibility of seizing a major port in occupied Europe and show Britain's commitment to opening a second front. In the event the raid was a catastrophe with over 50% infantry casualties and with the R.A.F. losing over 100 aeroplanes. http://tinyurl.com/Kilroy129.

The Battle of Berlin, Bomber Harris' plan for saturation bombing of Berlin, was supposed to win the war outright but was abandoned in March 1944, at a cost of over 1,000 aircraft. http://tinyurl.com/Kilroy130.

Operation Fustian, in July 1943, was supposed to take a bridge in Sicily with airborne troops, ahead of the Eighth Army. It failed and ultimately the bridge was captured by the advancing Eighth Army anyway. http://tinyurl.com/Kilroy131.

Operation Market Garden, in September 1944, was supposed to use airborne troops to seize a line of bridges, to provide a direct route for the land army into the heart of Germany, thus shortening the war. The operation was a messy failure with over 15,000 allied casualties. http://tinyurl.com/Kilroy132.

Three of these four operations depended upon airborne troops. Airborne operations could easily go awry, especially in the early days, with unanticipated weather resulting in glider crashes, other misadventures and wide scattering of troops.

About an hour later, the major and I were out in the open air, on the country lane that I had only recently been chased along by Weber. I'd got my days and nights mixed up below ground. It wasn't morning at all but evening, with the sun just setting. Marcel was standing alongside us, holding a bicycle – a tandem – as the major paced around it. I noticed he'd attempted to iron out his cap but it looked even worse now than before. He tweaked and prodded the bike as he worked his way around it. 'Tyres – checked. Brakes – checked.' He sounded all crisp efficiency, like he was on the parade ground, inspecting a tank battalion. 'Good. All present and correct. Now Marcel, is there *any* possibility of having that leopard?'

Marcel shook his head. 'Tiger.'

Well, that was a relief. The major seemed to think Vladimir might be useful for what he called "flank defence" but, idiotic as the idea was, it had been still-born as his trainer, Rosa, had refused to let him go. The major frowned but said nothing further. He extracted a torch and shone it on his map. 'Hmmm,' he said, 'sixty miles to Dunkirk. Countryside as flat as a flapper's tits. Five hours, I'd say. Would have been more like three when I was young and fit, but,' he looked at me and sniffed, 'we're carrying excess baggage these days.'

He pulled a compass out of his pocket and pointed it up the lane. 'Three Five Zero, I reckon. That should get us there, near enough.' He sniffed the night air. 'Right. Time to get disguised.'

'But...'

'No buts, young man. Disguise and surprise is the name of the game. You'll see. Disguise and surprise.'

Beatrice was with us, hovering in the background and carrying a large bundle, which she dumped at our feet.

'Now, I'm going to be the one up-front,' instructed the major, as he rummaged through it, 'which means you get the arse end I'm afraid.'

'But...'

'Not much point you being up-front. You'll get us lost and, besides, you don't speak the lingo.'

'Lingo? What language?' I asked.

The major threw his head back, cupped his hands, placing them around his mouth and loudly whinnied. I remember thinking that he might be the biggest idiot this side of Sandhurst but he could sure do a convincing whinny. It wasn't just me who was convinced either. There was an answering call from the other side of the hedge.

The major gave a snort, an ordinary human snort that is, while I had a last quick smooch with Beatrice and then, too soon, it was time to get suited up, in the saddle and on the road. As for Madame Mum, Beatrice, Gypsy Jingo, Henri and the others – many years later I tried to track them down. I found that they had all been smuggled back to Paris shortly after my departure but much good it did them as the Germans themselves were there a few days later. Surprisingly, I found Vladimir, saved by the Menagerie du Jardin des Plantes* but, of the rest, I could find no trace. Most likely the Gendarmerie had simply rounded them up, and from there they went the terrible way of so many Nazi undesirables.† ‡ Marcel and Pierre lasted a little longer than their charges but, today, their names can be found on the Memorial Wall in Arras Citadel, on the spot where the Nazis shot 218 patriots during their years of occupation.§ **

---

* Paris' famous zoo. http://tinyurl.com/Kilroy133.

† Under Nazi rule the plight of Slavs, Gypsies, Blacks, the disabled, mentally handicapped, physically deformed, homosexuals, Communists and many others was much the same as that of the Jews. During the course of the war there were an estimated 14 million Gentiles murdered by the Nazis, including over 3 million Soviet POWs, 2 million Russian civilians and 3 million Poles (in addition to the 6 million Jews). http://tinyurl.com/Kilroy141 (Jews), http://tinyurl.com/Kilroy135 (Romani), http://tinyurl.com/Kilroy136 (disabled), http://tinyurl.com/Kilroy137 (Soviet POWs), http://tinyurl.com/Kilroy138 (Soviet civilians), http://tinyurl.com/Kilroy139 (Poles), http://tinyurl.com/Kilroy140 (homosexuals).

The Vichy regime, headed by Marshal Phillipe Pétain, was the nominal government of France throughout the Nazi occupation. It embraced Nazi racial policies with enthusiasm and built numerous concentration camps, which it filled with Gypsies, Jews and others. After the war Petain was convicted of treason. His death sentence was commuted to life imprisonment on account of his advanced age. He died in 1951, aged 95. http://tinyurl.com/Kilroy142.

‡ It is likely that at least one of Kilroy's Arras acquaintances survived. Kilroy has almost certainly misspelled Gypsy Jingo's name incorrectly and it should read Django. Django Reinhardt, the famous jazz guitarist, was of Romani (Gypsy) extraction, based in Paris, where he performed in the 30s, 40s and 50s and, specifically, during the German occupation. The account here mentions a grande-bouche, a big-mouth guitar, otherwise known as the Selmer-Maccaferri, which was Reinhardt's favoured instrument. Reinhardt never forgot his roots and didn't just play on the big stage. At the height of his fame he still liked to mix with his old Romani acquaintances and it would seem this was how he crossed paths with Kilroy in Arras.

Reinhardt was spared the *Porojamos*, the Nazi genocide of the Romani, due to the protection of surreptitiously jazz-loving Germans, such as Luftwaffe Officer Dietrich Schulz-Köhn, nicknamed "Doktor Jazz" (the Nazis officially disapproved of jazz). http://tinyurl.com/Kilroy143 (Reinhardt), http://tinyurl.com/Kilroy144 (Selmer), http://tinyurl.com/Kilroy145 (short documentary).

Kilroy's remark about Gypsy Jingo's playing does him a disservice. Judge for yourself here: http://tinyurl.com/Kilroy146.

§ The Memorial Wall in Arras Citadel records the names of 218 patriots who were shot there by the Germans during the occupation. They were mainly French, but there were also Poles, Belgians, Russians and others. 70 were Communists. See

I've already commented on the daftness of the major's plan but the remarkable thing was that it worked. What he had noticed and I hadn't, was that along with abandoning their tanks, lorries and weaponry as they retreated, the Allies had left behind a lot of horse power. They should have shot them all of course, but soldiers can be sentimental creatures and don't always obey orders. Consequently, at that time, there were many Allied four footed beasts of burden galumphing up and down the Flanders highways and byways and, in the event, with it being dark, I suppose we must have just blended in with them. Disguise and surprise as the major would say (ad nauseam).*

There is little I can say about our journey as the rear half of a pantomime horse doesn't offer much in the way of vantage points. We just cycled through the night, hour after hour. It was pretty hot and uncomfortable stuck in the costume, with the major's sweaty backside

---

http://tinyurl.com/Kilroy147 (in French). In Kilroy's account, Pierre and Marcel are not their real names.

** The Arras Caves are a network of caves, caverns and tunnels under Arras, which were used by British Empire and Commonwealth troops during the First World War. Arras was close to the front line in WWI and had been mined and quarried for centuries. It was realised that these underground works could be of use to the military so, in 1916, miners from New Zealand and elsewhere were brought in to dig a network of connecting tunnels, working in great secrecy over several months. In the end over 20 kilometres of earthworks were dug, making for a complex that could house around 25 thousand troops, with electric lighting, sanitation, a railway and even a hospital. The underground network stretched from Arras railway station to the German front line, over one kilometre away. The Germans were taken by surprise on the opening day of the Arras Offensive, on 9th April 1917, when thousands of Allied troops suddenly popped out of the ground right in front of them. They were pushed back a remarkable 11 kilometres, but ultimately the Allied advance ground to a halt, with the usual terrible casualties ensuing.

After the war the tunnels were sealed, but were reopened in WWII when they were used as air raid shelters, before being sealed again after the liberation. There they lay, largely forgotten, until reopened in 1990. Then, after much research and negotiation, the Carrière Wellington Museum was finally opened in 2008 ("Wellington Quarry" in English – Wellington being the name given to it by the New Zealand miners). Much of the network has now collapsed and the remainder is deemed extremely unsafe but there is much of historical interest in the museum, including poignant graffiti scrawled on the walls by the men shortly before they went into action. http://tinyurl.com/Kilroy148 (museum), http://tinyurl.com/Kilroy149 and http://tinyurl.com/Kilroy150 (*Daily Mail* articles), http://tinyurl.com/Kilroy208 (interactive map).

* At the end of May 1940, the moon was in its third quarter, which would be ideal for this sort of operation. http://tinyurl.com/Kilroy152.

poking me in the nose, but I kept to the task. We must have encountered a number of Germans along the way, as every now and then the major started whinnying for all he was worth and I had to do my bit, clipping and clopping with some coconut shells hanging from his belt. I heard lots of traffic – tanks and lorries I guessed – grinding past us in the night but for all the difference they made, we might as well have been invisible. Once I heard some shots ring out and the major cried, 'Come on Copenhagen, pedal like billy-oh.' This was my cue to put some muscle in. Our pursuers must have quickly given up as that was an end to it. Copenhagen, by the way, was the major's name for our strange assemblage – after Wellington's horse at Waterloo I suppose, although I can't imagine Cirque Suprême would have called it that.

Memorial Wall for the 218 patriots, in the citadel at Arras. The post marks the place of execution.

After several hours of this torture it was getting light and I was guessing we must be nearly home and dry. As if he could hear my thoughts, the major shouted, 'The front line!' I felt a surge as the bike picked up speed. 'C'mon,' he shouted, 'it's Blighty boys ahead. Hurrah for St George! Copenhagen, Copenhagen, charge!'

I was pretty knackered by then but, encouraged by his words, I put in every last ounce of effort, pumping hard on the pedals and straining every sinew. Judging by the clamour, I guessed we'd arrived in the middle of a pitched battle. Thankfully I couldn't see anything but I could hear plenty. There was a roar of an explosion nearby and the thump of its shock wave and the continuous zipping of bullets all around us, sounding closer and closer by the second. I would have given anything to jump in a ditch but instead had to keep pedalling for all I was worth whilst bracing myself for the inevitable. Just when I thought the game must surely be up, the major braked hard. It caught me by surprise and as we screeched to a halt we fell over in an untidy heap.

It took a while to sort ourselves out, lying as we were with bike, horse and each other all tangled up. Meanwhile the clamour of battle surrounded us. At last I managed to disentangle myself enough to peel back a part of my costume and look around. I found that we were sheltering in the wreckage of an overturned army vehicle, an armoured car I guessed. The sun had well risen by then so I could see quite clearly and I counted one, two, three, four dead, lying alongside us, and one alive – a general, a British

Army general, who was moaning softly in a crumpled heap on the floor. 'Have we made it?' I shouted to the major.

'Of course not, you bloody fool. We're in the middle of...' The rest of his explanation was drowned out by several explosions, uncomfortably close.

'Who the what now?' I shouted.

'The Calonne Canal,' he shouted back, cupping his hands around his mouth and bellowing into my ear. 'On the Willem van Gulik Bridge. Our boys at that end.' He pointed. 'And Krauts at the other.'

He seemed to think my lack of response to this ghastly piece of news was a request for more information.

'Van Gulik. Slain at the Battle of Bulskamp, 1297. Build up to the Battle of the Spurs. Surely you've heard of him?'*

I wasn't really in the mood for a history lesson at that moment but there was no stopping the major.

'Look, see here, Bulskamp's just over there.' He was warming to his theme and stood up to get a better view. 'See the church spire, over there?'

He was beckoning me to get off the floor and look but I wasn't having any. Then he frowned. 'No, I've got it wrong. Silly me.' He smacked the side of his head and stood up again. 'That's Bulskamp there.' He produced his compass and pointed it in another direction. 'Two five zero. Over there see.'

He was beckoning at me to get up again but finally got the message that I was staying put. 'Well, no matter, but somebody's screwed up that's for sure. Sappers should have blown the bridge but their balls-up is our salvation. If it wasn't for that we'd be swimming across – and Christ knows what the Frogs drop in their canals. Probably need 20 injections afterwards.' He paused for a moment, collecting his thoughts. 'Right then, here's what we'll do. We'll get back into jolly old Copenhagen, a quick hundred yard sprint and we'll be breakfasting on Bully Beef and biscuits in next to no time.'

The general groaned at that moment and the major started. 'Crikey. Where'd he spring from? I thought they were all goners.'

The major might have seemed like an escapee from a lunatic asylum but he certainly had powers of persuasion. My natural inclination at that moment was to burrow into the wreckage and wait for nightfall but he wasn't having any of that. A few minutes later, we were suited up again, without the bike beneath us but *with* the groaning general perched on top of us. He must have looked like the Iron Duke on a decidedly off day, hat askew, trousers at half mast and a somewhat crumpled mount beneath him as we attempted to gallop towards the British front line, bullets flying all

* See http://tinyurl.com/Kilroy153 (in Dutch).

around. 'They won't shoot a horse – don't worry,' shouted the major above the clamour.

'Christ, but the Frogs'll bloody well eat 'em,' I thought but hadn't the breath to say. With only half the distance covered our gallop had slowed to a walk and, a few yards after that, to whatever horses do when too tired to walk – stroll I suppose. The bullets were still flying and I really didn't think we'd make it but somehow or other we strolled, staggered and limped across the last of the bridge – the last few yards seemed to take weeks. Mercifully the ground dropped away sharply at that point so for the final leg all we had to do was stumble down a steep slope to safety where, at last, we collapsed on the ground, in an exhausted heap, our chests heaving as we gasped for breath.

CHAPTER 11

The subaltern beckoned us to follow. 'The general would like to thank you personally,' he said as we followed him along a corridor. We were in a farmhouse, the regimental HQ, where the three of us had been taken after our inglorious arrival. The major and I had indeed dined on biscuits and Bully Beef, while the medicos had attended the general. The subaltern opened a door and gestured us to enter.

I'd rather expected to find him on a stretcher, but he was on his feet in the middle of the room, standing by a table with his back to us and, talking on a telephone. 'No, I'm fine,' he said, 'Mild concussion that's all. Never felt better. But get a vehicle here ASAP, car, carrier or motor bike – anything.' He laughed. 'And, look Nigel, do find a driver who knows how to get around without taking in a Panzer division en route.' He put down the phone and turned around as the subaltern announced, 'Gentlemen, I give you General Montgomery.'

We saluted and I stepped forward. 'Venereal disease,' I said as he pumped my hand.

He let go, blinked and stood back. I could see the others frowning at me too. 'And?' he replied cautiously.

'I read your memoranda, sir. When I was the squadron's Voodoo, that is the, er, VD Orderly Officer. Sound advice if I might say, sir.'

The others looked relieved at this point although I noticed the general still wore a frown. The Montgomery name meant little in those days. He was on the lowest rung of high command, a mere divisional commander, with his triumphs at El Alamein and in Normandy in the future. At this time his one claim to fame had been his liberal views on what was euphemistically called the men's "horizontal entertainment". I found out later it had got him into a lot of trouble so it wasn't the wisest subject to raise but, as his rescuer, it would seem he would let that pass.

'Gentlemen,' he said as he shook the major's hand, 'thank you for your kind assistance.'

'It was nothing, sir,' said the major with studied understatement, 'you have Copenhagen to thank really.'

Montgomery frowned in puzzlement momentarily, then his face cleared. 'Oh that stupid pantomime horse? Oh I get it. Har har. Copenhagen. Very good. Well, I'll tell you something, it might have been an idiotic way to go about things but I'm putting you up for a gong for this. Very brave. Wish we had more chaps like you in our front line.'*

An orderly entered the room and whispered in his ear. 'Excuse me gentlemen,' he said as he picked up the phone. 'What now, Nigel?' he barked into the mouthpiece.

There was a pause while Nigel, presumably, conveyed some news. 'What?' asked the general. 'They've done what?' He was getting louder. 'Jesus H Christ, no!' He paused for a moment tapping his teeth. 'Okay, let me think.' He paused a little longer. 'Right, here's what you'll do. We've still got the Guards in reserve haven't we? In Furnes? Get their nearest battalion to plug the gap. Time for them to earn their keep. Fixed bayonets and if any of those runaways won't return to their post they have my authority to use them. Got that?' He waved at us to go. 'And any of their officers not doing their duty,' he continued, 'shoot them. That's right – shoot them. That'll clarify my orders. No gaps in the front line and no retreat, I said. None at all or we'll all be sunk. Okay?' He banged down the phone without waiting for a response.

General Bernard Montgomery in North Africa, 1942.

From this I gathered that things were pretty desperate in Dunkirk. Until then I'd no idea.† In the aftermath of our recent dramatic arrival I'd merely

---

* It is possible that Kilroy's exploit with the pantomime horse was the inspiration for a Monty Python sketch filmed many years later – http://tinyurl.com/Kilroy154 (watch from 1min 32 seconds onwards).

† There are at least two recorded instances at Dunkirk of British troops being summarily shot for "retiring without permission". In one case, the 246th Field Company of the Royal Engineers, together with some of the Royal Suffolks and Royal Berks battalions, broke under heavy shell fire. A section from the Grenadier Guards 2nd Battalion was sent to fill the gap. One of the Guards officers found it necessary to shoot some of the Engineers, while his NCOs had to turn others at the point of the bayonet before they could be reorganised. The Guards officer, Lieutenant Jones, was awarded the Military Cross for restoring order and leading the remains of both battalions and the Royal Engineers company back to the front line. This action took place at Furnes on 31st May, in a section of the line commanded by General Montgomery. Kilroy was back in London by then so the phone call he overheard must have concerned some earlier similar incident. See: http://tinyurl.com/Kilroy155 (Amazon).

been relieved to be in one piece and back with the right side and was vaguely expecting to loaf around a few days until some opportunity presented itself to rejoin my squadron. But the subaltern soon put me straight. With the bulk of the British Expeditionary Force just down the road, sitting on the beach with pea-shooters and praying for salvation, all we had left were good men like himself and Montgomery, too, to marshal the perilously thin defensive line in the town's outskirts. We really were hanging by a thread.*

And so it was time for the major and me to part company – he to rejoin what was left of the Norfolks and me to head for the beach and queue for a berth home. I can't say I was sorry to see him go. I heard a rumour later that he made it back home with a flotilla of pedaloes but (mercifully) I never saw him again.

Not so Montgomery. Our paths crossed several times over the years and if there was a better general on any side, friend or foe, I never met him. Of course he'd been rather busy that day in Dunkirk, what with one thing and another and, not surprisingly, forgot all about his promise of a "gong" for our rescue efforts. I think it was in Italy in late '43, that I rather stupidly took the opportunity to remind him. 'Oh, yes,' he said, looking a tad prickly, 'I well remember that malarkey with "Copenhagen". But you saved my bacon that day that's for sure. So what do you want? The country's highest award for valour perhaps?' He waited for me to answer.

I gulped. I'd half expected a campaign medal or some such but if he wanted to put me up for the Victoria Cross I wasn't going to argue. I nodded.

'Leave it to me then,' he said.

And true to his word a few months later I received it, not at the Palace, but in a parcel by registered post. It wasn't a VC but it *was* indeed the country's highest award for valour – the DM or Dickin Medal as it's called. It sits on my desk as I write these words – a large bronze medallion bearing

---

* This was one of the few occasions in the whole dismal Battle of France when the Allies stood up to the Germans (for a while anyway), with the famous result that everybody, well everybody in Britain anyway, still speaks of. The famous Hitler/von Rundstedt Halt order gave the British and French a vital 48 hours to organize some sort of resistance but it was still desperate stuff. The landward approaches to Dunkirk all thread through a maze of canals and these, combined with some flooded lowlands, formed the basis of the defence – a 40 mile line held by French units to the west and British to the east. The commune of Bergues, the nearest point in the line to Dunkirk harbour, was still six miles away and thus the German artillery was kept out of range.

Four years later the boot was on the other foot. It was in the autumn of 1944 when the Allies laid siege to the Germans in the port. On this occasion the defenders were able to hold out for eight months, until the German surrender in May 1945. http://tinyurl.com/Kilroy156.

the words "For gallantry" and "We also serve", with a green, brown and blue striped ribbon. The citation reads:

*For outstanding gallantry and devotion to duty in rescuing the division's commanding officer the PDSA (Peoples Dispensary for Sick Animals) is proud to make this equine award to...**

---

* The Dickin Medal, sometimes called the animal's VC, was instituted by Maria Dickin, the founder of the PDSA, during WWII. Since its inception it has been awarded to 32 pigeons, 31 dogs, three horses and one cat, all for service in military conflict. Copenhagen is not listed among these awards, although it is possible it received an Honorary DM, as additional honorary awards have been made occasionally. http://tinyurl.com/Kilroy157 (Dickin Medal) and http://tinyurl.com/Kilroy207 (PDSA).

CHAPTER 12

Nowadays everyone speaks of the men on the beaches being ferried out to sea by the little boats, but at the time I arrived in Dunkirk the evacuation was mostly from the harbour and so that is where I headed. It had taken me over four hours to walk there from the front line, in a dreary procession of the defeated, through rubble and smouldering buildings. The driving rain and thunderstorms did little to cheer us, although at least the weather kept the Luftwaffe at bay.

As I neared my destination, the skies cleared and at last I could see what awaited me. The harbour was in ruins but there were two jetties untouched and the nearer one, which I guessed was over a mile long, was crammed with men, standing five deep. A further long queue was snaking around the harbourside, everyone patiently waiting. At the far end of the jetty the ships were moored – some Royal Navy destroyers but also all sorts of odd-ball craft – a paddle steamer, trawlers, tugs, everything really. Further out in the harbour floated the remains of some of those that hadn't made it. Planks and splintered wood drifted around, a large oil slick had formed and, in the middle of it all, was a lumbering cross-channel ferry, laying incongruously on its side but otherwise looking whole and undamaged.

Being R.A.F., I didn't have a unit to hook up with but rather expected that I would be allowed to just tag along with whoever would welcome me. I spotted an army captain with a clipboard and marched smartly up to him, saluted and asked what was the score.

He eyed me warily. 'R.A.F.?' he asked.

I nodded.

He coughed. At the time I thought he was clearing his throat but then I realised he had spat at me.

I wiped my face with my hand. I was wondering how to respond when he must have seen my look of puzzlement.

'Why don't you check in at the Castille?'

'Pardon?'

'Not much point you going back home is there? For all the good your lot are doing. You can wait there for your Nazi chums to show up.'

You've read my tale so will know this was a monstrous injustice but it was what most of the army thought of the R.A.F. at that time. All they could see was the Luftwaffe attacking them with our fighters nowhere to be found. In reality the R.A.F. *was* operating flat out but all the air battles were going on out of sight and the army just didn't know it. I guessed this might be the case and was trying to decide whether to poke the captain in the eye or give him a civil reply when I saw him look up at the sky. As if on cue, a formation of Stukas appeared.

All eyes around the harbour turned to watch them and we stood silently as they gracefully wheeled above us. One peeled off and went into a dive. It was heading for one of the ships a mile away, at the end of the jetty but it was still terrifying to witness. It looked like an enormous bird of prey, pointing vertically downwards with its siren blaring and doing its darnedest to dive straight down the ship's funnel. The Royal Navy answered in kind, pumping shells into the air but the plane remained unscathed and at the last second it released the bomb and pulled out of the dive, swooping over our heads. The bomb missed, throwing up an enormous column of water alongside the ship. Meanwhile the next plane was attacking. Then the remainder turned their attention on us. Those of us who could, ran for cover. I sprinted up a side street, into a café and threw myself under a table. Almost immediately there was a loud explosion, uncomfortably close, followed by a loud crash as the ceiling fell down, covering everything with plaster dust.

Evacuation from Dunkirk beach.

It took me some time to sort myself out. I was coughing and choking on all the dust and my ears were ringing but I gradually realised that I was otherwise in one piece and unhurt. There was no one else around and so no one to be helped or to help me and it took a while before I felt steady enough to scramble to my feet and stumble outside. By then the Stukas had gone and, I thought, at least their arrival had saved me from further grief from the army captain. I looked back down the street and there he was again, at the harbourside, with his clipboard. The queue had reformed too, presumably everyone politely back into the place they had recently vacated. I could see that one of the destroyers was ablaze and drifting across the harbour. I wondered whether I really wanted to queue for several days to end up like that.

An army lorry was parked across the street. This was unusual as most units had been made to abandon their transport before they entered the town and there weren't that many vehicles around in the centre. I'd seen scores of abandoned lorries and carriers that morning, in the fields and at the roadside as I was walking in from the front line.

An army lieutenant walked up to me. 'Best stand well away mate. There's going to be a bit of a bang in a minute.'

I looked behind him to the other end of the street and could see a couple of men coming out of a building on the corner and unrolling a wire from a spool they were carrying between them. There was a sandbag emplacement beside the lorry and they hurried towards it. Meanwhile the lieutenant was doing the rounds, warning other bystanders. Then he came back to me. 'Stand there much longer mate and you'll get your head blown off. Don't say I didn't warn you.'

'But what's up?' I asked.

He sighed and looked at his watch. I did wonder if I was going to get the hotel treatment again but this officer was a little more R.A.F.-tolerant. He pointed up the street to the building on the corner and started lecturing me, like I was a simpleton. 'That there is a bank. You can tell that by the word "Banque" above the door. In the basement of said bank there's a safe and said manager's buggered off. Christ knows what's in the safe but whatever is there the Jerries aren't going to get their sticky mitts on it. Might just be the manager's lunchbox for all I know but there might be something worth having too. My orders are to blow the safe, get what we can out of it, log it all carefully and then get everything safely back to London where, no doubt, it will all end up in another safe.'

I could see one of the men, standing on top of the sandbags and carefully attaching the wire to a plunger. I was about to ask another question when the Stukas reappeared. I turned and ran up the street, past the bank and around the corner, diving into a shop – a florist this time. It was just fate that I didn't follow the lieutenant to the safety of the sandbags. I just went the other way.

I won't say you can ever get used to being dive bombed but, with practice, you can become fatalistic about it. I think they hit another destroyer on that occasion but I knew by the closeness of the explosions around me that they had attacked the town too. After it was all over I walked back onto the street and returned to the bank, which was unscathed. There was hardly anyone around – just a few men like me, stumbling around in the rubble looking bewildered.

Looking back up the street towards the harbour I could see the army lorry was now on its side some way away and the sandbag emplacement had all but vanished. I walked over and looked around where it had once been. There were bits of fabric, an army boot, a cap badge and some grisly remains and that was all that was left of the lieutenant and his men. I guessed they had taken a direct hit. The sole survivor was, bizarrely, the plunger, with the lead attached, still in one piece and leading all the way to the bank. I don't know what came over me but, without thinking, I pushed it, ramming it hard into the box.

Nothing happened. I realised later that that was probably just as well as quite possibly I *would* have blown my head off if it had worked but at the time I thought, perhaps, the safe *had* blown and I just hadn't heard it. You see my ears were still ringing from the Stuka attack. So I followed the trail of the wire back up the street to the bank, through its open doorway, across the floor, through the open internal security door, past the counter, along a corridor and down some stairs. The safe was at the bottom of the stairs, built into the foundations and standing as high as me. The word "Chubb" was writ large on it, which surprised me as that's of course a British manufacturer. It had a combination lock – a precision engineered dial in the centre – and the explosive, which I guessed must be gelignite, was packed around it, with three detonators attached. All I knew about explosives could be written on the side of a penny banger so I stood there for a while, wondering what to do. I suppose I could have walked away and left it but it's not every day you get a chance to crack a safe and I was curious to see if I could.

Pater had a hefty Chatwood Milner safe in his study and always had difficulties working the combination mechanism. 'I'm just no good with numbers,' he'd say. This was rich coming from him, given what he did for a living, but there it is. In the manner of a typical nine year old I had no problem figuring it out, so I used to open it for him. Then, a couple of years later, when I was despatched to the Herne Bay House of Horrors he made me write out idiot-proof instructions for him to use while I was away. These instructions, which included the actual combination numbers, he imaginatively secreted in the top drawer of his desk.

I climbed back up the stairs to the manager's office. None of the drawers was locked and I wrenched them all open, but was disappointed to find only pencil shavings, stationery, a Health and Nature magazine and a blackened banana. There was nothing that looked remotely like a note with the combination.

Pater had still struggled with the safe, even with my instructions, and was always calling out the locksmith. The breakthrough came when the locksmith changed the combination to Pater's birth date.

I'd noticed some keys in the depths of the pencil shavings and figured they were for the line of filing cabinets, against one of the walls. I soon located the staff records, held in one of the drawers, the manager's name was on the brass plate on his door so in no time at all I was leaping back down the stairs, two at a time, with his birth date scrawled on a piece of paper.

It didn't work. I guessed that Messrs Chatwood and Milner's mechanism might be different from Lord Chubb's* so I tried some variations, adding extra intermediate turns, trying anti-clockwise first, then the numbers in a different order and so on. Then I idly twiddled the dial backwards and forwards but, of course, that was not going to work in a hundred years. I poked the explosive a couple of times but thought better of it and stood back. Then I noticed a business card stuck on the safe door – 'Robin Loutte et fils, Serrures et coffres-forts sont nos affaires,'† it proclaimed, together with his address and phone number.

Chubb Safes, advertisement in *The Times, Dec 2nd 1926.*

Robin Loutte – blimey, he'd struggle for work in the UK – wasn't in the staff file but it seemed he did have an account with the bank because he was in the customer file, and this told me he was born on 26th January 1877.

So... 26-01-77. I still had to experiment a bit but it really was the key and I heard the clunk as the lock sprung open, at which I threw the door lever hard down to withdraw the bolts and, at last, was able to heave the door open.

At first glance it looked disappointing. The top shelf contained what I guessed must be the cashiers' drawers, each rattling with change and, no doubt full of notes, but securely padlocked and far too heavy for one lone aviator on Shanks's Pony. The next two shelves were given over to documents. Some were rolled and tied with ribbon, while

---

* The Chubb family owned the business at that time but the title of the baronetcy was Lord Hayter.

† Robin Loutte and son, Locks and Safes are our Business.

others were in folders and a few fastened with bulldog clips. I glanced at one or two of them and tried to make sense of the French legalese – wills and title deeds at a guess. If the Germans could make any sense of that lot they were welcome to them I thought. There seemed to be nothing at all on the bottom shelf and I was about to call it a day when I spotted a small pouch. It was made of chamois and securely tied with a string, a label attached. The label read "Beurs voor Diamanthandel" with an address in Antwerp below. On the reverse was written "100 x Fine round/I.F./D/0.75 carat" and, below, in a different hand, in French, "To be collected on 20th May, by M. Pierre Solange from Paris – manager to authorise release." All that "I.F./D" stuff meant little to me at the time although I've looked it up since and know exactly what it means now – "top notch" in short.* I untied the drawstring, my hands trembling a little and carefully poured the contents of the bag into the palm of my hand. The light was poor in the cellar, but even so the sparkle of 100 mighty little rocks was impressive and the thought of what they must be worth even more so. My hands were sticky with sweat and grime so it seemed prudent to kneel on the floor to decant them back into the sack. I dropped a couple but managed to find them easily enough. Once everything was back in the bag I tightly tied the drawstring. M Solange was way overdue of course, the manager was AWOL and Jerry was knocking at the door so it would seem to be down to yours truly to do the right thing, I thought. I slipped the bag into my pocket and climbed back up the stairs.

* Diamonds are valued by the four "C"s – cut, clarity, colour and carats. These diamonds are fine round cut, internally flawless (I.F.) and colourless (D) – the finest quality and therefore the highest value. According to http://tinyurl.com/Kilroy159 a single 0.75 carat diamond of this quality (in 2016) would be worth about $US 10,000 and so 100 of them would therefore be worth around US$ 1,000,000. See also http://tinyurl.com/Kilroy160.

CHAPTER 13

Captain Clipboard was still on duty at the harbour so I decided to try my luck on the beach. I've already mentioned that there was little going on there but it was only a short walk away and I couldn't think what else to do. I caught sight of just a handful of men in the middle distance wading out into the shallows to board a couple of small boats but there was precious little else going on. For all the chance of rescue, I thought, the rest of them might just as well roll up their trousers, strip to the waist and build sand castles.

Like any other seaside town Dunkirk had its share of cafes, bars and hotels. In the main, the British Army was pretty well behaved, I thought, but there were a few I'd noticed who had decided to contribute to the war effort by making sure that there would be no precious liquor left for Jerry when he eventually showed up. I passed Café Carla, on the front. It had been drunk dry I guessed – the door was wide open and there were some overturned tables and broken glass outside but nothing happening within. Next door the Hotel Mirabelle was rather more lively, well, in uproar to be precise. I was wondering whether or not to pop in myself for a glass or two when I heard a shout from behind me.

'It's the Raff, the bloody Raff. Let's get the bass-turd.'

Before I could turn around I felt a hefty shove in my back. I stumbled forward, slipped and fell. As I tried to pick myself up a solid kick landed in my side and took the wind out of me. A bottle hit the pavement near my head and broke into smithereens. Then they were upon me, stinking of stale sweat and drink, and kicking, punching, scratching at me. I tried to slither away in the mêlée but it was hopeless and in the end all I could do was tuck myself into a ball with my arms over my head and pray for it to stop. I tried to brace myself against the blows and, strangely, it didn't hurt much at the time although I was sore enough afterwards. Just when I was wondering if they might tire and give up or perhaps render me unconscious or worse I heard a lorry screech to a halt nearby and a voice of authority, 'Right, you lot, pack it in. Right *now*. Attention. Attention I said.'

There was one last thump, a glancing blow on my shin and then, at last, the beating stopped. It took me a while to unwind, but eventually I managed to look up to see a half dozen dishevelled men being pushed into line with truncheons. It would seem that I'd been rescued by the MPs, the military police.

Their sergeant strode up and down the ragged line, lecturing on proper behaviour, like he was on the parade ground at Aldershot. No one seemed bothered about me at all. Unhelped and ignored I managed to roll over onto all fours. I was still struggling to get my breath back as the sergeant was finishing with a little homily on decorum in foreign fields, giving each miscreant a solid poke in the stomach with his truncheon as he sent him on his way. At last one of his men turned to me and helped me to my feet. 'Blimey, Sarge,' he said, 'It's an officer. Crikey, R.A.F. An R.A.F. officer, Sarge.'

'R.A.F., eh?' replied the sergeant as he saluted me. 'Don't see many of them these days, do we?'

I was still pretty winded, so couldn't reply.

'Can't have you hanging around here, sir, getting beaten up on the beach. We'll get you to the airfield.'

A few minutes later I was in the back of the lorry as it roared through the streets of Dunkirk. There was something odd about the sergeant's suggestion. I was wondering how we could possibly maintain an airfield anywhere nearby with the Luftwaffe so much in evidence, but then he had seemed pretty sure about it. It certainly sounded a better bet than enduring further pongo hospitality in the town. The MPs were all up-front in the lorry's cabin so I was alone in the back. I watched over the tailgate as we threaded our way through the streets – some buildings whole, many in ruins – and out into the countryside. We must have been going for quarter of an hour and I guessed would be nearing the perimeter when the lorry slowed and stopped. I heard the cabin door open and someone trudge around to the back. The tailgate came down with a bang. I was still pretty shaky after the beating but managed to slowly clamber down and onto the road.

The land is pretty flat around Dunkirk but we had stopped on a small rise and there was a good view all around. 'Here we are, sir,' said the sergeant, pointing towards the setting sun. 'There's the Mardyck Canal.'

The area in front of us was criss-crossed with railway lines, a sort of vast shunting yard for the port, I guessed. The sergeant was pointing just beyond that and, squinting into the sun's rays, I could just make out a straight cleft in the ground leading to the sea and took that to be the canal. I nodded.

'French army's holding this sector, sir.'

They'd taken pains to be well dug in so there wasn't much to see but I thought I could spot some artillery units nearby and even a squadron of tanks hidden in a coppice. 'And the airfield?' I asked.

'Ah, there's your airfield, sir.' He pointed to the far side of the canal, to a patch of green just by the sea.

'But?...' I said and turned around.

He was trudging back towards the lorry cabin.

I squinted into the sun and looked again. It was certainly a flat expanse of field and I rather fancied I could make out a windsock, some huts and a couple of wrecked aircraft. 'But how do I get there?' I asked.

'Shanks's Pony,' he grunted as he climbed into the cabin and banged the door shut. The engine roared and the lorry took off, leaving me at the roadside.

I continued to stare into the distance. I couldn't see any operational aeroplanes at all but after a while I noticed some movement. There was a column of vehicles trundling across the field. At first it was difficult making it out but eventually I was sure. They were Panzers.

There didn't seem much I could do other than trudge back into the town again. I took stock of my situation. On the plus side I was still alive and, to the east, the pall of smoke was not so far away, so I reckoned it wasn't going to be that long a walk. On the minus side I was pretty well knackered after my recent ordeals and didn't seem any too popular with the army there.

Somewhere along the way I got in step with Mickey, an army corporal and a veteran of some years to judge by his lined face. I never found out which unit he was from but in those days these things barely mattered. Wherever he'd been he'd been bombed rather too many times that was for sure. He was practically stone deaf.

You certainly wouldn't choose the countryside west of Dunkirk for your holidays. Let's just call it an industrial wasteland. I wondered if its recent mauling by the Wehrmacht and Luftwaffe had possibly improved it. I've already mentioned the railway. The tracks and yards seemed to extend for miles on both sides of our road. Of course normal operations were suspended for the time being and so all was quiet, the wagons and locomotives lying idle or in splintered ruin by the track side. Every now and then we passed an oil tank and I noticed that some of them were leaking their contents onto the road or into the canal. There were also signal boxes, water tanks and the odd coal bunker, without a tender to fill, but covered in filth and soot. Strangely we saw very little of any people. I don't suppose many waifs and strays such as ourselves were coming into Dunkirk from this direction and the Frenchies who were defending it were clearly keeping their heads down. It occurred to me that we should do the same. It was still light and the German line wasn't so far away. 'Let's walk a bit faster,' I suggested to Mickey.

'Rather not, sir. I only drink at Christmas,' he replied.

'What?'

'Not been plastered since my 20th birthday, sir.'

I opened my mouth to reply but then thought better of it and just quickened my pace anyway. Mickey caught on, hitched his pack high on his back and we set to "at the double" as the pongoes would have it. We strode along like that, in companionable silence, for perhaps a half hour. By then the sun was dipping below the horizon, but still warming our backs and turning the smoke hanging over the town into a soft golden hue. If you could overlook the fact that we and the rest of the British Army were in one hell of a jam you might say it all looked strangely beautiful. The landscape had improved as well. The rail yards had given way to open countryside and it was pleasantly rural, with farms and small holdings dotted around. It was still eerily quiet. There were no human beings to be seen or heard and no animals either, apart from the odd chicken clucking at the roadside. I guessed all the locals had somehow managed to escape the war zone or were sheltering in the cellars in the town. And presumably there had been no shortage of takers for the livestock, what with two hungry armies to feed.

We were just passing a rather ordinary looking farm – a delapidated barn alongside an untended meadow with a modest farmhouse just up the road, when there was a loud shriek. It must have been loud as even Mickey heard it. We exchanged looks. 'What the bloody hell was that, sir?' he asked.

The cry seemed to have come from the house so we broke into a run and, without a by-your-leave, barged through the front door. It was gloomy in the hallway, so we stopped, looking at each other and unsure of what to do next. 'Hello,' I cried, then in French, 'Allo.'

'Ici, ici,' a woman urgently cried. We strode up the hall and into what turned out to be the farmhouse kitchen. The room's only occupant was a young woman who was in some disarray, hair bedraggled and perspiration running down her cheeks. She was standing by the table supporting herself with one hand while clutching a large book to her stomach with the other. 'M'aidez, m'aidez,' she cried.

I've seen men who've just been bayoneted standing like that but, if anything, she looked worse. Even now I can recall the look of fear and desperation in her face. Mickey grabbed a chair while I rounded the table and guided her towards it. Beneath all the bedraggled panic I could see she was a pretty young chit and my first thought was that she had fallen victim to some rampant roving Poilus. I put my arm around her and helped her to sit down. 'Quel est le problème?' I asked.

She didn't answer but instead thrust the book into my hands. It was a weighty tome, leather bound, but had seen better days. The bindings were badly worn and, as I opened it, several pages came loose and fell to the floor. I rather expected it to be the family bible but it wasn't. I looked at the title page, attempted to translate, looked at the girl, did a double-take and gulped. 'Mickey,' I asked, 'are you a married man?'

Of course he couldn't hear me so I had to repeat the question, roaring unnecessarily loudly, which alarmed the girl.

'No need to shout, sir. Me and the missus been spliced these twelve years. Never a cross...'

'Any children, Mickey?'

'Two sir. Boy and a girl.'

'Well that's a bloody relief.'

'Beg pardon, sir?'

'Look, Mickey. Take a good look at the young lady.'

I was standing behind her and pointed. She had been quiet during our exchange but chose that moment to let out a long wail, grabbing her belly with both hands while rocking backwards and forwards in the chair.

'Blimey, sir. I can't be doing with that. Mrs Turnbull did for my missus. Went on for hours. I was in the billiard hall both times.'

I picked up a tea towel from the table and wiped the girl's forehead. She smiled weakly up at me. I turned to Mickey and pointed at the door. 'Well see if there's a blower anywhere in this dump and use it. The village bobby, Lord Gort, Mrs Turnbull or even blinking Lord Nelson, I don't care. Any one of them will do.'

He was only too glad to get out of the room, which gave Aimée and me a chance to get acquainted. I discovered it was possible to have some sort of reasonable conversation with her for a couple of minutes, before she was seized by the cramps again. 'Where's your family?' I asked, when I thought she might be able to answer.

'One of those terrible dive bombers,' she replied and gestured out the window. It looked out on a small garden and at the back, by the wall, there were three piles of freshly dug soil. 'Mama, Papa et Cecille,' she added softly.

I frowned. I was thinking it unlikely that a slight young thing, in her condition, could dig three graves.

She must have anticipated my question. 'Phillipe,' she said. 'My fiancé,' and pointed at her belly. 'It happened three days ago. He saw to the bodies but then, when this...' The cramps must have started at this moment. Her voice cut off and she just seized my hand and hung on tightly in silence.

Then Mickey reappeared. 'Phone's kaput, sir. I couldn't have done much anyway as I can't speak French. Shall I go and look for help?'

I knew what that meant. Once he was out that front door he'd go the same way as Phillipe. 'No, Mickey, you can stay here.'

Aimée was watching anxiously during this exchange. It was clear she couldn't understand us but had sensed some discord. 'You *will* both stay and help me?' she asked.

'Of course. In fact you are in luck. We are Royal Army Medical Corps. Why Mickey, here, has delivered lots of babies.' I repeated this nugget in English for his benefit and mimed that I wanted a nonchalant "yes" in reply. Of course he didn't catch on and instead gaped back at me, his eyes wide with horror.

I'm not sure Aimée was that convinced either but of course she wanted to believe so went along with it.

Things got rather busy after that. In those days childbirth was very much women's work, with the menfolk no nearer than the local pub, but strangely enough I *had* been at a birth and I'm not talking about my own. One Christmas, when I was about nine, Helga's sister was on a visit and chose that moment to enlarge the family – a month earlier than expected. So young Helmut, seven and a half pounds, was delivered on our kitchen table with Cook, Helga and one of the maids in attendance up top, while yours truly, forgotten in the general hullabaloo, was playing with his new train set down below.

I looked at my hands and fingernails. There was about two weeks worth of Flemish filth embedded in them. 'Water,' I shouted at Mickey. 'Boil some water.' I pointed at the kitchen range, with the large black saucepans hanging above it. It was dark by then and I could see a faint glow coming from the grate. I think Mickey was only too grateful to help but from a distance, so made a pretty good job of stoking the fire, lighting hurricane lamps and so on. Then, after I'd cleaned myself up, I started wondering what to do with Aimée. She was still seated in the chair but the cramps were by then coming more often which, I recalled from Helmut's grand arrival, meant that things were hotting up so as to speak and I'd have to get her to move somewhere more appropriate, somehow or other. She gestured at some fire irons lying on the table and I was about to pass them to Mickey when I realised what they were and looked at them with horror. I didn't *think* such things had been needed for Helmut but then, I reminded myself, I was under the table throughout so couldn't be sure.

With some difficulty I managed to persuade Mickey to hold the fort while I sloped off to the salon, with the irons, the weighty tome and a French-English dictionary which, by good fortune, Mickey happened to have in his pack, although he clearly had never looked at it.

First the tome: *ABRÉGÉ DE L'ART DES ACCOUCHEMENTS** it proudly proclaimed on the badly bashed cover, by someone called Madame du Coudray, published in 1759 for Christ's sake. I suspected there had been all sorts of medical advances over the years while this ancient work had been doing sterling service to the seven or so generations of Aimée's family but took heart that at least they had survived, well some of them anyway.

Further in, things didn't improve. After nearly a year of loyal service in a foreign field my everyday French wasn't at all bad but then childbirth hadn't exactly been a hot topic in the places I'd been visiting so I had to

---

* A brief treatise on childbirth.

keep resorting to Mickey's dictionary. It was heavy going. The diagrams were pretty ghastly too so all round it didn't take me long to realise that it just wasn't possible to swot up on post-renaissance naissance in the half an hour or so I had available while the subject of my ministrations was wailing in some distress in the room next door.

At that moment Mickey came charging into the room. 'Come quickly, sir. Quickly.'

'In a minute, Mickey. But first look at this...'

'No, sir. Come quickly.'

But I wasn't having it. 'No look at this, Mickey, tell me what you think. This is important,' I shouted and pointed at a diagram.

Mickey glanced at it and his cheeks reddened. 'Blimey, sir. I wouldn't know about any of this.' He scratched his cheek and frowned. 'The diesel engine. That's my cup of char. Can do a four litre Commer top-end overhaul in 90 minutes.'

Cover and title page of ***ABRÉGÉ DE L'ART DES ACCOUCHEMENTS,*** **published in 1777.**

'Well, well done Mickey. So now we'll have to have to do a bottom end under-haul won't we? See, it's all in the book,' I roared.

'Not me, sir. No way. *You* told her we were medicos, not me.'

I sighed. 'Okay, Mickey. But any idea what this is about? Come on, help me here... You're the married man. "Dilation of the cer-vix" it says. Seems to be important.'

'The what sir?'

'The cer-vix, Mickey. Cer-vix,' I shouted.

'Last time was Christmas '37. Had to leave early. My little girl was frightened of the clowns.'

'Not the bloody circus, Mickey, I said...' And at that moment there was a loud wail from next door. I slammed the book shut, threw it in the corner and we marched out the door leaving its pages wafting around the room.*

* The book's full title is: *Abrégé de l'art des accouchements, dans lequel on donne les preceptes necessaires pour le mettre heureusement en pratique, & auquel on a joint plusieurs observations intéressantes fur des cas singuliers*, by Madame le Boursier du Coudray. It can be downloaded, for free, in a variety of formats, from http://tinyurl.com/Kilroy161. See also http://tinyurl.com/Kilroy162.

I was surprised to find that Mickey had done some good deeds while I'd been doing my homework. He'd got Aimée onto the kitchen table and persuaded her to disrobe belowstairs. I'd been a bit worried about that bit. I'd never had much difficulty in that department when it came to the local women generally but, somehow, it seemed an entirely different proposition in a clinical context. 'But what about the fruit bowl?' I asked Mickey.

He spotted it and pulled it out from under her foot. And now, I thought, the decks were entirely clear for young frog's first look at the world. Aimée had stopped her shrieking by then. I don't know if she'd got used to the pain or if it just wasn't hurting as much, as the cramps seemed to be coming very regularly. She was mainly panting. Panting and straining. The sweat was pouring down her face but I suppose instinct had kicked in and she seemed to know what was needed, which was just as well, as she wasn't going to get much from Mickey and me.

As I reached down to mop her forehead her arm suddenly snaked up and grabbed me behind the neck. She was a strong lass and I couldn't get her to let go so I was held there by her, cheek to cheek, with her panting and straining all the while. Then the room resonated with a plaintive yowl. 'Ow. Owwww. Owwwwwww.'

'What is it, sir?' asked Mickey.

'Christ the little minx has bitten my bloody ear. That bloody well hurt. Owww. Owww. Owww. Bloody hell.' I was trying to rub it but couldn't get to it as she had such a tight grip around my neck.

Then the miracle happened. 'Bloody hell, Mickey. It's a joint of lamb. Oh no. Bugger me. It's a baby. Look.' And there he was, and it was a he, lying perfectly formed and peacefully between her legs on the table. I'd no idea what to do so picked him up and gave him to her. I guess Aimée must have read a little of the unlamented treatise as she carefully took him, expertly thrust her little finger into his mouth then slapped him gently on the back. There was a gentle cry and she smiled in response and slumped back down on the table.

I'll spare you the muddle over the umbilical cord but we got there in the end. Then there were more surprises for the uninitiated. 'What the effing 'ell's that, sir?' asked Mickey. 'I'm sorry. It reminds me of my mother-in-law's liver casserole. I've had enough of this.' He had his hand cupped over his mouth as he ran for the door.

I can't remember much after that. Aimée was exhausted and, although I couldn't claim to have done anything as clever as adding one small being to the human race I had been mighty busy over the previous 48 hours so was pretty well kaput too.

The next morning I was shaken awake by Aimée and handed a cup of coffee. I was still in the kitchen, having flaked out in an easy chair in the corner. Mickey was nowhere to be seen and at that moment Phillipe II was making his presence felt no more than his father, which was to say he was nowhere in evidence at all. Aimée herself was looking bright and perky, humming to herself as she fussed around, tidying things up. From what I've gathered since it had been an easy birth although it didn't seem like it to me at the time. And she was young – 16 at a guess – and the young bounce back from these things I suppose.

'The baby needs a name,' she said suddenly.

I nodded.

'What's yours?' she asked and I told her.

'No, your first name, your Christian name?'

I told her that too, rather warming to the idea of a child being named after me.

She pulled a face. 'Ach, I can't call him *that,*' she said. 'What about your friend, the one who ran away?'

'Who, Mickey?' I asked. So that's why he wasn't around, I thought. He'd absconded in the night, the sly old fox.

'Yes, Mick-ee I like. Runaway Mick-ee, yes.'

I suggested Phillipe. 'Him?' was all she said and pulled an even worse face than she had for my name. '*Him!?*'

Eventually she settled on Michel, which is of course both an English and French name. I've occasionally wondered if Mickey ever found out about his Godchild. I never saw him again to tell him.

'Are you really a doctor?' Aimée asked abruptly.

I coughed and spluttered, 'Well not exactly. More a sort of...'

'I knew it,' she said triumphantly and pointed at my battledress. 'R.A.F. Those are R.A.F. wings aren't they?'

I nodded.

'Good. I can get you home.'

A quarter of an hour later we were standing in the barn. Michel had joined us, tightly swaddled, at peace with the world and confidently clasped by his mother, looking like a woman of many years of matronly practice.

The light was dim and I couldn't really see anything much. 'But what is it?' I asked.

'You'll see,' she said, reaching up with her free hand to rattle something up and down.

This raised a cloud of dust which started me in a coughing fit.

'Come on,' she said, 'help me wheel it out.'

A few minutes later, it was parked on the grass outside. I walked around it, poking bits and pieces and feeling generally doubtful. 'Are you *sure* it can fly?' I asked.

'Of course, Papa, he...'

'But it's more like a kite. And held together with chewing gum and string I shouldn't wonder.' I dislodged a resinous lump that did indeed look like chewing gum.

'Stop that,' she said. 'Papa, he made this in his workshop and, before the war, flew it every weekend. Poor Papa,' she sighed and glanced back towards the house. 'But now you must use it to get home and fight the *boche*.'

Her bright eyes stared up at me and I found myself thinking what a fool Phillipe had been to flee the nest when he had this lively young spark waiting at home for him. And she was right too. I hadn't exactly made any headway with my own countrymen at the harbourside and on the beach and we neither of us were to know then that before the week was out about a third of a million of us would indeed be rescued. On the other hand this contraption, I thought, *if it flew at all,* would see me home and supping a mild and bitter within the hour.

It had rather passed me by but there had been a craze in France in the thirties for home-built aeroplanes. If you could put in the hours and had plenty of wood and canvas to hand you could take to the skies for the cost of a beaten-up Renault. This particular model, Aimée told me, was built to a plan by a Monsieur Mignet. I'd not heard of him then but he is still celebrated in aviation circles and indeed some of his wretched contraptions survive to the present day, God help anyone who flies in them.

The plane was really tiny and would fit in a moderate sized drawing room. It had two pairs of wings, arranged like a moth, and a large rudder behind. There was only room for one aboard of course and the engine, which I thought had come from a lawn mower but Aimée assured me was a motorcycle, was stuck right in front of the pilot's nose.

Aimée had regularly helped Papa with his flight preparations so knew all about the fuel cocks and so on and could even tell me about the unusual way the flight controls worked – not like a Hurricane, in short. There was no question of her coming as there was no room but even if we'd had a Dragon Rapide at our disposal I think she would have stayed behind. 'This is our home,' she said, glancing down at young Michel, 'and here we stay.'

There was no wind, which was good, and low cloud which, for something like this little operation, was also good, because I wasn't planning to go any higher than Beachy Head and I'd be well hidden under all the clag from the dastardly Luftwaffe up above.

Aimée gently laid young Michel down in the grass and prepared to swing the prop. I was sitting strapped in the seat, feeling a mite apprehensive, with one hand on the joystick and the other on the throttle.

'Ach,' she said after several failed attempts, 'Papa always said to check the spark plugs. They oil up quickly with a two stroke engine.' She marched into the barn and came back a few seconds later wielding a spanner.

Two of the plugs came out easily enough but, after several months sitting idle, the third seemed welded into place. Eventually we managed it between us. My knowledge of engine maintenance was limited but Aimée knew what was needed. She found some emery paper back in the barn, which we used to clean off all the gunk, then she checked each plug for the right gap (0.6 mm she informed me). I noticed the sky was darkening above and so was anxious to get going but she admonished me that it was essential to wipe off the last traces of residue before bolting the plugs back in the engine, otherwise we'd have to go through the whole exercise again. She was going to use her headscarf for this but I chivalrously provided my handkerchief (clean obviously, as per Helga's injunctions) and only a couple of minutes later the engine was roaring with me sitting precariously behind it, trying to get a feel for things as the plane bumped and trundled over the grass. There were no brakes and no real opportunity to bid farewell so I just did a couple of circles, waved cheerily at Aimée, pointed the plane at the far end of the field and fully opened the throttle.

British Prisoners of War captured at Dunkirk.

The plane was surprisingly responsive. And noisy too, with an antiquated *Aubier et Dunne* only inches from my nose and screeching like it was about to expel its innards out the exhaust. I'd no idea at what point I should ideally depart terra firma but just let the speed build up until I could stand the bouncing around no longer then pulled back gently on the stick. The bumps stopped immediately and, to my amazement, I found I was flying. I let the plane gently climb and levelled off just below the cloud base, which with no altimeter, I guessed must be at about 500 feet.

Thus far it had all been rather easy. Instrumentation was virtually non-existent but fortunately there was a compass, so I gently turned to head north. The plan was to get out to sea ASAP, away from all that weaponry below. After only a minute or so I was over the coastline, with the town on my right, still smoking ominously, the German army on my left and the French below. One of them took a potshot at me but must have failed to hit anything important as the plane just continued on its way without a twitch or murmur. Without instrumentation I realised I would just have to guess at the passage of 15 minutes before turning west.*

Rain began to fall, which was pretty unpleasant in the open cockpit with my head stuck out in the slipstream. I also had to drop down to a couple of hundred feet as the cloud base lowered. VFR it's called – visual flight rules – which boils down to this: without instruments or visible reference to the ground, it takes only about ten seconds before you're a goner.

Looking back now I can say this flight was one of the most frightening of my life and that's in a lifetime where I have had my fair share of terrifying experiences. To add to my woes I'd started out with the fuel tank only half full and that meant there would be only just enough petrol to see me home. With no margin for error accurate navigation was the key. On a fine day you can see right across the Channel – find the white cliffs and off you go – but at 200 feet and bouncing around in driving rain it's another story. If you look at a map, which by the way I didn't have that day, you will see that, heading due west from some point north of Dunkirk, it's only too easy to wander slightly south and it's next stop Philadelphia or slightly north to join Amy Johnson in the Thames estuary.†

A song in tribute to Amy Johnson from 1930.

Well, it didn't happen. The low point, in both senses of the word, was when I nearly collided with the mast of a trawler – a trawler crammed with British soldiers I noted. But then the weather brightened suddenly and I was able to gain some altitude and, after what seemed like five years sitting in

---

* Much has been written of the Dunkirk evacuation and Kilroy's account, although sketchy in places, is well in accord with the known history. The evacuation took place from 27th May to 4th June 1940, at the mid-point of the disastrous Battle of France, which ended with the French capitulation, hard on the heels of the Dutch and Belgian surrender, and just six and a half weeks after the initial German advance. See *End Note (12).*

† Amy Johnson, the famous aviatrix, died on 5th January 1941, which was some months after Kilroy's flight from Dunkirk. She was serving in the Air Transport Auxiliary, delivering an Airspeed Oxford, and crashed into the Thames estuary in very similar conditions to those described by Kilroy here. Her body was never recovered. http://tinyurl.com/Kilroy163.

that wretched machine, I caught sight of the famous white cliffs exactly where they should be, straight ahead of me. I'd just switched to the reserve tank so knew then there was enough to see me home. The sun chose that moment to come out too and I literally whooped for joy as I opened the throttle to gain height and admire the view.

The plane was heading towards the great port of Dover, more or less in the middle of the line of cliffs, but a landfall there didn't seem a great idea, with its fearsome defences, so I turned slightly to the right where I could make out the coastal town of Deal. I reflected that I hadn't had a good warm foaming pint of English beer in quite a while and Deal was home to a pub called the Admiral Penn, scene of many an illicit outing from my late and unlamented alma mater.* I was worried about my lack of funds, not knowing that at that moment, back home, any Dunkirk refugee could wander into any bar in the land and drink all night for nothing. Then I remembered the diamonds. I confess that by then I'd rather made up my mind not to hand them over to the authorities but instead was thinking along the lines of "spoils of war" which I might put to, ahem, better use elsewhere. I reckoned the Penn landlord would still remember me and most probably could be persuaded to take one of the rocks as security on a loan. He bloody well should too, I thought – a couple of them would be enough to buy his pub. I patted my pocket to reassure me I still had them. I felt nothing. That's odd I thought, as I switched hands on the joystick and patted the other pocket. Christ, there was nothing there either. I might easily have crashed into the sea in the next 20 seconds, what with the stick being held wedged between my knees as, with both hands, I frantically searched every nook and cranny of my trousers and battledress, turning pockets inside out and even rummaging around on the cockpit floor. Then it came to me. When I'd given my handkerchief to Aimée to wipe the spark plugs I'd first placed the bag of diamonds on the workbench alongside us and, well... you can guess the rest.

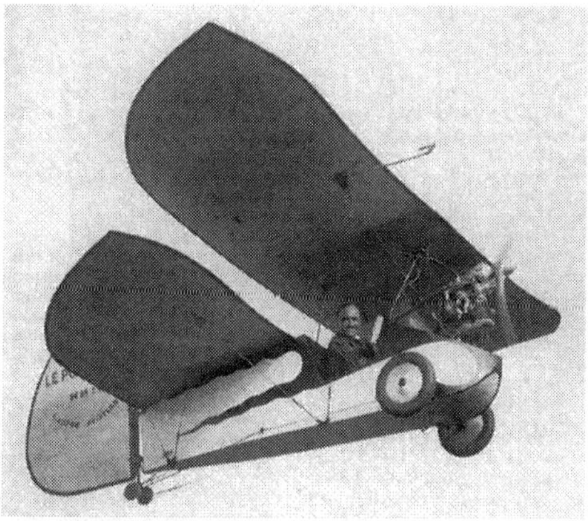

The HM-14 Pou-du-Ciel (Flying Flea) flown by its designer, Henri Mignet.

* The Admiral Penn was at 79 Beach Street in Deal. The building survives but the business has closed.

Human nature can be strange. Minutes before I was just glad to be alive but now I was grimly mourning my loss. Looking back, I can't believe I did this, but I really did turn the plane around and start heading back to Dunkirk. It was only the sight of those storm clouds mid-Channel that made me think again. It was just as well I did too, as I had only about ten minutes of petrol left anyway.

After that, my arrival in Deal was uneventful. I must have looked such an odd sight that the coastal defences held their fire and I landed without mishap on the beach. I didn't know it then but this was the most dangerous plane I ever flew, with the unfortunate idiosyncracy of going into an unrecoverable dive if slightly mishandled. The Pou du Ciel, it was nicknamed, or Flying Flea. Anyway it made for a memorable entry in my log book – the only aeroplane type I flew but never crashed. For all I know it's still there on Deal beach. If you find it you can keep it.*

* It's surprising that Kilroy had not heard of the Flying Flea as it was a noted plane in the '30s. It was one of a series of designs by Henri Mignet, the HM-14, that could be built in an ordinary home workshop for around £70 and was intended to be safe and easy to fly. It had a passable performance – a cruise speed of 65 mph and a range of 150 miles, with modest fuel consumption. Unfortunately it had a design defect that meant that, under certain conditions, it would go into an unrecoverable dive. After several fatalities the type was grounded by most aviation authorities. Eventually it was found that the defect could be remedied easily but by then Mignet's reputation was besmirched and, not surprisingly, enthusiasm for his designs had waned. After the war interest revived and, to this day, his planes are still flying and being built. http://tinyurl.com/Kilroy164.

Anyone wondering about the intricacies of building an HM-14 should follow the link to the rather charming English language reprint of Mignet's book at http://tinyurl.com/Kilroy165. There is a lot more material on Flying Fleas online but in particular there is some historic newsreel footage (courtesy of Movietone) at: http://tinyurl.com/Kilroy166 (Henri Mignet demonstrating his plane), http://tinyurl.com/Kilroy167 (a non-fatal crash, at Heston aerodrome, of a British build) http://tinyurl.com/Kilroy168 (an early cross-Channel flight).

PART FOUR: LONDON

1940

That certain night
The night we met
There was magic abroad in the air
There were angels dining at the Ritz
And a nightingale sang in Berkeley Square

First performed by Judy Campbell in *New Faces* (1940)
Words and music by Eric Maschwitz and Manning Sherwin
Recording by Anne Shelton with Ambrose and his orchestra (1940)
http://tinyurl.com/Kilroy004

CHAPTER 1

It was afternoon tea time at the Ritz and von Rundstedt, Leclabart, the dreadful Knöchlein and all the rest of them were safely on the other side of the Channel. My old family home was still out of bounds so Helga and I were meeting on neutral ground.

I'd barely been back a day but had had time to get smartened up, courtesy of a spare uniform, retrieved from Mac's place at Claremont. There had been no need to add to the single thin pilot officer rings on my sleeves, sewn on nearly a year before, but at least I *could* fix an improvised red and green barred ribbon of the Croix de Guerre just above my breast pocket.

I was surprised to see that Helga looked a tad dewy eyed when we met. 'You've grown, I think,' she said with a sniff, as she gave me a peck on the cheek and wiped some fluff from my shoulder, 'and looking quite handsome in your uniform. Quite the young gentleman.'

She stood back and her eyes alighted on my medal ribbon. 'What's that?' she asked with a frown. 'Is that a medal?'

'Well...' I hesitated. I was beginning to wish I hadn't worn it.

Tables set for afternoon tea at the Ritz.

'Well what?' she said, her face darkening some more. 'I hope you've not been doing anything stupid?'

I gulped, recalling how I had earned it and was wondering what to make up. 'Well, it's a long story...' I began but then stopped because I could see she wasn't paying attention. She was staring past me, with pursed lips.

I caught a waft of perfume and turned to see Candice, looking cooly elegant in a light pale blue summer frock, tottering on heels with peep toes and bare legs. 'Darling, how lovely to see you,' she said, presenting her cheek for me to kiss. I hesitated before delivering a peck. I hadn't seen her since the night of her supposed violation and my subsequent expulsion. I can't say I was any more pleased to see her than Helga was but wasn't sure what to do.

Candice was all innocence, behaving as if the horrible family drama had never happened. She pulled up a chair, sat down, grabbed a plate and helped herself to a scone, ladling on the cream and jam, while firing off questions to me about the war.

I answered noncommittally. Dunkirk was the word on everybody's lips right then so any information from the frontline was much sought after. In answer to further questions, I told her what I knew while Helga sat sipping her tea in silence.

Then Candice got up to go. 'Oh I nearly forgot,' she said. 'I'm going to the opera tonight. With some friends. There's a spare ticket. Would you like to come?'

Helga started a coughing fit and some tea spluttered into her saucer. I gently patted her on the back, handed her my serviette and while she carefully wiped herself I nodded to Candice.

'Good, it'll be fun, darling. Mo-zart I think it is. Or whatever his name is? Yes, Mo-zart. Sadler's Wells, in the foyer at eight.' And with that she breezed off.

We sat in silence as she swept out of the room. Helga turned to me, opened her mouth to say something, thought better of it, then sighed and picked up the teapot to pour herself a cup. 'I haven't told you about your mother,' she said. 'I think you should visit her. You'll just make it if you go now.' She looked at her watch. 'And, don't worry. You'll still have plenty of time for the opera.' This last remark was delivered with a frown.

Half an hour later I was wandering along the Camden Road clutching the piece of paper Helga had given me. 'A couple of stops on the tube and a short walk,' she'd assured me. 'You can't miss it.'

And there it was. I hesitantly walked up the forecourt and pressed the buzzer.

Ten minutes later we were sitting opposite each other, a table between us. I hadn't seen my mother for quite a while and now we were together I felt awkward and wasn't sure what to say. We eyed each other in silence. I thought she had aged. I couldn't imagine what she was thinking about me. 'Thanks for the sock, Mutti,' I think was my opening gambit. It wasn't a great line, I know, but that had been our last contact, when she'd knitted me the elephantine hosiery, just after I'd arrived in France.

She didn't answer but just looked back at me, downcast.

'Look, mother, how the hell did you end up here?' I gestured around at the stark bare walls and barred windows on high, heavy with grime.

'Ich hätte nach Deutschland gegangen,' she said, close to tears.

'English. Speak English,' boomed a voice behind me and we both started.

'Yes, Mutti,' I answered, 'perhaps you should have gone to Germany. You could have told me which city you were going to and then I could make sure I don't go and bomb it..'

'But it's not fair. I shouldn't be in here in the first place. I see you're doing alright. You're not locked up are you?'

I sighed. 'Well, Mutti, I'm *English*. I was *born* here, remember? And educated here *and* I joined up *plus* I'm not a bloody...' I realized just in time I was heading for dangerous ground. 'Look, Mutti, why can't you just try being a little more discreet?'

She nodded.

'Look at Helga,' I went on, 'she's still out and about, isn't she?'

I could see by my mother's look I'd said the wrong thing. 'That woman,' she said in measured tones, 'that woman has no loyalty.' She waved her finger at me. 'Not a gram of loyalty in her entire body.'

Lady Diana and Sir Oswald Mosely under house arrest in an Oxford hotel after their release from Holloway in 1943.

'Er, well then, not Helga but, er, what about your friends the Mosleys?' I went on, hoping for safer ground. 'They are still out and about, aren't they?'

'But that's just it. Diana's here! And Fay and Norah too.* It's been terrible. I think they've taken everyone. And Diana's frantic about Oswald. She doesn't know where he is, although we think the men have all been put in Wandsworth.' She sighed.

It was called Section 18B. With Britain on its knees the government wasn't taking any chances with enemy aliens or fascists rolling around the countryside like loose Panzers – especially with enemy aliens who were also fascists, like Mutti.†

'You remember Uncle William?' Mutti asked suddenly.

I nodded. I couldn't recall much about him but he'd visited us from

* Presumably racing driver Fay Taylour and former suffragette Norah Elam who were both interned at that time.

† Defence Regulation 18B allowed for the internment without trial of anyone suspected of being a Nazi sympathiser, in effect suspending the principle of *habeas corpus*. It was brought in at the beginning of the war but barely used until the worsening situation, in May 1940, made the government nervous of a right wing coup (as happened in Norway, where Vidkun Quisling deposed the legal government). By the end of 1940, around 1,000 arrests had been made, with Diana and Sir Oswald Mosley the best known of them. Initially apart, the Mosleys were held together thereafter, in a house in the grounds of Holloway. The detainees were gradually released as the war situation improved and by the end of the war there were just 11 people still held. See http://tinyurl.com/Kilroy169. A list of the detainees (with photos) can be found at Oswald Mosley website: http://tinyurl.com/Kilroy170.

time to time in my early childhood, when we were in London.

'He had the sense to get out. He went to Germany six months ago and he's on the radio now.'

'What?'

'Yes, on that station Reichssender Hamburg. You can get it here.'

'No?!'

'Yes, you can.'

'No, I mean, no way, I know you can get it. I've heard him. We all have. I thought I recognised that whiny voice – "Jairmany calling, Jairmany calling." Lord Haw Haw. That's him isn't it?'

William Joyce, Lord Haw Haw, after his arrest in Germany in 1945. He was shot in the buttocks while being taken.

'It's not a whiny voice,' she said tartly. 'Don't be so rude. I should think he's doing very well for himself – he's a close friend of Goebbels now so I hear.'

I was tempted to tell her that I'd only recently been hob-nobbing with Hitler himself but thought I'd better keep quiet or I'd have an 18B slapped on me. 'Well, he won't be doing so well after we win the war,' was all I could come up with.

And he didn't. He was hanged for treason, at Wandworth Prison after the war, on a legal technicality. I can't say I was overly sorry but he was pretty unlucky. He could hardly be said to have betrayed his own country as he wasn't even British – an Irish American who'd taken German citizenship. But then that's lawyers for you, and I've never trusted them.*

* William Joyce was born in New York and raised in Ireland. Unusually for a Catholic he was strongly Unionist. He moved to England in the 1920s, joining Sir Oswald Mosley's British Union of Fascists in 1932 and was heavily involved with right-wing politics throughout the thirties. He fled to Germany just before the outbreak of war and was soon recruited, with his signature "Jairmany calling" voice, for propaganda broadcasts, which he continued to make throughout the war. He was nicknamed "Lord Haw Haw". Listening to his broadcast was discouraged (but not illegal) and at the height of his influence he had an estimated six million regular listeners and 18 million occasional. He was captured by the British at the end of the war, put on trial for treason, convicted and hanged. His defence that he wasn't a British citizen was overturned on a technicality. http://tinyurl.com/Kilroy171.

And that was visiting time over. I realised that at least I would know where Mutti was while she was in Holloway. I promised her that, on my next leave, I'd bring a cake, with a file in it too, I joked, although even that failed to raise a smile.

Mac had an account at the famous Grosvenor House Hotel and had generously told me I could make use of it so I checked into one of their new-fangled rooms with an integral bathroom. I knew the Grosvenor well, from the outside at least, as it was on Park Lane, just around the corner from my old family home. Along with every other building in London, the war had changed it. There were over 10,000 sandbags piled up all around the outside, the porter proudly told me. There was also, he said, nearly five miles of blackout material, which had been stuck across every single window, rather spoiling the view out onto Hyde Park.

I only needed half an hour to get spruced up. The Sadlers Wells Theatre is fair a way outside London's West End, in Islington, but it was a fine evening and I had plenty of time to stroll there, arriving just as a taxi pulled up, spilling Candice and her chums out onto the pavement.

Candice did the introductions. There were two specimens of strapping American manhood, Sweeney and Todd, and her two ample and fruity girl-chums Babe and Ruth. You've probably guessed I've made that up. Well, you'd only be half right. The menfolk really were Todd and Sweeney, twins, but not identical fortunately and, I gathered, named in complete innocence by their New England parents. But, yes, as for Babe and Ruth – who knows? – I really can't remember now so their real names are lost to history I'm afraid.

That evening, the Yankee Dollar was much in evidence, something that has always endeared me to our American cousins. Todd and Sweeney just wouldn't hear of a war hero standing his round and, with my back-pay overdue, I didn't put up much of a fight. I think we'd managed three bottles of Dom Pérignon before the performance started.

We had a box, with just enough room for the six of us and two bottles, smuggled in. It soon became apparent that none of us knew a great deal about opera and especially about this one. It was called *l'Oca del Cairo* which means the Goose of Cairo and I can't say it made much sense to me at all. The best bit is about an hour into it, when the hero is propelled onto the stage, secreted inside a large mechanical goose. No, I'm not making this up, but you'll no doubt be drawing your own conclusions as to why the opera is seldom performed. Todd nudged me at this point and whispered, 'Goose? Call that a goose? I'll show you a goose,' reaching forward to Ruth, seated in front of him and delivering a sizable nip to her curvy bottom.

Mozart never finished *l'Oca del Cairo*, which is probably just as well as we'd most likely have been thrown out had it gone on much longer.* A quarter of an hour later we were out on the street. Todd hailed a taxi and we moved on to the Café de Paris. I'd not been there before but knew of it as the place where the Charleston craze had started in Britain. Fifteen years later it had become home to "swing" music, another American import. Candice started to explain it to me, but I silenced her. 'Want to dance?' I asked. 'Lindy hop, Jitterbug or Balboa? You name it...'

As I led her onto the dance floor, I thought she was looking mildly impressed at my knowledge of American culture. The truth was that Mimi, one of the girls at an establishment in Chalons called *la Boite à Bonbons*,† had a collection of swing records and always liked to precede the carnal act with an abbreviated dancing workshop. I'd learned that you got much better service after if you humoured her before so had picked up a few of the steps in passing. My personal favourite was a dance called the "Shag". Speaking only French, she'd no idea why it amused me so.

Ken "Snakehips" Johnson.

The resident band was fronted by someone called Ken "Snakehips" Johnson and, to Candice's surprise, I'd heard of him. This was also courtesy of Mimi's record collection of course but, unfortunately, Mimi had failed to impart on me any ability on the dance floor. Sticky Stevens had once told me that my enthusiasm and uninhibited energy made up for my obvious lack of technique or rhythm but I'm not sure Candice would agree. 'Can we sit this one out?' was all she could offer as we limped back to our seats after an embarrassing failure with my improvised aerial triple step.‡

* There is only enough material in *l'Oca del Cairo* for about a 45 minute performance – http://tinyurl.com/Kilroy172. Sadler's Wells Theatre staged it at the end of May 1940, with the last performance on 1st June.

† Box of Sweets.

‡ Ken "Snakehips" Johnson and his West Indian Orchestra had a residency at the Café de Paris in Coventry Street in London at this time. He had studied medicine at Edinburgh University but then turned to "swing" music – arguably the forerunner of "pop". He enjoyed some considerable celebrity until the Café de Paris was struck by a bomb during the Blitz, in March 1941, and he was killed along with over 30 others. The venue was

Some time later, and I can't recall now how it came about, we were back in Todd and Sweeney's flat. The brothers were working at the US Embassy and had their own apartment there – a baseball's throw from my hotel in fact. This was when the US Ambassador in London was Joseph Kennedy – a man whose pacifism (to put it politely) was not popular with the British. It was thanks to him I was there at all that evening. On the outbreak of war he had immediately despatched his children back to the US, that is all bar one, Rosemary, who had stayed on but had at last been sent home only a couple of days earlier. It was her ticket I'd been given for the opera.*

While Todd played some records on the gramophone, more swing, Sweeney poured the drinks. He also produced a long and misshapen cigarette – called a "reefer" he said. We all had a puff at it. I wasn't sure what the point of it was and at the time I didn't think it had any effect on me but now, I'm not so sure. Todd kept the music going while the others were talking about some baseball match. The discussion seemed to go on for hours. I suddenly realised I'd been spending a little long studying the pattern on the carpet and was thinking I should leave when Candice rose and came dancing and wiggling up to me. She had a champagne glass in one hand and pulled me to my feet with the other. For one horrible moment I thought I was going to have to dance again, but no, she just wiggled and skipped, tugging me along behind her, through a doorway, down the hallway, through another doorway, kicking the door shut behind us. It was a games room, with a small snooker table in the middle or a "pool" table as I subsequently found it was called. She turned to face me, leaning back on it, plonking her glass down on the side. Her free hand snaked around my neck and pulled me towards her.

Pool's a much better game than snooker. I've played it a lot over the years and found that, with a smaller table, it's much easier to pot the balls, although it takes considerable skill to play well. The rules are simpler too –

---

closed following the bomb but reopened after the war and is still in operation today. See http://tinyurl.com/Kilroy173 and http://tinyurl.com/Kilroy174 (video memorial to the bombing).

* Joseph Kennedy Sr, the US Ambassador in London from January 17th 1938 to October 22nd 1940, was the father of the famous Kennedy family – with his son, Jack, becoming US President in 1960. All his children departed the capital shortly after the outbreak of war except his daughter, Rose Marie, who remained until 30th May 1940 when she was sent home. She had probably been mentally incapacitated at birth, although she was fit enough to mix normally in London society whilst in the UK. A few years after she returned to the US she was subjected to a lobotomy, which left her needing institutional care for the rest of her life. http://tinyurl.com/Kilroy175 (Joseph) and http://tinyurl.com/Kilroy176 (Rosemary).

no complexities with colours, just spotted and striped balls and, of course, you can accommodate a full size pool table where you'd have to go down to quarter size for snooker. As I said, all round it's a much better game. And, like snooker, pool offers a convenient horizontal surface for other games although, with all that solid slate immediately under the baize, it isn't exactly built for comfort. You might recall my account of my previous and disastrous encounter with Candice, over a game of Monopoly, and are no doubt bracing yourself for 'two extra balls on the table', 'going in off the red' and so on, but I'll spare you that. Let's just say my elbows felt a little raw for a couple of weeks after, although I did find, that night, that US womanhood is made of stern stuff as Candice certainly didn't complain throughout – at least I think the yowls and whoops she made were of approval.

I've since wondered why I went anywhere near Candice again and I really don't know why, but I must say that, after our pool table encounter, I was feeling mightily well disposed towards her – she might have landed me in it on our previous triste but she certainly made up for it second time around.

A few minutes later, our dress adjusted and hair combed back in place, we were out in the street together, as I walked her home. It was only a short stroll away. We stood on the doorstep and I was about to deliver a farewell peck on the cheek when her hand sprung up and grabbed me behind the neck, in a repeat of her manoeuvre earlier in the games room. A few seconds before I'd been thinking of a brisk walk back to my hotel, but the silky smooth feel of her dress put that on hold, especially when I realised she wasn't wearing anything beneath it. 'Come inside,' she whispered as she thrust her tongue into my ear.

CHAPTER 2

I was on my way out, having just handed over my key at the Grosvenor's front desk, when I was hit by a whirlwind.

'Hey sweetie, darling, where've you been hiding?' said a familiar woman's voice from behind as a pair of arms wound around my neck.

I tried to turn to face her but this didn't work as she was off her feet and hanging onto me, piggy-back fashion. 'Hayley!' I exclaimed as I unwound her tight grip. 'How lovely to...'

'You're safe, thank God,' she said breathlessly. 'Safely back in London. But why didn't you phone me?'

We were facing each other at last and she was as desirable as ever, all the more so with her chest heaving as she looked accusingly at me. 'But I did phone you, at your, er, work and they always told me you were, er, busy.' This was true. I had tried to get hold of her several times.

'You could have made an appointment?' she asked.

'Well, I er..'

'Oh, I know,' she said, 'of course. No money! Oh you poor thing,' she pouted. 'There you've been, being a brave soldier,' she glanced at my medal ribbon, 'and the hero returns and they haven't paid him, eh?'

Grenadier Guards constructing defences around government buildings in London.

I nodded. I'd returned without a penny to my name. The R.A.F. pay clerks would no doubt catch up eventually but in the meantime all I had to hand was some cash from Mac and Helga, which was plenty for ordinary soldierly needs but not quite enough for Hayley's professional fees.

'But you've been wounded?' she said, frowning.

'Oh, it's nothing,' I replied with a nonchalant wave.

'But your leg. I can see. You're limping?'

I winced a little as I shifted my weight onto my other leg. 'Just a flesh wound, you know? Nothing to worry about.' In truth I'd sprained my ankle the previous night exiting via the drawing room window when Pater awoke and came crashing downstairs to see what his precious Candice was up to.

'Listen, darling, I'm busy right now, but I can see you later. Kensington Gardens. At the Peter Pan statue?' She looked at her watch. 'At four o' clock?'

I nodded.

'Good. See you then. Must dash.' She walked away, towards the far end of reception where there was a squadron leader sitting alone on a settee. He rose and they exchanged a few words before walking towards the lift. As the lift doors closed on them I caught him staring at me. There was something familiar about his look but I couldn't place it.

When I'd returned from my adventures with Candice the previous night I found that Mac had left a message for me. McNulty, AKA Jock McKnow-all, wanted to see me ASAP. You may recall he was, ahem, something in "security" on the Chamberlain mission to Munich and had been instrumental in restarting my career with the R.A.F. I really didn't know what he was about at the time but he seemed to think of me as some sort of long-term investment in his intelligence shenanigans. I certainly hadn't given him much thought since Munich and was wondering how he knew I was back – the best guess was that word had reached him after I visited Mutti. I thought it would be wise to humour him.

McNulty's office was only a short walk away but my ankle was feeling pretty sore. I stepped towards the main door and winced as it bore my weight. I realised I wasn't going to get very far at all without a walking stick, an item that doesn't figure often on my shopping list. I couldn't for the life of me think where I might buy one but, as I was heading towards the concierge to ask, I spotted a rather elegant darkwood crook with natty brass bands, propped up in the fireplace and without an owner to hand. I shuffled over, took a quick look around and discreetly liberated it.

It was a Sunday but with a war on, most of Whitehall was on a seven day week, so just half an hour later I limped into McNulty's office and, at his invitation, sat down before his desk. It was laden with files, and I could only just see his flushed face over the top. 'Where the devil have you been?' was his opening gambit. 'You should have reported to your squadron at once. You know that, laddie, don't you?' He wagged his finger at me. 'Another 24 hours and we'd have had a warrant out on you.'

I muttered some feeble excuse about my leg injury.

'Your leg, you say? Really?' He raised his eyebrows and puckered his lips. 'Well, no matter,' he went on with a sigh. 'I've no time for that now. More importantly what's all this bloody nonsense about some nutcase turning up at von Rundstedt's HQ?'

You've already heard my tale, so I won't repeat it here. I told him the whole caboodle, from the horrific mission in the Fairey Battle right through to my landing on Deal Beach, only skipping my botched attempt to purloin the diamonds, an episode which seemed so embarrassingly stupid on my part I thought it best forgotten. He didn't seem terribly interested in much of what I had to say but took copious notes on my encounter with Hitler and his High Command and also the massacre at le Paradis. 'The bastards,' was all he said as he wrote it down. 'The bloody bastards.'

When I had finished, he put down his notepad, stood up and strolled up and down in front of me, deep in thought. I said nothing, waiting for him to break the silence. 'You know what?' he said eventually, 'you remind me of myself when I was your age – a reckless idiot mostly and undisciplined too but, by Jove, when the chips are down, you get results, eh?'

I decided to take this as a compliment and nodded.

'Well, we can't have you tooling around any more in those Fairey Battle death-traps, that's for sure. Don't want to lose you in one of them, do we?' He walked up to his office door, opened it and looked up and down the corridor outside, before pushing it firmly shut. 'How about something rather different?' he asked in a low voice. 'It's very new and very hush-hush. You'll still be flying, mind, and it'll be dangerous too, but I think we'll make better use of your talents there and I think you'll find it more to your taste. What do you say?'

Well, I thought, anything that got me away from the Fairey Battle could only be a good thing. I nodded.

He picked up his notepad and wrote down a name and address. 'Your new CO,' he said, 'Go straight there now and report to him. By the time you arrive he'll know to expect you.'

I rose to leave.

'One final thing,' he said. 'What you've just told me, in this office, not a word to anyone, eh?' He tapped his nose.

***

Most summers in pre-war years I'd managed at least one outing to Lords cricket ground, but that June day in 1940 it was rather different. The sun was shining (for once) but cricket was suspended for the duration as the R.A.F. had taken it over as a recruitment centre. The fine old ground was looking pretty badly mauled. The pitch had been dug up in several places and there were tents all over the place, some issuing kit, others serving food. On the sidelines, new recruits were marching up and down while lorries laden with men and supplies trundled around the outfield.

My new CO, Squadron Leader Clarke, had an office tucked away in the member's pavilion. Eventually I located it, rapped smartly on the door and went in. Normal service protocol is to salute smartly on arrival but I think I was so surprised by what I saw that I just stopped, stood and gaped. 'You?' I said.

He was the man I'd seen with Hayley that morning.

Strangely he wasn't put out by seeing me at all. 'Ah, Pilot Officer Kilroy,' he said. 'I rather hoped we were getting *you* specifically and not just any old Kilroy.'

I didn't know what he was talking about. He gestured to me to sit down, leaning back in his chair and smiling as he studied me. 'But you don't recognise me do you?' he asked.

First day in the R.A.F. for these recruits, at Lords cricket ground.

'Well, of course I do sir. I saw you with the..., er, I mean at the hotel this morning, sir,' I replied.

'No, before then. Where have you seen me before, eh?'

I stared straight at him and studied him closely. Then it came to me. Nearly two years had gone by and a lot had happened since but it suddenly came to me that he was Mad Mungo – my old Geography teacher at Herne Bay and one-time collaborator in the betting scheme. 'Mr Clarke!' I exclaimed. 'Herne Bay, ha ha! I didn't recognise you without the beard. I must say, it suits you sir. Makes you look much younger. But I didn't know you were R.A.F., sir?'

He frowned at this. 'Well, I did my bit in the last show. R.F.C.* in 1914 right though to the R.A.F. at the end actually. And, now they've brought me back for this. I expect you want me to tell you about it?'

I nodded. I was thinking how hopeless he'd been at Geography, specifically with the map reading skills of a myopic lunatic and wondered how he squared that with distinguished service in aviation. But then I'd known trainees who could effortlessly plot a perfect course on the ground and then get lost while still within sight of the airfield so guessed it might also work the other way around.

Some boxes were stacked along one wall, each neatly punctured with air holes and he carefully reached for one and placed it on his desk. He opened one of his desk drawers and pulled out a pair of scissors and a sock. At that moment I was half expecting to be assigned another knitting detail but, no, he grabbed a portion of the sock toe between thumb and finger and carefully snipped it off. Then he opened the box, reached in and gently removed its occupant. Thirty seconds later it lay before us on the desk, bound up in the sock, staring me sullenly in the face with its head poking

* Royal Flying Corps, which merged with the Royal Naval Air Service (R.N.A.S.) in 1918 to form the Royal Air Force.

through the toe hole – a pigeon. 'What do you make of that?' he asked with, I thought, some measure of pride in his voice.

'Well sir,' I lied, 'it certainly seems impressive.'

'You're right there young man, bang on,' he cried, thumping his fist down on the desk and startling the pigeon, which blinked several times and started floundering around in a bid to escape. 'And, this has come right from the top,' he said, lowering his voice, as he shoved the pigeon back into the middle of the desk, 'from "Big C" himself.'

At first I didn't know who he meant. 'Churchill? The prime minister?' I whispered, wonderingly. He'd only become PM a couple of weeks earlier and, I thought, he would surely have more important matters to worry over.

Mad Mungo nodded and then he explained. The whole thing wasn't as idiotic as I first thought. The Battle of France was ongoing but with defeat seeming more and more likely by the day, Churchill was looking to a future covert campaign, one where agents would be dropped into occupied Europe, create havoc behind enemy lines and communicate back with radio and, yes, even homing pigeons if necessary. It would be the job of Mungo's squadron to provide transport for them and, as McNulty had intimated, this would be a line of work more suited to my taste than being blown to kingdom come in a Fairey Battle. I'd need conversion training first though, to fly at night and in the Lysander, an aeroplane which was ideal for discreetly hopping across the Channel. Mungo agreed to a week's leave first.*

A pigeon prepares to "set Europe ablaze."

That completed our official business but there were not a few questions hanging in the air. Mungo pulled out a cigarette case, took out a cigarette, offered me one, and we lit up. He leaned back in his chair, inhaling deeply.

'An unusual family you have, Kilroy?' he asked.

'Sir?'

'Your cousin, of course. Strange for her to be involved in... well, it's not my business I suppose.'

* Churchill ordered the formation of the famous Special Operations Executive (SOE) on 22nd July 1940, which was shortly after the French capitulation. His order, much quoted, was that they were to "set Europe ablaze". The SOE mission was to conduct espionage, sabotage and reconaissance in occupied Europe.

I didn't know what he was on about to begin with, then I twigged that Hayley must have told him I was a relative. 'Oh, I see, sir. Well, it's a long story. Our folks are a pretty liberal lot though – just live and let live I guess...' I shrugged and exhaled a puff of smoke, hoping he'd drop the subject.

'Yes, yes, of course,' he replied. Then he sat forward and fixed me with a penetrating stare. 'But let me be clear on this, young man – what happened in the Grosvenor, *stays* in the Grosvenor, yes? Do I make myself clear? Why Mrs Clark...'

'Of course, sir, and how is your charming wife?' I asked. I'd often wondered what had become of my comely matron after we'd all been expelled by the dastardly Blenkinsop.

'Not so good I'm afraid, after the arrival of the little one...'

'She's had a baby, sir?'

'Why, yes, the little blighter's 15 months old now. Victor. That was a surprise, I can tell you.' He took a long draw on his cigarette. 'Good to see there's still life in the old dog, eh, but, ha ha, time and fatherhood waits for no man, what?'

'Well congratulations, sir.'

'Yes, well, thank you. "Baby blues" the doctor calls it. Hopefully Flora'll snap out of it soon though. She'll be pleased to hear you're on the squadron. Ho ho, you being a pilot, that's a turn up isn't it? Come to dinner once you're settled in. She always had a soft spot for you back at the school – said she admired your enthusiasm for getting stuck in with the Classics.'

'Oh, she's too kind, sir. But really for me it was more a case of: *lectio brevior potior*,* I'd say?'

Mungo looked decidedly puzzled.

'Oh sorry sir, it means...'

'Hey, you cheeky monkey. You've got my bally walking stick. I wondered where it had gone.'

* The shorter reading is the better.

CHAPTER 3

Minus the walking stick I had to get a taxi, and had a fair wait for one. To cause further delay, the Peter Pan statue is slap in the middle of Kensington Gardens and I had to hobble the last leg along a long footpath. I arrived over a quarter of an hour late but was relieved to find that Hayley was still there. Hitherto when I'd seen her she'd been on-duty so as to speak, with a look that would ignite a vicar's cassock in a downpour but that afternoon she seemed almost demure. It was strange seeing her like that but, I thought, in a different way, she seemed even more fetching than usual.

Peter Pan statue, Kensington Gardens, London.

Hayley allowed me to lean on her arm as I hobbled alongside and we talked. There was a lot to catch up on. We'd exchanged a few letters while I'd been in France but otherwise we hadn't seen each other for nearly a year. Of course she was interested in my recent heroics and what I thought about the disastrous French campaign and so on but eventually I steered the conversation around to her.

'Business has been terrific,' she said, 'we've been flat out ever since the war declaration, absolutely flat out.'

I was having some trouble digesting that little nugget, but managed to nod sagely.

'Why,' she laughed. 'You'll never guess. Marie and I are having a competition. Generals versus Admirals. And I'm... hey, are you alright?'

'I'm fine,' I replied a little hoarsely.

'Well, as I was saying Marie is just in the lead with the Admirals but... look, do you want to take the weight off your feet? You really don't look alright.'

There was a vacant bench nearby and we plonked ourselves down on it. It was a relief to sit as I really was feeling a little light-headed. Hayley took my hand and snuggled up to me. Her perfume wafted over and I could feel her hair softly brushing against my cheek. 'Anyway, Marie and I've had some laughs,' she went on, 'why, only yesterday..'

'Look,' I interrupted, 'could you spare me...'

She drew back, looking startled. 'Why, blow me down, I do declare your face has gone red.'

I could sense my cheeks were a little warm and willed it to stop but, if someone tells you something like that, it makes it worse. I could feel them just getting hotter and hotter.

'Oooh look at you,' Hayley declared, 'I do believe you're jealous.' She grabbed a lock of her hair and tickling my ear with it. 'Jealous, jealous, jealous. Tee hee, tee hee. Jealous. Am I right?'

'Absolute rot,' I replied with as much conviction as I could muster, which was little enough.

LEAVE HITLER TO ME
SONNY — YOU OUGHT
TO BE OUT OF LONDON
ISSUED BY THE MINISTRY OF HEALTH

'But you can't be jealous of a *whore*. Why, it's just what I do for a living.' She paused and thought for a moment. 'Look, if I was a telephone operator you'd expect me to talk to men all day...'

'Yes, but you'd keep your blinking knickers on while you were doing it, wouldn't you? I exploded. I regretted opening my mouth immediately but the words had popped out before I knew it.

Hayley disengaged her hand, sat up straight and looked sternly at me. 'Now look,' she said, 'we won't have that sort of talk here. There are young ears nearby.' London's children had nearly all been evacuated but there were a few still around and she gestured across the grass to where a boy and a girl were flying a kite. 'And I don't bother you about what you might get up to do I?'

I nodded, reluctantly.

'I bet there are a few broken hearts back in France, eh?'

I felt a bit better at the thought of that and nodded again.

'And what about all those eager young English roses here, eh?'

I nodded again, wondering what she might know about that.

'So there you go,' she added, sounding triumphant, 'and you don't think I believe all that nonsense about a "flesh wound" to your ankle, do you? So show me the bullet wound, then. I bet you sprained it escaping from some damsel's boudoir. That's what I think. Am I right?'

Hayley pulled away to guage my reaction. Her last remark had set me back. It would seem that she had a nose for intelligence that might even surpass Helga but, I thought, but... but what? I sighed. 'Yes well, it might have been a little bit like that I suppose.'

'I knew it, I knew it,' she squealed with delight. 'Ha ha, wait till I tell Marie about it.' She reached into her handbag, pulled out two slips of paper and showed them to me. 'Gone with the Wind. Tonight at the Empire in Leicester Square. Do you want to come?'

At that time Gone with the Wind was spoken of in London almost as much as the war. It had come over from the States a few months earlier. Despite showing at three cinemas simultaneously it was extremely difficult to get hold of tickets. I nodded.

'I got them from one of my clients. He works at the Astoria. He's a projectionist actually.'

I took a deep breath. 'That must be nice for both of you,' I replied a little gruffly.

Hayley, slapped my arm and giggled. 'Now stop it, stop it, stop it and let's go and enjoy the film.'

I started to feel a little more perky once we were in the cinema foyer. Hayley was looking radiant, hanging on my arm as we waited to go in and I could see I was getting envious looks from the other men in the queue. I put my arm around her and gave her a squeeze. I wasn't so bothered about seeing the film but the thought of the delights to follow was certainly putting me in a good humour.

Hayley set the scene during the overture when she pulled out two pristine men's hankies from her gas mask bag and placed them in her lap. People say the film was pure escapism for us Londoners with all the terror awaiting us outside but it had its own horrors too – a scene of hundreds of dead after the Battle of Gettysberg to name but one. At any rate, with some jaw-dropping panoramas and a very fetching leading man and leading lady there was plenty to please everybody. And, I confess, there were a couple of moments I came close to borrowing one of Hayley's hankies.

Afterwards we threaded our way out into the blackout. Fortunately it was a clear starlit night so we could see well enough not to fall off the pavement or get run over by a bus. We called into a Joe Lyons for supper. 'If I have to lie, steal, cheat or kill, as God is my witness, I swear I'll never be hungry again,' I declared as I paid the nippy.* She sighed like someone who had heard that line 30 times already that week, exchanged a look with Hayley and they both raised their eyebrows.

'Tara, Tara, Tara. See me home, won't you?' asked Hayley once we were outside.

'Who the what now?' I replied.

Hayley blinked. 'Tara,' she said. '*Tara* remember? Did you nod off in the cinema or something?'

Home for Hayley was a flat near South Ken station, only a quarter hour away by tube. We stopped in the street outside and she turned for me to kiss her. 'You should be kissed by someone who knows how,' I declared as I stooped down to oblige.

'Stop it, stop it,' Hayley giggled. 'Now I must tell you, you can't sleep with me tonight.'

'Frankly, my dear, I don't give a damn,' I said, not believing a word of it, as I squeezed her bottom.

'No, you can come in for a drink, but no hanky-panky,' she replied, pulling my hand away and sounding ominously serious.

The door to her flat opened just as we reached the landing and I caught a glimpse of a figure inside. 'Oh, Daphne,' said Hayley, as she looked at her watch, 'I'm sorry we're late but do please go now.'

By the time we had made it to the door Daphne had her coat on. 'Goodnight Miss,' she said, nodding at me as she squeezed past us. 'See you tomorrow at twelve.'

* J Lyons café's and corner houses were an institution at that time. The waitresses were called "nippies". http://tinyurl.com/Kilroy177.

The flat was small – a kitchen on one side of the hall, a door, to the bedroom presumably, on the other. Further down the hall there was another door, which burst open, releasing what I can only describe as a bundle of pure energy – a young girl, eight or nine I guessed, who threw herself into Hayley's arms.

'C'est tard, ma petite,' said Hayley, 'tu devras être au lit.'

Hayley turned to me. 'This is Lara,' she said and introduced me.'

The youngster smiled at me. 'Is Mr Kilroy one of your clients, Maman?'

I nearly swallowed my tongue at this but Hayley rescued me. 'No darling, he's not interested in piano at all, he's just, er, just, er, a friend.'

'He's a *friend*... oooooh,' said young Lara as she waltzed down the hall and into the bedroom.

So, in five short minutes my plans for Hayley had been utterly derailed. After Lara had been put to bed and I was settled with a drink, Hayley proved surprisingly reluctant to be drawn. Yes, Lara was hers (I found myself revising estimates of her age) and was with her now in London because she kept running away from the evacuee programme. *Had* she spoken French to her?, she asked, in answer to my query. Well, it was a long story and she wasn't keen to go into it right then. 'I'm tired,' she declared as she stretched and suppressed a yawn. 'You can hear the whole of it another day,' she added as she gave me a peck on the cheek. She stood up and headed out of the room and to the bedroom.

I spent the night on the settee.

CHAPTER 4

I saw him before he saw me. 'Sticky Stevens, you old bastard, you made it,' I cried.

He was standing on the forecourt of Charing Cross Station and had indeed made it back, but only just by the look of him. His face cracked into a smile as he leaned on his crutches and pumped my hand. 'Kilroy, old fellow, I say, I say.' He sounded quite emotional but eventually let go to take a good look at me. 'I wasn't sure if that old McKenzie fellow would track you down but here you are and bang on time too. Bloody marvellous. Are you thirsty? I am.'

I'd "borrowed" another walking stick at the Grosvenor so the pair of us made an interesting spectacle, while we threaded our way down the street. Stevens told me our old squadron was now flying from Biggin Hill and a few days earlier he'd had what he called "a small disagreement" over Calais with a brace of 109s. He'd downed one of the blighters, but the other had got him "up the chuff". With flames licking around the cockpit, he had just managed to bail out, landing in the Channel and had been "dead lucky" to be picked up by the Navy.

I eyed him up and down. He was leaning heavily on his crutches, with swathes of bandages around his left thigh and an angry red scar across his forehead. I asked after the rest of the squadron.

'Baines, Friesegreen, Ellis, Jones and Bryant – all bought it I'm afraid.'

That was five gone. I realised with a jolt I'd been away only ten days. 'So who's left?' I asked.

'Well Barnes and Tucker of course. Jerries wouldn't dare take on the CO or his 2IC, ha ha. And Basher's okay as well. But I'm not sure you'd know any of the others now. Lots of new faces but they don't last long. The record is 45 minutes. Poor bastard rolled through the gates, was sent straight up and got caught by ground fire over Boulogne. Didn't even get to stow his kit.'

He asked how I'd made out with the Fairey Battle and I told him about my single terrifying operation, but bearing in mind McNulty's caution, I was sparing on the torturous aftermath.

Stevens knew just the place for us and it was only a short walk away. We turned down a side street, slid through a gateway, down some steps and tumbled into a cellar. 'Who needs an air raid shelter, when we've got this place?' he grinned as he we sat down at a table. He handed me the menu. 'What do you fancy, old chap?'

I looked at the list before me. There was something called Gordon's Tipple at the top, which sounded hideous. I scanned down further and took in a couple of ordinary Beaujolais in the middle and there at the bottom I spotted it. 'Crikey they've got a 1924 Petrus. A lot more pricey than in Chalons, mind you.'

'I'm more a Margaux man myself.' He yawned and glanced at the menu. 'Tell you what. We'll have one of each.' He gestured to the barman and made the order.

'Christ, what are you doing? I can't afford them,' I hissed at Stevens.

He looked at his watch. 'Don't worry about it old boy. I've got an account here.'

The waiter arrived and reverentially uncorked our bottles, carefully decanting the precious fluid into our glasses. Petrus. I've had it only a few times in my life and it always seems to get me into trouble. I am unsure if this is because of its unique molecular structures and their complex interactions with my brain cells or just simply because I like to guzzle it down so quickly. This occasion was to be no exception.

Gordon's Wine Bar, near Charing Cross station, London.

We were each about half way through our bottles when Stevens excused himself. 'Just off to the boys room, old fellow.' He left his crutches with me, with instructions to come and get him if he wasn't back in a few minutes. I noticed that we were at the bottom of a steep and narrow staircase, which was just behind our table. He staggered to his feet, made a lunge for the banister rail and hauled himself up the stairs, hand over hand.

I poured myself another glass. Stevens still hadn't reappeared when I'd finished it, so I picked up his crutches and went to investigate. I soon found him, leaning up against a wall at the top of the stairs. He gestured me to be silent. As I handed him the crutches, I noticed that there was a doorway behind him, opening onto the street. Abruptly he turned and, before I could react, headed through it. I could only follow as he sallied up the pavement, expertly swinging along between his crutches. With my own dicky ankle it was a struggle to keep up but something told me it would be a very good idea to do so, so I hobbled alongside as best I could.

There was a shout from behind and we quickened our pace, diving down a side street. We headed a short way along that and then down another side street before slowing to a halt. We were both breathing heavily and I was relieved to hear no sound of pursuit. 'I thought you said you had an account there?' I asked.

He grinned at me. 'Ah, yes, well that would be a running account I fear.' He looked at his watch and pointed up the street. 'The Lamb and Flag should be open by now. Let's get some beer.'

I will spare you the details of the next few hours. Eventually we realised that we needed to eat. I vaguely recall being thrown out of Rules before we had even ordered. As we stood in the street outside, Stevens suggested the Savoy Grill. I looked doubtful but he assured me we wouldn't have any problem there, as his uncle was on the board.

The Savoy Hotel, London.

'Would that be the board of directors or a diving board?' I asked, but he just grinned back at me.

Unfortunately we had mislaid one of his crutches at an earlier port of call, so progress was slow, but eventually we arrived at our destination, shuffling across the carpet towards the dining room.

At that time, in most places, you could get away with a lot if you were in service uniform and especially if you were carrying the scars of battle. Before the war, Stevens's uncle or not, I am sure we would have been shown the door, but the waiter merely smiled and ushered us to a corner table, which I noticed was some way away from the other diners.

I was hungry. For the past couple of weeks I'd been too busy romping around occupied Europe to get a decent bite to eat, and had had only the odd nibble since I'd been back. Now with all that Petrus and Watneys sloshing around in my stomach, I desperately needed something to soak it up.

The menu was somewhat diminished from my last visit. What was it I'd had that time with Mutti? Something pretentious like Seriously Stuffed Swan I think. Well, surprise, surprise, that was nowhere to be seen. And not even a dangerously depleted duck. But at least there was a note at the bottom of the menu apologising for the excisions "due to the current emergency". Well, I thought, it was nice to know that the Savoy patrons had to endure wartime hardship too. I looked over at one of the other tables and could see a po-faced diner being served with what appeared to be the steak and kidney pudding. It smelt pretty good, so I decided to go for that. Stevens thought so too, but commented rather loudly that he doubted the portions would satisfy a fasting ferret.

He was right. The helpings didn't look that large, but I knew a way around this. When the waiter arrived I asked for another place to be set, 'for Kaspar,' and stated that all three of us wanted the jolly old kate and sydney, with peaches and cream to follow. Stevens had no idea what I was on about and kept asking who the effing hell was Kaspar. I replied that if his uncle was on the board he really ought to know about these things. The waiter ignored us while he discreetly set an extra place. Shortly afterwards he came lumbering up with a large ebony carved cat, which he dumped in the vacant seat alongside me, before tying a napkin around its neck.

It was time to make the introductions. 'Stevens, meet Kaspar,' I said.*

Stevens eyed him suspiciously. 'Well if it gets us another portion, who cares? I only hope he's house trained.'

The grub turned up pretty sharpish and I recall that I chose a bottle of a fairly young Pinot Noir to wash it down. Not in the same league as the Petrus but I didn't rate our chances of a quick getaway this time and so chose something that we might just conceivably be able to pay for. We were divvying up Kaspar's portion, when there was a commotion behind us. The army had arrived.

There were four of them, in a similar celebratory state as ourselves. The major caught me watching him as they were shown to the table alongside. 'Oh ho, lads. The Brylcreem boys are here.' He nudged the captain alongside him and turned to me. 'Done any low flying recently, eh?' I knew what was coming next so pretended not to hear. 'Low flying over a WAAF that is.' All four were seated by then and made a point of guffawing at some length.

I thought it best to ignore them, but as we were served our dessert I was struck on the back of the head by what I guessed was a bread roll. I could hear the major's voice behind me. 'Nice shot, Stanley. You should be in Bomber Command. Fucking sight better use than these wallies.'

I turned around to see all four of them glaring at me. 'Gentlemen, can we be allowed to finish our meal in peace?'

The major piped up. 'Yes, peace, that's all your lot want. Fat lot of use you were when the Luftwaffe was shooting our arses off at Dunkirk.'

---

* Kaspar is a black alabaster Art Deco cat, carved by Basil Ionides in the 1920s, and has been joining guests at the Savoy ever since. If you book a table for 13, an extra place is set (and paid for) for Kaspar. The Kaspar tradition arose following an earlier dinner party for 13 when the first guest to rise after the meal was fatally shot shortly afterwards. Kilroy must have had special powers of persuasion to get a place for Kaspar when there were only the two diners at his table. http://tinyurl.com/Kilroy179.

I told them that we, that is Stevens and I, were the only survivors from our squadrons – a slight exaggeration I know but near enough.

The major sniffed and asked what we'd been flying.

'Hurricanes and Fairey Battles.'

'Fairey Battles? Well that fits, eh lads? Faireys for a bunch of fairies.' He smirked at his companions. 'See, what I mean, chaps? No fight in them at all.'

I don't know how it happened, but it felt like some unseen hand had propelled me to their table. 'What did you say?'

He didn't look quite so cocky now, with my face hard up against his, me all red in the cheeks and breathing wine and beer fumes over him. I could see his mind working as he looked around the table. Four to two. Good enough odds. He took a breath. 'I said you chaps have got no fight in you at all.' He put down his napkin. 'You couldn't fight over Dunkirk and you can't fight now.'

Kaspar prepares to dine, under a picture of Churchill, at the Savoy in London.

Having read this far you'll know that I'm not one for common brawling. But then I have my limits. 'I'll tell you what Major,' I roared, 'the R.A.F. will fight *you* anywhere.' Somehow or other I seemed to have my hands around his throat. 'For starters we will fight you here in this dining room.' Everyone had stopped eating, I noticed. 'We will fight you at your table or in your seat.' Both of which crashed to the floor as he tipped over backwards. 'We will fight you on the floor.' Which is where I was by then, with his comrades sitting on me.

'And we will fight you with peaches.' This was good old Stevens, waving his crutch in one hand and our dessert in the other.

'And we shall never surrender,' I thundered back. I was being a little optimistic here, given that a size 12 army boot was about to land in my essentials.

I braced myself for the worst, but nothing happened. Silence. My assailants slowly got off me, stood up and dusted themselves off. I caught a whiff of cigar smoke, looked up and blinked. I was staring straight into the concerned eyes of our newly appointed prime minister. He slowly clapped his hands. 'Well done young man, that was very good.' He straightened up and turned to the others. 'And if you fight the Hun as hard as you fight each other we've got nothing to fear.' He addressed his companion as they walked away. 'Very good. That was very good. Anthony, pass me my notebook. That little affray has given me an idea.'[*][†]

---

[*] Churchill was a regular diner at the Savoy both before and during the war. Kilroy does not mention it but he would have been concerned to see Kaspar in the middle of an affray. Churchill always insisted that Kaspar attend his "Other Club" meetings, claiming that he was an excellent and discrete dinner guest who would never repeat anything he heard. Later in the war Churchill had to rescue Kaspar and return him to the Savoy when two R.A.F. personnel stole him and flew him to Singapore.

.

[†] Here is the key part of Churchill's famous 'Fight them on the beaches' speech, delivered to the House of Commons on June 4th 1940 (my italics):

I have, myself, full confidence that if all do their duty, if nothing is neglected, and if the best arrangements are made, as they are being made, we shall prove ourselves once again able to defend our Island home, to ride out the storm of war, and to outlive the menace of tyranny, if necessary for years, if necessary alone. At any rate, that is what we are going to try to do. That is the resolve of His Majesty's Government-every man of them. That is the will of Parliament and the nation. The British Empire and the French Republic, linked together in their cause and in their need, will defend to the death their native soil, aiding each other like good comrades to the utmost of their strength. Even though large tracts of Europe and many old and famous States have fallen or may fall into the grip of the Gestapo and all the odious apparatus of Nazi rule, *we shall not flag or fail. We shall go on to the end, we shall fight in France, we shall fight on the seas and oceans, we shall fight with growing confidence and growing strength in the air, we shall defend our Island, whatever the cost may be, we shall fight on the beaches, we shall fight on the landing grounds, we shall fight in the fields and in the streets, we shall fight in the hills; we shall never surrender,* and even if, which I do not for a moment believe, this Island or a large part of it were subjugated and starving, then our Empire beyond the seas, armed and guarded by the British Fleet, would carry on the struggle, until, in God's good time, the New World, with all its power and might, steps forth to the rescue and the liberation of the old.

See also http://tinyurl.com/Kilroy206.

AFTERWORD

I made a promise at the start of this account that I'd explain how the "Kilroy Was Here" graffiti came about and, to date, I've not once mentioned anything about it. Thus far there has been nothing to tell. It played no part in my life until the morning after the fracas at the Savoy.

When I awoke I'd no idea where I was, but I knew I wasn't in the Grosvenor. I was still fully clothed and the sun was streaming into the room. Stevens was lying flat on his back on the floor, mouth agape and snoring gently. I, at least, had made it to the bed.

I stretched, yawned and stood up, rather gingerly. There was a small desk with some stationery on top and I gathered from that that we were in the Strand Palace Hotel. I stepped over the recumbent Sticky and opened the door. Outside was a typical hotel corridor, with a line of numbered doors, but I spotted, at the far end, one bearing a "Please leave this bathroom as you would wish to find it" sign. As I drew nearer, I noticed that someone had scrawled below "Why?" and then, underneath that, the witty riposte of "Fuck off".

I let myself in, locked the door and stood a while at the sink, gazing at my reflection in the mirror. I was bleary-eyed and a little bruised from the previous night but, I thought, there was nothing a good wash and scrub wouldn't put right. The toilet nearby was not too unwholesome, but there was no toilet paper, just an empty box lying on the floor. I picked it up, turned it over and that's when I saw it – a drawing of a little man with his head poking over a wall. It was rather expertly done I thought, with the legend "Kilroy Was Here" in tidy capitals underneath. Someone else had added "So wide he use all der fucking bog roll?" rather less elegantly below.

And here was a puzzle. My Kilroy surname is fairly common of course, but the drawing and inscription were horribly familiar and I couldn't figure out how someone else could possibly have come up with my little design, in the Strand Palace of all places.

Back in the room I woke Stevens. He yawned as he examined the box. 'Oh, blimey, it's found its way over here now has it? I guess someone from the squadron has been here before us. I wonder who it was?'

'Squadron?' I exclaimed, 'What the hell has that got to do with it?'

I make the excuse that a lot had happened to Stevens and me over the previous month and we were both very hung over. It took us a while to sort ourselves out.

'So, let's get this straight,' said Sticky eventually, 'you're saying you've got no knowledge of that awkward business at the airbase during the blitzkrieg?' He waggled the box up and down in front of me. 'None at all?'

I nodded. My memory was still a blank between my coming out of hospital, after the prang with Belfrey and being picked up by Ollie in Ypres.

'Christ. You must remember that writing on Belfrey's broken Bentley, just beforehand though?' asked Stevens, 'Ha ha. That was a laugh alright although Belfrey didn't think so.'

'What?' I exclaimed.

Sticky looked surprised but then smacked the side of his head. 'Oh, but of course, you were in hospital. That's how we knew it couldn't be you. Very witty though. First you land a Tiger Moth on top of his car, then you have that prang with him in the Magister, then later on that very day this slogan turns up on his car's one and only undamaged door panel. Ha ha. Belfrey was less than happy though. Had everyone lined up at the airfield the next morning. Read the riot act good and proper. Didn't stop it though. Just encouraged it if anything.'

I could only listen with mounting horror. Thereafter the graffiti had been found, not just in the ground crew lavatories but on the sergeants mess dartboard, Squadron Leader Barnes' hat and even, in gloss white, daubed on Tungsten's considerable left flank ('Brave chap who did that,' said Sticky).

This was interesting of course but didn't solve the mystery of how a drawing and slogan, which *I* knew well, had become common knowledge to every man and beast in the squadron. There was only one person I could ask. A couple of hours later, just outside the Fitzroy, I found a phone that worked.

'Oh you're safe, thank God.'

'Pamela I...'

'But you shouldn't have called me here,' she whispered.

'Pamela I...'

'Nigel has just gone for a walk but please be quick.'

'Pamela, this graffiti business...'

'Oh that. A frightful bore.' I could imagine her examining her nails, eyebrows arched, as she stood by the phone.

'But how did it get out?' I asked. I was trying not to sound irritated but I didn't seem to be getting any answers. All I knew was that only she and I should know about it. I'd only ever drawn that image once in my life and the one place that I drew it was at a lofty elevation on her left thigh.

'Well, *everyone* knows about it darling.'

'Yes but...' I was trying to find a delicate way to frame my question. 'Who have you been showing it to?'

'I just said. Everyone. Well, near enough.' she replied.

'Your husband?'

'Well not him of course. I managed to hide it from him.'

I exhaled. 'But why didn't you just wash it off ?'

'It wouldn't come off sweetie. That stupid pen of yours, the one invented by that boring old Beano chap.'

'Biro?' I said.

'Yes, that's it. It was indelible. Took me days to scrub it off.'

It wasn't supposed to be a picture of a little man at all but was just an inept attempt to draw my rough and ready accommodation when I was training at Kincardine in '39 – a Nissen hut in fact. And Kilroy *was* there alright, wasn't he? And, yes, I know it sounds an unlikely image to etch on a fair maid's thigh, but there it is. Take a look at one yourself if you can find one. No not a woman's thigh, a Nissen hut I mean. From a certain angle and in a certain light it looks very like a little bald man peering over a wall. And the fair maid hadn't seemed worried at the time I drew it, back in the cottage, all lovely and tousled and stretched out on the bed as she carelessly knocked back a G and T.

I took a deep breath. 'Look, Pamela, are you going to tell me how this silly bloody drawing got out so it's now even being scrawled in a London hotel?'

Nissen Hut.

'Really?' she asked, 'A hotel you say? Not the Dorchester I hope?'

'No, Pamela, not the bloody...' I took a deep breath. 'Listen sweetie can you just tell me what happened?'

I could hear a sigh. 'You remember a couple of days after we'd, um, well you know?'

I nodded and then, feeling rather foolish because, of course she couldn't see me, added a husky 'Yes.'

'You'd just been carted off to hospital after that crash with Nigel, remember? By the way did you know it was dear little Oscar's doing? Climbed up his trouser leg...'

'Pamela...'

'Anyway, a couple of hours later, the air chief marshal showed up.'

'Barratt?' I asked.

'Yes, "Ugly" Barratt. That's the fellow. God, he *is* ugly too. Nigel had everyone out on parade.'*

'And?'

'Well, it was a super hot day, although it was a bit windy. I was standing beside Nigel for the march-past, wearing that yellow frock you once told me you liked.'

I had a premonition as to what she was going to say next and, sure enough, it featured a sudden gust, a billowing dress and no stockings beneath.

'Good God.'

'That's just what Sergeant Oliver said.'

'And everyone saw...'

'Well only the other ranks. The top brass and Nigel missed it because they were facing the other way.'

'Well that's okay then.'

'Oh don't be so stuffy darling.'

'Well...'

'Nobody else minds and Nigel is none the wiser.'

'He must be furious with me over the bloody car though.'

'Oh, he's probably forgotten about it. Had to leave it behind anyway. We've got a Rolls now. And I forgot to tell you, I've got him to put you back on the squadron. We'll see lots of each other. But quickly now, he'll be back in a minute. Tell me how long you are on leave and when can I see you?'

* Air Chief Marshal Sir Arthur (Ugly) Barratt was Commander-in-chief of the British Air Forces in France (BAFF). http://tinyurl.com/Kilroy182.

für

TASSELS
in the AIR
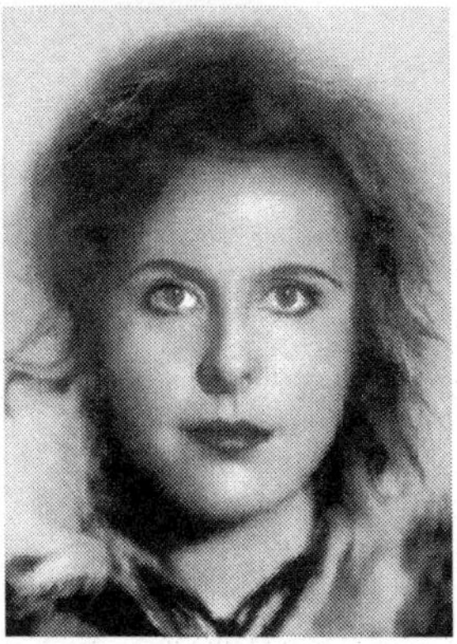
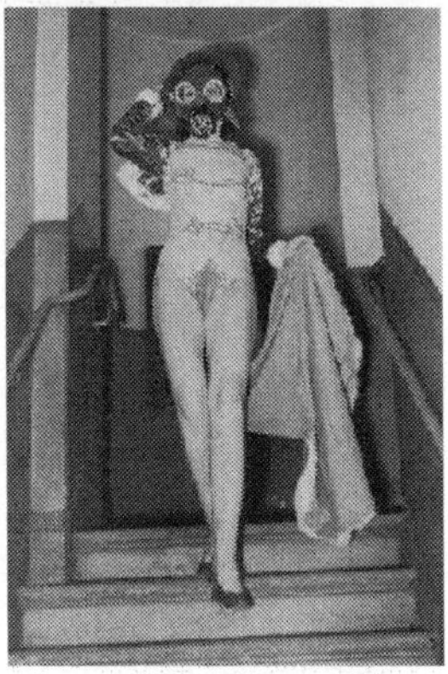

EDITOR'S POSTSCRIPT

In the summer of 1966 I was in my final year as a postgraduate student in the History Department at Edinburgh University and I was very busy writing up my doctoral thesis (*Uses and Abuses of Barbed Wire in the Eastern Mediterranean 1920-1932*, M. H. Liardet, PhD thesis Edinburgh University Library 1967). One day I was in my room, with papers, maps, reports and books strewn all around, when my landlady knocked and dropped a letter on my bed. It was from my mother. I didn't open it immediately. Maman had been writing weekly from back home in France ever since I'd come over to "Angleterre" (never "Écosse" despite my reminders) and I felt sure there would be nothing much requiring my immediate attention.

When I did open the letter, I found, along with Maman's news from home and her usual injunctions about ironing my shirts and so on, a clipping from an English newspaper about the football team's recent World Cup victory. Of course we knew about it in Scotland but I can't say the event had been greeted with much joy there (more the opposite) and, being French in any case and studying hard, I'd barely paid attention to the momentous events over the border. The clipping was a picture of jubilant England fans running onto the pitch at the end of the final game. Maman had circled one of the fans, who was clutching a foaming bottle of what looked like a Watneys beer. 'Would I track him down?' she asked.

Maman seemed to think there were only a few hundred people in the entire United Kingdom and that I was on first name terms with practically all of them. It seemed a hopeless task but a couple of days later, having dinner at a friend's house, I recalled that his father worked on the *Scotsman* newspaper and produced my clipping for him.

'The crowd are on the pitch – they think it's all over – it is now,' he intoned, as he smoothed out the paper on the table cloth.

It's now a famous line, often heard when England's victory is revisited, and that was the first time I heard it (but, sadly, not the last). To my surprise he got back to me a few days later with the news that he'd identified the mystery fan. 'I thought I recognised him,' he told me. 'We did a feature a few years back on "The man who survived 57 plane crashes". We had a double page spread of him surrounded by all these dinged aeroplanes – and I'm pretty sure that he's your man.' He handed me a piece of paper with a name and address on it.

A few weeks later I was in London, following up some leads for a course I was giving on the fourth Anglo-Mysore War. One morning I visited the Victoria and Albert Museum to obtain a photograph of the famous Tipu's Tiger (which plays some small part in the history). Afterwards, as I was walking out onto the street, it came to me that Maman's mystery man lived somewhere close by. I dug out the press cutting and piece of paper from my wallet and asked for directions. The street was Glendower something or other. It was indeed only a few minute's walk away and the man lived in a flat – 3B as I recall. I pressed the bell and waited.

There was a delay while he came down, then the door opened and I found myself face to face with the man who was in the crowd that was on the pitch. I introduced myself, showed him the press cutting and he was looking generally unimpressed until I mentioned Maman and where she lived.

'Grande Synthe?' he repeated. 'North East France, little village, near Fort Mardyck, by the coast? Surely not?!' He stepped back to get a good look at me. 'No, no, no – I don't believe it.' He chuckled. 'And you young man. Now let me think.' I could see him making a mental calculation. 'Twenty six years old and, er, four months to the day if I'm not mistaken?'

I nodded.

'So what happened to the blinking diamonds?'

***

Yes indeed, what *did* happen to the blinking diamonds? Maman had never mentioned them to me, that was for sure.

Kilroy invited me up to his flat and told me his half of the story but I could add very little, beyond some early memories of the cold winters and hard times we'd had during the German occupation. It occurred to me the diamonds might even still be lying around, unnoticed in a corner of the barn.

There the mystery stuck until I visited Maman a few months later. She didn't look best pleased to be asked, sat down, frowned, thought about it some, then frowned again. I thought she was going to tell me to mind my own business but instead she sighed, got out of her seat, walked over and tapped me, none too softly, on the head.

'The diamonds – they are in there,' she said and stood back.

Feeling rather foolish I rubbed my head, feeling nothing different of course and wondering how and why they'd be there in any case.

Maman laughed. 'No not literally in there,' she said. 'Where do you think your brains come from?'

Maman was talking in riddles and I was starting to feel a bit irritated with her. 'Yes but...' I began.

'Your education, Michel,' she interrupted, 'your *education*.'

Then it fell into place. It had been a subject of some gossip in the village that Maman had been able to send her one and only first to the famous Lycée Louis-le-Grand in Paris then on to the Sorbonne and finally overseas to Edinburgh, where I'd just been awarded my doctorate. And then I remembered all those mysterious trips to Antwerp that she made every six months or so. Now it fell into place.

'And they've all gone,' she cackled, 'Every single one. All gone now and all in there.' She tapped me on the head again.

Kilroy took the news rather well. 'Made better use of them than I'd have done,' was his response.

And that was the beginning of our friendship, which lasted many decades, and only ended when he died just a few years back.

I found the old boy had willed me a few hundred pounds along with his considerable collection of old home computers, data, disks and what-not. This sort of stuff is typically worthless and I was thinking of chucking it out but then, one day, I came across a box of floppy disks which looked like it might contain some interesting material.

I will skip over the difficulties I had in extracting Kilroy's writing from the 30 year old disks, and the minor obstacles I had to overcome with the family over the meaning of the words "to the beneficiary – for his pleasure and profit". Let's just say that one thing led to another and this story here is the outcome.

M. H. L. 2016

END NOTES

(1). The game of Nim is played by two players with several (usually three) piles of matches or other counters. Each plays in turn and removes any number of matches from *one* pile. The winner is the player to remove the last match/es.

These simple rules conceal a game of some complexity. It is not clear how to force a win but, surprisingly, a winning strategy for the game exists and in fact was first presented in a published paper in 1901, by Charles L. Bouton, a Mathematics professor at Harvard University. This paper was remarkable for its time, because it made use of binary arithmetic and Boolean logical operations (see Wikipedia on *Binary*: http://tinyurl.com/Kilroy185). With the advent of computers binary is well known nowadays and easily understood, by computer scientists at least. But in 1901 it was merely a mathematical curiosity and it certainly wasn't clear then that it would ever be of much practical value.

The "Nimatron" Machine at New York's World Fair 1939.

More than 30 years later, nuclear physicist Ed Condon of Westinghouse Electric Corporation spotted the potential for mechanising Bouton's method and developed the "Nimatron", a machine which was exhibited at New York's World Fair in 1940, where it beat all-comers. This predated by nearly ten years what we now call computers and, although it was not a general purpose computer itself, it was, arguably, the world's first game machine.

Bouton's paper describes some tricky calculations which would be beyond most people's mental arithmetic capabilities (see Wikipedia on *Nim*: http://tinyurl.com/Kilroy184) but it is possible to play a winning strategy if you can remember certain combinations (or indeed write them on your wrist):

- If there is only one pile left, remove all matches to win immediately.
- If there are two piles left, remove matches from the larger one so that the two piles are left equal.
- If there are three piles left and two (or more) are equal, remove all of the third to leave two equal piles.
- Otherwise there are three piles left, all different sizes. Remove some matches from one pile to leave your opponent with three piles comprising: 1/2/3 matches, 1/4/5 matches, 1/6/7, 1/8/9, 2/4/6, 2/5/7, 2/8/10, 3/4/7, 3/5/6 or 3/9/10 matches. (These combinations suffice for any game of Nim with up to 10 matches per pile.)
- If it is not possible to act on any of the above then your opponent is in a winning position and the best you can do is make a move at random and hope s/he makes a mistake. Once you *can* act on one of the above you will always be able to later find another winning position in reply, whatever your opponent does.

If you want to try this strategy and lack a human opponent there are many (free) Nim apps available for mobiles, laptops or desktops.

(2). Later in the war Ford-Werke and Opel manufactured armaments, transportation and aeroplanes using slave labour, although their US management subsequently claimed that the parent companies had lost control of their German subsidiaries by then. They weren't the only allied companies in a compromising position before and during the early stages of the war: Standard Oil, Woolworth and many other well known names continued doing business with the Nazis right up until the Japanese attack on Pearl Harbor, in December 1941.

According to *The Untold History of the United States* by Oliver Stone and Peter Kuznick (Ebury Press, 2013), during the war General Motors received a tax write-off of $22.7 million for the loss of Opel and, after the war, reparations of $33 million for damage to "its" factories by allied bombing.

See also:

http://tinyurl.com/Kilroy188 (Amazon link to *Trading with the Enemy* by Charles Higham (iUniverse Inc, 2007))
http://tinyurl.com/Kilroy186 (Jewish Telegraphic Agency)
http://tinyurl.com/Kilroy187 (Global Research).

(3). John Maynard Keynes was highly influential from the 1920s until the 1970s, when his ideas were superseded by Milton Friedman and others, but Keynesian economics has recently seen a revival following the global financial crisis of 2007-8.

Keynes' greatest work was *The General Theory of Employment, Interest and Money* (the title is a word-play on Einstein's General Theory of Relativity) was first published in 1936 (see http://tinyurl.com/Kilroy191, also available on Amazon at: http://tinyurl.com/Kilroy189). Keynes' thinking was heavily influenced by the economic misery of the slump following WWI. Until that time, free-market economics were based on the ideas of Adam Smith, David Ricardo and John Stuart Mill who opposed government intervention in the working of the economy. Keynes' earlier work, *Economic Consequences of the Peace in 1919* had warned prophetically that destroying the German economy would have serious implications for the rest of Europe. In the General Theory he argued that government action with market forces could alleviate distress and promote the general welfare of society. The book has been controversial ever since its publication. Here is one of Keynes more provocative statements:

> "If the Treasury were to fill old bottles with banknotes, bury them at suitable depths in disused coalmines which are then filled up to the surface with town rubbish, and leave it to private enterprise on well-tried principles of *laissez-faire* to dig the notes up again (the right to do so being obtained, of course, by tendering for leases of the note-bearing territory), there need be no more unemployment and, with the help of the repercussions, the real income of the community, and its capital wealth also, would probably become a good deal greater than it actually is. It would, indeed, be more sensible to build houses and the like; but if there are political and practical difficulties in the way of this, the above would be better than nothing." (p 129)

(4). It has not been possible to verify which aeroplane carried the prime minister to Munich but, at any rate, one of two (G-AFGN) crashed following an engine failure, at Saint Saveur in France in August 1939, with no fatalities. The other (G-AFGO) crashed only a month after Munich, at Walton Bay near Bristol, killing one of the Munich pilots (Eric Robinson) along with a trainee (Robert Leborgne). The other two members of British Airways' then Super Electra fleet (G-AFGP and G-AFGR) were also lost, "damaged beyond repair", in Sudan in 1941.

Aviation was certainly more hazardous in those days as evidenced by the remarkable number of crashes during the Super Electra's service career.

Of the 354 aircraft produced, 52 ended their days as "hull-losses", 27 of them involving fatalities. Some of these losses were under the stress of war but there were also many in peacetime. The losses are listed on *Aviation Safety Network* website: http://tinyurl.com/Kilroy194.

(5). Methamphetamine is classified as a "psycho-stimulant" and is one of a range drugs that, for several decades, were freely available worldwide and were widely used both by the military and in civilian medicine. The Germans gave Pervitin, known as "tank-chocolate", to their Panzer crews, the R.A.F. distributed "wakey-wakey" or "go" pills to Bomber Command and the Americans also used them, latterly in the Vietnam war (where they were known as "purple hearts", after the medal given for being wounded or killed in action). For civilian use these drugs were often prescribed for slimming, performance enhancement and to combat narcolepsy.

It is commonly believed that, after the war, Prime Minister Anthony Eden's poor decision making during the Suez Crisis was down to his heavy consumption of Benzedrine.

Amphetamines and the other stimulants are seldom prescribed nowadays but are still used by the military and widely used recreationally, where they are manufactured and supplied illegally. http://tinyurl.com/Kilroy195.

(6). Hitler's mysterious *Zweites Buch*, his second book of political theory and the sequel to *Mein Kampf*, was written in the late 1920s. It was not published initially because *Mein Kampf* was not selling well and EherVerlag, the publishers, were simply not interested. Subsequently, after sales of *Mein Kampf* took off, Hitler decided to suppress *Zweites Buch* because he thought it would be too revealing of his foreign policy objectives.

There were only ever two copies of the manuscript. The only one to survive the war was lodged in a safe in an air raid shelter in 1935. It remained there until its discovery by an American officer in 1945, then to be submerged in the Nazi records of the US National Archives until its rediscovery by the Jewish American historian Gerhard Weinberg in 1958. Kilroy's account raises the interesting possibility that Capello and/or "Helena" came by the other copy in Munich in 1938, but no trace of it exists today.

As far as is known, British Intelligence never did get any closer to the manuscript than the photograph Kilroy mentions in his memoir. It is debatable whether it would have been of much use if they had. The book mentions Hitler's desire for an Anglo-German alliance and praises the USA for its "racially successful" society that practised segregation, but as Hitler's stated policy aims and actual political direction often conflicted it would possibly not have been of much use at the time.

The book has been pirated several times since the war. There is now an authoritative English translation: *Hitler's Second Book: The Unpublished Sequel to Mein Kampf*, Enigma Books, New York 2003, (Amazon: http://tinyurl.com/Kilroy196).

(7). Georgina Shaw Baker portrayed many celebrated ships' mascots (cats and dogs) and several of her works are in the possession of the National Maritime Museum, now held in store (but they can be seen on request). According to the Museum, Oscar's first ship was the famous German battleship Bismarck, sunk on its maiden operation in May. He was rescued by the Royal Navy and adopted by the crew of HMS Cossack, only for it to be sunk later in the year, in October. He survived that sinking as well, to be given the nickname Unsinkable Sam, when he served on the aircraft carrier HMS Ark Royal. Oscar was indeed unsinkable but the Ark Royal wasn't. It was torpedoed in November. Having survived that third and final sinking, and after what must have been a very trying year, Oscar was confined to shore duties thereafter and spent the rest of his life in a seaman's home in Belfast, where he died in 1955.

Kilroy's account provides valuable information on Oscar's early life, apparently wreaking havoc in French agriculture and then with the R.A.F. If the Oscar of Bismarck fame and the Oscar of Kilroy's acquaintance were one and the same this begs the question of how he travelled from Condé-Vraux, where he was left in May 1940 to be on the Bismarck when it was sunk in the North Atlantic in May the following year. The most likely explanation is that after the occupation he was adopted by a German sailor, perhaps on his way back from leave in Paris and heading to Hamburg, where the Bismarck commenced sea trials in August 1940. He had been given a name tag at Condé-Vraux so it is not surprising he was known as Oscar by both Germans and British and that, with the likeness in the portrait and his heterochromatism, not to say his Jonah-like capabilities make it highly likely that Bismarck Oscar and R.A.F. Oscar were one and the same.

http://tinyurl.com/Kilroy197 (*Unsinkable Sam*)
http://tinyurl.com/Kilroy198 (*Heterochromatism in cats*)
http://tinyurl.com/Kilroy199 (*The Great Cat* website contains an image of the portrait).

Collage found after the war in Oscar's last home in Belfast. (Bottom to top) the Bismarck, HMS Ark Royal and HMS Cossack, Tiger Moth, Miles Magister and Hawker Hurricane; bus, bicycle saddlebag and tractor.

(8). Colonel T.E. Lawrence found fame for his exploits in the Arab Revolt in WWI and with his writing, most notably *Seven Pillars of Wisdom* (made into the celebrated film, *Lawrence of Arabia*, in 1962). He left the army in the 1920s and re-enlisted in the R.A.F. as Leading Aircraftman (a lowly rank) T. E. Shaw, presumably seeking anonymity. His fatal accident occurred in 1935, shortly after he had left military service. He was riding his motorbike, a high performance Brough Superior, from his home at Clouds Hill in Dorset to a nearby post office in Bovington Camp. While travelling at considerable speed on the way back he swerved to avoid two boys on bicycles heading in the same direction, Frank Fletcher and Albert Hargreaves, who later claimed they had been in single file at the road's edge. Lawrence was thrown from his machine and suffered head injuries, dying six days later, without regaining consciousness. Neither of the boys was seriously hurt.

Before his death Lawrence was tended by a specialist neuro-surgeon, Mr H. W. B. Cairns, from the London Hospital. Lawrence had not been wearing a crash helmet and Cairns subsequently campaigned for motorcyclists to wear them. A post-mortem revealed a large fissure fracture, nine inches long, extending from the left side of the head backwards and also a small fracture of the left orbital plate. With this injury, Cairns claimed that, had Lawrence lived, he would have been unable to speak, he would have lost his memory and been paralysed.

An inquest was held at the Wool Military Hospital at Bovington Camp shortly after his death, with the jury returning a verdict of accidental death. Lawrence's Brough Superior is on display in the Imperial War Museum at Kennington in London. http://tinyurl.com/Kilroy200

(9). The Abbeville Massacre took place on 20th May 1940, in the French town of Abbeville, just before it fell to the Germans. A group of 79 detainees, supposedly spies or Nazi sympathisers, had been transported there the previous day, only just ahead of the German advance. With the town about to fall, 21 of them were summarily executed by a reservist company of the French army. Of the 58 survivors, many were taken to Auschwitz during the occupation, never to return.

The detainees had originally been arrested in Belgium, immediately following the German invasion of 10th May. Some of them *were* pro-Nazis – for example Joris Van Severen, a co-founder of a Belgian extreme-right group called Verdinaso and Leon Degrelle, the founder of the far-right Catholic and nationalist "Rexist" party. There were some genuine German agents who had been picked up as well but there were also Communists and neutrals – innocent people who had just happened to lack identity documents or who were simply in the wrong place at the wrong time.

With the fall of Belgium imminent, the detainees were moved west from their prison in Bruges on 15th May, in a convoy of three buses routing through Dunkirk and Ostend to Bethune. At Dunkirk, Leon Degrelle was recognised by the French, who pulled him from the convoy and beat him up. The convoy moved on without him, arriving in Bethune, where the prisoners were handed over to the French Sûreté for questioning. They remained at Bethune until May 19th when, again, they had to be evacuated just ahead of the German advance. Upon departure, a young Belgian who was living in France but had refused to be drafted into the French army, was added to their number.

On arrival in Abbeville on 19th May, the detainees were secured in an improvised lock-up, in the cellar beneath the bandstand in the Jardin d'Argos. The next day, Abbeville was in chaos with the German occupation imminent. After the event it was established that most of the men involved in the massacre, officers and men from the French reservist 28th Regional Guard Regiment, were drunk. The officer in charge was Captain Marcel Dingeon. He was not present at the scene but, without instructions from his superiors, he gave a verbal order for Chief Sergeant François Molet and his men to carry out the summary execution of all of the detainees immediately.

In an attempt to get it over with quickly, one of the men threw a grenade down the hatch of the cellar but it failed to explode. It was at this point that Molet was joined by Lieutenant Rene Caron, from the same regiment, a teacher in civilian life, who just happened to be passing. The executions started with the detainees being removed from the cellar in groups of four and bayonetted or shot. There were frequent interruptions because of German bombing. Finally, with the body count at 21, Lieutenant Jean Leclabart, also of the French 28th Regional Guard Regiment – the 5th company of the 2nd Batallion – arrived and, being well-versed in army regulations, he accused Caron and the men of being crazy and demanded to see a written execution order. Since nobody could show him such an order he put a stop to the massacre.

Only a few of the executions would likely have been carried out had there been a fair trial – most probably Joris van Severin, Jan Ryckoort, René Wéry and van Gijsegem from the Flemish far right, and De Bruyne and Vanderkelen who were spies for the Abwehr. The rest were innocent. Among the dead were Lucien Monami and Van Dijcke, both Communists (who would hardly likely be collaborators), Robert Bell, a Canadian, who had been a coach for the German national ice hockey team, Maria Geerolf-Ceuterick, who had been arrested instead of her son, Adolf Wybon, the Belgian who had refused to serve in the French army, four Jews, four Italians, a mentally deranged Austrian (no, not Herr Hitler) and even one of the convoy's bus drivers who had been mistakenly detained. Leon Degrelle, the Rexist who was beaten up in Dunkirk and removed from the convoy there, escaped their fate. He survived his ordeal and during the occupation he collaborated with the Nazis, serving in the Waffen SS. He fled to Fascist Spain after the war to escape retribution and ultimately died there, of natural causes, in 1994.

After the occupation the Germans conducted an inquest into the tragedy. Captain Marcel Dingeon escaped this as he happened to be in the Vichy France free zone but in any case he committed suicide, in Pau, on 21st January 1941. Sergeant François Molet and Lieutenant René Caron were condemned to death and executed at Mont Valerian in Paris on 7th April 1942. Mont Valerian was infamous during the war as the place of execution of many French resistance fighters and, as such Lieutenant Caron was honoured as a war hero after the war. There is a street in Abbeville, very near the site of the massacre, which is named after him.

There are several accounts of the massacre that have been published. Gabby Warris, who was detained with her mother and whose grandmother was one of the victims, wrote movingly of it in *Het van bloedbad Abbeville /The massacre of Abbeville*, Hadewijch, Antwerp 1994. There are other works referenced in the French Wikipedia *Massacre d'Abbeville*: http://tinyurl.com/Kilroy202.

(10). The Fairey Battle was, arguably, the R.A.F.'s worst operational aircraft of the entire war. It was a single-engine light bomber, fitted with the same Merlin engine as the Spitfire and Hurricane (and later the highly successful Mosquito and Lancaster) but it was overladen with three crew and 1,500 lbs of bombs. Thus overburdened its maximum speed only just topped 250 mph. To make things worse, from the rear, its sole defence was an upward pointing machine gun, which meant that enemy fighters could attack it with impunity from below. This type of attack could be avoided by flying low, but this left the plane exposed to anti-aircraft fire, which was murderous in daylight which, unfortunately, was when the plane was mainly operated.

On the opening day of the Battle of France, three out of eight Battles were shot down in their first sortie and ten out of 24 in the second. The next day six out of nine (from the Belgian Air Force) were lost, followed by seven out of eight from the R.A.F.'s No 12 Squadron later on. For this latter operation two Victoria Crosses (both posthumous) were awarded – the R.A.F.'s first of the war. After yet more losses, on 14th May an operation was mounted with 71 Blenheim and Battle bombers. Forty did not return and 35 of them were Battles. This remains the highest casualty rate ever on a full-scale R.A.F. operation.

The appalling losses only lessened when the Battle was switched to night operations (for which the crews were not properly trained). By the end of the Battle of France, nearly 200 Battles had been lost in just six weeks. The planes continued to be used through the summer of 1940 in operations against shipping massed in the Channel ports for Operation Sealion – Hitler's planned invasion of Britain. The Battle's last combat sorties were mounted on the night of 15/16 October 1940 by No. 301 (Polish) Squadron in a raid on Boulogne, and Nos 12 and 142 Squadrons bombing Calais. Thereafter, it continued to be used for training and other purposes but was never again used for frontline operations.

(11). Most historians acknowledge that the Dunkirk "miracle" started with the colossal blunder made by the Germans to halt their armour on the outskirts of the town, when they could have taken it easily. The first decision, by von Rundstedt, was made on 23rd May. The following day Hitler visited von Rundstedt's headquarters, confirming the decision. The nearby port of Boulogne fell shortly after, on 25th May, with Calais on the 26th. Thereafter Dunkirk was the only port available to the surrounded Allies but, with the German armour at a standstill, they had just enough time to strengthen its defences and, in the event, managed to hold out until 5th June. By then a third of a million troops had been embarked from the beaches and from what was left of the harbour. The Luftwaffe played only a small part in the proceedings as for much of the time its planes were grounded by low cloud.

There has been much speculation ever since as to why the Germans made this mistake, not helped by the high ranking Germans who survived the war having little motivation to tell the truth afterwards. One theory is that Hitler didn't want to annihilate the British as he hoped that that would encourage them to sue for peace but this is contradicted by Führer Directive 13, *Next Object in the West*, which was issued on May 24th.and called for the Luftwaffe to defeat the trapped Allied forces and stop their escape
http://tinyurl.com/Kilroy203.

(12) The Dunkirk evacuation was the end of British land operations in Europe for several years and the prelude to the French capitulation which came only two weeks later. The death blow, as far as the French and British were concerned, had been the earlier German armour breakthrough in the north of France, the so-called *sichelschnitt* (meaning "sickle cut", a phrase coined by Churchill), from Sedan near the German border to the coast near Abbeville. The allied armies were split in two by this manoeuvre and never managed to rejoin. Most of the British Expeditionary Force, together with three French armies and some Belgian forces, found themselves cut off in a northern "pocket" and in some disarray, especially after Belgium's sudden surrender. Plans to break through to the south came to nothing and, with much muddle and improvisation, the troops retreated to the coast. By then Dunkirk was the only port accessible to them. With numerous waterways and old fortifications it was a good town to defend (the Allies never captured it when the boot was on the other foot in 1945) and it also possessed the longest sand beach in Europe, which in the event proved very useful for the evacuation.

The evacuation almost never happened. The Germans could easily have taken Dunkirk earlier, had it not been for the infamous "Halt" order, issued by Hitler and General von Rundstedt, which stopped the Panzer advance for three days (discussed further in *End Note (11)*). This gave the Allies just long enough to establish a defensive perimeter, a 40 mile line encompassing the town and substantial surrounding territory. French forces held the western half of the perimeter with British to the east. It was nearly breached on several occasions.

The British had started preparing for "Operation Dynamo" – the evacuation – as early as 20th May, without telling the French. It amounted to an improvised fleet of pleasure craft, trawlers and ferries with the Royal Navy and later some French vessels as well, that had to make the hazardous journey to Dunkirk's beach and harbour and pull the troops out, landing them at Dover and other ports on England's south coast. The first evacuees arrived home on the 27th May.

Fortunately the weather precluded Luftwaffe operations on several days but there *were* clear days when the German planes took full advantage. They virtually destroyed the harbour and sank numerous ships, including six Royal Navy destroyers, not to mention making attacks on the men on shore who were awaiting rescue. The R.A.F., flying from British bases, mounted substantial operations to defend Dunkirk but much of the air combat took place out of range of the town so the troops on the ground were unaware of it. Consequently much of the British army had a very low opinion of the R.A.F. at that time, that is until it distinguished itself a few months later, during the Battle of Britain.

It is often overlooked that, of the third of a million troops pulled out from Dunkirk, over 100,000 of them were French and many of them went straight back to France (to Cherbourg) to continue the fight. Despite the recurring images of troops on the beach the majority of troops boarded ships home from one of the harbour walls, "the mole", which survived all the Luftwaffe attacks. Virtually no heavy equipment came back, leaving Britain in a desperate position, with only enough armament at home to equip one division (commanded by Montgomery) to defend against a possible German invasion. And not every one got out. After the evacuation the defenders surrendered and they were mainly French, around 35,000 of them. The British Expeditionary Force suffered 68,000 casualties in the campaign as a whole, with around 50,000 captured, destined to be prisoners of war for the next five years.

There is newsreel footage of the evacuation, filmed from the ships or harbourside (in Britain) but (as far as I am aware) no footage in Dunkirk itself (see http://tinyurl.com/Kilroy209). An excellent portrayal of what it it might have been like can be found in the film Atonement (based on Ian McEwan's book of the same name). For example, see the five minute tracking shot in http://tinyurl.com/Kilroy210.

For references for further reading, films, or more online material see http://tinyurl.com/Kilroy204.

WEB LINKS

All web links are tabulated here, in their "TinyURL" and expanded "actual" forms. The TinyURLs are all in the form http://tinyurl.com/KilroyNNN (where "NNN" is some number). Either form of web address will take you to the described page but the TinyURLs are easier to type.

Tiny URL	Description	Actual URL
http://tinyurl.com/Kilroy001	YouTube: Let's Face the Music and Dance...	https://www.youtube.com/watch?v=c08wiEyVuak
http://tinyurl.com/Kilroy002	YouTube: We'll meet again...	https://www.youtube.com/watch?v=OvgM_xcx2GI
http://tinyurl.com/Kilroy003	YouTube: Run Adolf, Run Adolf...	https://www.youtube.com/watch?v=bvETi4KNZgg
http://tinyurl.com/Kilroy004	YouTube: Nightingales sang in Berkeley...	https://www.youtube.com/watch?v=2gnTkgCusMc
http://tinyurl.com/Kilroy005	Website: Kilroy Was Here	http://www.kilroywashere.org/
http://tinyurl.com/Kilroy006	Wikipedia: Kilroy Was Here	https://en.wikipedia.org/wiki/Kilroy_was_here
http://tinyurl.com/Kilroy007	Wikipedia: Lord Reading	http://en.wikipedia.org/wiki/Rufus_Isaacs,_1st_Marquess_of_Reading
http://tinyurl.com/Kilroy008	Streetview: Lord Reading's House	http://goo.gl/maps/3NLQErugnVC2
http://tinyurl.com/Kilroy009	Wikipedia: SS Bremen	http://en.wikipedia.org/wiki/SS_Bremen_(1928)
http://tinyurl.com/Kilroy010	Website: The Russian Tea Room	http://russiantearoomnyc.com/
http://tinyurl.com/Kilroy011	Streetview: The Russian Tea Room	http://goo.gl/maps/mhsw8
http://tinyurl.com/Kilroy012	Website: The Roosevelt Hotel	http://www.theroosevelthotel.com/history.aspx
http://tinyurl.com/Kilroy013	Streetview: TheRoosevelt Hotel	http://goo.gl/maps/7WNQ3ifCbrj
http://tinyurl.com/Kilroy014	Wikipedia: Wall Street Crash 1929	http://en.wikipedia.org/wiki/Wall_Street_Crash_of_1929
http://tinyurl.com/Kilroy015	Wikipedia: SS Albertic	http://en.wikipedia.org/wiki/SS_Albertic
http://tinyurl.com/Kilroy016	Wikipedia: George VI Coronation	https://en.wikipedia.org/wiki/Coronation_of_King_George_VI_and_Queen_Elizabeth
http://tinyurl.com/Kilroy017	Wikipedia: Hossbach Memo...	https://en.wikipedia.org/wiki/Hossbach_Memorandum

Tiny URL	Description	Actual URL
http://tinyurl.com/Kilroy018	Wikipedia: Blomberg-Fritsch	https://en.wikipedia.org/wiki/Blomberg%E2%80%93Fritsch_affair
http://tinyurl.com/Kilroy019	Gutenberg: The 12 Caesars	http://www.gutenberg.org/ebooks/6400
http://tinyurl.com/Kilroy020	Daily Mail: Jonathon Burrows	http://www.dailymail.co.uk/news/article-85112/Boy-11-expelled-day-school.html
http://tinyurl.com/Kilroy021	Wikipedia: Burke and Wills	https://en.wikipedia.org/wiki/Burke_and_Wills_expedition
http://tinyurl.com/Kilroy022	Gutenberg: Keynes on probabilities	http://www.gutenberg.org/ebooks/32625
http://tinyurl.com/Kilroy023	Wikipedia: Austrian Anschluss	https://en.wikipedia.org/wiki/Anschluss
http://tinyurl.com/Kilroy024	Wikipedia: Moscow Trials	https://en.wikipedia.org/wiki/Moscow_Trials
http://tinyurl.com/Kilroy025	Wikipedia: Max Schmeling	https://en.wikipedia.org/wiki/Joe_Louis_vs._Max_Schmeling
http://tinyurl.com/Kilroy026	Wikipedia: English Electric Lightning	https://en.wikipedia.org/wiki/English_Electric_Lightning
http://tinyurl.com/Kilroy027	Wikipedia: Charles K. McNeil	https://en.wikipedia.org/wiki/Charles_K._McNeil
http://tinyurl.com/Kilroy028	Wikipedia: Monopoly game	https://en.wikipedia.org/wiki/Monopoly_(game)
http://tinyurl.com/Kilroy029	Gutenberg: Works of Rabbie Burns	http://www.gutenberg.org/ebooks/18500
http://tinyurl.com/Kilroy030	Wikipedia: Nylon	https://en.wikipedia.org/wiki/Nylon
http://tinyurl.com/Kilroy031	Wikipedia: Electric razor	https://en.wikipedia.org/wiki/Electric_razor
http://tinyurl.com/Kilroy032	Wikipedia: László Bíró	https://en.wikipedia.org/wiki/L%C3%A1szl%C3%B3_B%C3%ADr%C3%B3
http://tinyurl.com/Kilroy033	Wikipedia: Enigma Machine	https://en.wikipedia.org/wiki/Enigma_machine
http://tinyurl.com/Kilroy034	Streetview: Claremont estate	https://goo.gl/maps/RsJNfMt6Ab72
http://tinyurl.com/Kilroy035	Website: Claremont school	http://www.claremont-school.co.uk/
http://tinyurl.com/Kilroy036	Website: Claremont garden	http://www.nationaltrust.org.uk/claremont-landscape-garden/
http://tinyurl.com/Kilroy037	Wikipedia: Anderson Shelter	https://en.wikipedia.org/wiki/Air-raid_shelter#Anderson_shelter
http://tinyurl.com/Kilroy038	Wikipedia: R.A.F. Balloon Command	https://en.wikipedia.org/wiki/RAF_Balloon_Command
http://tinyurl.com/Kilroy039	Wikipedia: Heston Aerodrome	https://en.wikipedia.org/wiki/Heston_Aerodrome
http://tinyurl.com/Kilroy040	Wikipedia: Neville Chamberlain	https://en.wikipedia.org/wiki/Neville_Chamberlain

Tiny URL	Description	Actual URL
http://tinyurl.com/Kilroy041	Wikipedia: Minox camera	https://en.wikipedia.org/wiki/Minox
http://tinyurl.com/Kilroy042	Wikipedia: Horace Wilson	https://en.wikipedia.org/wiki/Horace_Wilson_(civil_servant)
http://tinyurl.com/Kilroy043	Wikipedia: Alec Douglas-Home	https://en.wikipedia.org/wiki/Alec_Douglas-Home
http://tinyurl.com/Kilroy044	Wikipedia:Dachau concentration camp	https://en.wikipedia.org/wiki/Dachau_concentration_camp
http://tinyurl.com/Kilroy045	Wikipedia: Oberwiesenfeld airfield	https://en.wikipedia.org/wiki/Oberwiesenfeld_Army_Airfield
http://tinyurl.com/Kilroy046	Wikipedia: Messerschmitt 109	http://en.wikipedia.org/wiki/Messerschmitt_Bf_109
http://tinyurl.com/Kilroy047	Wikipedia: Condor Legion	http://en.wikipedia.org/wiki/Condor_Legion
http://tinyurl.com/Kilroy048	Wikipedia: Alex. von Dörnberg	https://en.wikipedia.org/wiki/Alexander_von_D%C3%B6rnberg
http://tinyurl.com/Kilroy049	Wikipedia: Königsplatz, Munich	https://en.wikipedia.org/wiki/K%C3%B6nigsplatz,_Munich
http://tinyurl.com/Kilroy050	Wikipedia: Ardabil Carpet	https://en.wikipedia.org/wiki/Ardabil_Carpet
http://tinyurl.com/Kilroy051	Wikipedia: Theodor Morell	https://en.wikipedia.org/wiki/Theodor_Morell
http://tinyurl.com/Kilroy052	Wikipedia: Ludwig Beck v Hitler	https://en.wikipedia.org/wiki/Ludwig_Beck#Pre-war_conflict_with_Hitler
http://tinyurl.com/Kilroy053	Website: Text of Munich agreement	http://avalon.law.yale.edu/imt/munich1.asp
http://tinyurl.com/Kilroy054	Wikipedia: Shakespeare Coriolanus	https://en.wikipedia.org/wiki/Coriolanus
http://tinyurl.com/Kilroy055	Website: Künstlerhaus	http://www.kuenstlerhaus-muc.de/
http://tinyurl.com/Kilroy056	German Wikipedia: Künstlerhaus	http://de.wikipedia.org/wiki/K%C3%BCnstlerhaus_am_Lenbachplatz
http://tinyurl.com/Kilroy057	Website: Synagogue memorial	http://en.tracesofwar.com/article/12935/Memorial-Main-Synagogue-Munich.htm
http://tinyurl.com/Kilroy058	Wikipedia: Eva Braun	https://en.wikipedia.org/wiki/Eva_Braun
http://tinyurl.com/Kilroy059	Amazon: Wagner and the holocaust	https://www.amazon.co.uk/Richard-Adolf-Wagner-Incite-Holocaust/dp/9652293601

Tiny URL	Description	Actual URL
http://tinyurl.com/Kilroy060	Google Books: Karl Ernst	https://books.google.co.uk/books?id=X5q6SsVTK3EC&pg=PA105&dq=unholy+alliance+peter+levenda+karl+ernst&hl=en&sa=X&ei=AXKhVOPxOoqrabb2grgI&ved=0CCAQ6AEwAA#v=onepage&q=unholy%20alliance%20peter%20levenda%20karl%20ernst&f=false)
http://tinyurl.com/Kilroy061	Wikipedia: Leni Riefenstahl	https://en.wikipedia.org/wiki/Leni_Riefenstahl
http://tinyurl.com/Kilroy062	Wikipedia: Mercedes Benz 770	http://en.wikipedia.org/wiki/Mercedes-Benz_770
http://tinyurl.com/Kilroy063	Website: Chartwell	http://www.nationaltrust.org.uk/chartwell/
http://tinyurl.com/Kilroy064	Facebook: Jock VI (cat) of Chartwell	https://www.facebook.com/chartwellnt
http://tinyurl.com/Kilroy065	Youtube: Chamberlain at Heston	https://www.youtube.com/watch?v=t_EEhUgon7w
http://tinyurl.com/Kilroy066	Wikipedia: Romeo and Juliet	https://en.wikipedia.org/wiki/Romeo_and_Juliet#Synopsis
http://tinyurl.com/Kilroy067	Wikipedia: Munich agreement	https://en.wikipedia.org/wiki/Munich_Agreement
http://tinyurl.com/Kilroy068	Website: Anglo-German agreement	www.iwm.org.uk/collections/item/object/205132693
http://tinyurl.com/Kilroy069	Wikipedia: Duff Cooper	https://en.wikipedia.org/wiki/Duff_Cooper
http://tinyurl.com/Kilroy070	Wikipedia: Enid Blyton	https://en.wikipedia.org/wiki/Enid_Blyton
http://tinyurl.com/Kilroy071	Wikipedia: Gloster Gladiator	https://en.wikipedia.org/wiki/Gloster_Gladiator
http://tinyurl.com/Kilroy072	Wikipedia: Hawker Hurricane	https://en.wikipedia.org/wiki/Hawker_Hurricane
http://tinyurl.com/Kilroy073	Wikipedia: Supermarine Spitfire	https://en.wikipedia.org/wiki/Supermarine_Spitfire
http://tinyurl.com/Kilroy074	Wikipedia: Boulton Paul Defiant	https://en.wikipedia.org/wiki/Boulton_Paul_Defiant
http://tinyurl.com/Kilroy075	Wikipedia: Phoney War	https://en.wikipedia.org/wiki/Phoney_War
http://tinyurl.com/Kilroy076	Website: Museum at Condé-Vraux	http://www.amrvraux.com/
http://tinyurl.com/Kilroy077	Website: Château de Juvigny	http://www.chateaudejuvigny.com/
http://tinyurl.com/Kilroy078	Wikipedia: Picture Post	https://en.wikipedia.org/wiki/Picture_Post
http://tinyurl.com/Kilroy079	Website: Santa Claus' reindeer names	http://german.about.com/library/blgermyth05.htm

Tiny URL	Description	Actual URL
http://tinyurl.com/Kilroy080	Wikipedia: Rudolh the red-nosed reindeer	https://en.wikipedia.org/wiki/Rudolph_the_Red-Nosed_Reindeer
http://tinyurl.com/Kilroy081	Wikipedia: Reinhard Heydrich	https://en.wikipedia.org/wiki/Reinhard_Heydrich
http://tinyurl.com/Kilroy082	Wikipedia: Mechelen incident	https://en.wikipedia.org/wiki/Mechelen_incident
http://tinyurl.com/Kilroy083	Wikipedia: Pierre Bosquet	https://en.wikipedia.org/wiki/Pierre_Bosquet
http://tinyurl.com/Kilroy084	Wikipedia: Joseph Vuillemin	https://en.wikipedia.org/wiki/Joseph_Vuillemin
http://tinyurl.com/Kilroy085	Wikipedia: Marcel Petiot	https://en.wikipedia.org/wiki/Marcel_Petiot
http://tinyurl.com/Kilroy086	Wikipedia: Albert Ball	https://en.wikipedia.org/wiki/Albert_Ball
http://tinyurl.com/Kilroy087	Wikipedia: Meredith effect	https://en.wikipedia.org/wiki/Meredith_effect
http://tinyurl.com/Kilroy088	Wikipedia: De Haviland DH 88	https://en.wikipedia.org/wiki/De_Havilland_DH.88
http://tinyurl.com/Kilroy089	Website: Early aerobatics world champs	http://www.france-voltige.org/Docs/OriginsWAC.PDF
http://tinyurl.com/Kilroy090	Wikipedia: Morris Oxford flatnose	https://en.wikipedia.org/wiki/Morris_Oxford_flatnose
http://tinyurl.com/Kilroy091	Wikipedia: Miles Magister	https://en.wikipedia.org/wiki/Miles_Magister
http://tinyurl.com/Kilroy092	Wikipedia: Battle of Thermopylae	https://en.wikipedia.org/wiki/Battle_of_Thermopylae
http://tinyurl.com/Kilroy093	Wikipedia: Hector	https://en.wikipedia.org/wiki/Hector
http://tinyurl.com/Kilroy094	Website Cat torture in France	http://xroads.virginia.edu/~DRBR/cat.html
http://tinyurl.com/Kilroy095	Youtube: Remove cat before flight	https://www.youtube.com/watch?v=J_8mdH20qTQ
http://tinyurl.com/Kilroy096	Website: The Goldfish Club	http://www.thegoldfishclub.co.uk/
http://tinyurl.com/Kilroy097	Wikipedia: Patrick Playfair	https://en.wikipedia.org/wiki/Patrick_Playfair
http://tinyurl.com/Kilroy098	Website: Château Crayeres	http://chateaucrayeres.com/?lang=en
http://tinyurl.com/Kilroy099	Wikipedia: Reims-Champagne air base	https://en.wikipedia.org/wiki/Reims_%E2%80%93_Champagne_Air_Base#History
http://tinyurl.com/Kilroy100	Amazon: R.A.F. Field Service pocket book	https://www.amazon.co.uk/Royal-Force-Field-Service-Pocket/dp/B0015HPDDQ
http://tinyurl.com/Kilroy101	Wikipedia: Edmund Ironside in the Battle of France	https://en.wikipedia.org/wiki/Edmund_Ironside,_1st_Baron_Ironside#Battle_of_France

Tiny URL	Description	Actual URL
http://tinyurl.com/Kilroy102	Wikipedia: Citroën Traction Avant	https://en.wikipedia.org/wiki/Citro%C3%ABn_Traction_Avant
http://tinyurl.com/Kilroy103	Wikipedia: Suicide doors	https://en.wikipedia.org/wiki/Suicide_door
http://tinyurl.com/Kilroy104	Wikipedia: Gaston Billotte	https://en.wikipedia.org/wiki/Gaston_Billotte
http://tinyurl.com/Kilroy105	Wikipedia: Dewoitine D.520	https://en.wikipedia.org/wiki/Dewoitine_D.520
http://tinyurl.com/Kilroy106	Wikipedia: Fairey Battle	https://en.wikipedia.org/wiki/Fairey_Battle
http://tinyurl.com/Kilroy107	Wikipedia: Doric dialect	https://en.wikipedia.org/wiki/Doric_dialect_(Scotland)
http://tinyurl.com/Kilroy108	Website: Maison de l'Ardenne – von Rundstedt's HQ	http://www.monumentum.fr/maison-lardenne-ancienne-maison-blairon-pa00078413.html
http://tinyurl.com/Kilroy109	Wikipedia: Gerd von Rundstedt	https://en.wikipedia.org/wiki/Gerd_von_Rundstedt
http://tinyurl.com/Kilroy110	Wikipedia: White's	https://en.wikipedia.org/wiki/White%27s
http://tinyurl.com/Kilroy111	Wikipedia: Georg von Sodenstern	https://en.wikipedia.org/wiki/Georg_von_Sodenstern
http://tinyurl.com/Kilroy112	Wikipedia: Messerschmitt 109, Emil	https://en.wikipedia.org/wiki/Messerschmitt_Bf_109_variants#Bf_109E
http://tinyurl.com/Kilroy113	Amazon: Hitler's directives	https://www.amazon.co.uk/Hitlers-Directives-1939-1945-Hugh-Trevor-Roper/dp/1843410141
http://tinyurl.com/Kilroy114	Wikipedia: List of Hitler's directives	https://en.wikipedia.org/wiki/List_of_Adolf_Hitler%27s_directives
http://tinyurl.com/Kilroy115	Wikipedia: Wilhelm Keitel	https://en.wikipedia.org/wiki/Wilhelm_Keitel
http://tinyurl.com/Kilroy116	Wikipedia: Alfred Jodl	https://en.wikipedia.org/wiki/Alfred_Jodl
http://tinyurl.com/Kilroy117	Wikipedia: The Lone Ranger	https://en.wikipedia.org/wiki/Lone_Ranger
http://tinyurl.com/Kilroy118	Wikipedia: Messerschmitt 110	https://en.wikipedia.org/wiki/Messerschmitt_Bf_110
http://tinyurl.com/Kilroy119	Wikipedia: Jagdgeschwader 2 wing	https://en.wikipedia.org/wiki/Jagdgeschwader_2
http://tinyurl.com/Kilroy120	Wikipedia: Blondi	https://en.wikipedia.org/wiki/Blondi
http://tinyurl.com/Kilroy121	Website: Hitler in Liverpool	http://streetsofliverpool.co.uk/the-hitlers-of-liverpool/
http://tinyurl.com/Kilroy122	Wikipedia: Godesberg Memorandum	https://en.wikipedia.org/wiki/Godesberg_Memorandum#Chronology

Tiny URL	Description	Actual URL
http://tinyurl.com/Kilroy124	Wikipedia: Leon Trotsky	https://en.wikipedia.org/wiki/Leon_Trotsky
http://tinyurl.com/Kilroy125	Wikipedia: George Joseph Smith	https://en.wikipedia.org/wiki/George_Joseph_Smith
http://tinyurl.com/Kilroy126	Wikipedia: Junkers Ju 87	https://en.wikipedia.org/wiki/Junkers_Ju_87
http://tinyurl.com/Kilroy127	Wikipedia: Le Paradis Massacre	https://en.wikipedia.org/wiki/Le_Paradis_massacre
http://tinyurl.com/Kilroy128	Wikipedia: Fritz Knöchlein	https://en.wikipedia.org/wiki/Fritz_Knoechlein
http://tinyurl.com/Kilroy129	Wikipedia: Dieppe raid	https://en.wikipedia.org/wiki/Dieppe_Raid
http://tinyurl.com/Kilroy130	Wikipedia: Battle of Berlin (R.A.F.)	https://en.wikipedia.org/wiki/Battle_of_Berlin_(R.A.F._campaign)
http://tinyurl.com/Kilroy131	Wikipedia: Operation Fustian	https://en.wikipedia.org/wiki/Operation_Fustian
http://tinyurl.com/Kilroy132	Wikipedia: Operation Market Garden	https://en.wikipedia.org/wiki/Operation_Market_Garden
http://tinyurl.com/Kilroy133	Wikipedia: Ménagerie du Jardin des plantes	https://en.wikipedia.org/wiki/M%C3%A9nagerie_du_Jardin_des_plantes
http://tinyurl.com/Kilroy134	Wikipedia: German and Nazi genocides	https://en.wikipedia.org/wiki/Genocides_in_history#Germany_and_Nazi-occupied
http://tinyurl.com/Kilroy135	Wikipedia: Porajmos	https://en.wikipedia.org/wiki/Porajmos
http://tinyurl.com/Kilroy136	Wikipedia: Aktion T4	https://en.wikipedia.org/wiki/Aktion_T4
http://tinyurl.com/Kilroy137	Wikipedia: Mistreatment of Soviet POWs	https://en.wikipedia.org/wiki/German_mistreatment_of_Soviet_prisoners_of_war
http://tinyurl.com/Kilroy138	Wikipedia: Genocide of Soviet civilians	https://en.wikipedia.org/wiki/Genocides_in_history#Soviet_civilians
http://tinyurl.com/Kilroy139	Wikipedia: Nazi crimes against the Poles	https://en.wikipedia.org/wiki/Nazi_crimes_against_the_Polish_nation
http://tinyurl.com/Kilroy140	Wikipedia: Nazi persecution of homosexuals	https://en.wikipedia.org/wiki/Persecution_of_homosexuals_in_Nazi_Germany_and_the_Holocaust
http://tinyurl.com/Kilroy141	Wikipedia: Nazi genocides in occupied Europe	https://en.wikipedia.org/wiki/Genocides_in_history#Germany_and_Nazi-occupied_Europe
http://tinyurl.com/Kilroy142	Wikipedia: Vichy France	https://en.wikipedia.org/wiki/Vichy_France
http://tinyurl.com/Kilroy143	Wikipedia: Django Reinhardt	https://en.wikipedia.org/wiki/Django_Reinhardt
http://tinyurl.com/Kilroy144	Wikipedia: Selmer guitar	https://en.wikipedia.org/wiki/Selmer_guitar

Tiny URL	Description	Actual URL
http://tinyurl.com/Kilroy145	Youtube: Reinhardt documentary	https://www.youtube.com/watch?v=PQhTpgicdx4
http://tinyurl.com/Kilroy146	Youtube: Reinhardt performance (1945)	https://www.youtube.com/watch?v=aZ308aOOX04&feature=share
http://tinyurl.com/Kilroy147	Website: Memorial wall at Arras	http://memoiresdepierre.pagesperso-orange.fr/alphabetnew/a/arrasmurfusilles.html
http://tinyurl.com/Kilroy148	Wikipedia: Carrière Wellington	https://en.wikipedia.org/wiki/Carri%C3%A8re_Wellington
http://tinyurl.com/Kilroy149	Daily Mail: Arras "Cave City"	http://www.dailymail.co.uk/news/article-534236/Inside-amazing-cave-city-housed-25-000-Allied-troops-German-noses-WWI.html
http://tinyurl.com/Kilroy150	Daily Mail: WWI graffiti in Arras tunnels	http://www.dailymail.co.uk/news/article-3026250/WWI-graffiti-sheds-light-soldiers-experience.html
http://tinyurl.com/Kilroy152	Website: Moon phases 1940	http://www.calendar-12.com/moon_phases/1940
http://tinyurl.com/Kilroy153	Dutch Wikipedia: Bulskamp	https://nl.wikipedia.org/wiki/Bulskamp
http://tinyurl.com/Kilroy154	Youtube: Monty Python Pantomime...	https://www.youtube.com/watch?v=dkLsdQhZsw0
http://tinyurl.com/Kilroy155	Amazon: Dunkirk – Fight to the last man	https://www.amazon.co.uk/Dunkirk-Fight-Last-Hugh-Sebag-Montefiore/dp/0141024372
http://tinyurl.com/Kilroy156	Wikipedia: Siege of Dunkirk	https://en.wikipedia.org/wiki/Siege_of_Dunkirk_(1944%E2%80%9345)
http://tinyurl.com/Kilroy157	Wikipedia: Dickin Medal	https://en.wikipedia.org/wiki/Dickin_Medal
http://tinyurl.com/Kilroy159	Website: Diamond prices	http://www.diamondregistry.com/price.htm
http://tinyurl.com/Kilroy160	Website: Diamond Buyer's Guide	http://www.adiamondbuyingguide.com/
http://tinyurl.com/Kilroy161	Archive: Abrégé de l'art des...	https://archive.org/details/abrgdelartdesacc01lebo
http://tinyurl.com/Kilroy162	Wikipedia: Angélique du Coudray	https://en.wikipedia.org/wiki/Ang%C3%A9lique_du_Coudray
http://tinyurl.com/Kilroy163	Wikipedia: Amy Johnson	https://en.wikipedia.org/wiki/Amy_Johnson
http://tinyurl.com/Kilroy164	Wikipedia: Mignet Pou-du-Ciel	https://en.wikipedia.org/wiki/Mignet_Pou-du-Ciel
http://tinyurl.com/Kilroy165	Wikipedia: HM 14 external links	https://en.wikipedia.org/wiki/Mignet_HM.14#External_links
http://tinyurl.com/Kilroy166	Movietone: Mignet flies the HM 14	http://www.movietone.com/N_POPUP_Player.cfm?action=playVideo&assetno=88121

Tiny URL	Description	Actual URL
http://tinyurl.com/Kilroy167	Movietine: HM 14 crash at Heston	http://www.movietone.com/N_POPUP_Player.cfm?action=playVideo&assetno=88079
http://tinyurl.com/Kilroy168	Movietone: HM 14 flies cross-Channel	http://www.movietone.com/N_POPUP_Player.cfm?action=playVideo&assetno=86436
http://tinyurl.com/Kilroy169	Wikipedia: Defence Regulation 18B	https://en.wikipedia.org/wiki/Defence_Regulation_18B
http://tinyurl.com/Kilroy170	Website: List of 18B detainees	https://www.oswaldmosley.com/downloads/18b%20Detainees%20List.pdf
http://tinyurl.com/Kilroy171	Wikipedia: William Joyce	https://en.wikipedia.org/wiki/William_Joyce
http://tinyurl.com/Kilroy172	Wikipedia: L'Oca del Cairo	https://en.wikipedia.org/wiki/L%27oca_del_Cairo
http://tinyurl.com/Kilroy173	Wikipedia: Ken (Snakehips) Johnson	https://en.wikipedia.org/wiki/Ken_Snakehips_Johnson
http://tinyurl.com/Kilroy174	Youtube: Café de Paris bombing	https://www.youtube.com/watch?v=zz3zVpLl2kw
http://tinyurl.com/Kilroy175	Wikipedia: Joseph Kennedy	https://en.wikipedia.org/wiki/Joseph_P._Kennedy_Sr
http://tinyurl.com/Kilroy176	Wikipedia: Rosemary Kennedy	https://en.wikipedia.org/wiki/Rosemary_Kennedy
http://tinyurl.com/Kilroy177	Wikipedia: J. Lyons and Co.	https://en.wikipedia.org/wiki/J._Lyons_and_Co.
http://tinyurl.com/Kilroy178	Website: Gordon's Wine Bar	http://gordonswinebar.com/#!/history
http://tinyurl.com/Kilroy179	Wikipedia: Savoy Hotel	https://en.wikipedia.org/wiki/Savoy_Hotel#Music_and_fine_art
http://tinyurl.com/Kilroy181	Wikipedia: We shall fight on the beaches	https://en.wikipedia.org/wiki/We_shall_fight_on_the_beaches
http://tinyurl.com/Kilroy182	Wikipedia: Arthur Barratt	https://en.wikipedia.org/wiki/Arthur_Barratt
http://tinyurl.com/Kilroy183	Website: Nimatron US patent 002215544	http://pdfpiw.uspto.gov/.piw?Docid=02215544
http://tinyurl.com/Kilroy184	Wikipedia: Nim	https://en.wikipedia.org/wiki/Nim
http://tinyurl.com/Kilroy185	Wikipedia: Binary number	https://en.wikipedia.org/wiki/Binary_number
http://tinyurl.com/Kilroy186	Website: Hitler's carmaker (1)	http://www.jta.org/2006/12/01/archive/hitlers-carmaker-part-2-as-the-nazis-amassed-power-what-did-gm-know-and-when
http://tinyurl.com/Kilroy187	Website: Hitler's car-maker (2)	http://www.globalresearch.ca/hitler-s-carmaker-the-inside-story-of-how-general-motors-helped-mobilize-the-third-reich/5571

Tiny URL	Description	Actual URL
http://tinyurl.com/Kilroy188	Amazon: Trading with the Enemy	https://www.amazon.co.uk/Trading-Enemy-Nazi-American-1933%C3%BD1949-1933-1949/dp/0595431666/
http://tinyurl.com/Kilroy189	Amazon: Keynes Theory of Employment, Interest, Money	https://www.amazon.co.uk/General-Theory-Employment-Interest-Money/dp/1535221984/
http://tinyurl.com/Kilroy191	Wikipedia: Keynes Theory of Employment, Interest, Money	https://en.wikipedia.org/wiki/The_General_Theory_of_Employment,_Interest_and_Money
http://tinyurl.com/Kilroy192	Wikipedia: Lockheed Hudson	https://en.wikipedia.org/wiki/Lockheed_Hudson
http://tinyurl.com/Kilroy193	Wikipedia: Lockheed 14 Super Electra	http://en.wikipedia.org/wiki/Lockheed_Model_14_Super_Electra
http://tinyurl.com/Kilroy194	Website: Super Electra losses	http://aviation-safety.net/database/types/Lockheed-L-14-Super-Electra/losses
http://tinyurl.com/Kilroy195	Wikipedia: History of amphetamines	https://en.wikipedia.org/wiki/History_and_culture_of_substituted_amphetamines
http://tinyurl.com/Kilroy196	Amazon: Hitler's second book	https://www.amazon.co.uk/Hitlers-Second-Book-Unpublished-Sequel-ebook/dp/1929631618/
http://tinyurl.com/Kilroy197	Wikipedia: Unsinkable Sam	https://en.wikipedia.org/wiki/Unsinkable_Sam
http://tinyurl.com/Kilroy198	Wikipedia: Odd-eyed cat	https://en.wikipedia.org/wiki/Odd-eyed_cat
http://tinyurl.com/Kilroy199	Website: Cats in war and Unsinkable Sam	http://www.thegreatcat.org/cats-in-20th-century-history-cats-in-war-unsinkable-sam/
http://tinyurl.com/Kilroy200	Wikipedia: T. E. Lawrence	https://en.wikipedia.org/wiki/T._E._Lawrence
http://tinyurl.com/Kilroy201	Streetview: Abbeville Bandstand	https://www.google.com/maps/@50.1101646,1.8416421,3a,75y,240.37h,90t/data=!3m6!1e1!3m4!1sgqmflw8uLwEXRltsUVJlJg!2e0!7i13312!8i6656?hl=fr
http://tinyurl.com/Kilroy202	French Wikipedia: Abbeville massacre	https://fr.wikipedia.org/wiki/Massacre_d%27Abbeville
http://tinyurl.com/Kilroy203	Wikipedia: Dunkirk Halt order	https://en.wikipedia.org/wiki/Battle_of_Dunkirk#Halt_order
http://tinyurl.com/Kilroy204	Wikipedia: Dunkirk evacuation	https://en.wikipedia.org/wiki/Dunkirk_evacuation
http://tinyurl.com/Kilroy205	Youtube: White Cliffs of Dover	https://www.youtube.com/watch?v=Hqtaoz4QFX8

Tiny URL	Description	Actual URL
http://tinyurl.com/Kilroy206	Website: Full text of Churchill's "Fight on the beaches" speech	http://www.winstonchurchill.org/resources/speeches/1940-the-finest-hour/128-we-shall-fight-on-the-beaches
http://tinyurl.com/Kilroy207	Website: Dickin Medal recipients	https://www.pdsa.org.uk/what-we-do/animal-honours/the-dickin-medal
http://tinyurl.com/Kilroy208	Website: Arras tunnels interactive map	http://www.nzhistory.net.nz/media/interactive/arras-tunnels-map
http://tinyurl.com/Kilroy209	Movietone: Dunkirk evacuation	http://www.movietone.com/N_POPUP_Player.cfm?action=playVideo&assetno=87110
http://tinyurl.com/Kilroy210	Youtube: Dunkirk in "Atonement"	https://www.youtube.com/watch?v=m_yhuhp880s
http://tinyurl.com/Kilroy211	Website: Visit Ardennes	http://visitardennes.e-monsite.com/pages/est-ce-vrai/hitler-a-charleville.html
http://tinyurl.com/Kilroy212	Wikipedia: Harold Balfour	https://en.wikipedia.org/wiki/Harold_Balfour,_1st_Baron_Balfour_of_Inchrye
http://tinyurl.com/Kilroy213	Authentication of Hitler's poem	http://www.ifz-muenchen.de/archiv/ed_0416.pdf
http://tinyurl.com/Kilroy214	Hitler's poem, in English and German	https://en.m.wikiquote.org/wiki/Adolf_Hitler
http://tinyurl.com/Kilroy215	Wikipedia: Bierstein	https://en.wikipedia.org/wiki/Beer_stein
http://tinyurl.com/Kilroy216	Wikipedia: Zimmermann	https://en.wikipedia.org/wiki/Zimmermann_Telegram

PICTURE CREDITS

There follows an itemisation of all the photos, drawings and artwork featured in this volume. Much of the material was extracted from the Internet and is in the Public Domain but it is possible that some pictures, subject to copyright, have been inadvertently used here. If anyone gets in touch with proof of ownership, I'll be pleased to credit them in future editions and, if requested, make a reasonable payment to them, or a charity or, if they wish to have the picture removed, this will be respected where possible. Contact: ThreeBPub@Hotmail.Com.

(Cover) Hawker Hurricane R4118 – veteran of the Battle of Britain – photographed by Adrian Pingstone in July 2008 – public domain; 4 silhouettes designed by Freepik.Com; Alpha Smoke font by Beeline – freeware; (Dedication) Royal Air Force Memorial, Victoria Embankment, London; (Foreword P3) Kilroy Was Here Grafitti; (Foreword P4) Cave painting by Kilroy's ancestor

(PART ONE:PEACE P5) Fred Astaire and Ginger Rogers over WWII collage; (Ch 1 P9) SS Albertic, White Star Line; (Ch 2 P13) Nim, AKA "Limbo"; (Ch 2 P14) Victoria Station, London; (Ch 2 P19) George VI Coronation; (Ch2 P23) Ford Werke army lorry; (Ch2 P24) Opel Blitz trucks in convoy; (Ch2 P26) German Embassy; (Ch 3 P30) Herne Bay College; (Ch4 P38) Hitler Ovation in the Reichstag; (Ch4 P42) Raleigh Bicycle Advert; (Ch4 P43) England 903 scoreboard; (Ch4 P44) Supermarine Spitfire K9795, the 9th production Mk I, with R.A.F. 19 Squadron in 1938; (Ch4 P 45) English Electric Lightning; (Ch5 P48) Cranwell; (Ch6 P56) Claremont Estate, Esher, near London; (Ch6 P57) US Patent for Enigma; (Ch6 P58) Anderson air-raid shelter; (Ch7 P61) Lockheed Super Electra with Howard Hughes; (Ch7 P62) Minox camera; (CH7 P63) British Airways Advert; (Ch7 P69) Services Watches Have to be shockproof Advert; (Ch7 P71) Konzentrationslager Dachau; (Ch8 P75) Führerbau; (Ch8 P76) Death mask of Frederick the Great; (Ch8 P82) Pervitin; (Ch9 P84) Postcard image of the Regina Palast Hotel, Munich; (Ch9 P85) Map of the Czechoslovakian partition; (Ch9 P88) At the Führerbau in Munich; (Ch10 P91) Künstlerhaus and synagogue Munich; (Ch10 P93) Eva Braun; (Ch10 P95) Eight inch howitzer; (Ch11 P99) Mercedes Benz 770 with Hitler; (Ch11 P100) Leni Riefenstahl (1902-2003); (Ch12 P105) Chamberlain's first speech on returning from Munich, at Heston aerodrome; (Ch12 P106) Chamberlain's "Piece of Paper" – the Anglo-German declaration; (Ch12 P108) Chamberlain waves the Anglo-German declaration; (Ch13 P110) Winston Churchill in 1941; (Ch13 P111) Hitler passes through Graslitz.

(PART TWO: PHONEY WAR P117) Fond farewells at the station; (Ch 1 P121) Noddy and the Aeroplane; (Ch1 P122) Gloster Gladiator serving the Luftwaffe; (Ch2 P125) Our Boys need sox – knit your bit – poster; (Ch2 P127) Booby trap – Venereal Disease poster; (Ch2 P128) Mark 1 Hawker Hurricanes in France, inspected by King George VI, with the Duke of Gloucester and Viscount Lord Gort. Note the two bladed propellors; (Ch2 P130) A

Dornier 17 – the flying pencil; (Ch3 P133) Morgan Super Sports, 1937; (Ch3 P134) *Picture Post* cover; (Ch4 P142) Air Marshal Hugh Dowding; (Ch5 P150) Messerschmitt Bf108 "Taifun"; (Ch6 P163) Remains of the German plans captured at Mechelen, now in the collection of the Royal Museum of the Armed Forces and Military History in Brussels; (Ch7 P168) A Tiger Moth. Note instructor to the front and trainee pilot to the rear; (Ch7 P170) A Browning 303 machine gun with fighter mounts; (Ch7 P172) Bentley 3.5 Litre Cabriolet (Ch8 P179) Captain Albert Ball, VC, DSO and two bars, MC (14th August 1896 – 7th May 1917); (Ch8 P183) Miles Magister; (Ch8 P190) Oscar/Unsinkable Sam on gangplank – ship unknown.

(PART THREE:WAR P193) White Cliffs of Dover – Vera Lynn; (Ch1 P197) Dewoitine D.520; (Ch1 P193) Citroën Traction Avant; (Ch2 P203) Belgian refugees – Public Domain US National Archives and Records Administration; (Ch2 P206) Abbeville's "kiosque" still stands; (Ch3 P210) Fairey Battle cutaway in R.A.F.'s Pilots Notes; (Ch3 P211) Fairey Battles (and Bristol Blenheims) for scrap; (Ch4 P215) Briefing R.A.F. bomber crews; (Ch4 P219) Ballater Station, Aberdeenshire; (Ch5 P223) Fiesler Fi156 Storch; (Ch6 P230) Maison de l'Ardenne – Von Rundstedt's 1940 HQ – NEUVENS Francis – Sous licence Creative Commons 3.0 (Ch6 P232) Generalfeldmarschall Gerd von Rundstedt; (Ch6 P238) Cheese baguette, similar to Kilroy's, on display in the Imperial War Museum (cafeteria), London; (Ch7 P241) Hitler's arrival at von Rundstedt's HQ; (Ch7 P242) Hitler briefing his generals; (Ch7 P249) "The Mother" by Adolf Hitler; (Ch8 P255) Junkers Ju 88; (Ch9 P263) Le Paradis farmhouse where the Royal Norfolks surrendered; (Ch9 P265) Luger P08 of the German Reichswehr; (Ch9 P267) BMW Motorcycle combination; (Ch10 P272) Map of the Arras tunnels; (Ch10 P275)Cirque Pinder poster; (Ch10 P275) Memorial Wall at Arras; (Ch11 P284) General Bernard Montgomery in North Africa, 1942; (Ch12 P287) Evacuation from Dunkirk beach; (Ch12 P290) Chubb Safes advert; (Ch13 P298) Cover and title page of ABRÉGÉ DE L'ART DES ACCOUCHEMENTS, published in 1777; (Ch13 P302) British Prisoners of War captured at Dunkirk – Public Domain US National Archives and Records Administration; (Ch13 P303) A song in tribute to Amy Johnson from 1930; (Ch13 P304) The HM-14 Pou-du-Ciel (Flying Flea) flown by its designer, Henri Mignet.

(PART FOUR: LONDON P307) London by Night; (Ch1 P309) Tables set for afternoon tea at the Ritz; (Ch1 P311)Lady Diana and Sir Oswald Mosely under house arrest in an Oxford hotel after their release from Holloway in 1943; (Ch1 P312) William Joyce, Lord Haw Haw, after his arrest in Germany in 1945. He was shot in the buttocks during his arrest; (Ch1 P314) Ken "Snakehips" Johnson; (Ch2 P315) Grenadier Guards constructing defences around government buildings, May 1940 in London; (Ch2 P318) First day in the R.A.F for these recruits, at Lords cricket ground; (Ch2 P321) A pigeon prepares to "set Europe ablaze".; (Ch3 P323) Peter Pan statue, Kensington Gardens, London; (Ch3 P324) Leave Hitler to me sonny. You ought to be out of London – poster; (Ch3 P326) Gone with the Wind film poster; (Ch4 P329) Gordon's Wine Bar, near Charing Cross station, London; (Ch4 P330) The Savoy Hotel, London; (Ch4 P332) Kaspar prepares to dine under a picture of Churchill, at the Savoy in London

(Afterword P337) Biro Advert; (Afterword P337) Nissen Hut; (Afterword P339) Some of of Kilroy's women

(End notes P345) The Nimatron machine; (End notes P350) Oscar's trophy wall

65247491R00226

Made in the USA
Charleston, SC
24 December 2016